COSTLY AFFAIR

LOVE, LIES and LIAISONS

COSTLY AFFAIR
LOVE, LIES and LIAISONS

BY

LES COCHRAN

www.bookstandpublishing.com

Published by
Bookstand Publishing
Morgan Hill, CA 95037
4158_4

ISBN 978-1-61863-912-7

Library of Congress Control Number: 2014911051

First Edition

Printed in the United States of America

DEDICATION

To my wife, Lin, who inspired me to write a novel then stood by and supported me just as she had throughout my career. She reminded me of the "red corrections" I had made on staff memos; and that the red ink from the editor was payback time — my turn to learn.

Then she started the next phase. Organizing and planning, hosting book launch parties, issuing news releases and arranging a book tour. I thought I'd come out of retirement.

She proofed and edited my books then did it again. She tolerated my frustrations and reassured me, staying positive through the entire process. And when I made more changes, she was still there smiling and encouraging.

Now, she's onto a new venue, social media marketing and promoting. She navigated a tremendous learning curve, but once again, thank to Lin we're on our way. I love you, sweetheart!

ACKNOWLEDGEMENTS

I'm indebted to my editor, LinDee Rochelle of Penchant for Penning, whose attention to detail and strategic questioning complemented her tedious task of editing and critiquing. Thanks too, for inserting humorous comments into the painstaking process.

I am grateful, also, for the professional assistance of Dr. Francis R. Valenti and Eileen McBriarty who shared their professional expertise on addictive behavior.

A special thanks to Barbara Bender and Charlie McBriarty whose eagle eyes scrutinized the manuscript one more time, circling and astutely noting needed changes. And to the many friends who lent a helping hand, thanks again.

CHAPTER ONE

Steve Schilling slammed on the brakes of his new '94 Cadillac and grabbed a parking ticket from the valet. It was a short sprint inside Mercy Hospital to the information desk. Catching his breath, he finger combed his hair and tried not to shout. "What room is Elizabeth Webster in?"

A woman with tight blue curls and a sweet smile glanced at the printout on her desk then made eye contact with him. "She's in 732."

"Thanks." He ran for the elevator. Thrumming his fingers against his thighs impatiently, as the creaky lift discharged passengers at floors two through six, he could hardly wait for it to stop again. The doors parted.

Seeing Brittany Haywood, Elizabeth's administrative assistant, speaking with a nurse, he took two quick, long strides to meet them outside of Elizabeth's room.

"You can go in," Brittany said.

He cracked the door and peered in. A cocoon of tubes and wires enveloped the patient. Her vital-signs monitor beeped steadily. Tip-toeing to the bed, he kissed Elizabeth on the forehead and touched her raven hair, lying limp and damp against her scalp.

Her eyelids fluttered.

"How are you doing, sweetie?"

She gave him a half-smile. "Better now that you're here."

He pressed his fingers to her lips. "Sh, we can talk later."

Her eyes closed.

The door opened silently as Brittany walked softly through it. "They've done an MRI," she whispered to Steve. "The results will be available after lunch."

"Is her head still throbbing?"

"Less since the morphine kicked in." Brittany turned back to the door. "I'm going to grab a sandwich and call Lizbeth's father with an update. Can I bring you something?"

Steve shook his head. "I can't eat a thing."

He pulled a chair next to the bed and said a prayer, then leafed through a *Sports Illustrated.*

"Mr. Webster is on his way up," Brittany said when she returned.

Brittany and Steve made small talk.

Lizbeth's eyes cracked open and she stared wearily at the ceiling.

Moments later chief of staff Dr. Charles Woods, with Elizabeth's father, led a team of interns into the soothing pale green suite.

In a firm voice, Dr. Woods asked, "How are you feeling, Elizabeth?"

"About the same," she said weakly. "Things are still fuzzy."

"That's to be expected. We have the results of the MRI."

Her eyes opened wide and she squeezed Steve's hand. "Go ahead, Dr. Woods."

"You have a tumor on your brain the size of a tennis ball."

She gasped. Steve tightened his grip.

"The good news is that it's not malignant."

"Thank God. Are you sure?"

"I'm ninety-nine percent certain. It's a meningioma — with a smooth surface and no tentacles."

Elizabeth frowned.

Dr. Woods continued, "Think of the meninges membrane as a hairnet holding your brain in place. Technically, your tumor is not attached to the brain. Do you want to see the MRI?"

She glanced at Steve. He nodded.

"Yes, I would."

The doctor held up the film of her skull and pointed to a white area over the left eye. "It may be blurry to you but this large mass is the tumor. It's pressing on your optic nerve, causing your blurred vision and creating pressure on your brain. That's the reason for the headaches."

"Can you remove it?"

"Yes, but I can't. There are specialists who can. I'll be conferring with them. For now, I want you to rest and try not to worry."

***

In his hotel room that night, Steve fell to his knees and clasped his hands as he had done countless times since he was a boy. "God, please take care of her," he sobbed. *I don't know what I'd do without her. She's my everything. I can't lose her.*

Unbuttoning his shirt, he stretched out on the king-size bed — recalled the first time they'd talked in a social setting — the Pacesetters Winter Ball in the Omni's Grand Ballroom. His breath had quickened as he watched her graceful moves. She was exquisite in a navy georgette cocktail dress with a deep V neckline. Hobnobbing at Charlotte's most prominent black-tie event, he couldn't keep his eyes off of her. He had wanted to undress her, unfasten her chignon — one hairpin at a time — and make love all night.

But she was much more than eye candy. Elizabeth seemed to know everyone: the governor, North Carolina's senators, and East Coast media bigwigs. *And her voluptuous breasts, what a turn-on.*

Ed Barkley, one of his top fundraising prospects, had walked over, interrupting Steve's sexual fantasy. "What brings the president of Mountain State to a high-powered event like this?"

"I'm meeting influential people like you, selling the university wherever I can."

"Sounds like you're buttering me up."

Steve flashed his megawatt smile. "Well, that goes with the territory. I'm organizing a presidential task force of community leaders."

"Sounds interesting. What's your intent?"

"We'll bring a group of prominent leaders to campus to shape our five-year plan. What surfaces from a series of focused groups this spring will form the cornerstone of our future. May I count on you?"

"I'd look forward to that. But you don't have to sell me on Mountain State. I met my wife there and our three kids are graduates."

"Alums like you play an important role in shaping our future. Ideas from the community and campus reps will help us forge a strong institutional partnership."

"Sounds good. You developed good practices at Eastern Arkansas University. Your reputation as a strong leader is widely known and admired."

Steve blushed. "We had a good leadership team."

"C'mon. You went Division I, scheduled SEC schools and added a doctorate in education. Don't be modest. You built a new stadium, increased enrollment and engineered several million-dollar gifts."

"We had a good run. Now I'm focused on Mountain State."

"Are you approaching Lizbeth tonight?"

"Lizbeth?"

"Elizabeth Webster. She's Elizabeth in the office, but she's Lizbeth to friends."

"Thanks for the tip. And yes, I plan to pitch her."

"Saving the best for last?" Ed grinned. "Her son graduated from Mountain State. He goes by his dad's name. Webster is her maiden name. She has a daughter in graduate school, too."

"You must know her well."

"Lizbeth and I serve on several community boards. You're asking her for a biggie, right?"

"I need to learn more about her interests first."

Ed stepped closer to Steve. "Don't beat around the bush with her. She's a woman of action, not one to piddle around. If I were you, I'd ask for ten million dollars. But that's off the record."

"Ten million?"

"She can afford to do whatever she wants — and usually does. She's big on technology, runs corporate-wide meetings from her office. And don't ignore basketball. She's a fanatic."

"I'll have to rethink …"

Ed cut him off. "Don't play guessing games with her. Be bold or you'll get nothing. Tell her you need a new basketball arena and you want her to pay for it."

"Ask her to foot the whole bill?" Steve's face flushed. "That could cost fifteen million or more."

"She follows the Tarheels and the Blue Devils. If North Carolina or Duke is in the final four, she'll be there. Tell her you'll put her daddy's name on it."

"Are you sure?"

"Is my name Ed Barkley? Of course, I'm sure. You have any other naming opportunities associated with the basketball arena?"

"There'll be two or three in the million-dollar range — the press box, loges, reception area."

"Put Lizbeth's name on the press box. Who knows? Maybe she'll broadcast your basketball games. Consider what that would do for recruitment in Charlotte."

"I'll think about it."

"Don't think too much. Hit it off with her and you can write your own ticket." Ed paused and pointed to a tall, Spanish-looking guy. "See that stud on the other side of the ballroom?"

"Sure. You can't miss him."

"Two or three like him show up at every event — thirty-something, good-looking, and with all the right moves. He's going to hit on Lizbeth."

"Really?"

"You bet. Once in a while one of them will strike it rich with a hot socialite. He screws her until daddy finds out. Before you know it he's back on the prowl, his pockets bulging with cash."

"I thought that only happened on TV."

"Think again. Here he comes."

Watching the gigolo saunter across the dance floor, Steve finger-combed his dark, wavy hair. The playboy stopped and waited reverentially behind Lizbeth. When she finished her conversation and turned to face him, he whispered in her ear.

She smiled and strolled over to the band leader. Moments later the band struck up "El Choclo," (He recalled his aunt swaying to Ángel Villoldo's Argentine tango that translates to "Kiss of Fire," a popular cover song for several American vocalists in the 1950s).

Lizbeth unpinned her hair and shook it free. Burnished brown curls cascaded over her shoulders. Steve's gaze turned to the large diamond-studded pendant hanging in her cleavage. Lizbeth wrapped her arms around her partner's back and pressed her breasts into his chest. He thrust his hips into hers. Her upper body arched gracefully as he guided her across the floor. Over her shoulder, she caught Steve's eye and winked.

"Did you see that?" Ed asked.

"See what?"

Ed slapped him on the back. "You saw it. She winked at you."

"I thought she was winking at you."

"Come on, Steve, you know her better than you've led me to believe."

"We've spoken a few times at the regional economic development forum. Last month I stopped by her place at Lake Lure to drop off a report."

"Lake Lure? You've been to her mountain home? Hell, I'd go for the whole enchilada."

The two men continued their conversation over another drink before Ed excused himself. When the crowd had thinned Steve walked slowly over to her table. After ending a conversation with the woman next to her, Lizbeth looked up. "I wondered how long it would take you. I'd like you to meet my administrative assistant, Brittany Hayward."

"It's a pleasure to meet you." He reached for her hand. "I'm Steve Schilling."

"Yes. You're taller than I expected."

"That'll be all, Brittany," Lizbeth said.

"Nice to meet you, Mr. President." Brittany flipped her waist-length blonde hair over her shoulder and walked away.

Steve sat down in Brittany's seat. "Ed Barkley said you prefer to be called Lizbeth. Do you?"

"Yes, I do."

"You're a very popular woman. And a good dancer too."

"You noticed?" She smirked. "That was for you."

"Me? I thought you winked at Ed."

"I don't think so."

"He thinks very highly of you."

"He's a difference maker. We serve together on several committees."

"So he said."

"Is that all he said?"

"No."

"What else?"

"That your son is a graduate of Mountain State, and you're a basketball nut."

"And that you should ask me for a big donation, I bet."

"That too, but mostly we talked about you."

Lizbeth's eyebrows shot up with a quizzical expression. "So what do you know about Elizabeth Webster?"

"Not enough. Why don't you tell me more?"

She pursed her lips. "Do you always answer a question with a question?"

"Only when I'm interested in learning more."

"Smooth," she said, her eyes holding steady on his. "What would you like to know?"

Steve shrugged. "Do you have a hobby? Where do you go after work? What do you do for fun?"

"Is this twenty questions?"

"Sort of."

"My age and weight are classified," she warned.

Steve morphed into a robot, arms flailing. "Warning! Warning! Critical data missing."

She laughed. "Okay. I'm the president and CEO of Webster International Media Group. I do what most Fortune 500 presidents do — work too much. And I love to shop. I'm divorced and have two grown children. The rest of the bio is on the website."

"Yes, I know. I've read it."

"Then why all the questions?"

"I'm interested in hearing it from you."

"Brittany said you're not like most men. What did she mean?"

"Beats me. I guess you'll have to find out." He winked. "Tell me about your kids."

"Richie is thirty-one. I'm grooming him to become our financial VP."

"And your daughter?"

"You are on top of things, aren't you?"

"I try."

"She's a lot like me." Lizbeth paused. "No, that's not right. She's like I wanted to be. She's very attractive and has had several small movie roles."

"She must be a knockout."

"She's beautiful alright, but she takes after Arnold's side."

"Arnold?"

"He's my ex. He runs our paper here in Charlotte."

"He works for you?"

Lizbeth nodded. "Some people think that's strange, but he's a damn good newspaperman. I just don't sleep with him."

Steve fell silent.

She cocked her head. "Aren't you going to ask who I sleep with?"

"I thought that would be forward. And gauche."

"You're probably right. But I'll tell you anyway. I don't have a significant other. And I don't sleep around."

Steve tried a new tack. "What do you know about Steve Schilling?"

"A lot. I had Brittany run a search on you."

"Do you run a search on everyone?"

"Almost always on people I don't know. I want to know where I'm walking."

"Interesting." Steve rubbed his chin. "Where'd you pick that up?"

"My daddy always said, 'You need to know the other person's path before you take a step with them.'"

"Makes sense."

"When I read Brittany's report, I said, 'This guy has had an impressive career.'"

"I've worked hard all of my life."

"You won extra points in the receiving line."

"What do you mean?"

"You were the only man who didn't sneak a peek."

Steve smiled. "You're talking about the diamond pendant, of course."

She gave him a sexy smile. "You looked me straight in the eye. I liked that."

"I peeked before."

"Aren't you the sly one?"

"Anything else you want to know?"

"I've read your resume and some stories in the *Ruston Daily Gazette*. I know you're recently divorced and you have a reservation at the Sheraton."

"You know just about everything."

"Not quite. Want to dance?"

Steve grinned and took her hand; they fell into the rhythm of a familiar waltz. He liked her self-confident air — and the way her firm breasts pressed against him. He willed himself not to react. It wasn't easy.

She snuggled closer, slid her hands under his tuxedo jacket to the small of his back.

He looked into her sparkling brown eyes. "Are you trying to turn me on?"

"Maybe," she whispered.

"May I talk about Mountain State for a few minutes?"

"I thought you'd never ask."

***

In the hospital room Brittany and Steve stood when Dr. Woods and Lizbeth's dad walked in. "I have wonderful news," the doctor said.

"What is it?" Lizbeth asked.

"Dr. Hans Beamer at Johns Hopkins has agreed to review your case. He's the head of their meningioma center. It's ranked number one in the world."

"That's terrific."

"I overnighted a CD of your MRI. His team of surgeons evaluated it this morning. The panel meets regularly to determine which doctor is best qualified for each case. I had Dr. Beamer's conference call transferred to your room. It should be coming any time."

Before a significant word could be spoken, Dr. Woods turned and picked up the ringing phone. "Yes, Dr. Beamer. I'm putting you on speakerphone." He pressed the button.

"Lizbeth, this is Dr. Beamer. Can you hear me?"

She detected a slight German accent. "Yes, please go ahead."

"I want to be very candid. The size of your tumor is a major concern. Left unchecked, it could be fatal." She gasped. "I'd like to put you on steroids immediately to shrink its size. Do you understand?"

"Yes. Will the steroids produce any side effects?"

"Only short-term. We can talk about that before surgery. Since you're experiencing headaches and blurred vision, I'd like to schedule you for surgery as soon as possible. Would next Tuesday work?"

She hesitated, her eyes opened wide at the urgency. "Ah … yes."

"I've done hundreds of these procedures. Your tumor is one of the largest I've seen, but I don't anticipate any problems."

Lizbeth turned to Steve. "Can you be there?"

"Of course, dear."

"Tuesday is fine, Dr. Beamer."

"I don't want you to fly," the surgeon said. "We can't risk a change in the air-pressure."

Lizbeth's dad spoke. "Earl will drive you and Brittany to Baltimore. Steve and I will fly up on the weekend."

"That sounds ideal. We'll do your pre-op on Monday," Dr. Beamer said. "I'll see you then."

CHAPTER TWO

Steve gazed out the window at the lifeless trees. Dark circles hung under his normally warm brown eyes. *Cities look dreary in the wintertime.* He turned back toward the waiting room — four drab, gray walls — people packed in rows of dark green and blue plastic chairs. A silver-haired volunteer at a small desk in the front of the room cast a casual glance his way.

He ignored her and headed for the coffeepot stationed by the water cooler. Not an eye looked up as relatives and friends waited, quietly, patiently.

Mr. Webster paced the room for the umpteenth time. He peered up at the clock — 2:30. "She's been in surgery for seven hours. You'd think they'd tell us something."

"Dr. Beamer said the operation would take ten to twelve hours," Brittany said, tossing a magazine in the rack. "I'm going down to pick up a sandwich. Can I bring anybody something?"

The two men shrugged. Mr. Webster said, "I'll have a chocolate shake."

Steve opened his wallet and handed her a twenty. "I'll have one too."

Two hours passed.

The three watched the clock hands move as if in slow motion.

A doctor walked in, removed his mask and headed for the mother and daughter huddled in the corner. Saying a few words, the mother broke into tears. The daughter cried out, "No, no, it can't be."

The doctor encircled them with his arms and whispered. They continued to sob. An older doctor, his face lined with fatigue, joined them and talked at great length, then left.

The clock ticked toward seven.

Mr. Webster folded his hands in prayer, while Brittany sat in an unfocused daze. Steve stood to stretch his legs; his square-shoulders drooped as he meticulously rearranged the chairs to the five original rows.

Dr. Beamer walked in. All eyes shifted anxiously toward him.

"Everything went smoothly," he said his German accent more pronounced with weariness. "She's going to be fine."

A collective sigh filled the room.

"Thank God." Mr. Webster shook Dr. Beamer's hand then gave him a bear hug.

"Did you remove it all?" Steve asked.

"Yes. The size of the tumor made the surgery more complex than usual. Her brain has been under tremendous pressure. When we removed a portion of her skull, half of the tumor popped out. It'll likely to take several months for her brain to move back into its normal position."

"Will that be a problem?" Mr. Webster asked.

"No, it'll be very gradual. The tumor was sitting on top of the optic nerve. Fortunately it was not attached."

"Will she have any lasting problems?" her father asked.

"No. The meninges membrane acted as a cushion between the brain and tumor."

"Thank God," Mr. Webster repeated.

"The membrane is about the thickness of a piece of paper. The team worked hard to manage the flow of blood while I sliced down the middle of the membrane."

"I can't imagine slicing something that thin," Steve said.

Dr. Beamer smiled. "That's what I'm paid to do. There'll be some swelling for a few months until everything normalizes. In effect, her brain has been working overtime the last several years to compensate for the pressure it's been under. When everything is back in place, she'll have more energy than she's had in the past five or six years."

Her dad grinned. "We'll have to hire another Brittany."

"What causes a tumor like this?" Steve asked.

"That's the $64,000 question. We know it's more common for women in their fifties and sixties. We still don't understand the source of the problem."

"I don't understand how something like this can happen," her dad confessed.

"It's a real puzzle. The best analogy I can provide is for you to imagine that every cell has a clock inside it. The clock in your bone cells turns off at eighteen or so and you stop growing. Hair cells keep growing, some stop and you lose your hair. For some reason Elizabeth's clock in the meninges membrane turned on roughly twenty years ago. And the tumor started growing."

"Twenty years ago?" Mr. Webster covered his mouth. "It's been growing that long?"

"Meningiomas are slow growing. They're hard to detect because they produce gradual changes over a long period of time."

"What can we expect in the next few weeks?" Steve asked.

"It'll take her two or three days before she remembers much. When she starts asking about the bandages wrapped around her head, I'll walk all of you through the surgery step by step."

"Thank you," Mr. Webster said. "We appreciate what you've done."

"Yes, thank you," the group echoed.

"My reward will be Elizabeth's full recovery," the doctor said.

***

"I understand you're anxious to see the incision," Dr. Beamer said.

Lizbeth grinned. "Yes, I am."

"I think you'll be pleased." He removed the tape and gauze from her head and tossed the dome-shaped mass on the foot of the bed. "Are you ready to see it?"

Lizbeth nodded.

The nurse handed her a mirror.

She hesitated slightly, then looked and smiled. "I have my hair."

Dr. Beamer pulled off his horn-rimmed glasses, his eyes twinkled. "We shaved a three-quarter inch strip for the incision from your forehead-hairline back across the top of your skull then looped around in front of your left ear."

"It looks like a big question mark-shaped railroad track."

"Once your hair grows back you won't see the scar."

"How many staples do I have?"

"Sixty-nine," he said. "We'll remove them in two weeks. And a month from now you won't see any evidence of the surgery."

"That's amazing," Steve said.

"When will I be able to go back to work?" she asked.

"We'll talk about phasing in later. Right now I want you to rebuild your strength. It's one step at a time. By your six-month MRI, you'll be back to full speed."

"That's it?"

"It takes time and a lot of rest. You can't hurry the body, it'll heal at its own pace. You'll be taking several naps a day for the next six weeks. Don't worry, that's normal. You can do most anything you feel like doing. Of course I don't want you standing on your head."

***

Steve gazed across Baltimore's Inner Harbor from a Hyatt Regency suite as he had for the last several nights. For the first time he saw the glow of the shops below, the waving lights strung atop the mass of the Chesapeake, and the twinkling harbor lights running toward Fell's Point.

Sucking on the last of three olives, he took a sip of Tanqueray. He realized he loved Lizbeth more than ever. He grinned to himself, recalling that hint of a smile she'd revealed when he'd passed his handkerchief dabbed with Beautiful — the perfume he'd given her for her birthday — under her nose. *Oh how she loved the tender bouquet of lilies and roses.*

Somehow praying for her survival, watching her lay helpless, and then seeing her smile when she sensed his touch, had brought him closer to her.

He refilled his water glass with ice and gin and walked back to the picture window and gazed at the Inner Harbor. He recalled the appointment he'd had with Dr. Benderman only two days after that encounter with her at the Omni.

"Mr. Schilling," the receptionist had called.

Lost in thought, remembering how he'd slid sideways off the dance floor so as not to reveal his hard-on, he giggled to himself. *I can't believe how sexy she looked. I wanted to jump her right there.*

"Mr. Schilling," the woman repeated for the benefit of the entire room.

"Yes, right here," he had said.

Holding a folder in her hand, the pencil-thin nurse guided him down a narrow hallway and motioned to a chair in a small office. She placed the folder in a tray on the outside wall, and closed the door. "The doctor will be here in a minute."

14

The door opened a few minutes later and a stout, imposing man walked in. Dr. Benderman removed his glasses and laid them with the folder on the end table between the two men. "When we met eight months ago I had little hope about the progress you'd make with your addiction. You've done quite well."

"I almost blew it Saturday night."

"Why, what happened?"

"I attended a big gala downtown at the Omni."

"Yes, I read about it in Sunday's paper. It sounded like a celebrity ball."

"The room was filled with media bigwigs and the state's top officials. I met with one of our alums, Ed Barkley; he's a heavy-weight in the furniture industry."

"Yes, I've heard his name. He's involved in several civic groups."

"Right. He shared several insights about Elizabeth Webster."

"Lizbeth? Funny you mention her. My wife was so upset with the photo of her in the receiving line — showing off everything — she almost wrote a letter to the editor."

Steve's eyes lit up. "You're telling me. She's the sexist woman I've ever seen."

"Not many men would disagree. And probably the richest woman in North Carolina too."

"We talked for a spell. Next thing I know she was pressing her body against me on the dance floor. I made a dumb remark about the pendant she was wearing and ended asking her if she was trying to turn me on."

"Not good. Then what?"

"I had those old feelings. I've been thinking about her ever since."

"Did you masturbate?"

"No, but she's on my mind all the time."

"I think you're being a little hard on yourself. You can't snap your fingers and make your sex addiction go away. Those urges will always be there."

"But doc … nothing has happened for nine months."

"Nine months, nine years, it doesn't matter. I've had smokers tell me after twenty years they still crave a cigarette with their morning coffee."

"How am I going to explain this to Kate?"

"Just like always. You made an agreement with her to share everything. You can't pick and choose what you tell her. She's more than someone you sleep with; she's your confidant, your adviser — she listens and recommends. Treat her like always. Be honest."

"Do I have to tell her I had a hard-on?"

"Steve, you have to be truthful and express your feelings so she can continue to help you."

"I don't know."

"Put yourself in her shoes, Steve. You had a twenty-year affair with her and she's still standing beside you trying to help, willing to be a part of your life."

***

Makes sense to tell Kate. But how? I can't tell her I had a hard-on when I was dancing with another woman. She might say screw you. Maybe I shouldn't tell her. One little white lie won't hurt.

Steve's thoughts bounced back and forth before he convinced himself Dr. Benderman was right — he had to be honest with her.

He picked up the phone and dialed.

"Kate Blanchard," a sleepy voice answered.

"Did I wake you?" he asked.

"I was reading. I must have dozed off. How are things going?"

"Fine."

Kate paused. "That doesn't sound like the Steve Schilling I know. Are you positive?"

"Hmm … I'm kind of down."

"Steve Schilling down? What's wrong?"

"Some of those old feelings have crept back in."

"What did you expect? Dr. Jones in Little Rock said those urges would always be there. We haven't seen each other for two months. How many times do you think I've felt that way?"

"A lot I suppose."

"Do you want to have sex over the phone?"

"It's not that Kate, I have …"

She interrupted. "Steve, what happened?"

"Nothing, really."

"Steve, we agreed. You have to be truthful with me."

"You won't be mad, will you?"

"Look, we're a team. I may be five hundred miles away but I'm still here for you."

"You're so sweet, Kate. I love you."

"Tell me what happened."

"I attended that gala Saturday night in Charlotte. Remember I told you it was coming up."

"Yes, what's the point?"

"I felt strange."

"Did someone hit on you?"

"Kind of … but nothing happened."

"She turned you on, didn't she?"

"No, it wasn't like that."

"Did you take her to bed?"

"Kate, no."

"Steve, you're bound to have ups and downs. I guess this was an up." She laughed.

"It's not funny."

"I'm sorry, honey. We have to learn how to laugh. It'll help us in the long run."

"You're right, Kate. You're always right."

"How long before we can be together again?"

"I'm thinking about spring break? We could meet in Myrtle Beach."

"That'd be wonderful."

"I'll pick up tickets for a country and western show."

"Sounds perfect."

Steve hung up the phone and wiped the perspiration from his brow. One down, he thought, recalling the doctor's conversation about dealing with his sister's experience. One to go! His upper lip had quivered when the doctor had mentioned her name.

"Whaddaya mean?" he had said to Dr. Benderman.

"You have to tell Sally how you feel about her and how sorry you are for what she had to go through."

He remembered sitting in a cold sweat. "I can't do that, doc."

"Steve, you have to. It will help you and most important it will help her."

"Help her, how?"

"She's carried the burden of your father raping her, all her life. You've had nightmares about being locked in the tool shed with your mother and brother while your dad did it. You have to let her know how you feel. Think about how she must have felt."

Steve's eyes had moistened. "I can still see her standing there in her Sunday dress. She had such a sad look when she unlocked the door. I felt so bad for her."

"You have to unload that burden. Express your feelings to her."

"You mean go to Kentucky?"

"Hmm, you could call her but it'd be best if you were there."

Steve bit his lip. "It's about expressing my feelings, isn't it?"

Dr. Benderman had nodded. "You have to develop a pattern of truthfulness with yourself, and letting others know how you feel about them."

***

Steve threw an overnight bag into his car and headed for his sister's in Hazard, Kentucky. Driving west on I-40, he picked up a soda at McDonald's in Knoxville then took I-75 north. By the time he turned onto the Cumberland Parkway and headed east at London, his shirt was moist through — over all of these years he had never mentioned to Sally the ordeal she had endured.

In Hazard he drove north on State Road 15 for a few minutes then slowed when he saw the mailbox for Greg and Sally Henderson. He turned down the gravel lane and stopped out front.

Pausing for a moment, he collected his thoughts. *This was worse than giving his first state of the university address.* "I have to do it," he said to the rearview mirror.

He grabbed his bag and walked slowly toward the house.

The front door flew open. Sally raced toward him with her arms wide open. "Oh Steve, it's so good to see you. Did you have a good trip?"

He hugged her and spoke softly in her ear. "I love you, sis."

She pulled back. "Steve … you … you've never said that."

"I should have said it lots of times but I …"

"Oh you," she interrupted. "I knew you loved me. I could tell by your actions."

"Hmm maybe, but I should have said more."

"Don't worry about it. I'm fine." They walked arm-in-arm up toward the house. "Want a sandwich or a bowl of soup?"

"How about a BLT and some chips?"

She grabbed his hand and tugged him inside. "I knew you'd say that."

Steve looked around the small living room. "You've made several changes since the last time I was here."

"It's almost ten years ago. Suzanne and you were on your way to Cincinnati for some kind of a meeting."

"I like the printed drapes. Are they new too?"

"Everything is new." She pointed to a short hallway. "We even have a new bedroom set for the spare room where you're staying."

"Great. I'm going to freshen up. I'll be right back," he said, walking down the hallway.

By the time he returned a sandwich and large plate of chips were on the table, along with a bowl of pickles and hot peppers.

"Did you make the hot peppers?"

"Yep, the pickles too. I canned twenty-five quarts just like mom used to do."

Steve dug in and stuffed a hot pepper in his mouth. "God, these are hot," he said, gulping down half a glass of sweet iced tea.

"What did you expect? They're mom's recipe." She laughed and quickly refilled his glass.

"How are things in the Smokies?"

"Couldn't be better. We're talking about building a new basketball arena."

"Wouldn't that be something? I remember when they built Rupp Arena. It was a big deal."

"Same thing is true for us. North Carolina is a big basketball state."

Steve hesitated, pressed his fingers into his temple. "Sally, there's something I want to say. Can we talk?"

"Sure. The kids won't be home till four. And Greg is having the truck repaired."

Steve didn't respond.

"Steve?"

"It's something I should have said long ago."

"About mom?"

"Ah … it's about dad."

Sally's face flushed. Her fingers fiddled with her apron strings.

"You don't have to say anything, just listen." He swallowed hard. "I love you, Sally. I'm so proud of you, raising two perfect kids, running a daycare facility and having such a wonderful husband. You've done everything mom would have wanted."

She stared, caught between a tear and a smile.

He blew his nose and wiped a tear. "I'm so ashamed I didn't protect you. I should have kicked him in the balls and tossed him in the river."

"Steve, there's nothing you could have done. We were kids."

"I know …"

She cut him off. "Mom and the minister helped me a lot. And Greg's been terrific."

"I should have said something earlier."

"I knew how you felt. I could tell by the way you looked at me. Besides, I'm so proud of all the things you've done. Becoming a university president. Who could have a better brother?"

"You're the best, Sally."

Steve put his arms around her and the two talked about the good times they'd shared with their mother.

"Thanks." She hugged him. "I really appreciate the things you said. You're the best."

"What's that noise?"

"It's the school bus." Sally stood. "I'm going outside to watch the kids walk down the lane."

Steve grinned. *How lucky can a guy be? I'm so proud of her.*

***

Still reminiscing, Steve recalled watching Kate stride through security at Myrtle Beach International. *God, she hasn't changed a bit. Other than her ponytail being gone, she looks the same as in college — slim and trim like when she was captain of the cheerleading squad.*

The security guard's eyes followed her through the gate.

"Steve," she called, waving her hand.

He stepped toward her and planted a big smacker on her cheek. "It's good to see you, sweetie."

"I can't wait until we're in the hotel," she said.

"Me too." He grinned like a teenage boy then picked up her carry-on and tugged her over-sized suitcase out of the baggage claim area. "Are you staying more than a week," he jested.

"I thought about it." She giggled. "Figured you wouldn't be up to it."

Steve laughed. "You're probably right."

"What kind of tickets did you buy?"

"Reba McEntire, for tonight."

"Reba? That's wonderful."

He put her suitcase in the trunk and pulled out of short-term parking.

Kate jabbered excitedly about nothing.

Steve drove across town and stopped in front of the hotel. Jumping out, he raced around the car, opened the door and swept his arm in a bowing-like motion. "Welcome to the Breakers."

"You're a crazy man."

"Crazy about you."

Hustling through the lobby to the elevator, he hit the button for their floor and waited impatiently. The door opened and he pulled her suitcase to their room. Unlocking the door, he set the suitcase inside then lifted her in his arms and carried her to the sliders overlooking the ocean.

She waved her arms and giggled. "What are you doing?"

"Practicing for our wedding." He kissed her on the cheek and eased her down.

Kate opened the sliders and stepped outside. "It's spectacular. I love the ocean."

"I do too." He nestled a kiss on the side of her neck. "You're the best."

"I am so happy to see you," she said, running her fingers through his hair. "Each time, I can't wait until we're together again."

He slid down on one knee.

"Don't tell me you're practicing again," she joked.

"It a fantasy I have every time I see you on the beach."

"We're not on the beach."

He glanced over the railing. "Close enough." He loosened her belt.

"What are you doing?"

"What do you think?"

"What if someone comes to the door?"

"It's bolted."

"We can't do it on the balcony."

"Why not? You said you could hardly wait until we were in the room."

"What if someone sees us?"

Steve pulled her onto the lounger then glanced over his shoulder. "I don't see any skydivers." He grinned, slipping off her slacks and running his fingers around the edge of her panties.

Kate pulled him tight and kissed him wildly. "I love you, Steve Schilling."

She unbuttoned her blouse and unhooked her bra.

Steve's hands searched her body as if it were the first time. He ripped off his pants and shirt, and gave out a Tarzan-like yell.

"You're a wild man."

"I'm just starting." Looping his fingers under her bikini panties, he pulled them down.

***

The next morning the two enjoyed a leisurely breakfast on the balcony. Kate replayed Reba's songs. Steve played an air guitar like the lead guitarist. They talked about the good ol' days in Arkansas and got caught up on recent happenings.

Finishing off a second carafe of coffee, Kate raised the topic. "Tell me about that night in Charlotte."

"It wasn't a big deal."

"It sounded like it was when we talked on the phone. I want to hear about it."

Gathering his thoughts, Steve gazed across the horizon. "It was Charlotte's biggest event of the year. All of the bigwigs were there …"

She cut him off. "You told me that. I want to hear about her."

"Okay. I had two fundraising targets — Ed Barkley and Elizabeth Webster."

"Elizabeth Webster? Was she the one?"

"Yes. I'd just finished a positive conversation with Ed and was on a real high when I walked over to Lizbeth's table."

"Lizbeth?"

"She prefers Lizbeth socially. It's Elizabeth in the office."

"Is she attractive?"

"Very."

"I suppose she has big boobs too, right?"

Steve nodded.

"No wonder you got turned on."

"It wasn't like that. We were chatting when she asked me to dance."

"She asked you to dance?"

"Kate, it was a social event. She danced with everyone."

"Did you?"

"No, she was the hostess."

"Did she come on to you?"

"Kind of."

"Did you get a hard-on?"

"A little," he fibbed. "Why are you giving me the first degree?"

"Because I'm trying to help. And … I'm a little jealous, too."

"My God, Kate, nothing happened. I love you."

She backed off and smiled. "I'm so proud of you, Steve. It sounds like you handled it just fine," she said, loosening her robe. "Maybe we should go inside where it's more comfortable."

CHAPTER THREE

Driving east on I–40, Steve tapped the steering wheel to the beat of the up-tempo electric guitar in Tracy Lawrence's "If the Good Die Young." It'd been slightly over a month since he'd raced down the same stretch of highway to be by Lizbeth's bedside. *What a whirlwind series of events — the diagnosis, surgery and wait, then the glimmer of a smile on her face. God, I love her.*

He turned south on I–77, cruised for almost an hour, exited the freeway then drove through downtown Charlotte and parked behind Ed Barkley's office building.

Walking briskly inside, he saw Ed standing in the lobby, and strolled toward him. "Thanks, for squeezing me in."

Ed nodded and the two shook hands.

"I'd like to talk about some university business."

"Of course, come in my office and have a chair," Ed said, continuing down the hallway. "How's Lizbeth doing?"

"She's doing better. It's a long haul, one step at a time."

"I can't imagine what she's gone through."

"Just being there was something else."

Steve followed Ed into his office. "I'm going to see her after our meeting."

"Please give her my regards."

"Will do."

Steve sat down and ran his hand over the finely handcrafted-cherry chair. "Looks like you know something about making quality furniture."

"Thirty-two years in the business. I took over from my dad when I was twenty-eight. The business has grown ten-fold."

"Wow … that's impressive."

"Like you my boy, we had a good team. So what's on your mind?"

"I received a confidential call from the Governor's chief of staff this week. He said the Governor wants two or three names of potential trustees for Mountain State and asked if I could help him."

"Why was it a confidential call?"

"President's don't usually get asked. The Governor likes to keep some distance between the board and the president. His assistant said they were making an exception because of the good things they've been hearing about MSU."

"Good for him. I'm glad I wasn't the only one who noticed. Whataya you think I ought to do?"

"It's a lot of work but you'd be terrific. University boards need strong people like you. I think you should do it."

"Sounds interesting."

"So is it okay for me to call him back with your name."

"Sure." Ed paused, as if contemplating something else. "Do you have a minute?"

"Of course, what's on your mind?"

"I've been thinking about those task force meetings we had last spring. Are the faculty always so engaged?"

"What do you mean?"

"I was surprised by their level of involvement in the focused groups. They really got into the discussions."

"The faculty are extraordinarily capable and have great pride in what they do — in many ways they see the university as their place."

"I suppose that could be a concern sometimes."

"You bet."

"Does that happen often?"

"No, but when they get their dander up they can be a real problem — some get out of whack and think they run the place. Then it's more like herding." Steve laughed.

Ed shifted to another point. "I saw how you finessed the faculty, getting them to endorse your proposal to change the title of the academic vice president to provost. Why was that so important?"

"I like the provost model. It makes a clear statement that academics are number one."

"There seemed to be something more than that."

"You're quite perceptive, Ed. Most people don't pick up on that subtlety. Faculty members are leery about everything. They see four vice presidents in the cabinet meeting and automatically assume the academic vice president can be out-voted. With a provost in place it's easy for me to say the provost has one more vote than the other VPs combined. And when I'm off campus everyone knows who's in charge."

"How do the other VPs feel about that?"

"They understand the symbolism."

"Interesting." Ed hesitated. "How did you finagle the retirement of the old basketball coach? Getting him to step down without a fuss had to be a real coup."

"Like always I was upfront, and told him straight out 'we're going to play the big guys.' He saw the handwriting on the wall. After twenty years of coaching, a position in alumni affairs, even at a reduced salary, sounded better than the alternative."

"And a lot easier too." Ed nodded. "Last question. There seemed to be a lot of interest in that KidsStyle program. What's that all about?"

"Several of our education faculty members are working with teachers in the local schools on a new and unique approach to teaching social skills. It provides tools for students and teachers to deal with confrontation and bullying."

"You're going to be all right." Ed nodded and smiled. "You have any of those naming opportunities left in the arena?"

"Everything except the press box. I mentioned that to Lizbeth."

"Hmm." Ed paused. "I'll do the reception area."

"For a million dollars?"

Ed gave him a questioning look. "You offering a discount?"

"One mil."

Ed extended his hand.

"Deal." Steve shook his hand and clasped his free hand on top of Ed's.

***

Steve parked his black Caddy in front of the garage door, picked up a dozen red roses and headed up the front steps.

Brittany opened the door of Lizbeth's mountain home on Lake Lure, with a flourish. "I saw you coming up the driveway and I ran to the door. I thought you might like to surprise her. She's in the sunroom."

He winked and tiptoed across the huge oak-floored great room then leaned over the back of the chair and kissed Lizbeth on the neck.

She flinched then catching a glimpse of him, smiled. "What a pleasant surprise. How did you get in?"

"Brittany opened the door." He pulled the bouquet of roses from behind his back. "Red roses for the beautiful lady."

"You're so sweet, thank you." Lizbeth motioned to Brittany. "Would you put these in a vase?"

Brittany nodded and took the flowers into the kitchen.

"How have you been sweetheart?" he asked.

"Hmm, about the same. Brittany says I'm better but my energy is zip-o. After combing my hair in the morning, I have to take a nap."

"Your color is better."

Lizbeth shrugged. "My head's fuzzy. I can't wait till the meds wear off."

"Dr. Beamer said it would be at least six weeks. You still have a couple of weeks to go."

"Two weeks of sitting in this chair … sounds like an eternity."

"I've worked out my schedule so I can be here every other weekend. Maybe that'll make the time go by faster?"

A glow surrounded her face. "It sure will."

"Good. What's for dinner?"

"Brittany is baking Cornish hens."

"Terrific. They're my favorite. Want a drink before?"

"That'd be perfect."

***

The next time Steve arrived Lizbeth greeted him in her jogging suit and tennies at the front door. Her body language conveyed a new sense of resolve.

"I'm ready," she said spontaneously.

"Who *is* this person?" he joked.

"The meds are gone. My energy is up. I walked by the lake twice this week. It felt good."

"Great, maybe we can take a walk this afternoon."

"I'd like that."

Steve glanced toward the kitchen. "I'm starved. What's for lunch?"

"Brittany made your favorite — BLTs, German potato salad and iced tea."

"What more could a man ask for? Two beautiful women and a perfect lunch."

"It's almost ready," Brittany called.

"Sit down, sweetie," Lizbeth said. "I'll bring out the tea."

"Are you sure?" Steve questioned. "I can do that."

"I'm fine," she said, giving a hint of her old self.

Steve watched Brittany balance a platter of BLT halves and a large bowl of potato salad, on her way to the morning room.

"Is company coming?" he jested.

"I figured you'd need two sandwiches apiece. Lizbeth's appetite has really picked up."

The three had a leisurely lunch. Steve cleaned up the last of the potato salad and said, "What's for dessert?"

"See Brittany, I told you he would ask."

"There's a pecan pie in the oven," Brittany said. "I thought you might like a warm piece when the two of you return from your walk."

"Perfect." Steve jumped up and reached for Lizbeth's hand. "Ready to go, darling?"

"I've been waiting all week." She grabbed his hand and gave him a light tug.

Steve put on his old St. Louis Cardinal ball cap, and the two walked slowly down to the lake then headed west along the shoreline. "We've talked about a lot of things but you've never said much about your job," Lizbeth said. "What's it like running a university?"

Steve stared across the lake. "That's a difficult question. Managing the staff is the same as what you do." He paused. "But ... dealing with the faculty — that's something else. Sometimes I feel like I'm the head zookeeper. Other times I feel like I'm herding elephants. Then again, I admire them for their commitment to students. It's exciting to see the students succeed."

"How do you manage four hundred Ph.D.'s?"

"Very carefully." He laughed. "I can't manage the university the way you run your corporation."

Lizbeth wrinkled her brow. "Why not?"

"Universities operate under a concept of shared governance."

"You mean everyone is equal?"

"Not equal. We treat each other as peers; each person has different responsibilities. The curriculum is the faculty's domain. I can't tell them what to teach, what should be in a major or how to go about organizing the content."

"That seems kind of dumb. Why not?"

"Faculty members are experts in their disciplines. I can't know every field of study so I have to rely on their expertise."

"That makes sense."

"Sweetie, it's time to turn around. We've walked far enough for the first time."

"But Steve, I have more questions."

"Save them. Right now my mind is on a piece of warm pecan pie."

***

When the lovers walked two weeks later, Lizbeth peppered him with more questions about the university. Steve rambled for an hour. And they walked twice as far.

"Enough," he said, turning back toward the house. "What's for dessert?"

"Hot fudge sundaes if you tell me about dealing with athletics."

"Athletics?" He shook his head. "That could take all night."

"I want to know, Steve. I want to understand the world you live in."

Steve opened the lakeside door and hung his ball cap on the back of a chair. Plopping down on the sofa in the sunroom, he dug into his sundae then looked up. "Okay, what would you like to know?"

"Everything. To start with why are so many people on campus anti-athletics?"

"It's a real dichotomy. On Saturdays everyone roots for the football team. Faculty members, like everyone else, party and have a good time. That's where the common ground ends. The rest of the time it's a clash of cultures."

"Cultures?"

"Athletics is about winning. And, of course, we all want them to win. But not at all costs."

"What's that mean?"

"There are a lot of good coaches, don't get me wrong. And honest ones too." He hesitated. "But to tell you the truth, I wouldn't give you a hill of beans for most of them. They say the right words but when push comes to shove — they are a bunch of cheats."

"Cheats?"

"Well … maybe not cheats but they live on the fringe, an inch from a NCAA violation. They're always crossing the line creating one problem after another. It's an ongoing headache."

"How do they get away with it?"

"It's part of their culture. Coaches stick together like bugs on flypaper. They lie … and cover up for each other."

"I can't imagine dealing with that every day."

He shrugged. "It's something you learn to cope with."

"No wonder there's such tension."

"Right. The rest of the campus operates under a consensus-building concept. There are issues and disagreements but people work together for the betterment of the whole."

"Good for them," Lizbeth interjected.

"Most faculty members see athletics as being in it for themselves."

"That sounds kind of harsh."

"Maybe so, but it's reality. Athletics is similar to the military. Neither one fits within their organizational structure. And both have a win-win, no compromise philosophy. As I've said before we want them to win … but their modus operandi runs counter to internal campus operations. It's the same way things work in Washington — someone is always at odds with the military."

"What's the other choice?"

"That's the problem. What we have is probably the best structure we can hope for. I'm grateful our forefathers placed the military under the president. Who knows what would have evolved if the military had been out on their own?"

"Sounds like the same is true for athletics in universities."

"You bet." He smiled.

"What else do I need to know about athletics?"

"Lots. We've barely touched the tip of the iceberg."

"Tell me more," she requested.

Steve reflected, briefly. "Athletics raises all kinds of questions about money, time and attention."

Lizbeth cocked her head to the side. "They bring in millions of dollars. How can that be a problem?"

"They spend millions more. Only eight of the hundred and twenty-five biggest Division I football schools in the country make money."

"I can't believe that. I bet nine out of ten people would say athletics is a cash cow."

"I know, it's crazy. But faculty members know the full story, they see those losses as real dollars that could be used to enhance the academic programs. It's a big issue!"

"How can athletics run programs that regularly operate with deficits?"

"That's part of the dilemma most presidents face. Most cave to public pressure. Some hope for a bowl game. Bowl game or not, most campuses have to eat it — there's lots of red ink."

"Eat it. If I were president I wouldn't do that."

"That's only part of the problem. Over the years athletics has inched its way out of control. Now it seems more important to keep up with the Jones' than to maintain institutional integrity."

"That's unbelievable."

"You're telling me?"

"Last question. How is time a factor?"

"I devote more time to athletics than any other entity on campus. And the faculty know it. They see athletics consuming far more time and attention than it deserves, way out of proportion to what they contribute."

Steve glanced toward the kitchen. "What did Brittany prepare for dinner?"

Lizbeth snuggled against his chest. "I sent her home. I thought we'd start with dessert in the bedroom."

"Are you sure?"

"Absolutely. Let's get naked."

CHAPTER FOUR

Steve slid the stack of mail to the side of his white-oak desk and glanced at his calendar — call Martha Brown was printed in red. He remembered the love letters he'd received from her, and then suddenly, a Dear John letter. It'd been well over a year now. *How could she have done that? We'd planned to be married and honeymoon in Ireland. Why didn't she call? I know we could have worked it out.*

Steve dialed directory assistance then shook his head and placed the phone back in the cradle. He'd had this conversation with himself countless times — *what do I say to her? I have to figure out something; her athletic facilities construction management expertise is critical to our success.*

He buzzed Joyce, his administrative assistant.

She appeared within an instant. "Yes, Mr. President," the petite, fortyish brunette said. Pulling the collar of her blouse together, she eased onto the chair next to his desk.

"Please set up a meeting with Martha Brown at Global Sports in Charlotte. They're a world-class company that specializes in building athletic facilities. She's a former colleague of mine and a vice president there. I need to meet her before my May meeting with Ms. Webster."

"Anything else?"

"Yes." He looked her in the eye. "I've decided to create an assistant to the president position."

"Good for you. There's no way you can continue to carry the load like you've been doing."

"I'd like someone who knows Mountain State and could help avoid the pitfalls of the past."

"That's a good idea. People are nervous about the number of changes you're suggesting. Having an insider in the cabinet would make them feel more comfortable."

"I'd like someone who's well respected, who could be my right arm."

"There aren't many like that."

"So I've learned. I've narrowed my list to three — Harry Lounsbury, Fred Panzow and Charlie McBride."

Joyce raised her hand. "I can save you a lot of time."

Steve gave her a quizzical look.

"Interview Charlie McBride first. He knows everyone and has the right temperament. Would you like to see his personnel file?"

"You're positive he's the right guy?"

"Absolutely."

"My old mentor used to say, 'Trust your staff.' Go ahead, set up the meeting."

***

Joyce buzzed Steve. "Dr. McBride is here."

"Send him in, please."

Balding and round-faced, a short man with wire-rim glasses extended his hand. "Good morning, Mr. President."

Steve stared at a young image of Ben Franklin. "Morning. I understand you prefer Charlie."

"That's right."

"Good. It's Steve."

The old man smiled. "I hear you're looking for an assistant to the president."

Steve cocked his head. "How did you know?"

"You can't do much around here without someone knowing."

Steve frowned, not knowing the full scope of the comment. "Joyce thinks you'd be the best candidate. What do you think?"

"My daughter is always right."

"Your daughter? You mean Joyce is your …"

"No," Charlie jumped in. "I was just putting you on."

"Sneaky, aren't you?"

"I'd rather say sly. Anyway, yes, I'd be honored to be your assistant."

Steve frowned. "I haven't asked you, yet."

"Sorry, I retract my acceptance," Charlie said, folding his arms across his chest.

"Fine." Steve smiled. "Will you be my assistant?"

"Yes."

"Just like that? We haven't talked about your duties or what your salary will be."

"I know what an assistant does — all of the work."

Steve laughed.

"You're working your butt off. I know you'll be fair."

"How did you know about my plans?"

"You've scheduled appointments with two others. After thirty-one years around here I have a good sense of what's going on."

***

Steve parked outside Martha's office and strolled up the sidewalk. Opening the door, he paused to examine the art deco furnishings — a twenty-foot vaulted space splashed with purples, lime-green and reds. Spotlights beamed on the wall art and the glass-encased sports arena models arranged throughout the reception area.

A soft, southern accent interrupted his gaze. "May I help you?"

Steve's eyes shifted to the plunging neckline of a well-endowed receptionist. "Yes, I'm Steve Schilling. I have an appointment with Martha Brown."

"She'll be with you shortly. Her conference call with the mayor of Savannah is running longer than expected. Please, make yourself comfortable."

She motioned to a cluster of multi-colored lounge chairs in the center of the room.

"I'll check out the arena models," Steve said, knowing that he'd rather be checking her out.

"If you have any questions please let me know. We have a brochure for each one."

"Thanks." Steve made a quick tour of the displays then sat down in one of the cushy chairs. Leafing through an *Architectural Digest,* he heard her voice and looked up.

"These projects might be of interest." Handing him a couple of brochures, she leaned over, revealing her full cleavage. "If there's anything you'd like, please let me know."

Steve glimpsed down her gaping sweater.

She gave him a come-on smile.

You bet your sweet ass there is. "No, I'm fine."

Martha appeared, looking as stunning as she had years ago when they first met. Steve stood to shake her hand. She turned away and headed down the hallway. His heart raced as he walked behind her, watching her firm ass and red hair bounce like a Victoria's Secret model.

She gave him a politically correct smile and motioned for him to be seated at the end of an eight-foot long walnut conference table. Easing into a black high-back executive chair at the other end, she smirked.

Steve shifted uncomfortably.

"Mr. President, our organization is pleased you're considering us as your design consultants."

Steve stared, not knowing what to say.

Martha returned his stare with an icy glare, her eyes shooting daggers.

He opened his notebook and lowered his head. "I-I don't …"

"Don't say a word," she said, turning over her pad. She hesitated for what seemed like an eternity then straightened her broad shoulders.

"Steve, I'm meeting with you as a professional courtesy on behalf of our corporation. I want you to know my personal feelings have nothing to do with the corporation's decision. Do you understand?"

He nodded.

Martha sighed. "I've thought about this for five hundred and fourteen days. Some days I thought it would never happen. Other times I *hoped* it would never happen."

"Can I say something?" he asked in a soft tone.

"No." Her cold expression said more than words.

He wished he could hide.

"Steve, I'll never forgive you. I gave you my all, everything and more. For seven years I was the other woman, waiting for your call, hoping you'd stop by. I was thrilled when you told me you were divorcing Suzanne. You got down on your knee and proposed to me." She choked and wiped a tear. "We made honeymoon plans to see my grandparents' home. Then I found out about the others."

"Martha, I can explain."

She slammed her hand on the table. "Fuck you!"

Steve wilted into his chair.

"You can't explain screwing four others. You told me I was the only one. Did you tell Sandra she was the only one when you screwed her in Memphis? I suppose that's what you told your doctor friend when you fucked her on the gazebo?"

"Martha, it wasn't like that. I loved you."

"You didn't love me. You've never loved anyone but yourself."

"Can I say something?"

"Fuck no." She glanced at her notes and composed herself. "Here's the last thing I'll ever say to you. Yes, our corporation would be pleased to serve as design consultants. If you're interested, Paul Curtis will be the project manager. Here's his business card." She flipped it to the center of the table and looked up. "If you ever contact me, I'll void any agreements you've signed with our company. Do you understand?"

Steve lowered his head.

Martha stood and marched out.

Moments later the door reopened. A tall, slender man with a crisp business attitude walked in. "Good afternoon, Dr. Schilling, I'm Paul Curtis. I would be pleased to handle your project."

"I'd like that."

The two men talked about the planned arena for the next two hours.

It was after six when Steve walked out and plopped down in his car. *How could I have betrayed her? She was the best thing to ever happen to me.*

***

Steve exited the elevator at the executive level of Webster Media International. The glass doors to the suite opened automatically. He stepped in. High-end walnut furniture with deep red and orange damask fabric covered the reception area. On the left, two large fig trees framed a twenty-foot picture window. A large Monet hung on the right. *Surely it was an original.*

A cute short receptionist looked up. "Dr. Schilling, how are you today?"

"Fine, thank you."

"Ms. Webster is waiting. Please follow me."

She opened a set of double doors. "Ms. Webster, Dr. Schilling is here."

"Wonderful. Send him in."

Dressed in a dark blue pinstriped suit, she greeted him with a professional hug and a peck on the cheek. "How do you like my office?"

"It's lovely but not as lovely as you."

She smiled, retaining her professional demeanor. "It sounds like you've been a busy man."

"The projects keep adding up."

"Ed Barkley told me about the focused groups. I look forward to hearing more about them."

"The process works particularly well when you're on a fast track."

"Sounds like it," she said, motioning him to the conversation area centered in front of the picture window.

"Do we have assigned seats?" he jested.

"No, but I'd take the loveseat on the end. It has the best view. Would you like a soda?"

"A diet something would be fine."

Lizbeth buzzed her assistant. "Ashley, we'll have two Diet Cokes and some munchies."

"Right away."

"You look fabulous," Steve said.

"I can't believe six months has past. I feel better than ever."

"Remember, that's what Dr. Beamer said would happen."

"I know but I never imagined the change would be so dramatic."

"Good for you." Steve spooned a few almonds from a crystal bowl on the coffee table and placed them on a plate. "I'd like to walk you through the arena prospectus."

"Great. I've been thinking about it ever since that night at the Omni. Daddy's so excited about the idea."

"I've talked to Paul Curtis at Global Sports. He'll be the project manager."

"Excellent, I was hoping you'd involve them."

"We've had a pre-bid meeting with several construction contractors. Gurley Construction really looks good. Mark Gurley is topnotch."

Are they the ones out of Raleigh?"

"Yes." Steve nodded.

"You can't do better. They have an outstanding track record and are always on time."

"That's good to know."

Steve spread a folder in front of her and opened his. She patted the seat next to her. "Please, join me. It'll be easier for us to work off the same copy."

Steve slid his soda and plate next to hers then eased next to her on the sofa. Handing her some brochures, he said, "These are pictures of similar projects they've done in Minnesota and Texas. What do you think?"

Lizbeth studied the photos. "They're terrific."

"I thought you'd like them. I have a possible naming plaque too."

"I can hardly wait to see it."

"Mr. Curtis recommended that we call it the James E. Webster Convocation Center."

She looked like she wanted to jump for joy. "Daddy will be so pleased. He was afraid you'd propose something with athletics in the title. This will be perfect."

"It'll be appropriate for us too. We can host concerts, commencement and other events in it."

"This calls for a celebration. Is it too early for Tanqueray?"

Steve glanced at his watch — 4:20, then smiled. "It must be five o'clock somewhere."

Lizbeth walked toward the liquor cabinet. "Ashley, could you come in for a minute."

She popped her head in the doorway. "Yes, Ms. Webster."

"Call daddy at the paper and ask him come over. Tell him to bring his checkbook we have something special to tell him."

Lizbeth poured a Royal Crown on the rocks then fixed Steve his usual. Handing him his gin, she asked, "Would you like to make a toast?"

"Yes, but first I have a question."

"Sure, go ahead."

"I didn't understand your comment about the checkbook. We haven't talked about the size of the gift."

Lizbeth grinned. "I was checking to see how alert you were."

He wrinkled his brow. "I'm sorry to be dense, but I don't …"

"I cheated." She laughed. "When you opened your file I saw the numbers $13-14. My staff came up with $13.5 to $14 million. I propose we agree on a $15 million naming gift."

"Fifteen?" Steve gulped.

"I figure you'll need a little extra. There's no reason to cut corners, agreed?"

"Right."

"So how about that toast?"

Steve stood and flashed his megawatt smile. "Here's to the opening of the James E. Webster Convocation Center."

She clinked his glass and took a sip. "And here's to our future."

Her father walked in. "What's going on?"

***

A black limo turned down Church Street and stopped in front of the McNinchouse. The driver jumped out, hurried around to open the door and extended his white glove just as he had, almost a year ago to the day, when they'd dined here for the first time. She had worn a strapless Carolina blue cocktail dress. Four strands of pearls had filled her cleavage.

He remembered taking in an eyeful. "I love your dress. You look beautiful," he had said.

She placed her hand on his arm and the two strolled into one of Charlotte's finest restaurants. The maître d' greeted her with a nod. "Good evening, Ms. Webster. Your table is ready."

He escorted the couple upstairs to a small, dimly-lit private room. Following behind, Steve admired the richly molded woodwork, the hand-crafted furniture and tiled fireplaces.

The maître d' pulled out her chair.

"What do you think?" she asked Steve.

"It's spectacular. I love the deep red drapery."

"It's one of the most romantic restaurants in town. The same Victorian craftsmen who worked on the Biltmore Estate built this house back in the 1890s. Wait till you see the menu — encrusted rack of lamb, spice marinated venison and brown sugar-rubbed filet."

"Sounds scrumptious. If I eat too much I might have to stay all night."

Lizbeth flipped her long black hair aside. "I was hoping you might consider something else."

"I'm open to that. What do you have in mind?"

"The driver will be back at nine-thirty. We can talk about it after dessert."

Steve changed the subject. "I want to hear about your trip. Did you have time to shop? I love shopping."

"You're putting me on."

"No. It's exciting to see a woman's glow when she steps out of the dressing room and twirls. It turns me on."

"Really? I'll have to try that sometime."

"Don't get my hopes up," Steve joked.

"I was thinking about more than that." She snickered.

Steve leaned back with a Cheshire smile. "Well then … maybe we should pass on dinner."

"I had my mind set on the filet," she said, licking her lips.

"That'll work."

They shared two bottles of wine with their gourmet dinners and talked about places they'd traveled and the favorite things they liked to do.

Steve shoved his plate aside. "I can't eat one more bite."

"What, no dessert?"

Steve gave her a blank look.

"Our corporation rents the Mecklenburg suite in the Omni for twenty nights a year. It has a comfortable living room, dining area and a wet bar."

"Sounds like a good start to me." He laughed.

Brittany's made arrangements for tonight. Should I say more?"

"Are you serious?"

"I don't make frivolous proposals."

Steve feigned surprise. "Why, I'm just a country boy. I've never been invited to a beautiful woman's room," he jested.

"Sure, and I'm a country lawyer." With a grin, she played along. "I've never done anything like this."

"Do you always have things arranged or planned?"

"Most of the time. Brittany does most of it."

"Sounds like she thinks of everything."

"That's what I pay her for. She also reserved the rooftop pool from midnight 'til two and arranged for a lobster and shrimp snack."

"I can handle that."

"Wake-up call will be at eight o'clock. Breakfast will be served in the room at nine-thirty. And at eleven, the limo will pick you up. Are you up to it?"

"I'll stay up as long as I can."

"You devil you."

***

That night, a year ago, Lizbeth had unlocked the door to the suite and motioned to him. Steve stepped in and studied the elegant maple furniture. Walking further, he peeked into the partially open doorway — white terrycloth robes folded on each side of the open bed. "Did Brittany do that too?"

She nodded. "Would you open the champagne while I slip on a robe?"

"Of course." Steve popped the cork and filled their glasses then sat at the bar next to a bouquet of yellow roses. *This woman is hard to figure. She's powerful, in charge to the nth degree. Next thing I know she's warm and compassionate, like the girl next door.*

Lizbeth floated out of the darkness, her robe loosely tied, picked up a glass and offered a toast. "Here's to our state's most wonderful university president."

"And here's to the most beautiful CEO I've ever met."

She eyed him. "What was it like growing up in Kentucky?"

"Hmm … that's a long story, not very interesting I'm afraid."

"To the contrary, I want to know."

"Well, my dad was a coal miner." Steve hesitated. "A real asshole I'm sorry to say. He treated mom like crap. He never did anything for her, never bought her a new dress, nothing."

"That's sad. I can't imagine what it must have been like for you."

"I got regular beatings, sometimes twice a day."

She scowled. "That's horrible."

"The only time my mom was happy was Thanksgiving of my junior year, a couple of years after dad died from Black Lung. His younger brother, Uncle Freddie, drove up from Corbin. His old Cadillac trunk was loaded with canned goods, frozen pot pies and a turkey. He gave me a football. And a white-laced dress to my mom. I can still see her holding it in front of her as she danced around the kitchen. You'd thought she was the queen of the ball."

"That must have been something."

"It was. Uncle Freddie poured the champagne into juice glasses. Can you imagine?"

"Not really."

"I asked mom if I could stay overnight at my friend's house. She was reluctant but he convinced her it'd be okay. I was halfway down the hill when I realized I'd forgotten my kicking tee. When I returned the lights were out. I peaked in the kitchen window. My mom was standing there, her long dark hair hanging over her bare shoulders, the top of her dress pulled to her waist. I'd never seen her breasts. God, she was beautiful."

"I can't imagine what thoughts must have gone through your head."

"I ran down the hill, crying."

Lizbeth held back a tear. "Oh Steve, you're so sincere." She stood and walked over to the full-length mirror. "Would you unlock my pearls, please?"

Steve slid behind her, watched her remove her earrings and loosen her robe. Gazing into the mirror, his eyes moved down to her black panties and back, zeroing in on her perfectly shaped breasts. *She looks thirty-five rather than the fifty-five she must be.*

"Do you work out regularly?" he asked.

"Every day. And in case you're wondering — they're real."

"I figured," he said. "Otherwise you wouldn't have a double-locked clasp."

"Not the pearls, silly," she quipped then paused with a giggle. "That's one for you."

She turned to the side showing off her nipples, poised like rockets.

He pulled her tight, kissed her on the forehead then French kissed her until he could hardly breathe.

Lizbeth gasped, took a step back then ran her hands down his well-trimmed frame. Unzipping his pants, she let them drop to the floor.

Steve stood erect, waiting, hoping for more.

She wrapped her hand around his protruding boxers and fondled him, kissing him softly; then tugged him into the bedroom. Pushing him on the bed, she snuggled beside him and toyed with the buttons on his shirt, slowly unbuttoning each. Her velvet-like lips crisscrossed his chest.

Steve's insides somersaulted.

She pulled off his shorts and grinned. "You're much larger than Arnold."

"And luckier, too."

Lizbeth slid between his legs, caressing one leg then the other. Reaching the top of his thighs, she nibbled and teased, her tongue circling his erection. Her mouth engulfed him.

Steve took a deep breath and gasped. "I can't hold off any longer."

"Hold off?" She laughed. "We haven't had the first course yet."

Steve blinked his blurry eyes, and mumbled. "How many courses are there?"

"I haven't decided." She straddled him. "Entrees won't be ready for another hour."

"An hour?" He bit his lip trying not to come.

She rose and gazed at his naked body. "Not bad for a university president."

She grabbed his shoulders, pulled herself on top of him and eased him in.

CHAPTER FIVE

Steve read the morning story about today's board meeting then tossed *The Mountaineer* on the kitchen table. Pouring a third cup of coffee, he glanced at the clock and smiled. *Plenty of time.* Ed Barkley had captured the essence of each task-force meeting, and with his million dollar gift, deserves the Distinguished Alumni Award he'll receive today.

Steve looked at the clock again.

"Shit, my meeting with Ed is in ten minutes," he said to himself, grabbing his jacket from the kitchen chair and hurrying out the door.

He raced across town and pulled into his designated parking space.

Ed was waiting in Steve's reception area when he rushed in. "Sorry, my breakfast meeting with the students ran a little overtime," he fibbed.

"Hey, that's why you're here."

Steve pointed to the meeting area in his office. "Have a chair."

Ed sucked in his gut, unbuttoned his suit jacket, and sat down. "Thanks for sending me a preview of today's agenda. What's the game plan?"

"It'll be fairly routine."

"Maybe for you but I've never appeared before a university board."

"It'll be like talking to your own."

"Sure."

"I'll give them a brief synopsis of your background and the many ways in which you've contributed to MSU — highlight your outstanding leadership on the task force and you're million-dollar donation. They'll vote on your award, and then the chair will motion you to the dais and present your plaque."

"I want to say some things about your leadership. Anything special you want me to say?"

"It's your call, do your thing. The microphone will be on the right."

"It's important for board members to understand the quality of leadership you exhibited."

"Thanks, I appreciate that."

Ed glanced at the clock. "Since we have a few minutes, I'd be interested in your assessment of your second year. Do you feel good about it?"

"I do. I had some anxiety at the beginning — still a little guarded — but overall it went well."

"You were feeling your way; people were watching and waiting for your next agenda."

"After I commended the faculty senate for upgrading the promotion standards it all changed."

Ed smiled. "They were looking for your stamp of approval."

"Probably so."

"By the way, how are things going with Lizbeth?"

"Couldn't be better. She's recovered and going like gangbusters. We'll be announcing her daddy's fifteen million-dollar naming gift later in the month."

"I told you to go for the big kahuna."

"It's costing *you* a million dollars."

"My pleasure."

"Thanks." Steve glanced at his watch. "We better leave now. I want to chat with the board chairman before the meeting."

***

Steve chatted with Ed on the way to his car and thanked him again. "I hope you have a proper place for your award."

Ed slid behind the wheel. "I've already picked out the space behind my desk."

"Thanks, again," Steve said, turning toward his office.

"I enjoyed it. Look forward to the next time we can team up."

Steve walked briskly to his office, unloaded his briefcase and handed Joyce the board materials.

"How'd it go," she asked.

"Like clockwork. I've made a few notes on the agenda for you to follow up on."

"I'll have the drafts ready when you arrive in the morning."

"I'd appreciate that."

Steve closed his office door and plopped down on his executive chair. *Phew, if people only knew what it's like to run a board meeting. I never know when a board member is going to say something out of line or propose a harebrained idea.* He eased back on the swivel-rocker and read the lone message slip — Brittany called at 2:10.

He smiled and dialed.

"Brittany Hayward," she answered.

"Brittany, it's Steve."

"Thanks, Mr. President for returning my call. I want to confirm the schedule of events for the arena groundbreaking ceremony."

"Hang on." Steve pulled a folder from his drawer. "I have it. Lunch for the special guests will be at twelve-thirty in the university center. I'll fax you directions and where to park. The campus bus for the ceremony will leave at two o'clock. At two-thirty, I'll give a brief welcome and introduce Lizbeth and her father. After his remarks there'll be a photo op when we unveil his portrait and the naming plaque."

"He doesn't know the plaque is coming. Mr. Webster will love that."

"Would you ask him to make a few remarks?"

"Don't worry." Brittany giggled. "He'll have plenty to say."

"Next, we'll do the heavy lifting — pose with the shovels — and that'll be it."

Brittany laughed. "Knowing Mr. Webster, he might dig the entire footing before nightfall."

"It should be over by three o'clock."

"Sounds perfect. Mr. Webster's driver will be able to take him home before dark. He has another commitment that evening."

"That shouldn't be a problem."

"I've reserved a suite for Ms. Webster at the Comfort Inn for Friday and Saturday night. I hope that's okay?"

"It's not the Ritz."

"They said it opened last fall and still has that shiny newness about it. I'm sure it'll be fine."

***

Wiping the tears from her eyes, Lizbeth applauded as her father stepped back from the portable podium. She jumped from her folding chair and rushed to his side. "Daddy, I'm so proud of you. What you said about mother and the meaning of today's dedication was wonderful."

"You made it all possible, sweetie. None of this would have happened had it not been for you. Thank you, so much." He looked around. "Where's the food?"

"I might have known." Lizbeth laughed and pointed to the right. "It's in the white tent."

"Sounds good." Mr. Webster led a small group inside and filled a plate.

Steve caught up with him a few minutes later, and gave him a bear-sized hug. "I want to personally thank you Mr. Webster. You've made a significant difference for the campus. We'll be eternally grateful for your commitment."

"The pleasure is mine."

Steve introduced Mr. Webster to the board chairman then mingled with the other guests and dignitaries.

After cleaning his plate one more time, Mr. Webster motioned to his driver. "It's time to go, Earl."

Overhearing the request, Lizbeth asked Earl to transfer her bags to Steve's car. She gave her father a farewell peck on the cheek and turned to Steve. "Can we leave now?"

"In a minute. I have to make one final round. Go ahead to my car I'll catch up with you."

Steve said his goodbyes then joined Lizbeth in his Caddy. She snuggled close and kissed him lightly on the cheek. "That was a wonderful program. Daddy loved it. Did Brittany tell you pecan pie was his favorite?"

"No. I guess I lucked out on that one."

"You really impressed daddy. He'd like to invite a large group of his friends in Charlotte for a similar event at the Omni. It'd be good press for the university. What do you think?"

"Sounds perfect. Any time in June would be fine."

She glimpsed at her pocket calendar. "Let's shoot for Friday the ninth. I'll have Brittany confirm that and reserve the Mecklenburg suite for that weekend. That is if it's okay?"

"Okay? I can hardly wait."

***

Steve dropped Lizbeth off at the entrance to the Comfort Inn and parked in a nearby spot. When he arrived inside with her bags, she was holding the elevator door. "Hurry up, honey. I can't wait much longer."

"Do you have to go to the bathroom?" he asked.

"Yes but that's not the main reason."

Getting the message Steve hurriedly unlocked the door.

Lizbeth rushed in.

He placed her suitcase on the stand and flopped down on the only lounge chair. *What a day, fifteen million dollars. That's three times more than the university has ever raised.* He kicked off his shoes and dozed off.

Hearing the toilet flush, he cracked an eye open.

"Are you ready?" Lizbeth called.

"Not yet." Steve jumped up, pulled off his pants and shirt, and slid in bed.

Lizbeth opened the door and strutted out in her high heels, a bath towel barely covering her breasts and vital parts.

"Aren't you something?" he said.

"You haven't seen anything yet," she said, loosening the towel at the top and teasing him with a short stripper routine before letting the towel fall to the floor.

Steve extended his arms. "You look terrific."

Lizbeth ripped off the sheet and gazed at him lying spread-eagle in his boxers. She eased in beside him, and fondled and teased. He erected a tent in his boxers.

"Take those off," she said, flipping her bra and panties on the chair.

"You're the most beautiful woman in the world."

"What makes you such an expert?"

"I've seen a few." He grinned. "But I have never met anyone quite like you. You're beautiful, worldly, and know everything."

"Everything?"

Steve gazed at her nipples, aiming for his mouth. "Everything." He smiled then nibbled on the right one while caressing the other.

"I love your wit." She planted a wet kiss on his mouth and slid on top of him.

He caressed her shoulders then ran his hands down her graceful back. Pulling her close, he gently eased inside. She pushed back slowly, consuming him.

Picking up the pace, the two rolled in rhythm together for a few long moments then she slammed against him. Steve maintained the pace for a while then gasped and began to falter, unable to hold off any longer.

Lizbeth hammered against him wildly, driving herself home. She gasped then snuggled beside him.

Sometime later Steve opened an eye and searched for the clock radio — 7:10 p.m. Turning over, he reached for her.

The bed was empty.

He saw light flowing beneath the bathroom door. *I can't believe how fast things have happened. The dance, the Mecklenburg suite, Lake Lure, her surgery, and here I am.*

Lizbeth opened the door. Steve covered his eyes to shield the light. "Your turn," she said.

Steve squinted, trying to adjust to the brightness. "Where did you find those loungers?"

"Atlanta. They're pure silk."

"Let me feel them."

"One touch that's all. You're not getting any more.

"Why not?"

"Because it'd take a crane to get you up."

"So you say."

She changed the subject. "How about going to Las Vegas?"

"Vegas? What brought that up?"

"You mentioned your calendar was free in June. I have a timeshare there."

"Geez, I don't know. I …"

"Think about it. I'm starved now. Want a pizza?"

"I had something else in mind."

"You always do. Take a cold shower. I'm ordering a pizza."

***

Dr. Benderman poked his head around the door frame and motioned to him. Steve followed him to his office.

"Thanks for squeezing me in," Steve said when the doctor turned to him.

"No problem." The doctor sat behind his desk and skimmed down Steve's file then laid it aside. "You've cancelled the last two sessions. You okay?"

"Couldn't be better. This is the best I've felt since I moved to North Carolina."

"Really. What's going on?"

"The board approved our five-year master plan. We're searching for a provost and looking for a new basketball coach. Things are coming together."

"What's this I hear about a fifteen million dollar donation from the Webster's?"

"Isn't that something? Who'd ever thought that would happen?"

"It's the talk of the town. How did you pull it off?"

"One of our alums gave me an inside tip. Next thing you know I was shaking Mr. Webster's hand."

"Did Lizbeth help you pull it off?"

"She did it all."

"Isn't she something?"

"Something? I've never met anyone like her. She's got it all."

The doctor opened his file. "How's it going with Kate?"

"I followed your advice. We had several long conversations, and met in Myrtle Beach over spring break. Things are working out perfectly."

"Good. It's important to have someone you can confide in. Anything else happening?"

"Not much." Steve fidgeted and ran his fingers along the arm of the chair.

"You seem a little uneasy." The doctor cocked his head. "Are you positive there's nothing else?"

Steve glanced out the window then shifted uncomfortably.

"Steve, what's bothering you?"

"I've been seeing Lizbeth."

"Yes, you mentioned that."

"No. I mean I have been *seeing* her."

The doctor scowled. "Steve, you're involved with Kate. She's helping you work things out. You can't be sleeping with Lizbeth."

"It happened. I couldn't help it.

"Things don't just happen. I've told you before — one relationship — that's it. Seeing two women at a time is a problem for you."

"I'm not married. It's not like I'm having an affair."

Dr. Benderman took a deep breath. "Technically, you're right. And for most guys I'd let it slide. But for you, it's different. You're a sex addict."

"Geez, doc, I'm only human. What'd you expect me to do when Lizbeth comes on to me? Wouldn't you jump at the opportunity?"

Not responding, the doctor shook his head.

"Steve, you've made a commitment to Kate. You can't be having sex with Lizbeth." The doctor stood and paced to the window and back. "Look, I've told you countless times. It doesn't matter how long it's been. The urge will always be there. You're rationalizing."

"I love Lizbeth. I really do."

"How much do you actually know about her?"

"I've never met a woman like her before. We're going to Vegas in a couple of weeks."

"Vegas? Have you told Kate?"

"No. Why should I?"

"Because you've pledged to share everything with her. You have to tell her."

"She'll leave me."

"That's the point. Lizbeth is supplying sex … feeding your addiction. She's the same as a cigarette for a smoker or a hundred dollars for a gambler."

"She's not like that. I love her."

"You can't say that. One minute you say you're in love with Kate. Five minutes later you tell me you're in love with Lizbeth. I've told you before you can't do that."

Steve gave him a blank look.

Dr. Benderman waved his hands in front of Steve's face. "Hello, is anyone home?"

Looking startled, Steve shook his head. "Doc, I-I … don't know, I …"

The doctor placed his hands on Steve's shoulder and looked him in the eye. "Doesn't anything I've said ring a bell? Before you moved to North Carolina you were involved with five women. You're headed down the same road."

"That was different."

"How was it different?" The doctor probed. "You're telling me you're in love with two women. It doesn't matter, two, three, four, five."

"This time it's different. Kate is in Arkansas. Lizbeth is here."

"Location doesn't matter. You're grasping for straws, rationalizing."

"I'm not rationalizing. I love them both."

The doctor shook his head. "Steve, we've gone over this before. You can't be in love with two women. Your urges are normal — that's part of your natural instincts, your desire for sex. Anyone could have an urge when they see a woman like Lizbeth. That doesn't mean they're in love with her. You're equating sex with love."

"It's different for me, doc. I love her."

Once again, the doctor shook his head. "Love involves feelings for another individual — compassion, affection, relationships. Sex is only one way of expressing it."

Steve smirked. "Doc, I love each one."

Dr. Benderman scratched his head. "We have to meet more often. How about next week?"

"I'll be in Las Vegas."

The doctor pressed his lips. "How about Monday after you return?"

"Fine."

CHAPTER SIX

"Last week in Vegas was like a dream come true."

Lizbeth hugged Steve. "You're the one who made it perfect. I can still see the look on that guy's face when you hit the thousand-dollar jackpot on the slots."

"His look? I thought he'd had a heart attack when he fell off the stool. I was afraid I'd have to resuscitate a three-hundred pounder."

"The look on your face was priceless."

"I thought the guy was dying. Silver dollars were bouncing all over him. I could see security coming any time."

"I love you, sweetie." Lizbeth kissed him goodbye. Steve slid out of the limo. "Call me when you get home," she said.

"Will do." Steve hopped on the Douglass International shuttle and bounced to the end of the long-term lot. He tipped the driver, fished his keys from his pocket and drove to the Airport Sheraton.

After checking in, he called Kate.

"Darling, it's so good to hear your voice," she said.

"I was going to call you all week but the pace was unreal."

"How are you doing?"

"Fine, and thanks again, for listening in Myrtle Beach. I haven't had a problem ever since."

"That's good to hear. You have to stay focused."

"Don't worry, dear. How about meeting me in Nashville? I'm free three weeks from now. We could stay at the Opryland Hotel like before."

"That'd be wonderful."

"Great. I'll make hotel reservations and get tickets for a show."

***

Sitting in Dr. Benderman's office, Steve thought about his upcoming meeting. *Doc is all caught up in theory. Why can't I be in love with two women? He doesn't know how I feel. I was with Lizbeth all week — I love her. I talked to Kate last night — I love her, too. Why can't he understand?*

The receptionist called his name. Steve took his usual position in the doctor's office, waiting a little longer than normal.

Dr. Benderman popped in. "Sorry, I got caught in a telephone dispute. It looks like the couple is headed for a messy divorce. How was your trip to Las Vegas?"

"I came home with four hundred and ten dollars in my pocket. Can you believe that?"

"Hardly. I always donate. How'd it work out with Lizbeth?"

"Fabulous. There's no other way to explain it."

"Did you think about the issues we discussed last time?"

"I gave it some thought."

"What did you come up with?"

Steve hesitated.

"Go ahead I want to know your feelings."

"I don't want to be critical, doc …"

He waved his hand. "Don't worry about me, I'm trying to help you."

"Everything makes sense when you say it. By the time I get home it doesn't fit the way I feel."

"How do you feel?"

"Like I've said before, when I'm with Lizbeth she's the greatest. I never had a thought about anyone else the whole time I was in Vegas. I love her."

"And when you returned?"

"I felt fine. I called Kate. We made plans to meet in Nashville."

"Steve, you can't do that. You're digging a hole for yourself. Did you tell her about Vegas?"

He frowned. "No, why should I?"

"She's your confidant. You know why you didn't tell her."

Steve mumbled under his breath.

"What was that?"

"She'd be pissed. Probably would have hung up."

"Doesn't that say anything to you?"

"Ah …"

"Steve, you have to be truthful with her. You're rationalizing your actions, like before."

"I'm not. I'm not having an affair. I'm not out there looking for action."

"You're involved with two women. How long do you think it'll be before there's another?"

Steve stopped cold, gave him a questioning look. "Why do you ask that?"

"Because it's only a matter of time. Remember the smoking analogy?"

"That doesn't fit me."

"Listen. It doesn't matter whether it's smoking, drinking or gambling. First, it's Kate then it's Lizbeth. "There'll be another. Either way it's an addiction."

"No. I won't let that happen."

"Steve, look me in the eye." The doctor paused and spoke slowing. "It's … only … a … matter … of … time. It's … going … to … happen. You'll be in bed with another woman."

Steve gave him a blank look. "You're positive?"

"Absolutely. If you don't stay focused you'll be in the same situation as before."

Steve ran his fingers through his hair. "I don't want to be like that again."

"That's what you say but you're not doing anything to prevent it."

"I'm trying."

"You're not. You keep telling yourself you're in love with both of them. Your life is about to spin out of control."

"I don't want to go through that pain and agony again."

"You have to do more than say it. You have to take action."

A crease crossed Steve's forehead. "Like stop seeing one of them?"

The doctor nodded. "That'd be a start."

"A start?"

"Dealing with your sex addiction is not about picking one." Dr. Benderman pursed his lips. "You have to change your lifestyle, make a commitment to a person, honor your word and share your feelings openly."

***

On the drive home Steve's brain played tennis. He volleyed to Kate. Served to Lizbeth. *Love one. How can I do that?* He shook his head. *Make a commitment to one and honor it. Doc doesn't understand.* Steve pulled in the garage and called Lizbeth.

"Webster's," she perked.

"Lizbeth, it's Steve."

"I'm so glad you called. I've been thinking about you all day. I can't get our trip to Vegas out of my mind. When can I see you again?"

Steve hesitated. "What works for you?"

"I have corporate meetings all next week. How about the weekend after the fourth?"

"That'll work."

"Lake Lure or the suite?"

"Let's do the suite. That way you won't have to do anything in the kitchen."

"You just want Brittany to reserve the pool."

"So?" He laughed. "What's wrong with that?"

He hung up and fiddled with the telephone cord, twisting it around his fingers, unwinding it, twisting it again. He dropped the cord, picked up the phone and dialed.

"Kate Blanchard."

"You sound peppy, what's happening?"

"I saw your name on call waiting, two days in a row. Why am I so privileged?"

"I thought about you all the way home from Charlotte."

"How sweet."

"I'm counting down the days until Nashville."

"Me too."

Steve waited for Kate to say more — the phone was silent.

"Is something troubling you?" she asked.

"Not really."

"What's on your mind?" Her voice trailed off. He didn't respond. "Steve, what's wrong?"

"Nothing, I'm just sorting things out."

"You met someone else, didn't you?"

"No. It isn't like that."

"Steve. You're not a good liar. How long ago?"

"Kate, you don't understand."

"Steve. You've been seeing her for a long time, haven't you?"

"No. I told you, it isn't like that."

"You're lying. You've been screwing her, haven't you?"

"No. I haven't."

"It started last spring, didn't it?"

"Why do you say that?" *How does she know these things?*

"I sensed it in Myrtle Beach. When I got back home I said something to one of my girlfriends. She unloaded everything she'd heard about you; lots of things I'd never heard."

"Like what?"

"Being with other women in Ruston when you were committed to me."

"Kate, I told you about those rumors. They're not true."

"Funny. Not one of my friends said a word while you were in Ruston. Now, my friends are spilling the beans."

"Who told you those kinds of things?"

"It doesn't matter. They've given me specifics. One saw you at the Little Rock airport with a hot redhead. Another saw you at the Peabody in Memphis with a busty broad. There's too much smoke not to have fire."

"Kate, those arc long over."

"Steve, I've heard that so many times — twenty years — I must have had my head buried in the sand."

"But Kate, none of it was true. I love you."

"I want to believe you but I can't. There are too many stories."

"They're not true. Doc says I'm making real progress. I'm better."

"That's what you say. You haven't changed, you can't. My friends agree."

"I have, Kate."

"Steve, I'm not going to live my life like Suzanne. She should have divorced you sooner. I'm not going down that road. I'm sorry Steve, goodbye."

"Wait, Kate, you …"

***

Steve staggered to the bathroom for the fifth time and sat on the toilet, not sure if he'd have to reverse his course of action. After taking care of business, he made a quick call to Joyce and had her cancel his morning meetings.

Unable able to think clearly, he went back to bed. He thought about calling Kate. *Certainly she'd reconsider — she always had. Then again, she had never talked in that tone.*

At ten Steve walked slowly to the bathroom and looked in the mirror. "You look like shit," he said to his reflection. His five o'clock shadow nodded with him. "Shape up or go down the tubes."

Options rolled through his mind. After an hour, he kicked himself in the butt and stood erect. "Get your shit together. Clean up, put on a new tie and go to the office."

Joyce looked up an hour later. "What kind of medication do you take?"

"It's an old family remedy from my mom."

"It worked. You look great."

"Thanks." He grinned. "Could you come in?"

"Of course." She followed him in and took her usual position.

He gave her a broad smile. "Joyce, I want to thank you for everything you have done. You made my transition much easier."

"Thank you, Mr. President. We're a team."

"You're right. That's why I want your advice."

"My advice? About what?"

"In two months I'll be giving my state of the university address. My old mentor once said, 'You have to have something in it for everyone.'"

"Sounds prolific."

"He also told me to rely on people closest to you. They'll give you good advice."

Her eyes brightened. "I'll do what I can."

"If you were giving my speech what would you emphasize?"

"Gosh, I don't know. I never thought about anything like that."

"I'd like you to think about it. Will you do that?"

"Okay … but don't expect too much."

He winked. "Think about it."

"Is that it?"

"Yes. I want to review the head basketball coach materials one more time before I meet with them."

"Good luck," she said on the way out.

Steve checked out her ass then buried himself in the files. *Everyone thinks their man is the best one. I don't trust any of them.* He smiled again as he read the message from the governor. "Steve, I don't want to place undue pressure on you. I'm telling you Ashley Rooks is one helluva coach. There are lots of people around here that would like to see him coaching at Mountain State."

He reread the key line in his notes from a twenty-minute call from the board chairman. "I'm telling you, Steve, there's only one choice. This guy is a winner. He gives the team a blessing before games and says a prayer at halftime."

He read a note from the legendary Dean Smith. "Willie Williams is a little young. In a couple of years he'll be one of the hottest items in the country."

The Asheville superintendent of schools wrote: "Jerry can't miss. He's a perfect fit for State. He'll recruit the best kids in the western part of the state. He'd be a real asset for all of us."

Steve picked up the last folder and read the two-page resume for Bo Willard — no reference letters, no reference calls. He mumbled aloud. "Why in the hell is this guy in the final group?"

He read the two pages again. He'd coached the state high school champs in Mississippi twenty years ago and was runner up in the NCAA Division II finals seven years ago. "What's he been doing the rest of the time?"

Joyce poked her head in the doorway. "Mr. President, Coach Willard is here."

"Send him in please."

Wearing scuffed sneakers, an old blue blazer and tattered brown slacks, the fiftyish coach shuffled in. Steve extended his hand. "Coach Willard, I'm pleased to meet you."

The old coach didn't look up. "You can call me Bo," he said with a slow southern drawl.

"Tell me about your coaching career, Bo."

"There's not much to say, doc. It's all in my resume. I just want to win ballgames."

"I'm interested in that too. Why should I hire you?"

"'Cause I'm the best candidate."

"What makes you say that?"

"I've done my research."

"Well then, why is Bo Willard the best coach in the pool?"

"I don't want to say anything bad about the other guys …"

"Of course not," Steve said, cutting him off. "I'm asking for your assessment."

"You really want to know?"

Steve nodded. "That's why I asked."

Unaccustomed to being asked for his opinion, Bo straightened his shoulders. "Here's what the pool looks like to me. You've got a graduate assistant who thinks he can transform a bunch of Division II losers into a winning Division I team. That's hogwash. There's another candidate who figures his bible will win ballgames. I haven't heard the prayer yet that wins the game. Players have to hit free throws."

"That's for sure."

"Then there are those politicians in Raleigh who think some good ol' boy can coach basketball. I've checked him out. He doesn't know his rear end from a hole in the ground. And finally, you have a local guy who can recruit local kids. If you think a bunch of white boys from the Smokies are going to beat Duke's national recruits you better have another smoke."

Steve chuckled to himself. *This guy is nobody's fool.* "Fair enough, Bo. What gives you the edge over the others?"

"It's simple, doc. I know how to win. I recruit good kids and they graduate. That's a hard combination to beat."

Steve nodded. "The other candidates have complained about our cracker-box gym. What do you think?"

"It's our home court advantage. Players from other schools will come in and laugh. They'll say, 'Hey, we've played in bigger gyms in junior high.'" Bo laughed. "We just won the game."

"You can't win all of the games because of the gym."

"No, but I can recruit players who want to play in that new arena of yours."

"You make a lot of sense, Bo. Anything else you want to say on your behalf."

"No, I guess the decision is up to you."

Steve closed his folder. "I do have one last question. Is Bo your given name?"

"It is now. I changed it fifteen year ago. My given name was Jess. My folks named me after the heavy-weight boxer Jess Willard."

"Why did you change it?"

"I like to win but sometimes that doesn't happen and I say things I shouldn't."

"We all fly off the handle once in a while."

"It's a little more than that. Some of my comments are quite pointed. I've been known to fire arrows. My buddies started calling me Bo. It stuck so I changed my name."

***

It was ten o'clock when Steve returned from his downtown breakfast meeting. Joyce waved a pink slip at him. "Your Dr. La Russa called. He said it was important."

"Did he sound excited?"

"Not particularly."

"He's the only viable provost candidate we have." Steve grabbed the slip and closed his office door.

Five minutes later, Joyce heard him shout, "Yahoo!"

Steve ripped open the door. "Carl accepted. He'll be here in two weeks. I'll be able to introduce him at the state of the university address."

Joyce gave Steve a thumbs-up. "Good for you."

"Good for *us*. We're going to be a real team. Now I can focus on my remarks." Steve looked at her. "Had any ideas?"

"Ah … yes. The early retirement program should be a point of emphasis. Put a positive spin on it so the deadwood will opt out," Joyce said; then covered her mouth. "Guess, I shouldn't have said deadwood."

Steve grinned. "I'll make it positive. That reminds me, would you set up a meeting with Bev Harrington? She's the vice chancellor of finance, and knows all there is to know about the state's early retirement program."

"You're meeting with the chancellor in September. Is that soon enough?"

"That'll be perfect. An hour will be fine."

"I have another idea for your speech."

"What is that?"

"We should open the new arena with a big-name school. Maybe North Carolina or NC State."

"How do you figure I'll be able to pull that off?"

"You asked for the idea. You're the president — that's why you're paid the big bucks."

"Thanks." He laughed.

***

Steve and the provost walked out of the university auditorium. "What do you think, Carl?"

He shook his head. "I've heard a lot of speeches in my career, Mr. President. None came close to what I just heard. You came off so sincere. It was like you were talking to each person in the auditorium. People were listening, literally holding their breath. And when you hit them with the closer, I thought the roof was going to explode. I've never heard such thunderous applause."

"Thanks, I appreciate that."

"Go home and have one of your Tanquerays," the new provost said.

"I'm going to do just that."

Steve strolled to his Caddy and drove home, visualizing the headline in tomorrow's *Mountaineer* — RED HENS TO OPEN ARENA AGAINST DUKE.

He poured himself a gin and headed for the den. *I'll have to thank Lizbeth, again, for pulling this one off. She knows everyone in the state.* He plopped down and took a sip. "How could things be any better?" *A five-year master plan approved. A new provost on board. Bo's already recruited three new players. I feel great — the best ever. Doc had it right after all. All these years I've rationalized my behavior. Lizbeth is the only one for me. I love her so much.*

CHAPTER SEVEN

Joyce noticed the moisture leaking through Carl's normally crisp, pressed white shirt. "You had better rest for a while."

"It must a hundred outside." He placed a large box of paper on the table next to her desk.

"There's some bottled water in the backroom."

"Thanks, I'll take you up on that." Carl stepped into the backroom and returned with a bottle in his hand.

"Are those the accreditation materials?" she asked.

He wiped his brow. "Yes, I poured over them all weekend."

"The team has been working on it for two years. Looks like a mess to me."

"You're right about that."

"President Schilling slipped down to the finance office. He'll be back in a minute."

"Fine, I'll rest a bit." Carl leaned back on a straight-back chair and took a long sip of water. He'd thought all night about what he'd say to Steve — he'd been on fifteen accreditation teams but this was the first time he had to tell his boss, of one month, the bad news.

Hearing the door open, he looked up. "Good morning, Mr. President."

"Morning Carl. I have a message for Joyce. Have a chair in my office I'll be right in."

Carl walked into the office and surveyed the seating arrangement; two settees and two chairs clustered around an oak coffee table. He paused, wondering which one was Steve's favorite.

"Take the one on the end," he heard from behind.

Carl eased into the chair and sat upright, facing Steve and his steaming MSU mug. "I hope you had a productive weekend. Are you settled in, yet?"

"We've unpacked the boxes. Jamie and Lisa like their teachers. And Margaret has been invited to several socials already. We're overwhelmed by the friendliness of our new neighbors."

"That's what I found too." Steve took a sip of coffee. "Whataya think about the accreditation material?" Carl hesitated. "Don't hold back, say what you think."

Carl shifted uneasily. "There are a few good sections but overall it's sad."

"I was afraid you'd say that. Whataya think we ought to do?"

He looked the president in the eye. "Ask for a year's extension."

"Damn!" Steve startled Carl who looked taken back. "That's what we did last year," the president said.

After a deep breath Carl said, "Well, no extension …sounds like we have a lot of work to do."

"We? You're the provost. It's an academic issue," Steve jested.

Carl frowned and said hesitantly, "I guess you're right."

Steve laughed. "I'm just joshing you. It's *our* problem. How can I help?"

"I'd like to know more about the committee members."

"What do you need?"

"Who are the four best writers?"

"That's easy — Shelia, Bert, John and Tom."

"Fine. I'll build my leadership teams around them."

"That could be a problem."

"Why?"

"Some of the members don't talk to each other. One talks over the rest of the committee. And the researcher doesn't say anything."

"Who picked these people?"

"The faculty senate."

"That was a mistake." Carl shook his head. "How strong is Shelia?"

"She's a dynamo. Give her a task and she'll deliver the goods."

"Good. I'll assign the blow-bag to her. Which ones are the least argumentative?"

"Bert and Tom."

"They can have the agitators, Henry Timken and Allen Dougherty. That leaves the researcher for John."

"Sounds like a plan." Steve was pleased with Carl's resolution.

* * *

Steve walked down the hallway and tapped on Dr. Harrington's door. "Come in," she said.

He peeked in, and took a double-take. *Holy shit. She's not the frumpy-looking, horn-rimmed analyst I expected.* He collected his composure and stepped inside. "Hi, I'm Steve Schilling."

"Yes, I know," said the tall, large-boned Swedish-looking blonde. "Your picture was in our paper. Congratulations on receiving that fifteen million-dollar donation."

"Thanks, it was a biggie for us."

"I understand you're interested in knowing more about the nuances of our early retirement program."

"Yes. I assume it's somewhat similar to the one we had in Arkansas."

"We have a few different twists."

Steve gave her a questioning look. "Have you worked in Arkansas?"

"No. I picked up a few tidbits from your financial VP."

"You talked to Ed Sawatzky?"

She nodded. "During your selection process. We're both from Minnesota and hit it off. He told me about your budgeting expertise. How'd you develop such an interest?"

"My old mentor said it was important for the CEO to know as much about the overall budget as the financial folks. I've always had a good handle on what was going on."

"That's cogent advice. Most of your colleagues don't have a clue about the budget."

"Numbers have always been easy. I guess that's why I'm such a stickler on the dollars."

"I admire you for that," she said, gazing into his eyes. "I've prepared a folder for you that includes state regulations, sample programs, and a list of the key points."

"Sounds good."

Bev motioned him to the small conference table in the corner of her office then walked him through the material. Pausing after the overview, she said. "That should get you started."

"I guess so," Steve said, taking a deep breath.

"Here's my card and direct number. If you have any questions, please give me a call."

"Thanks, I might take you up on that."

She gave him a pleasant smile. "Please do."

Steve walked slowly toward the parking structure, knowing Bev knew far more than she'd alluded to. He recalled his mentor in Ruston saying someone in the chancellor's office had talked to Ed Sawatzky and had been referred to Charles Bergmann, his long-time nemesis. *I know he told her about the rumors. The telephone calls. Probably filled her ears with the crap about the vote of no confidence and the letters about my affairs.*

***

Joyce buzzed Steve. "Bev Harrington is on the line. She says it's important."

"Thanks, Joyce. I'll take it." Steve pushed the blinking button. "Bev, how are you?"

"I'm fine, Mr. President. How are things progressing for you?"

"Couldn't be better."

"Do you have a minute?"

"Of course, take all the time you want."

"I have some great news. The chancellor has named your KidsStyle program as one of the state's most innovative programs."

"Terrific, wait until professor Tarpley hears about that."

"The news release will be sent out tomorrow. I'm faxing you an advanced copy."

"Thanks, I appreciate the heads-up."

"We'll be arranging a series of statewide conferences to highlight the five programs. I hope you can attend one so we can take a photo of you accepting the fifty thousand dollar check."

"Where are the meetings being held?"

"There'll be seven sites — Asheville, Fayetteville, Greenville, Morehead City, Rocky Mount, and a couple of others. They're listed in the news release."

"I'll probably attend the one in Asheville."

"Whatever works." She paused. "The second point is a little more sensitive. Could you stop by after your December meeting with the chancellor?"

"Yes. I could come to Raleigh earlier if it's really important."

"I don't want to send up any red flags. Let's keep it between the two of us."

"Sounds ominous. I'd be glad to come sooner."

"No. We can talk in December."

"Okay." Steve hung up. *Damn, I knew something was going on.*

***

Steve poked his head in her doorway. "Good afternoon, Bev."

"Dr. Schilling, come on in."

She stood and motioned him to the conference table. "How have you been?" she asked.

"The fall was crazy. And, I've thought often about your call."

"I should have said more but I wanted to double-check the numbers."

"Numbers?"

Bev flipped her wavy blonde hair. "In January Mountain State will go under fiscal watch."

"Fiscal watch? Does that mean what I think?"

"I'm afraid so."

"Why? What's wrong?"

"Based on our calculations the university is on the verge of being insolvent."

"Insolvent? That can't be. I've run the numbers personally. When our early retirement program is fully implemented we'll be in the black."

"That's down the road. In January you'll have a $1.1 million deficit."

"That's only a temporary phenomenon. We'll be in the black when the dollar savings from the early retirement program are counted in at the end of the year."

"I have to run the year-end numbers next month." She handed him the *State Fiscal Regulations.* "Here's the problem. I've marked the pertinent points."

"You can't put us on fiscal watch — that'll kill us. We've turned the corner. Student recruitment will dry up. Some of our current students will leave."

"That's why I wanted to talk with you."

"There has to be something we can do. You can't let a formula make the decision. There must be some flexibility."

"I've checked every possibility. Questions like that came up during the legislative hearings. The legislature did not want to leave any leeway. They knew people would try to make a deal."

"Jesus Christ, Bev, there has to be a way around this."

"Here, read it for yourself." She pointed to the highlighted section in the regulations.

Steve read the paragraphs then paused. "What does the last sentence mean? 'The agency administrator may supplement the formula with related data.' Is that you?"

"Yes. I can substitute one piece of data for another."

"Well then, substitute our projected early retirement numbers for your mid-year numbers."

"I can't do that. Your numbers are projections; they're not real. It'd be like creating data."

"Bev, you're missing the point. The purpose of a fiscal watch is to set off bells and avert a problem, right?"

"Basically, yes."

"We've already averted the problem. We've taken action. Your formula won't set off alarms — it'll create a crisis."

"That's the system. I don't have a choice."

"There are always choices. That's why people are in charge and not computers."

"That makes sense but I don't have any flexibility."

"A fiscal watch will throw us into an irreversible downward spiral. There must be something I can do."

She pursed her lips. "I'll think about it."

"Think about it? For God's sake, Bev, what do you want from me?"

She closed her folder. "Steve, I said I'll think about it."

"What does that mean?"

She gazed into his brown eyes then slid her hand on top of his. "How about we talk over dinner at my place tonight."

Catching her drift, Steve smirked. "What kind of wine do you like?"

"A red, not too expensive. Rodney Strong or something in that price range."

***

Steve pulled into Bev's driveway and rang the bell. She opened the door and motioned him in.

"You look great." *That's putting it mildly.* His eyes zeroed in on her cleavage bulging from her half-buttoned blouse, tied in a loose knot at the bottom, her mid-drift fully exposed.

"Thank you." She turned and led him to the kitchen. "I'm having a tequila and lime. Would you like a drink?"

"Do you have any gin?"

"There's Beefeaters and Tanqueray in the cabinet above the fridge. Olives are on the top shelve of the fridge. Help yourself. I'm finishing a Caesar."

Steve filled his glass with ice and Tanqueray, added three olives then pulled a stool up to the bar between the dinette and kitchen. His eyes followed her boobs and tight-ass stretch slacks as she paraded around the kitchen.

"What part of Minnesota are you from," he asked.

"Bemidji, the headwaters of the Mississippi," she said, proudly.

"And a great place for walleye fishing. What brought you south?"

"I was a budget analyst for the state department in St. Paul and one winter said 'who needs this?' Do you want your steak rare?" Steve nodded. "Want to freshen up our drinks? The coals are not quite ready."

"How long have you worked in the chancellor's office?"

"Eight years. I was named vice chancellor three years ago."

"Congratulations."

"The steaks are almost ready. You can put a potato on our plates and get the salad out."

"Will do." Steve hustled into the kitchen.

"Wanta pour the wine and fill our water glasses?"

"Sure." Steve grabbed the tongs, opened the oven door and flipped a potato on each plate. He pulled the salad bowls from the fridge, placed them on the table then filled the water glasses and poured the wine.

Bev added the steaks to their plates and dimmed the lights.

He held his glass of cabernet high and toasted. "Here's to the woman who can do it all."

"And to the state's newest budget expert," she added.

Steve dug in. Bev nibbled, glancing regularly at his sexy five-o'clock-shadow. "Dr. Bergmann told me about the telephone calls. What was that all about?"

Steve looked up. *I knew it. Here it comes.* "That was a bunch of crap. The chancellor followed up on it."

"Yeah, I got the word — crackpot — book closed."

"That's a good summary."

"Seems like there was a lot of smoke for such little fire; a hundred letters about you being seen with other women."

Steve sliced through his steak. "The New York strip is perfect."

She was a terrier. "I'm interested in knowing more about the calls. It'll stay between the two of us."

"Bergmann blew it way out of proportion."

"And your wife divorced you over that?"

"She had a drinking problem," he lied.

"No one mentioned anything about that."

"Bergmann tried to make something out of nothing. I played golf with a female donor. He received ten calls and recorded them as ten events. He did the same thing when I had a business luncheon with a woman at the country club, five more calls each listed as events. Let's leave it at that."

Finished eating, Bev gave him a questioning look then stood. "You can open another bottle of wine while I fill the dishwasher."

"Gladly."

Steve placed the bottle in the center of the tile-topped coffee table and eased onto the sofa across from it. She turned off the kitchen light and slid on the sofa, next to him.

"What's the real Beverly Harrington like?"

"That's what I've been wondering about Steve Schilling."

"You go first."

She paused, their eyes connected.

"There's nothing special. She's a small town girl who likes to read and cook." Bev wrinkled her nose. "Kind of a stick-in-the-mud."

"You don't look like a stick-in-the-mud."

She twisted to the side giving him a profile shot then leaned forward, showing off her cleavage. "Do you like my outfit?"

"You look fabulous — attractive — and sexy too."

"Do you really think so?"

"Of course, look at yourself."

"Really?" She acted surprised and subtly changed the subject. "What keeps you busy?"

"Work. I haven't had much time to think about anything else."

Switching gears again, she asked, "Are you seeing anyone special?"

"Nah, that's not important right now … too many irons in the fire."

Bev leaned back into the corner of her U-shaped sofa and placed her arms on top. "I've been thinking about the numbers you suggested. Maybe we could work something out."

"I hope so," he said, sliding close to her.

Bev bit her lip; she seemed pensive. "What did you mean by that?"

"Nothing." His mind raced for a proper response. "It'd be a shame if a lot of people had to suffer for no reason."

"Oh."

He placed his hand on her shoulder. "Bev, if I've said something wrong I'll leave."

"No, no." She hesitated. "It isn't you. I haven't been honest with you. I'm not …"

He placed his fingertips over her lips. "Bev, I came here to see you, the Beverly Harrington from Bemidji. Nothing more." He hesitated. "You don't usually dress like this, do you?"

She shook her head slowly. "No."

"And this is not the Bev Harrington from St. Paul?"

Her eyes welled. "I wanted it to be. I thought I could …"

"Bev, I'm here because of you. Nothing else."

She gazed into his dark brown eyes. "I gave you a false impression."

"You told me you'd think about it. That's all." His index finger circled her mouth then her nose. "You're extremely attractive."

"The women in the office think you're something. I figured you'd never look at me so …"

Steve interrupted. "A beautiful woman like you. I bet you have the guys standing in line."

"Not really."

"You're playing it cool." He laughed.

"I'm not."

He slid closer and kissed her lightly on the lips. She kissed him softly once then more firmly. He pulled her tight and kissed her again. Bev wrapped her arms around his neck and they kissed wildly.

"Wow." Steve gasped. "It's a good thing you've not been out with a lot of guys."

Seeming embarrassed, she smiled shyly.

"I bet you play that shy girl from Bemidji all the time."

She giggled.

"And maybe not so shy tonight." He loosened the knot holding the bottom of her blouse and toyed with each button as he slipped them open. Pulling the blouse aside, he walked his fingers around her breasts bulging from her bra. He tenderly kissed one side then the other.

Her breathing shortened. "Steve, I'm not sure we should …"

He placed his finger tip over her lips. "You don't have to say anything."

She gazed into his eyes. "Steve, I …"

He planted a heavy kiss on her.

Gasping, she stood and tugged him toward the bedroom.

Steve grinned to himself knowing she was his. *I have to move easy, not come too soon. Take her to the peak then slow it down — make her want more.*

With a shy, blushing smile Bev laid back on the bed. Steve followed, hovering above her on his arms, straddling her body with his. He continued exploring her, first with his fingers, then with his lips. Kissing the side of her neck, he trailed his way slowly down between her heaving breasts, stopping to tease her navel.

Bev panted lightly, anticipating where he would move next.

Steve didn't disappoint. *Take her beyond her limits and score.*

CHAPTER EIGHT

"Red Hens trail the High Point Panthers, sixteen to nine." The announcer paused, "We'll be back after this commercial timeout."

"We have to win this one," Steve said to himself. He set the dial on his car radio for WFNC, Charlotte. *Can you imagine? Last year the station in Midville wanted us to pay them to air our games. Now we're being beamed halfway across the state. Lizbeth can do it all.*

"The ball is under the Red Hens' basket. Coach Willard loves to run the double-pick down low," the announcer prognosticated. "There it is; Riley slam-dunks and he's fouled. Riley is at the line, he double pumps and … it's good! The Red Hens are down sixteen to twelve. Here's the inbound pass, Rankin steals the ball and lays it in. Red Hens are down two. Timeout, Panthers."

"I can't take any more of this." Steve surfed for a country and western station while he drove into the night. Gassing up in Black Mountain, he turned the game back on.

The announcer's voice had dropped an octave in disappointment. "That'll do it sports fans. The Red Hens lose their fifth in a row. You have to go back seventeen years since they started a season that poorly."

Steve reached for the dial. The announcer continued, "Stay tuned for Coach Willard's highlight show."

He waited.

The commercials droned on.

"All right, we have Coach Willard with us. The guys mounted a real comeback but they couldn't overcome that second-half fifteen point run by the Panthers."

"They played their hearts out," coach began. "Too bad no one else around here cares. The fans left at halftime."

"Coach … Riley really pounded the boards."

"Hey, the team did everything I asked. Too bad I can't say that about the administration."

Steve's face reddened. *What the fuck is he talking about? I'm the administration. Who the hell does he think he is?* Steve turned the volume up.

"I saw short stints of brilliance, coach. It looks like the guys are coming around."

"They're the only ones who show any brilliance around here," coach stated.

"Well, Coach Willard, anything else you want to say?"

"Hey, we got our ass kicked. The fans are with us win or win."

Steve snapped off the radio and slammed the dashboard with his fist.

***

Early the next morning Steve flipped on the office lights and called the basketball office. The phone rang several times. "C'mon coach I know you're there."

"Hello."

"Coach, this is President Schilling."

"Yeah doc."

"I want your ass in my office in five minutes," he said, then slammed the receiver down.

Steve stalked his office replaying every word Bo had said. Sitting down on a winged-back chair facing an oak coffee table with a glass insert top, a settee on each side and a matching winged-back at the other end, he waited like a cat ready to pounce.

Coach Bo shuffled in, looking like the morning after — unshaven, hair frazzled and wearing a sweatsuit that looked like it hadn't been cleaned in a month. "Have a chair." Steve pointed to the wing-back facing him.

Bo slouched down in the chair and stared at the floor.

"I listened to the game last night on the way home. I thought we were going to pull it out."

"Yeah, so did I, doc. The kids played good. We just couldn't get over the hump," Bo said, without looking up.

"I was surprised you said the fans didn't support the team."

"It's true, doc. There was twelve hundred at game time. At the end there weren't twelve."

76

"Twelve? It couldn't have been that bad."

"Twelve, a hundred and twelve, it doesn't matter. No one said a word. Half of the cheerleaders were gone before the game ended."

"And, I was surprised by your comments about the administration."

"I guess I shouldn't have said that."

"You *guess*?" Steve's face reddened. "Who the hell do you think the listeners thought you were talking about?"

"The guys in the administration building."

"Damn, it Bo, *I'm* the administration."

"It isn't you, doc. It's the other guys."

"Who? The vice presidents? Which one are you talking about?"

"Not them, the maintenance department. They haven't mopped the floor or cleaned the locker room all week. It smells like shit."

"Do you think your ranting about the maintenance man gained you any support?"

"Probably not."

"How many of the vice presidents do you think will go out of their way to help you?"

"Probably none."

"Have you talked to the head of maintenance?"

"I talked to the guy that cleans our building. He sleeps most of the time."

"What did he say?"

"He grunted, said he's been doing it that way for fifteen years … and if I didn't like it I could clean it myself."

"Did you report that to his supervisor?"

"Nope."

"Don't you think it would make more sense to go up the chain of command rather than spouting off on the radio?"

"I suppose. I was frustrated."

"Do you think I'm frustrated?"

"Yes. I'm sorry, doc."

"Whataya think I ought to say at Rotary today when someone asks about your comments?"

"Don't know, doc. I've never been in your shoes."

Steve's face flushed; he pressed his lips together trying not to blow a gasket. "I'll tell you what I'm going to say."

Bo looked up.

"I'm going to introduce you so *you* can tell them. Go home and clean up, put on a coat and tie, I'll pick you up at your office at eleven forty-five."

***

"How'd the accreditation committee meeting go today?" Steve asked.

Wearing a million dollar smile, Carl eased into the same chair Bo had used earlier in the day. "It couldn't have gone better. The group is meeting at the Road House for pizza and beer at five o'clock."

"The whole committee, Timken and Dougherty too?"

"Yep."

"I thought the two of them were mad at the world."

"Turns out the two of them were the best workers on the committee. We're all good buddies now."

"How'd you do that?"

"I had a sidebar with each one of them. Then I lectured the committee about teamwork. Next thing I know the two were cranking it out."

"You have a lot more patience than I."

Carl smiled. "I have more practice, two hours twice a month with the faculty senate."

"I couldn't handle that." Steve gave him a quizzical look. "Why's the group going out?"

"We're celebrating. The committee signed off and authorized me to edit the final report."

"How'd you pull that off?"

Carl laughed. "Patience."

"I guess." Steve shook his head. "How did you deal with planning criteria?"

"I told them plain out we had to 'face reality — we don't have an academic planning process.' We can't dance around that."

"How'd they react?"

"Several were leery. They thought it'd be a sign of weakness to admit a shortcoming. I told them we can't hide it. We have to be honest with ourselves. If not, the association will zing us."

"Did they get the message?"

"Shelia picked up the ball and carried it, said, 'The provost can't make a purse out of a sow's ear,' Dougherty chimed in by saying, 'We have to face the facts.' And the committee agreed."

"Sounds like you laid it on the line. Will the accreditation folks buy it?"

"Absolutely, it's a self-study. The worst thing you can do is not be truthful. We asked for a single-focused visit in three years on academic planning; then laid out the kind of planning process we'd have in place when the team returns."

Steve shook Carl's hand and smiled. "It's a good life if you don't weaken."

"Thanks, Steve." Carl gave him a questioning look, as if he wasn't sure of the full meaning of Steve's comment.

"What's next?"

"I'll edit the report. After the first of the year we can distribute it across campus for comment. It should be ready for the March board meeting. I'd like to send it to the Southern Association of Colleges and Schools in April so we can be on their summer agenda."

"Perfect. I'll make it the centerpiece of my state of the university address."

***

"The fall semester is over and done." Steve poured himself a tall gin, flipped on the fireplace and dialed Lizbeth.

"Lizbeth Webster," she answered.

"How are you doing, dear?"

"I've never felt better. I've been thinking about Christmas and being with you."

"I'd love to, but you ought to be with your family, like always."

"I enjoy being with dad and my son's family but I want to see you."

"It's important for you to be with the kids. You only see them all together once a year."

"I know but ..."

Steve interrupted. "I have a meeting on Monday in Charlotte. Afterward I'll stop by your place for a few days before Christmas. What do you think?"

"Oh Steve, would you?"

"I'd love to." He paused. "Did I tell you that our KidsStyle program has been designated as one of the state's most innovative programs? We're going to be showing it off in seven sites."

"Tremendous. That'll get a lot of PR for you."

"I need to attend one of the statewide meetings for a photo op."

"Where are they?"

"The ones that fit in my schedule are in Asheville, Fayetteville, Rocky Mount and Morehead City."

"Pick Morehead City. You have to stay at the Pecan Tree Inn in Beaufort. It's my favorite B & B. When is the meeting?"

"February fourteenth thru the sixteenth."

"Oh no. I'll be in New Orleans for my national conference."

"I'll pick a different place so we can be together."

"No. You have to go to Beaufort."

"What's so special about Beaufort?"

Lizbeth paused. "Memories, I guess. We used to spend the summers there with the kids. They loved it. Arnold still has the yacht there."

"Have you been there lately?"

"No. I signed off on the yacht as a part of our settlement. I figured he'd make more use of it than I."

"I'll call you after my meeting Monday. I should arrive in Lake Lure around three o'clock."

"I'll be ready."

***

Steve walked into Dr. Benderman's office. The receptionist immediately stood and motioned him in. "I'm sorry Dr. Schilling, we're really backed up. He asked me to take you to his private office. He'll slip in as soon as he can."

"Thanks." Steve picked up a surprisingly recent *Sports Illustrated* and followed her down the hall.

"Would you like a soda?" she asked.

"A diet would be fine."

Steve eased into a leather chair and looked around the doctor's personal office — family vacation pictures filled the walls. He read the magazine's lead story then glanced up when the door opened.

"Good to see you, Steve. This place has been a zoo ever since Thanksgiving."

"A zoo? You ought to try thirty Ph.D.'s in a faculty senate meeting."

"I can't imagine." The doctor chuckled. "We're not even in peak season."

"Peak season?"

"It happens all over. I remember when I was in med school in Michigan we called it 'cabin fever.' Statistics there show January through March have the highest rate of suicides, spousal-abuse and divorces."

"Maybe it's sunlight deprivation."

Dr. Benderman gave him a nod. "How are you doing?"

"Terrific, thanks to you. Since I broke it off with Kate, my life has changed totally."

"That's great news. How long has that been?"

"Spring break last year, almost eight months now."

"And all of that time you've been seeing Lizbeth?"

"Right. I've never met a woman like her."

"There are not many women like her. And you've not been with another woman?"

"That's what I said, isn't it?" Steve said, in an elevated tone.

Dr. Benderman stepped back. "Have you had the urge to be with someone?"

"No."

"And you haven't looked at a woman's ass and wondered what it'd be like to grab a little?"

"Nope."

The doctor pursed his lips. "Steve, you're not being truthful."

"What do you mean?"

"You're suggesting that you've gone cold turkey. An addict can't do that. You might go without sex but the urge is always there."

"Why?"

"If I had that answer I'd be a millionaire. An addict's sensors are always on the lookout. When he sees a woman, he automatically checks out her boobs and ass or vice versa."

"No one compares to Lizbeth."

"Sex addicts don't compare. They see each woman for what she is — an opportunity."

"Every woman?"

"It happens without thinking. His antenna is always searching. We've covered this before, but maybe now you'll understand. When he finds one, she's the most important one. When he's with another one he has the same feeling about *her*. Does that make sense?"

"I guess."

"Tell me more about being with Lizbeth. What do you really like about her?"

"Everything. We hit it off like gangbusters. I'm seeing her this afternoon."

"Everything? Like what?"

"Jesus doc, you've seen her. She's beautiful, has a great body and is smart. I love her.

***

"Merry Christmas," Steve chimed over the phone.

"Steve? Is that you?" Bev asked.

"Who did you think it was?"

"I don't know. No one has called all week."

"What are you doing over the holidays?"

"Not much, maybe read a book. I might go out for a movie. Why?"

"How about going on a cruise?"

"A cruise? Are you crazy?"

"You said you weren't doing anything."

"I know but we've only been together once."

"For two and a half days. It wasn't like I stopped by for a Coke. I thought it was wonderful."

"It was. I've never felt that way before."

"Well then, what's wrong with a five-day cruise?"

"Nothing, I suppose. I …"

Steve cut her off. "I checked out a cruise from Charleston. It's only a four-and-a-half-hour drive for you. Five days in the Bahamas. Last minute tickets are dirt cheap. Whaddaya think?"

"It may be a good deal …"

"Bev, it's not about the costs. I want to be with you, Beverly Harrington. What can I say to convince you? I want to go on a cruise with you."

"Oh my God, Steve, I never thought about us getting together again," she fibbed.

"You can pack on Christmas Day and drive down the next morning. The cruise doesn't depart until four on the twenty-sixth."

"I don't know what to wear!"

"It's mostly casual. One night is dressy, so you'll need an evening gown. Come on, I'll meet you in the check-in area between two and three, okay?"

She didn't respond.

"Bev, are you there?"

"Okay. I'll be there around two o'clock."

***

Drums rolled. Steve stood and applauded with the other guests in the ship's grand ballroom. Lights flickered and strobes flashed — a spotlight landed on the captain at the top of an elaborately-carved two-story stairway. A second light circled the room then beamed on a tall, well-endowed blonde. The captain extended his arm and the orchestra struck "The Grand March."

The couple paraded down the stairs to the main floor, promenading arm-in-arm around the dining room. Steve's eyes followed her breasts, extending beyond the limits of her black, strapless-gown — a very large diamond necklace hung in her cleavage, on loan from Diamond's International — it seemed dwarfed.

Stopping at the captain's table, Bev leaned over to Steve, "How did you pull this off?"

He smiled. "I saw the captain eye you at the reception on the first night. I told his first mate that you'd like to dine at the captain's table."

"Coming down the stairs I felt like a queen."

"You looked like one too." Steve gave her a peck on the cheek.

The captain stood to deliver his welcome. As he finished, the band struck a chord and he asked for Bev's hand.

"One dance," Steve winked.

Champagne flowed the rest of the night. The two chatted over dinner like they'd known each other for years. Steve talked about the KidsStyle program then asked, "Did I tell you I've signed up for the conference in Morehead City?"

"Oh. I've signed up to host the one in Asheville."

"I'm meeting a donor in New Bern the same week as the Morehead meeting so I changed. Can you do both?"

"Sure. I'll rearrange things." Bev kissed him on the lips then leaned back. "I ran the numbers like you suggested. You'll be two hundred thousand dollars in the black when the January report comes out."

"I knew you could work it out. I've had enough of this hoopla, let's go to the room."

CHAPTER NINE

A month later, Steve strolled the grounds of the La Bastide Inn in western North Carolina. Standing in the center of the gardens, he gazed at the mountain tops. *Spending the weekend with Bev in this mountain hide-a-way, what could be better?* He walked back to his room, stretched out on the sofa and dozed off.

A knock startled him awake. He jumped up and opened the door.

Bev stepped in. "What have you done, Steve? This is wonderful — yellow roses, music, and a fire crackling. How did you ever come upon this place?" she asked.

"I checked the Western Carolina directory for the best inns."

"I love it. It's beautiful."

Slipping in behind her, he placed a small package in her hand.

"What's this?"

"Something special, open it."

She loosened the small bow and unwrapped the box. "Beautiful!" she exclaimed. "It's from Estee Lauder. It has a wonderful scent but you didn't have to give me a gift."

He kissed her on the cheek and whispered in her ear. "You're the beautiful one."

"You're such a sweetheart," she said, pressing her arms against his. "The fireplace is mesmerizing. I could watch it all night."

"I'm ready for that." He loosened a button on her blouse, slid a hand inside, and crooned, "Take the ribbon from her hair. Touch her gently everywhere."

"Steve, it doesn't go like that."

"Sounds good to me."

She laughed and squeezed his hand. "You're crazy."

"I could hardly wait for you to arrive." He kissed her softly on one ear then along the back of her neck. "Would you like some wine to help you unwind?"

"That'd be terrific."

Steve filled two glasses with a moderate priced chardonnay and joined her on the sofa. "How was your trip from Raleigh?"

"Okay, kind of long."

He gave her a questioning look. "Are you okay, sweetie?"

"Hmm … a little tired."

"You seem to be a little down."

"It isn't important."

"What is it, dear?"

"It's none of my business."

He kissed her lightly on the cheek. "If you're thinking about it, it's your business."

She bit her lip. "It's Bergmann. I thought about his comments all the way here."

Steve slid closer to her. "I'm an open book," he fibbed. "Ask me anything. I don't want you to have any misgivings."

"I don't want to be a nag."

"You're not." He pressed his index finger over her lips. "No reservations, Bev, come on."

"I've been reluctant to say anything."

"Say whatever you want. Trust is at the heart of any relationship. If we don't have that we don't have anything."

She leaned back on the sofa. "Oh Steve, you're so understanding."

He topped off her chardonnay. "Here's the full story."

She took a sip; her eyes glued on him.

"My wife Suzanne and I had a wonderful marriage. After I became president things changed," he lied. "She started drinking and wearing revealing outfits. Next thing I knew she was gone all night."

"I can't believe she'd do that to you."

"I tried everything, nothing worked. She was staying out at night then she was gone all weekend."

"How awful."

"Whatever I tried seemed to make it worse." Tears welled in his eyes. "It didn't take long before the rumors were flying. I talked to a couple of her good friends for advice."

"How were you able to end it?"

"One of her friends told the truth. By that time there was nothing left of our marriage. I got a divorce and Bergmann had egg on his face. His report never saw the light of day." Steve sniffled, pulled out his handkerchief and wiped a tear.

"Poor baby. I'm so sorry." Bev slid close to him and snuggled. "I didn't mean to put you through that."

He gave her a half-smile. "I feel better now that you know."

She leaned over and kissed him firmly. "You're such a sweetheart."

"How about we go down for dinner?"

"I'd love to. Give me five minutes."

She freshened up, and took his hand as they exited the room. Halfway down the stairs she stopped and gazed across the dining room below. "This looks like an old French inn."

"It was modeled after a countryside inn in Provence, southern France."

"It's lovely."

Reaching the main floor, Steve inquired with the hostess.

"Yes, Mr. Schilling, your table is ready." She led them to a corner table for two.

"How delightful — a stone fireplace and sconces flickering like candles."

"La Bastide is part of the Cliff's developments. They use this as a place to host their guests. It's one of the most romantic restaurants in this part of the state."

"Maybe the entire state," Bev said, gazing at the flames dancing in the fireplace. "There's nothing like this in Raleigh." She gazed into his eyes and blew him a kiss.

Steve winked. "I'm having a steak. Would you like red wine?"

"A pinot noir would be fine. The rosemary grilled veal chops sound wonderful."

The two ordered and chatted through a second bottle of wine. Steve asked her the standard questions: What was it like growing up in Bemidji? What were your parents like? Where did you go to college? She countered with much the same, asking him about his youth, growing up in Kentucky, playing football in college, and becoming a university president.

Bev circled her index finger over the top of his hand. "I feel like I'm living a dream. A cruise over the holidays, being here with you in France tonight, and next month we'll be on the beach in Morehead City. What could be better?"

Steve grinned. "Being with you every night."

"You always know what to say. How about we skip dessert?"

Steve raised his eyebrows. "Hmm, I like that."

He signed the tab and the two took a short stroll through the inn's gardens. "It's a gorgeous evening — a full moon — you can see every star in the galaxy," he whispered.

She tugged on his hand. "Let's go upstairs."

Surreptitiously caressing each other when no one else was around, the two walked slowly upstairs. Steve unlocked the door. Bev headed for the bathroom. "Would you turn on the music and fireplace? I'll be right back."

He willingly followed her directions.

Bev returned wearing a thigh-length, blue silky top and barely visible matching shorts.

"You look sexy as hell."

She pulled him tight and the two danced to the rhythm of the soft jazz tape. Snuggling close, she pressed against his pelvis. Steve felt her heart pounding on his chest. He slid his hands down her back and fondled her perfectly rounded cheeks.

Running her fingers through his hair, she made a half-step back and took her time unbuttoning his shirt. She tossed it aside and kissed him on the chest. Steve caressed her neck and shoulders. She loosened his belt and watched his pants fall to the floor. Stepping back again, she admired his trim body and motioned for him to step out of his pants.

He did so then placed his hands behind his head and wiggled his butt. "What do you think about that?" he joked.

"I'd like to see more."

"More?"

Her eyes searched his body, head to toe then back again. "I've had this fantasy about a man dancing."

Steve raised his hand. "Don't look at me that way."

She ran her fingers over his pecks and around his abs. "Why not? I think you'd look sexy slow dancing in front of the fireplace."

"Me dancing? I don't think so."

"Come on, you wouldn't think twice about asking me to do a little strip show."

"That's different."

"I don't think so." She picked up her glass and eased onto the sofa. "I'm ready."

"Ready for what?"

"You said you'd do anything for me." She flicked her hand. "Let's see a little sex show."

"You have to be kidding."

"Let's see it … slow dance like a male stripper."

"Bev?"

"Come on, I'm going to enjoy my wine."

Steve pursed his lips and began to sway.

"Now we're getting somewhere." Watching him, she took a long sip. "Let's see a little more action. Caress your butt and move it around."

Steve did so then slowly picked up the pace. "How's that?"

"I'd like to see some fondling and stroking."

"Seriously?"

"Come on, let's see what you can do."

Steve slipped into a stripper routine, slinking and rolling his hips. He ran his hands over his protruding boxers. "Am I close to the finish line?"

"You're almost there. I want to see you naked."

"Naked? Come on, Bev." He started to say more.

She motioned to him. "Take off your shorts."

"Bev, I …"

"Come on, it's no different than being in bed. Let's see your moves."

Steve hesitated then slipped off his shorts and began a slow, rhythmic routine. Running his hands over his body, he fondled and stroked.

"Yes, yes," she cheered. "Turn around so I can see those cheeks in action."

He turned side to side and back and forth.

"Perfect." Bev stood and slinked toward the bed. "Come on, I'll show you some real action."

***

Waiting in his tux, Steve adjusted his red bow tie and gazed at Lizbeth ahead in the receiving line. *It's been a whirlwind year. I can't believe how much we have in common. What could be better than spending the rest of my life with her?*

He stepped in front of Lizbeth. She smiled and gave him a peck on the cheek. "Do you realize this is our second anniversary?"

"Funny you mention that. I was having the same thought."

"Ed Barkley is at my table. You can chat with him until I'm finished here."

"Good. We haven't talked in ages." Steve squeezed her hand and walked across the floor.

Ed gave him a bear hug. "It's good to see you again. How's it going?"

"Couldn't be better. I hope things are well for you and your family."

"I'm going to be a grandpa this summer."

"Congratulations."

"How's the arena progressing?"

"It's right on schedule. The foundation is in and they're erecting the walls. I never thought it'd be so large."

"When will the Barkley Reception Center be finished?"

"Less than a year. It'll be ready for the Duke opener."

"It looks like that Coach Bo of yours is building a winner."

"Can you believe it? He's won ten in a row and is leading the conference. We could make the NCAA tournament for the first time."

"Wouldn't that be something?"

"We had our first sellout last week; over thirty-seven hundred."

"And after what he'd said earlier in the season. I'm surprised anyone showed up."

"Wasn't that ugly?"

"Did you have a set-down talk with him?"

"Sure did. We agreed his assistant would do the post-game show after a loss."

"Maybe that's why he hasn't lost." Ed laughed then pointed. "The stud is back."

"Do you think he'll hit on Lizbeth?"

"Nah, he's after some young stuff. He's had his eye on the hot little blonde over there with the guys. How's it going with Lizbeth?"

"We had a wonderful time at her place before Christmas; three days up in the mountains. I could spend the rest of my life with her."

"Sounds serious."

"I didn't mean it that way. We haven't talked about anything."

"I'm receiving good vibes from her."

"We better drop it. Here she comes now."

Lizbeth pulled a chair between them. "What are you two talking about?" she asked.

"Guy talk." Ed laughed.

"I bet it's about that cute little blonde across the dance floor."

"Guilty." Steve threw his arms in the air. "You caught us dead to rights."

***

"Phew," Lizbeth said, unlocking the door to the Mecklenburg suite. "I'm glad that's over. No more chairing that event."

She threw her arms in the air. "Four years is enough. Want to fix me a drink? I'm going to slip on a robe."

"Sure."

Steve opened the liquor cabinet and grabbed bottles of Crown Royal and Tanqueray. Filling their glasses with ice, he tossed three olives in his, and added the booze.

Lizbeth slipped up behind him, wrapped her hands around his waist and snuggled close. He turned and gave her a light kiss then stepped back. Handing her a Crown Royal, he said, "Here's to the most beautiful woman in the world."

She turned her cheek. "Can you smell it?"

He pressed his nose against her earlobe. "It's Beautiful. There's a hint of citrus."

"Yes, I wondered if you could tell."

She clinked his glass. "Thanks, you're such a sweetie. Brittany said there'd be some appetizers in the fridge. I'll warm them up in the micro."

"Great. I didn't have a chance to eat a bite."

Steve walked into the living area. Lizbeth entered shortly and placed a large platter of hors d'oeuvre on the coffee table in front of him.

"It looks like a feast."

"Brittany always goes overboard."

"I'm not complaining," he said.

"You never complain. You're so gentle and sweet." She reached for a stuffed mini-pocket. "What's ahead for you this spring?"

Steve shrugged. "We have an accreditation report and a hundred more projects."

"You ought to take some time off. You've been pushing too hard."

"Look who's talking. Last year you had a tumor on your brain and here you are back in charge."

"You make it sound like I'm always in charge."

"You're not?" He cocked his head. "I can't recall a time when you're not."

She scowled. "How can you say that?"

"Because it's true. You're the one who's always on top."

"You said you like it that way."

"That's not the point. We're talking about you being in charge."

"Fine, I won't be in charge tonight." She tugged him into the bedroom.

"See, there you go again."

Lizbeth frowned. "How do you propose we do it?"

"I'll have to think about it."

"Fine, you think about it." She tossed her robe aside, flopped on the bed — in her bra and panties — and buried her face in the pillow.

Steve tiptoed into the bathroom, picked up her body lotion and knelt at the foot of the bed. Rubbing the lotion in his hand, he gently massaged her right heel, arch and toes, taking time to caress each toe, twice. She moaned and stretched out.

He repeated the routine on the left foot then added a small amount of lotion to his hands and moved up her calves. Taking his time, he massaged her caves and thighs then slid his fingers under the bottom of her panties and fondled. Her cheeks twinged and her butt tightened. Steve smiled to himself having seen that happen countless times. *I'm moving easy. Going to watch her make it on her own.*

He pulled himself onto the bed and straddled her legs. Placing a pillow under her stomach, he pushed his erection between the crease in her panties. She pressed her cheeks against him. Loading his hand with lotion, he rubbed them together and messaged her neck and shoulders and watched her body seemingly melt onto the bed. *I've never seen her so relaxed.*

Inching his way along, Steve ran his soft hands gently down her back, circling his fingertips around each vertebra. He unhooked her bra and gently massaged. Beads of moisture filled her back. She turned slowly side to side and pressed against the pillow. Her breaths shortened.

Steve slid off to her side.

"Oh Steve," she begged. "Don't stop."

Knowing she was close, he grinned as he slipped off her panties, caressed her cheeks and fondled between them. Lizbeth spread her legs slightly and pushed, rhythmically, against the pillow.

He watched her pace increase, and then smiled as her body shot out of control.

***

"I see your basketball team won their fifteenth in a row last night," Dr. Benderman said.

"Can you believe it? We're on a roll."

"I heard that coach of yours … Bo … what's-his-name?"

"Willard. Bo Willard."

"He sounds like quite a character. Does he always talk in one-liners?

Steve gave him a questioning look. "Why?"

"I heard a clip of him on the sports talk radio. He had me in stitches."

Steve mimicked Bo's slow, southern drawl. "Well, doc. I thought we played good."

"That's it."

"He's fine as long as we win."

"Nothing wrong with that. I don't like to lose either."

"You don't have to listen to him after we lose. I made sure of that."

"No one is perfect," The doctor said, then opened his notepad. "Are things still going well with Lizbeth?"

"Better than ever."

"Good for you," the doctor said. "Remember Steve, temptation is just around the corner."

"Don't worry, doc. I'm always on guard."

"It's more than that, Steve. Your mind can play tricks on you."

"Like what?"

"The literature suggests you could become involved with another woman *and* not see anything wrong with it."

"Oh."

"I'm just alerting you to what I know about sex addicts. Have you ever had that feeling?"

"Ah, yes. When I met Lizbeth, Kate and I were hot and heavy. It seemed okay to me."

"Was that the only time?"

"It happened lots of times in college. I never thought much about it."

"It didn't bother you to be seeing one woman and be involved with another one?"

"No. I felt the same way when I met Bev."

"Bev? Who's Bev?"

"She lives in Raleigh, works in the department of higher education."

"You're seeing her?"

Steve looked away. "For the last five or six months."

"You never told me …"

"It didn't seem important."

"Not important. Steve, that's exactly what I'm talking about. You can't fluff this off."

***

"On behalf of Mountain State University and the KidsStyle program, I am pleased to accept the state's highest award for excellence in education," Steve said, ending his remarks.

Bev moved to the microphone. "Mr. President, as the representative of the State of North Carolina, I'm pleased to present to you this check for fifty thousand dollars. We are happy to support KidsStyle and your efforts to deal with bullying and other social challenges facing our youth."

She shook his hand then held an oversized check in front of them. Cameras flashed.

The two walked off the stage, and Steve asked, "What's your agenda for the day?"

"I have workshops all day then a banquet at six-thirty. It'll be after nine before I can get away."

"I'll be waiting." He winked and handed her a business card. "Here's the address for the Pecan Tree Inn." She smiled.

Steve headed for the parking lot then drove across the Beaufort bridge, pulled up in front of the Inn and unloaded his bags. After taking a shower he planted himself on an old rocker on the front porch and drifted off. What seemed like minutes later, a horn interrupted his cat nap.

Leaping to his feet, he took the steps two at a time and planted a wet kiss on Bev's lips.

"Wow," she said. "Had I known that was coming I would have wrapped it up sooner."

"Wait till you see the place. We're in the Queen Anne room on the second floor."

Steve grabbed her bag and led the way upstairs. He pushed open the door and Bev walked in. "A four-poster with a lace canopy," she exclaimed. "And over there …"

"A Jacuzzi," Steve finished for her, leading her to the adjoining area on the right.

"How'd you find this place?"

"A donor recommended it."

"Can we use the Jacuzzi now? My feet are killing me."

"I thought you'd never ask." He grinned.

While the tub was filling, Steve poured a couple glasses of wine, stripped, and slid in. "Hurry up, sweetie."

Bev opened the bathroom door and, wrapped in a towel, waltzed toward him. "I can't stay too long. I have to leave for Rocky Mount tonight."

"How long will it take?"

"A couple of hours." She dropped the towel and sank down in the warm water. "What did you do today?"

"The donor I was supposed to meet in New Bern cancelled out. Some kind of a medical procedure, I guess. We had to reschedule."

"Too bad."

"I had to rough it; spent the whole day sightseeing."

"Poor baby." She kissed him on the forehead. "Where did you go for dinner?"

"Beaufort Grocery Company. It's a block or two from here. I had shrimp and scallops over cappellini. Next time we're here we'll have to go there."

"I'd like that."

"Have you ever done it in a Jacuzzi?"

CHAPTER TEN

"Back again?" the tall attractive barmaid said. "Tanqueray with three olives, right?"

Steve nodded and slid one leg over a barstool in the rear of the Grocery Company restaurant. Watching her fix a tray of drinks, he knew she wasn't the typical barmaid. *Too classy. Too elegant.*

"You from around here?" he asked.

"Wilmington. I work up here part-time."

"It seems quite pleasant."

"You should see it in the summer. There are yachts from all over the world."

"That must be something."

"It's special. I love sitting on the marina watching servants in white gloves on the yachts, women wearing long dresses and guys in tuxes. It's like a fairytale."

"Sounds spectacular. I'll have to come back sometime."

"Your table is ready, sir." Steve turned, assuming the words were for him.

"Thanks," he said to the blonde. "I enjoyed chatting with you."

Sitting at a table not too far from the bar, he periodically glanced her way. *God, she's beautiful. She can't be more than twenty-eight or twenty-nine. What a great body. And something else. What is it?*

He finished his New York strip bulgogi and opened the dessert menu — double-chocolate cake, pecan pie, and chocolate brownie with ice cream. Knowing he had to cut back on calories, he folded the menu and looked up. Standing before him, she held a piece of pecan pie with caramel drizzled over the ice cream. *Her smile, that's it — sweet yet sensual — like the girl next door.*

"I saved the last piece for you. I figured after two Tanquerays, a Caesar and strip steak, you'd want pecan pie."

"It's my favorite. Thank you."

"You're welcome." She smiled and turned for the door. "It's on the house."

***

I need to take a walk after scarfing down the pie. Steve strolled down the marina boardwalk. Walking into a balmy sea breeze, he thought about the bartender's smile, her body. *What was a woman like her doing in Beaufort? Who was she?*

He stopped under the warm glow of an 1890s light post and gazed across the dark harbor — sporadic soft lights twinkled from the moored sailboats. A blue light blinked steadily as the harbor patrol passed. A half-block further down the boardwalk his eye followed the moonbeam across the harbor to the bright lights of an outdoor restaurant. Under a large green Heineken umbrella, he saw that smile — that perfect smile — sitting with a glass of white wine at a table in the corner.

He moseyed over and asked, "May I join you?"

She gave him a who-cares expression. Feeling he had nothing to lose, he pulled out a wire-framed chair and sat across from her. "Thanks, for the pie."

Gazing out into the night, she gave him a half-smile.

Steve pointed to the yacht docked in front of them. "How'd you like to own something like that?"

"Wouldn't that be something?"

"How big do you think it is?"

"It's a 120-foot Ocean Alexander."

Steve leaned back. "You sound sure of yourself. How do you know?"

"My dad taught me a lot about boats. He's cruised the entire Caribbean."

"Sounds like fun."

"It's the best. We used to cruise every weekend when I was a kid."

"That must have been a great experience." With an impish smile, and knowing he was stuffed, he said, "I saw an ice cream shop back down the street. Would you like to get a cone?"

She cocked her head. "Why not?" Rising, she folded a ten under her wine glass and looked up at him. "I'm Brooke Hart."

He extended his hand. "Glad to meet you, Brooke Hart. I'm Steve Schilling."

The two walked to the next intersection then turned right and joined the tourists milling along Front Street. Steve made small talk as they passed a novelty shop. She pointed to a swimsuit on display in an upscale women's store next door then paused in front of an art gallery.

"Which of the paintings do you like?" she asked.

"I lean toward the impressionist. Is the one in the corner a Monet?"

"Very good." She smiled. "A print." She gave his hand a tug and led the way into the General Store. Weaving her way between display cabinets in the middle of the store, she stopped in the back by the old-fashion ice cream cooler and studied the containers.

"May I help you," a cute young black girl asked.

"Yes. I'll have a sugar cone and a scoop of chocolate black cherry."

Steve stared, knowing he'd love to have one. "I'll pass."

He paid for her cone and followed her outside.

The two strolled down the other side of Front Street making occasional comments as they window-shopped. At the end of the street, she took a small bite of her ice cream and turned. "Thanks for the cone."

Steve stood, dumbfounded, as she disappeared into the night.

***

After a restless night, Steve rose early the next morning. He took a quick shower, slipped on his sweatsuit and walked gingerly down the creaky stairs of the old B & B. Grabbing a cup of coffee, he plopped down on a wicker rocker on the front porch. He skimmed the *Carteret County News-Times,* and tried his hand at the crossword puzzle, but soon gave up.

"Damn." *Who is she? What is she doing here? One moment she seems distant. Then she's warm and appealing ... and disappears. I've never met a woman like her.* He slammed the paper on the table and bolted down the steps. Walking briskly down Queen Street, he passed Front Street then turned west on the boardwalk.

Seeing the only lighted café ahead, he walked past the wrought-iron fence and entered through the open gate. He ordered a large coffee then pulled out a second-hand chair.

Sunrays reflected off the 120-footer into the water below. Out of the corner of his eye he glimpsed a jogger heading his way. He studied the perfect stride then tried to catch a peek as the light-blue jogging suit and UNC-W cap flashed by. *Was that her? Nah ... maybe so. She said she was from Wilmington.*

He refilled his coffee, pointed to a Danish in the glass cabinet and paid the waitress. Mesmerized by the water lapping at the yacht's hull, he sipped his mug dry then saw an image shadowed in front of him by the glittering sun. He cupped his hand over his eyes — a jogger was running in place.

She popped off her ball cap and fluffed her long blonde hair. Her rosy cheeks looked like silk. *My God, it's her.*

"Hi," she said. "You're up early."

"I wanted to see the sun come up over the harbor."

"Wasn't it beautiful?"

"It sure was. Want a coffee?"

"Black." She pointed to his Danish. "I'll have one of those too."

Steve picked up her order and refilled his mug. "Where are you from?" she asked.

"I grew up in Kentucky. Went to college in Arkansas."

"Fayetteville?"

"No, Eastern Arkansas. I played football there."

"What position?"

"End. I wasn't very good but I caught the game winning touchdown pass in the championship game. Now, the ol' timers think I was an All-American." He laughed.

"Funny, how things turn out. I was a quarterback in Pop Warner football."

"A quarterback?" Steve scowled. "What'd you do, run the ball all the time?"

Her mouth turned down at the corners. "What do you mean by that?"

"Nothing, nothing at all. It's just that most girls can't throw a football very well."

She bristled. "I wasn't like most girls. I could throw as well as anyone."

"How did you learn?"

"My dad wanted my brother to be a quarterback so I read up on it and practiced. Turned out I was the only quarterback in the family. My mother made me stop playing when I was thirteen."

"Why?"

"She didn't think it was ladylike. She always had to be right." She turned the conversation. "What do you do?"

"I work in the administration at Mountain State University."

"My brother graduated from there. You're a long way from home."

Steve nodded. "I'm meeting with an alum in New Bern this weekend."

"Tough duty, being here for another day."

"I plan to spend some time at the museum down the street."

"You'll enjoy that. They have several artifacts from the Queen's Revenge, Blackbeard's ship. He used to control the waters around here."

"Really. I might pick up a book. I'm a real history buff. What do you do?"

She finished her Danish. "I'm a grad student at UNC-Wilmington. Try to spend as much time up here as I can."

"Why Beaufort?"

"Memories, I guess. My family came here when I was a kid. We had a cozy cottage on one of the side streets. And we boated. My dad loves the water."

"And your mom?"

Brooke twisted her mouth. "She went along for the ride. I guess she felt she had to. She was into her career. It all ended when they got divorced."

"That's too bad."

"I still go on trips with my dad. Do you know much about boating?"

"Nah, going down the Mississippi on a riverboat was the closest I ever got."

She eyed him and paused. "Would you like to go on a boat ride today? The shuttle for Shackleford Banks leaves at eleven. There's a lighthouse on the island with lots of interesting history."

"Really?"

"We could have a picnic lunch on the beach."

"I'll tell you what. You bring lunch and I'll buy dinner. What's the best place in town?"

She stood and pulled on her cap. "I'll meet you at the pier at ten forty-five, two blocks east of here." She tucked her hair under her cap, started jogging in place then headed down the marina. After several strides she turned her head back. "Front Street Grill."

"What kind of wine do you like?" he shouted.

"Pinot grigio," she called back.

***

Walking slowly toward the bed and breakfast, he saw the closed sign for Front Street Grill. He cupped his hands around his face and peered in the window. Thinking he saw something move, he tapped on the glass. A bearded man appeared and pointed to the sign.

"Can I make a reservation?" Steve mouthed.

Looking unhappy, the guy opened the door. "What time?"

"A table for two at eight."

"What's the name?"

"Steve Schilling."

The old man started to close the door.

"Do you know where I can buy a good bottle of pinot grigio?" Steve asked.

"For tonight?"

"For lunch. I'm going on a picnic with an attractive young woman."

The man paused. "An attractive woman. Was she blonde?"

"Yes. The most beautiful woman I've ever seen."

He stared at Steve. "Not Brooke Hart?"

"Yeah, how'd you know?"

"A bottle of pinot, an attractive woman … she's a regular here. Give me your credit card and I'll put a bottle of Trentinio Pinot Grigio on it."

"Great." Steve gave him his credit card.

The man returned in a minute and handed Steve a brown bag and his card. "Are you really having dinner with Brooke?"

Steve nodded.

"Other than her dad she's never had dinner with anyone else around here."

***

Steve waited near the shuttle ticket booth with one hand over his sunglasses trying to block the late morning sun. He held the brown paper bag in the other. A red Porsche raced down Queen Street, rolled through the stop sign and sped east on Front Street. Slamming to a halt, the car made a quick U-turn and parked across the street, in front of the Inlet Inn.

Steve watched a woman jump out. *That's her.* Popping the trunk, she bent over — her cream-colored, crocheted wrap slid over the bottom of her orange bikini. *What an ass.* Reaching further, the crease of her cheeks came into full view. "Holy shit."

Brooke pulled a large, flowery beach bag and small cooler out then slammed the trunk. "Looks like the tourists are back early," she called as several cars zoomed by.

Steve's eyes were glued on her orange top pressing through the loops of her wrap. "I hadn't noticed." His eyes raced up and down her body.

Crossing the street, she gave him a thank-you-very-much smile. "Think you're smart, don't you. Catching me with my hands full."

Not pursuing his thoughts, he reached for the small cooler. "Here, let me help you."

"Thanks." She pulled the tickets from her bag. "What's in the brown bag?" she asked.

"A bottle of wine."

She smiled, handed the agent their tickets and climbed onboard. "Let's sit up front so we can see the dolphins."

"Great idea."

She slid her bag under the seat. Steve squeezed in next to her and propped his feet on the cooler. "Looks like they are sold out."

Brooke grinned. "Shelling on the beach is popular this time of the year. There are sand dollars all over."

"Sand dollars?"

"Sorry, I forget." She fumbled through the beach bag then handed him one.

"Neat."

"Most of the people will head for the lighthouse so let's go to the beach before it gets overcrowded."

"Aye, aye, captain." Steve saluted.

She smiled.

At the dock Steve grabbed the cooler and followed her to the beach. She pulled a blanket from her bag and spread it out. "Want to play catch?"

"Sure."

She grabbed her football from the bag. "Go deep."

Steve trotted a few yards and turned. "Come on, go deep. This is not an up and in."

Steve jogged five or six more yards and turned. She waved for him to go further and heaved a perfect thirty-yard spiral. Steve raced trying to catch up and watched the ball fall off his fingers.

"I hit you in the hands — you should have had it."

He picked up the ball and, red-faced, walked back and handed it to her. "Where did you learn to throw like that?"

"I told you I was a quarterback."

"I've never seen a guy throw like that. So, what's for lunch?" he asked.

"Tuna fish or a BLT."

"I like both. Let's split."

She grinned. "I knew you'd say that."

"Why?"

"That's what my dad would have said. You're a lot like him."

Steve pulled the bottle from the bag. "How about a glass of wine?"

She grabbed the bottle. "Trentinio Pinot Grigio. My favorite, how did you know?"

"I said to myself, she's a very attractive woman. What kind of wine would she like? I thought, distinctively fruity, a hint of ripe pear. That's it!" He laughed. "Trentinio Pinot Grigio."

She gave him a quizzical look. "For some reason I don't believe you."

He raised his clear plastic cup. "Here's to the most attractive woman I've ever met."

She clicked his cup. "I bet you've said that to lots of women."

He winked. "A few maybe, but none measure up to you."

"Want some chips?

"Okay."

"Let me refill your glass."

She held it out for him. "Tell me about your first girlfriend."

"My first girlfriend?" Steve frowned. "Why?"

"I have a theory. Was she tall? Thin?"

Steve grinned. "Mary Lou Kitchen lived down the road, two farms over the hill. She was a freshman in high school. I was a junior."

"Did you date her long?"

"It wasn't like a date. We knew each other as kids. Sometimes we'd meet at the old fishing hole. Once in a while we'd have a picnic — nothing fancy like today. And we talked."

"Did you fool around?"

"No, I'd never do anything like that," he fibbed. "She was special."

Brooke grinned and lay down on her stomach. Loosening her halter-top strings, she asked, "Would you put some suntan lotion on my back? It's in the bag."

"Of course." Steve inspected her perfectively tanned back then poured lotion in one hand and rubbed his hands together.

"Do you always warm the lotion in your hands?"

"I guess … I never thought about it."

He gently massaged her back.

She raised her head. "Have you ever worked as a masseur?"

"No, why?"

"You are very good."

He noticed her cheeks tighten, ever so slightly. "How's that," he said, putting the bottle back in the bag.

"Perfect."

***

Steve adjusted his sport coat and tie then looked up when she entered the restaurant. Dressed in a tastefully-cut flowery sundress, she waved.

Patron heads turned.

Steve took a deep breath and stood. "You look beautiful. I love your lavender broach. It matches the colors in your dress."

"Thank you."

He pulled out her chair. "My dad bought it in Freeport."

The waiter filled her glass with pinot grigio. She looked at the familiar bottle. "Come on, now, tell me the truth."

Steve grinned. "I'm guilty. The manager here told me when I made reservations."

"Darn, why didn't I think of that?"

"How about an appetizer?"

"Their baked oysters and crispy calamari are wonderful."

"Let's have an order of each; we can share."

The two made small talk then ordered dinner. Steve motioned for another bottle of wine. "Do you have a place here?"

"Yes, a small two-bedroom house. My dad uses it when he takes the yacht out."

"He has a yacht?"

She smiled. "The 120-footer across from the café is his."

"Really? And you acted so …"

She cut him off. "I was checking you out."

"Sneaky I'd say."

"Maybe … you never know who you're talking to. It's better to be safe than sorry."

"And your daddy taught you that?"

"Yes. He also told me to 'be a girl with a mind, a woman with an attitude and a lady with class.' I've tried to follow that standard all of my life."

"You've done amazingly well." Steve pushed his empty plate to the side. "I'm sure he's proud of you."

She blushed. "I have to leave early in the morning to drive back to Wilmington. Thanks for a wonderful day," she said, standing. "And good luck on your meeting."

Steve stood and watched her walk out then eased back into his chair.

The bartender headed his way. "Looks like you were a big hit."

"What makes you say that? She's gone."

"I saw the way she looked at you."

"What do you know about her?"

"She's a classy young lady. The Hart family has been coming here for twenty years or more. Her dad is a bigwig in Charlotte. She stays here all summer, fills in here when I'm short-handed."

CHAPTER ELEVEN

The boys gathered daily for morning coffee at Mott's General Store in downtown Midville, North Carolina. Shelves of canned goods and household supplies filled three walls of the back room. In one corner a weathered green hutch holds mugs and a twenty-five-cup coffee pot that had seen better days. Other than replacing the potbelly stove with a butcher-block table, not much had changed since their fathers started the gabfest forty years ago.

They still grouse about the six-block pedestrian mall built in the center of town ten years ago. "Can you imagine replacing those brick pavers with asphalt?"

"No different than replacing a perfectly good street with the tables and green umbrellas."

"I don't mind the park benches but who in the hell picked out those art sculptures?"

"Art? One looks like an old plow shear with some rusty cans hanging on it."

A gray-haired geezer laughed. "That's the best description I've heard yet."

Today was no different, except they had a new citified complaint to chew on. Overnight, town workers had installed two fifteen x twenty-foot billboards on each end of the main drag — GO RED HENS BEAT TARHEELS.

Ralph McNeil, the elder statesman of the group pounded the butcher-block. "I can't believe the town council approved them. They wouldn't let me put a small, portable sign up in front of my shop."

"They've lost their mind."

"Double standard," Sam, the gray-bearded old codger said. "You scratch my back and I'll scratch yours. The university gets whatever it wants. That's a bunch of bullshit if you ask me."

"Here! Here!" the group shouted.

"In spite of that, I like that Bo fella. He's quite a coach," an overweight farmer chimed in.

Heads nodded around the table.

"There are not many other decent guys up there," said, Ned, as he pulled on one strap of his bib overalls.

"They're all crazier than a loon," the farmer said.

"The president is okay," chimed in Earl. A stereotypical bank manager, he waved his horn-rimmed glasses for emphasis. "I like him."

"That's two," the farmer agreed. "I bet you can't name two more."

Blank stares looked back at him from his buddies' faces.

A hand pulled open the curtain divider. Everyone looked up.

"Do you have an extra mug?"

"Of course, Mr. President." The bank manager grabbed a cup from the hutch.

"Thanks," Steve said, drawing up the last chair. "Driving to the office I noticed the new billboards — they're a lot bigger than I thought they'd be."

"They're huge," one of the old geezers said.

"The kids are really excited about playing the Tarheels."

"Yeah, that's something," Sam agreed, tugging at a gray lock of hair. "Do you think we have a chance?"

"Hey, that's why we play the game. There is always a chance." Steve took a slug then turned to Ralph who acted as the group's boss man. "Mr. McNeil, I stopped by your auto shop. They said you were down here."

"Yeah, whaddaya want?"

"I have four extra tickets. I thought you might like to take a few of the boys to the game."

Smiles greeted Ralph's glance around the table. "I've never been to anything like that," he said.

"I won't take no as an answer," Steve insisted. "I'm positive you can find someone to go with you."

"Ralph, you ought to do it," the farmer said.

"Yeah," the rest of the group agreed.

"Good enough." Steve stood. "Right now I'm headed for the press conference with Coach Bo. Wanna ride to campus with me?" he asked Ralph.

"Well, I …"

"Go ahead, Ralph. We'll hold down the fort," someone in the group shouted.

"Come on." Steve tugged on the old man's plaid flannel shirt. "My assistant, Charlie McBride, will bring you back with the tickets."

Ralph smiled and followed Steve to the car.

***

Sports director Bodie Both ended his remarks and pointed to coach. "And here's Coach Bo Willard."

Bo stepped to the podium. "Thanks, Bodie. And thanks to all of you for coming out. I'm so proud of our young men. Who could have asked for more? Twenty-two wins in a row and a NCAA bid."

A spontaneous chant broke out from the boosters. "Bo, Bo, twenty-two in a row, Bo, Bo, twenty-two in a row."

Coach raised his hands and the clamoring tailed off, as the press took notes and snapped pictures.

"Hey, coach," a journalist called from the rear. "Whaddaya think about playing the Tarheels?"

"It's a real honor. Who would have ever thunk it?"

Chuckles filled the room and the crowd cheered. "We want the Tarheels! We want the Tarheels!"

"Hold on. Hold on," Coach said, grinning, but trying to stop the chanting. The outburst continued for a few more long seconds. "We want the Tarheels!"

Bo held his hand high. The group stopped.

Steve and Ralph took seats in the last row.

"A lot of people deserve credit for this season. The team and I appreciate everyone's support but there's one person I want to personally acknowledge. He's the one who made all of this possible. My boss, President Schilling — please stand."

Steve stood and raised a two-finger victory symbol over his head. A cheer went up. "MSU! MSU!"

Steve gave coach a thumbs-up and sat down. Mr. McNeil watched in awe.

Bo quieted the group. "I remember sitting in Doc Schilling's office after that fifth loss. Prez said 'Bo I wasn't pleased with your comments after the game.'" Snickers filled the room. "'Yeah, doc,' I said. 'I shouldn't have said what I did.' Doc stuck his finger in my face, and said, 'Well, it's not going to happen again, right?' I nodded. 'Here's the deal,' he said. 'Bo, whenever you lose, your assistant does the post-game show. Got it?'"

"'Okay, doc,' I said. On the way back to my office I scratched my head, and thought, 'Damn, I receive a hundred bucks for every show.' Didn't take me long to figure out how much money I could lose. Mama Willard didn't raise no fool, I can't afford to lose."

The crowd stood and cheered. "Bo, twenty-two in a row!"

"That Bo is quite a guy," Mr. McNeil whispered to Steve. He nodded.

Bodie came to the podium. "Do we have any questions?"

Hands flew up from every direction.

Steve listened for a half hour then nudged Ralph. "We need to go."

Ralph grinned and the two men walked out of the room.

Steve chuckled. *I don't know how that guy does it. I chew him out one day and the next thing I know he has the crowd cheering about it.*

Ralph laughed. "Coach is all right. He's got a real sense of humor."

***

Lizbeth turned side to side, her black knit dress revealing every inch of her perfectly shaped figure. "What do you think about this one?" she asked.

Steve glanced over the top of the sport's page. "You look sexy as hell."

"Sexy? I don't want to look sexy. We're going to a banquet for the basketball team."

"Do you have a red scarf to go with it?" he asked. "Our colors are red and white."

"Gosh, how could I forget?" She turned and slipped back into the bedroom. Moments later she opened the door and paraded out in a red sporty outfit. "How about *this* one?"

"Perfect."

"Are you positive? I don't what to be the center of attention."

"Lizbeth, it's the first time the two of us have been together at a university event. Every eye will be on you."

"Maybe I should wear something more conservative."

"Sweetie, the boosters will love you in red."

"How long before we have to go downstairs?"

Steve looked at his watch. "Hmm, a half hour or so. I want to work the crowd before the players arrive."

"What's the agenda?"

"I've heard these events are well done. There'll be team banners in each corner of the banquet room designating where we should sit. We'll be there with our delegation. When the lights dim the cheerleaders and teams will march out singing their fight songs. Strobe lights will be flashing all over."

"It sounds kind of elaborate."

"Elaborate? Wait until we go to the NCAA national conference. They spend money like it's water — ice carvings, caviar, steak, lobster — you won't believe it."

"Sounds exciting."

"Tonight the focus will be on the players. After dinner each team will be asked to come forward. The players are individually introduced, and then walk across the stage for a photo op as they receive their commemorative tournament gift. Each coach will make a few comments, and it'll be over."

"Do we have to do anything?"

"Smile and stay close to me, everyone will want to meet you."

"What am I supposed to say?"

"Nothing special. Just smile and be yourself, they'll love you."

"And that's it?"

"Yes, unless you see me pause when I'm introducing you. That means I can't remember the person's name … go ahead and introduce yourself. They want to tell their friends that they met you."

"Met me … I don't understand."

"You're the future first lady. Trust me it's a big deal on campus."

Three hours later the couple walked back into their suite. "Well sweetie, what do you think?"

"It was just like you said. I can't believe how the people were so forthcoming and gracious. It was like I am some kind of a celebrity."

"You are to them. Most of them have never shaken hands with a person like you."

"But Steve I'm just …"

He cut her off. "Honey, it's a big deal for them. You'll get accustomed to it."

***

"Welcome to March Madness, folks," Brent Musburger announced to the national television audience. "Sixty-four of the nation's top basketball teams are ready to rumble. The countdown begins tonight with the number one ranked North Carolina Tarheels at 28 and 1, playing the sixty-fourth seed upstarts from Mountain State University with a 22 and 5 record. Dick, what can we expect tonight?"

"On paper it looks like we could have a real barnburner," Dick Vitale said. "The two teams match each other's statistics but that's where the similarity ends. All of the Tarheel opponents have been ranked in the top fifty. The Red Hens haven't played anyone ranked higher than a hundred and fifty."

"Sounds like we might be going home early tonight," Musburger chimed in.

"We have Coach Willard with us. Let's hear what he has to say. Coach Willard, welcome to primetime," Vitale announced heartily.

"Thanks, it's a real privilege to be here," he said in his typical slow southern drawl. "We're proud to be in our first tournament."

"How's it feel playing North Carolina? They're making their thirty-first appearance."

"They're like us. It's their first appearance this year."

"Good point … you have to agree, though, Dean Smith has an advantage with seven hundred and ninety-four Division I wins over your twenty-two."

"None of those count tonight. They'll have five guys out there and we'll have five. It'll be zero-zero when the game starts."

"You're right, coach but they've knocked off some of the nation's best — Kentucky, Duke, and Indiana."

"They haven't beaten *us*."

"Thanks coach, for taking a couple of minutes with us," Dick said, then turned. "Well, Brent. Sounds like we have some mountain boys ready to play."

"I'm sure Coach Bo feels they're ready but this will be a forty minute test against one of the best teams in the country. Sports fans, it's time to take a TV timeout."

Musburger rolled his eyes. Vitale shrugged his shoulders.

***

"Well, Dick, it looks like the Las Vegas odds-makers had it right, giving North Carolina a forty-point edge tonight. They're up by twenty-three at halftime."

"That's hard to disagree with, Brent. The Tarheel back line of 6-10, 7-2, and 6-9 is just too much for the outmanned Red Hens. It could be over."

"With Mountain State down forty-two to nineteen, it'll be interesting to hear what Coach Willard has to say when the teams come out for the second half." The camera switched to courtside. "Here come the Red Hens and we're back, with Dick Vitale."

"Coach, a tough first half. What are you going to do differently in the second half?"

"We're not changing. We're pounding it inside."

"But Coach … that strategy didn't work in the first half. You're down by twenty-three. They have six players bigger than your tallest player."

"They can't play them all at the same time. We're going inside. Their All-American center has three fouls and their other two trees each have two. If anyone on our team takes a shot from beyond fifteen feet, I'm taking him out."

"Wow, Brent. Whataya think of that?"

"I think he's in for a long night. Here we go folks … the tip for the second half … and we're underway."

***

"This place is going crazy, Dick. We've got five seconds to go. There's a basket by Raheed Wallace. The Tarheels are up sixty-four to sixty-one. That might put it out of reach. Two seconds to go. Here's a timeout by the Red Hens. We're staying right here, Dick. What do you think?"

"I have to give the boys from the Smokies a lot of credit. Early on, the game looked to be a rout. But they came back to give the Tarheels all they could handle."

"What do you expect now?"

"The Red Hens will probably make a long inbounds pass and throw up a prayer. North Carolina will likely put a big man on the inbound passer, so they'll have to pass over him."

The camera focused on the end line under the Tarheel's basket. "They're lining up just like you said, Dick. Here we go … two seconds on the clock. The official motions that the Red Hens player can run the baseline. He hands him the ball. The Red Hen guard fakes to the right, takes three steps to the left and sprints back to the right. He makes a long heave past the center-court line. A Red Hens player takes a thirty-footer at the buzzer. It's good! It's good! The place is going wild. The crowd is mobbing the Red Hens."

"Hold on, Brent. One of the officials is waving his arms."

"What's going on?"

"It looks like he's waving off the three pointer. They're going to review it on instant replay. Whataya see, Dick?"

"They're replaying the shot in slow-motion video. It's hard to tell from that angle. Here's another view. Hmm, I don't know … it looks like his toe is on the line. Can you blow it up?"

"You're right, Dick. Yep, there it is. The officials are signaling two points. North Carolina wins sixty-four to sixty-three. Looks like the Tarheels are going to escape Dodge unscathed."

CHAPTER TWELVE

Steve sat at the dais nodding in approval as provost La Russa presented the accreditation self-study to the board. *He did in six months what I couldn't do in two years. He's a good man.*

Carl ended, "Are there any questions?"

Two hands shot up. Carl seemed surprised. He acknowledged the heavy-set woman sitting next to Steve. "Mr. Provost, we approved the university priorities a few months ago. Why are you recommending a focused-team visit?"

"Good question." He grinned. "There are two differences. First, what you approved earlier were institutional goals. They provide overall direction for the university. In the self-study we're talking about academic goals and objectives. Second, the report outlines a grassroots process starting at the department level that flows upward. The other one was top down."

"What's wrong with a top down process?"

"It works in lots of situations but the curriculum is the responsibility of the faculty. They're the experts. Program changes start with them and move up on the approval ladder."

"That sounds crazy to me. I'd never run my business that way."

"Neither would I." Carl chuckled. "The faculty have Ph.D.'s in their disciplines and the most qualified individuals available, to design academic programs and ensure they are up-to-date."

Carl recognized the other hand. "Mr. Provost, why does the Southern (Accreditation) Association have to send a team back in three years?"

"It's a validation process. The report outlines the steps we'll take over the next few years. Then the association will send a team to determine the extent to which we've done what we said we would do."

"Mr. Provost," another member queried, "we're telling them that we have a deficiency. Isn't that a sign of weakness?"

Carl wiped his brow. "Not at all, we're simply being truthful. The association will see that as a strength. It's a self-assessment. We're obligated to disclose our strengths and weaknesses. And then we have to eliminate the weak points."

"How does a weakness translate into a strength?" the board member continued.

"Mr. Chairman," Steve interjected. "The self-study has been reviewed campus wide. After fumbling the ball for two years, Provost La Russa efficiently pulled our game plan together. It's time to call the question and praise Dr. La Russa for his leadership."

"Yes I agree," the chairman said. "I call the question."

***

Looking like a whipped dog, Carl plopped down in Steve's office. Charlie grinned. "Welcome to Mountain State."

"Is it always like that?" Carl asked. "I covered those questions in my presentation. I felt like I was defending my dissertation."

Steve laughed. "Sorry. I should have mentioned it to you."

"Mentioned what?"

"Those two always ask questions. They have to see their names in the paper."

"If I have to go through many more meetings like that I'll be drinking Tanqueray like you."

"Ha. Ha." Charlie laughed. "That's why you guys are paid the big bucks."

"Seriously, Carl." Steve paused. "The report is right on target. You did a great job."

"Thanks."

Charlie pursed his lips. "There's more to the questions than you may think."

"Why so?" Steve asked.

"There was a sharpness in the board's tone. Those questions came from the faculty."

"What makes you say that?" Carl asked.

"I've been picking up some scuttlebutt. There's an undercurrent; something is brewing."

"Brewing? Like what?" Steve asked.

"Some of the old timers think the changes are coming too fast. They're looking to slow things down, maybe derail a change or two."

"We've barely started," Carl said.

"That's what they're afraid of."

Steve leaned back in his chair. "What do you think is going on, Charlie?"

"I haven't figured it out. Hal Durocher called me yesterday. He's the assistant editor at *The Mountaineer*. He asked me a series of questions about your past, Steve. He said he had a two-page epistle from a Dr. Bergmann at Eastern Arkansas. I'd like to talk about that."

"I'll leave," Carl said.

"No need, Carl. We're a team." Steve turned to Charlie. "Okay, let's hear it."

"Hal asked me if I could verify Bergmann's accusations. I told him I'd call him back."

"Here's the scoop. Bergmann and I got into a pissing contest early in our careers. He's had a vendetta against me ever since — long before I was named president at Eastern Arkansas. Every year he'd come up with something new to hammer me. After my divorce he claimed that over a hundred calls about my personal behavior had been made to the senate office. Apparently he grouped them under the code of ethics and was ready to call for a vote of no confidence. Hearsay, it was a bunch of crap."

"Seems like a lot of smoke for no fire." Charlie looked puzzled. "And your wife divorced you over that?"

Steve squirmed in his chair.

"Come on, Steve. We're all in this together I want to know the truth." Charlie's eyes zeroed in on him. "Mr. President."

Steve walked over to the window then abruptly turned around. "Yeah, I fooled around. The chancellor heard about the rumors. He did his due diligence. Call the vice chancellor, Beverly Harrington, she talked to Dr. Bergmann."

"Can Hal call her?"

"Absolutely."

"That ought to set *that* aside." Charlie turned to Carl. "You're next."

"Me? I didn't do anything."

"Harold has four letters to the editor on you."

"What about?"

"Two weeks ago you laid out the changes you wanted the senate to make in the tenure policy, right?"

"Yes, our policy is something out of the past."

"That's a good way to win friends and influence people," Charlie said, not missing Carl's tone of mock sarcasm.

"I'm talking about standard stuff. I plan to kick off the debate this spring and wrap it up in the fall."

"Sounds like a good strategy." Steve interjected. "What do you think, Charlie?"

"He's headed for shit city."

Steve frowned. "What?"

"Carl has pissed off half of the senate by saying their policy is a throwback to the '50s."

"Well … it is."

"Maybe so, but you didn't have to say it. There are ways to imply that without ruffling feathers. Then you added insult to injury by saying it was standard stuff. It's not standard here. The senate chair called your former school. They said you tried to eliminate tenure and there was a lot of turmoil. Is that true?"

"There was turmoil, okay; it was focused on the president. He wanted to eliminate tenure. Several national groups got involved. He got fired. I salvaged the situation with a compromise."

"That explains the letters," Charlie acknowledged.

"What do you think we should do?" Carl asked.

"I'll give Hal a call and lay it out. We can talk after that."

"Good idea, "Steve said.

***

A few days later Charlie walked into Steve's office and closed the door. Steve and Carl looked up and gave him their full attention.

"Sorry I'm late," Charlie said. "I laid everything out for Hal; ten minutes later I had to repeat everything for his boss."

"What'd he say?" Steve asked.

"He called Dr. Harrington while I was there then said they're not going to run the Bergmann stuff — that's water over the dam."

"Good." Steve grinned. "What about the tenure letters?"

"They're going to run them. Hal said they're related to ongoing activity."

"Sounds like they want to sell more papers, if you ask me," Steve said.

"Probably so," Charlie agreed.

Steve turned to Carl. "Well, at least only one of us will be in the pressure cooker."

"I'd rather have it be you. I'm not very good riding in the hot seat."

"Someday you'll be a president. You might as well learn how to take the heat. The best thing is both of us are not in the pressure cooker at the same time. That'd shut the place down."

"You're right about that," Charlie chipped in.

"We need to be on the same page, Carl. What changes have you planned?" Steve asked.

"First, we have to define tenure as a process that builds upon academic freedom and due process. It's a protection for the faculty."

"No one can dispute that," Steve said.

"Don't be so sure. Someone will find an issue with every word," Charlie pointed out.

"Second, awarding tenure is a process that shifts the burden of proof from the individual to the university," Carl added.

"Burden of proof?" Charlie questioned.

"Prior to awarding tenure it's the faculty member's responsibility to demonstrate that he or she should be reappointed. After tenure is earned it's the university's responsibility to prove the faculty member should *not* be reappointed. That's a big difference."

"You mean a person who is no longer functioning at an acceptable level should be fired?" Charlie asked.

"Of course."

"You better not say that in a senate meeting."

Carl looked puzzled. "Okay … the next point is even more controversial. We need to increase academic standards and move from three-year reviews to the national standard of six."

"Shit," Charlie said. "All hell will break loose."

"Charlie, it's all standard stuff."

"Don't shoot me, I'm only the messenger. I'm telling you — you're talking about working conditions — the campus will explode."

"What's the last point?" Steve asked.

"The procedure for termination of those who fail to live up to the expectations."

"Termination." Charlie bolted out of his chair and faced Carl. "You'll be the one who is terminated. You'll never pass something like that."

"Charlie, we're only upgrading the policy. We're not doing away with it. We must make it clear what is expected in the future," Carl emphasized.

Steve rubbed his chin. "What if we segment the bill and push for three separate votes?"

Charlie rolled his eyes. "That'll be fine if you can avoid a vote on the entire policy."

"What do you think, Carl?"

"Sounds like a plan. I'll try it."

***

Twiddling his fingers on the top of an elegant Ethan Allen table, Steve heard a soft rap on the inn door. "Yes, who is it?"

"Room service." He scowled then opened the door. "I didn't call ..." Bev pushed her tight sweater toward him. "You called for room service?"

Steve pulled her tight. "Welcome to the French Quarter Inn, the finest in Charleston. I'm sorry, madam, I didn't catch your name," he jested.

"Call me Delight."

Steve rubbed his hands together. "Maybe I should cancel dinner reservations."

"Forget the Delight." She laughed. "I'm starved. Do I have time for a quick shower?"

"Make it super-quick. I'll bring your luggage up from the car."

Shortly, the two walked downstairs to the restaurant. "Schilling," he said.

"Yes, Mr. Schilling, right this way." The waiter guided them through the dimly lit garden-dining area, to a secluded table.

"It's beautiful, Steve, so romantic. It reminds me of New Orleans."

"Well, we *are* in the French Quarter Inn."

Bev smiled. "It's so authentic — the trickling fountain, fleur-de-lis and colorful artwork."

"They're not as lovely as you."

"You always say the right thing. How do you keep coming up with places like this?"

"I do my research." Steve placed his hand on top of hers and gently caressed.

"Champagne?" the waiter asked.

"Yes, of course." Steve said.

The two lovebirds toasted without taking their eyes off each other. Steve ran his index finger around hers then gently caressed her hand, one finger at a time.

"You're so special, Bev, I want to make love to you all night."

"You're so sweet. You don't have to do anything special. You're the special one."

"Bev, I have never felt this way about anyone."

She kissed his fingertips. "I love you, Steve. You can have me any way you want."

Steve cocked his head. "I'll have to think about that."

"Fine, you do that." She smiled coyly. "While I visit the ladies' room."

When she returned, Steve stood and pulled out her chair.

She wrinkled her brow. "Okay, what are you thinking about?"

"Nothing."

"Come on, I can tell."

Steve motioned to the waiter then whispered in his ear. He nodded and scurried away.

"What's going on?" Bev asked.

"Something special." Steve paid the bill and guided her to the door. "I've ordered a carriage so we can tour the historic district."

"You didn't have to do that."

"You said I can have you anyway I want."

Bev frowned, hoping he didn't mean *in* the carriage. The driver took her hand and helped her into the carriage. Steve slid in and pulled a blanket over her legs.

"I hope I don't fall asleep," she said.

He smirked. "I'll keep you awake."

Bev leaned back in the carriage. "I bet."

Moving slowly through the historic district, the two glanced left then right as the carriage driver pointed out famous sites.

"Steve, I've never had an experience like this. What could be better?"

He slipped his hand under the blanket onto her thigh. "I can only imagine."

She gave him a questioning look. "Steve?"

"You said what could be better? I was just seeing if …"

"I didn't mean it that way."

"Why not?"

"Because … I couldn't."

Steve's fingertips explored upward. "Don't you just love that mansion over there?"

"Don't try to distract me. I know what you're doing."

"I love you, Bev."

"I think you should stop. The French Quarter is right up there."

"Don't worry sweetheart. I asked the driver to take us on an extended trip. We're only halfway," he said, as they approached the inn. "Do you want me to stop him?"

Bev leaned her head back and closed her eyes. "No … I'm only halfway."

***

Charlie grabbed a bottle of water and sat in a straight-back chair across from Joyce. "Did you do anything special over spring break," he said.

"Not really. I did a little shopping in Ashville," she said. "How about you?"

"Ellen and I slipped over to Myrtle Beach to catch the Glenn Campbell show. She hummed 'Rhinestone Cowboy' all the way home."

"That's one of my old-time favorites too."

Steve walked in.

"Good morning, Mr. President," Joyce said.

"Morning, Joyce." Steve glanced across the room. "Morning, Charlie."

"Do you have a minute?" Charlie asked.

"Of course, go on in; I'm grabbing a cup of coffee."

Steve closed the office door and sat on the settee across the coffee table from Charlie. He chuckled. "I had a busy break, need to rest up."

"So I heard," Charlie said.

Steve frowned. "Whataya mean by that?"

"Sounds like you were busy in Charleston."

"I met an old friend. How'd you know?"

"I had three calls to return when I got home last night. Each one wanted to know about the big-busted blonde you were escorting about town."

"Jesus Christ, can't a guy go out with a friend? What's the big deal?"

"No big deal. I just thought you'd want to know that people are watching."

"People are always watching. The bastards are always looking for something wrong."

"Steve, everyone knows that Elizabeth and you are a thing. When they see you with some hussy in Charleston, they begin to wonder."

"She's not a hussy."

"You know what I mean."

Steve raised his voice. "No, I don't."

"Sorry. When people add one and one they expect to get two … not three," Charlie stated on his way out.

CHAPTER THIRTEEN

"We'll have a Sam Adams and a Budweiser," Charlie said to the bartender, grabbing a handful of peanuts from the bucket in the center of the table. "Want any wings, Carl?"

"Might as well. It sounds like we'll be here awhile," he said, turning his head to check out the place. "You come here often?"

Charlie gazed at the tired country and western bar then pointed toward the old North Carolina license plates nailed on the wall. "See that one over there — 1957. It's off my Nash Rambler. I used to take Ellen to the drive-in down the road and then we'd stop here for a beer."

"That's almost forty years ago."

"Yep." Charlie grinned and rubbed his bald head. "Been comin' here awhile."

Carl laughed. "I was in diapers."

"Don't rub it in." Charlie took a slug of his Sam Adams. "So what's your plan for the faculty senate?"

Carl loosened his tie and leaned back on the old rickety-chair. "I figured I'd lay out the three segments like we agreed."

"That's good, but what's your plan when they nail you?"

Carl wrinkled his brow. "What do you mean?"

"Changing the tenure policy is a major decision. Do you think the senators are just going to sit there and agree with everything you have to say?"

"What I'm proposing is totally logical. Changes like this are occurring all over."

"Right. And how many of those places lost the academic vice president or president?"

Carl shrugged. "I-I don't know."

"If we're not careful your ass will be on a hot griddle sizzling like bacon." Charlie rubbed his extended forehead. "My job is to make sure that doesn't happen."

"I'm for that." Carl swiveled toward Charlie. "What would *you* do?"

"I'd meet with senate chairman Bert Sharpton and share my well-planned strategy."

"Why would you do that?"

"You need his support and that of the executive committee. They're the level heads on campus. Without them on board you can't pull it off." Charlie paused. "Not all of the good guys are in the administration. They're respected by their peers and want Mountain State to be better too."

"I never thought of it that way."

"The execs will bring along their colleagues."

"Are you positive?"

"Is that a 1957 license plate up there?"

***

Bert Sharpton opened the door to his cluttered office in the biology department and motioned Carl in. "Mr. Provost, you're early."

"I like to be on time for my meetings, particularly important ones."

"So why do I deserve a visit from our distinguished provost?"

"To be candid, I need your help."

"*My* help?" Bert raised his eyebrows. "Have a chair."

Carl outlined the plan that took him the better part of three days to create, then waited.

Bert made a series of phone calls before turning back to Carl. "Here's the deal."

Carl straightened in his chair.

"I'll call a special meeting of the senate in two weeks. You appear with your plan and do your thing; just make sure you don't reference this meeting."

"Okay."

"Follow my lead and I'll see how far we can go."

Carl's eyes brightened. He smoothed the sharp crease in his slacks. "But … I'll tell you right now, if you lose your cool, the deal is off. I can't be seen picking up the pieces."

"Fair enough," Carl said. He stood and shook Bert's hand.

Unable to restrain himself when he left Bert's office, Carl quickened his pace across campus to a near run and burst into Charlie's office.

Charlie glanced up. "What's with you?"

"I pulled it off. I mean … we pulled it off."

"Pulled off what?"

"The meeting with Sharpton. He agreed."

Charlie sat back in his chair. "Good. Let's hear about it."

"I did exactly what you said," Carl stated, then summarized the meeting with Bert.

"I knew you could do it."

Carl stood and headed for the door. "Wait until Margaret hears about this."

***

Carl was still on cloud nine when he walked into the faculty senate meeting, ten minutes early. He glanced around the room — faculty members filled the gallery, standing shoulder to shoulder. Every chair around the senate's square table was taken except for his spot. He felt beads of moisture ooze under his arms.

Dr. Sharpton called the noisy room to order. "I've scheduled this meeting to start a discussion on the university's tenure policy. And I've invited Provost La Russa to make opening remarks. Mr. Provost."

"Thank you, Bert." Carl cleared his throat. "As you know, President Schilling is committed to taking Mountain State to the next level. And long term, to make us one of the foremost universities in the state. His vision compels us to evaluate every aspect of the university."

A murmur filled the room.

"Our tenure policy is the cornerstone of academic life."

"Mr. Provost is it true that you tried to eliminate tenure at your last school?" a bearded faculty member shouted from the back of the room.

A stir rippled through the gallery.

Bert gaveled the wooden block on the table. "We'll have order! There will be no more outbursts like that. I've asked the provost to make his remarks and … we'll honor that commitment. Mr. Provost …"

"That's a good question and the answer is no. The president there publicly stated his goal to eliminate tenure. As a matter of fact, I proposed the compromise that passed the senate. It's the same plan that I will present to this body."

"How do we know you won't hoodwink us?" another faculty member called out.

"You'll have to judge that for yourself. I can tell you I believe in tenure. It's a procedure that combines two of my most cherished principles — academic freedom and due process."

"Then why are you trying to eliminate it?" a short woman demanded.

Bert hammered the gavel. "One more comment like that and I'll clear the room. Please Mr. Provost, continue."

"As I said, I am not interested in eliminating tenure. My goal is to strengthen the policy."

"What's wrong with the current policy?" a faculty member shouted from the standing-room-only gallery.

"That's it," Bert said. "Sergeant-at-Arms, clear the room. The senate is going into executive session. Only those seated around the table may stay."

The disgruntled group shuffled slowly out of the room, grousing so all could hear. The Sergeant-at-Arms closed the door and stood against it, his arms folded.

"Mr. Provost, you may continue."

Carl described the key points in the first section of the policy. "Are there any questions?"

"I think we've heard enough for one day," Bert said, halting further discussion. "We'll reconvene in two weeks. May I have a motion to adjourn?"

***

Carl took a deep breath then walked into Charlie's office.

"Well, how'd it go?" he asked.

Carl sunk into a lounge chair. "I'm still here. I guess that's good."

"I'm sure you were fine." Charlie chuckled. "Now you know why I said being the provost is the toughest job on campus."

"You're telling me. Whataya think it'll be like next time?"

"Most senators will be civil but a few will continue to push."

"Thanks. That's just what I wanted to hear," Carl replied sardonically.

"Well, you wanted the truth, didn't you?"

"Yes, but I'd hoped you'd be a little more positive."

"Hey, Bert is on your side. All you have to do is be patient and not lose it. More heat is coming. Hal told me they have seven letters to the editor on tenure."

"Great," Carl jested. He brushed a hand over his short, black hair. "I'm sure my wife will appreciate that."

"You'll learn to develop a thick skin."

"What about my wife?"

"She'll shed a tear. Remind her, this is not about you; it's simply part of the process."

"She's a Christian person."

"So are most of the senators … until it comes to issues affecting them." Charlie rubbed his head. "One more thing. Make sure you read the letters to the editor. They'll provide good insights into what's coming next. Address the points in your introduction without reference to the newspaper. There's no use giving the rag any credence."

Carl pulled himself out of the chair. "Got it."

***

Following two more contentious senate meetings, Carl walked into the final meeting of the year. The room was packed. Television cameras scrutinized them from the two back corners.

Bert whispered in Carl's ear. "I'm expecting several parliamentary motions. Don't say a word; just smile. I'll take care of everything."

Bert gaveled the meeting to order. Carl sat quietly and grinned.

One of the senate members raised his hand. "Mr. Chairman, I move to amend."

"We faced that issue earlier," Bert said. "A motion to amend is not in order."

The guests standing in the back grumbled. Bert gaveled firmly. "Quiet, please."

"Mr. Chairman, I move a substitute motion."

"Out of order," Bert ruled.

The senator was persistent. "Mr. Chairman, I move to table the motion."

"A motion to table is not debatable," Bert said, "It requires a majority vote." He looked around at the confirming nods. "All those in favor of tabling the motion, raise your hand." Bert counted each hand aloud and ended with twelve. "All those interested in continuing the discussion, raise your hand." He counted aloud then stopped. "Seventeen. Motion to table fails, seventeen to twelve."

"Mr. Chairman," the vice-chair stated. "I move we approve resolution 95-42, as printed."

"I second the motion," another executive member said.

"Mr. Chairman, I move to suspend …"

"Out of order," Bert interrupted. "We have a motion on the floor."

"We are voting to approve resolution 95-42. All those in favor, raise your hand." Bert counted aloud, ending again with seventeen.

"Those opposed." He pointed at the last hand. "Twelve. Motion passes seventeen to twelve. A motion to adjourn is in order."

"So move," said the vice chairman.

"Second," came from the senate secretary.

"All in favor say 'aye.' Motion passes."

Carl turned to shake Bert's hand.

"Don't move," Bert said under his breath.

Carl watched the senators file out then slipped out the side door.

***

Carl strolled into Steve's office wearing a mega-smile. "It passed, seventeen to twelve."

"Congratulations," Charlie exclaimed, getting up from an overstuffed leather chair. He grabbed Carl and gave him a bear hug.

"You're the one. Without your advice I'd never gotten beyond day one. Thanks again."

"No need. It's one down and two to go."

Steve, sitting behind the desk, shook his head. "I don't know how the two of you put up with all of the crap. Those bastards are crazy. I would have lost it."

"That's what they were hoping for," Charlie said. "Carl stayed the course."

Joyce poked her head in. "Mr. President, can you take a call from Brittany Hayward?"

Steve looked at Carl then Charlie. "Anything else?"

The two men shook their heads and walked out.

"Put her through, Joyce."

Steve picked up the phone. "Brittany."

"Mr. President, I'm sorry to interrupt you but I'm at my wits' end with Lizbeth."

"Why? What's wrong?"

"She's overdoing herself — has gone bananas. Mr. Webster agrees. We're encouraging her to take some time off, maybe take a vacation. She says she won't go anywhere without you."

"What do you think we ought to do?"

"I've checked her favorite hotel in St. Amour. They have a vacancy. It's in the northern part of France's Beaujolais region. I think she would go there."

"When are you thinking?"

"I'm sure I could get her to go for two weeks if you would come for the third week."

"Hmm, commencement coming up. How about the middle of June?"

"That'll work. I can make all of the arrangements, if it's okay?"

"That'll be fine."

***

Brittany waited for the airplane in Lyon, France. "Mr. President, over here," she called to Steve and waved.

He caught her eye. "Brittany, it's great to see you. How is Lizbeth doing?"

"Much, much better. She's acting like the Lizbeth of old. It's like she flipped a switch. She must be eighty percent of normal."

"That's wonderful. I can't wait to see her," Steve said, then motioned for the driver to pick up his bags. He placed Steve's luggage in the trunk and began the drive north.

Brittany briefed Steve on their stay so far, then pointed to the hotel driveway. "There it is on the right."

The driver pulled in, jumped out and opened the door. Steve helped Brittany out and they walked inside the Hotel Auberge du Paradis. Spotting Lizbeth at a small table for two in the hotel bar, he slipped up behind her, leaned over and kissed her lightly on the neck.

She turned and grabbed him around the waist. "Oh Steve, I've missed you so much. I've been counting the hours."

He pulled her up and kissed her firmly on the lips. "I've missed *you* so much."

She squeezed him tight, almost hanging on his neck. "It's so good to see you. I've been on pins and needles all day. Did you have a good trip?'

"Yes, but seeing you is the best part. You look wonderful."

"The last few days have been like night and day. I feel like a million dollars."

"You look like two million."

"Just being with you, darling … I can't explain it. Wait until you see our suite." Lizbeth started up the steps then turned and blew him a kiss.

"I didn't travel this far for a kiss on the wind."

She grinned. "You devil, you."

***

The week passed quickly and before they knew it the last day had arrived. Lizbeth woke up early and ran her fingers through Steve's abundant, dark wavy hair. "You awake?" she asked.

"I am now."

"What are you thinking about?"

"It has been a whirlwind week. I can't believe it's almost over."

"What was the best part?"

He glanced down at her naked body.

"No, not that. Something we did."

"I enjoyed the two days in Lyon — the Fouviere Basilica and the Cathedral of St. John the Baptist were spectacular. The opera and shopping at those upscale fashion boutiques. Buying that dark green dress for you was a real turn-on. And the wineries. I'll never forget them."

"How many cases did you buy?"

Steve looked down sheepishly. "Ten. I bought a case of everything you liked."

"Wonderful. We'll have plenty to reminisce over when we get home. Want to get up now?"

Steve cracked an eye open. "Again?"

Lizbeth shook her head. "Do you have anything else on your mind? Go back to sleep."

She read the morning paper then tipped-toed into the bedroom. Seeing Steve spread-eagle in his shorts, she grabbed a belt from the closet and gently tied his right wrist to the bedpost. Pulling another belt from his pants draped over a side-chair, she headed for the other side of the bed.

Steve slowly opened one eye. "What are you doing?"

"What do you think?"

***

Later that morning, Lizbeth sat by the window, a French novel in hand. Steve strolled out in a pair of dark navy-blue silk loungers. "What do you think about these?"

"They're sexy as hell. I was hoping they'd fit you."

"Have you been up long?"

"A lot longer than you were last night." She laughed.

"Funny, funny. What are your plans for today?"

"There's one specialty shop I'd like to visit before we leave."

"Your wish is my command."

"Let's go this morning. There's a quaint deli we can stop at on the way home."

"Good. I'll be ready in a flash."

"I'll have the driver bring the car around and meet you out front."

Shortly, Steve stepped out of the front door. Lizbeth rolled down the window of a sleek, black town car, waving her hand. "Over here, dear."

Steve smiled and slid into the limo.

"This is André," she said, motioning toward the driver.

"Morning André."

He nodded.

Lizbeth gave André directions then snuggled against Steve's chest.

"What a perfect week," Steve said. "I don't know how it could have been any better."

Lizbeth grinned and slid her hand up his thigh.

"Lizbeth …"

"You said you didn't know it could have been any better. I'm just checking out the equipment for possibilities," she said, fondling his jewels.

"It's been working all week." Steve nodded toward André and whispered, "He can see us."

Lizbeth turned toward the driver. "André, would you close the window please?"

The black window slid silently upward and clicked shut.

"I hope that makes you happy." She loosened Steve's belt, unzipped his pants, pushed him down on the seat and began to stroke.

"I hope that makes *you* happy," Steve jested.

"Me?" She smiled. "The shop is a forty-five minutes away."

***

Lizbeth tapped on the smoked-glass window. It cracked open. "Are we almost there?"

"Five minutes."

"Thank you." The window slid shut.

Lizbeth combed her hair and added lipstick. Steve tucked in his shirt. "Ready to go?" she asked.

Steve nodded.

André opened the door and extended his grey-gloved hand. "Madame."

Lizbeth slid out, tugging Steve toward a small shop on the corner. "This is my favorite place. Wait until you see inside."

Steve followed her and stopped in the doorway. *Holy shit, I've never seen so much jewelry in all of my life. The inventory must be worth millions.*

"Whataya think?" she asked.

"It's fabulous. I've never been in a place like this."

"Wait until you see the good stuff."

Lizbeth headed for the counter in the back. A tall slender man with a pencil mustache appeared from the curtained doorway. "May I help you, madame?"

"Yes. Last week I talked to a woman about a diamond ring," she said, pointing to a glass countertop. "It was right here."

"Yes, my wife said there was an attractive American woman in, looking at an engagement ring. She put it aside in case you returned. Just a minute, I'll be right back."

He disappeared through the curtained entry to the back rooms. Steve browsed the shop while Lizbeth waited.

"Here it is." The shopkeeper opened the felt box and extended it toward Lizbeth, so the overhead lights caught the sparkle in each faceted diamond.

"It's lovely, don't you think so?" she gushed.

"It's spectacular," Steve said, hoping he wouldn't have to pay for it.

"I'm thinking about buying it."

"Buying it?" Steve swallowed.

"It fits perfectly. Would you like to slip it on my finger?"

Steve hesitated then looked her in the eye. "Are you saying what I think you're saying?"

"You know full well what I'm saying," she said, her face aglow.

"You're serious, aren't you?"

"Did you ever know when I wasn't?"

The shopkeeper called. "Maria, come out here. Hurry."

A short, heavy-set woman opened the curtain. "What is it dear?"

He grinned. "We're going to witness a proposal." His wife rushed to his side.

Steve kneeled on one knee and slid the ring on her finger. "Lizbeth, will you marry me?"

"Yes, oh yes, Steve. I love you."

CHAPTER FOURTEEN

Steve walked into his den, grabbed a pad of paper and pushed the blinking light. "You have twenty-three new messages," the computer voice announced.

He clicked. "Welcome home, sweetie, it's Bev. I hope the university exchange program went as planned. I miss you terribly. See you Friday night. Love you."

He deleted the hang-ups and marketing calls, double checked his reminder for the dentist appointment then clicked the last message. "Steve, it's Brooke in Beaufort. In six weeks we're staging a Civil War reenactment on the beach at Fort Macon. Because of your interest in history, I thought you might like to go. Give me a call."

Steve stared at the phone unable to believe what he had just heard. After double checking his calendar, he picked up the phone and dialed.

"Good evening. This is Brooke Hart."

He admired her sultry voice. "Brooke, it's Steve. Sorry I didn't call sooner. I just returned from France."

"France? What were you doing there?"

"Setting up a university exchange program in Lyon."

"That's a wonderful town. I've been there several times."

"The architecture is spectacular and the restaurants are out of this world."

"Have you ever had better wine?"

"Never. I enjoyed several wineries. Each one was better than the one before."

"I can't wait to hear more." She hesitated. "Do you have your calendar handy?"

"Yes, it's right here."

"I'm looking at the weekend of July twenty and twenty-one. Would you be interested in going to a Civil War reenactment?"

"Let me look," Steve said, counting to ten. "Geez, I'm sorry. I have a long-standing commitment I can't change."

Brooke's voice dipped. "Oh … I'd hoped we might …"

"I'll be in Beaufort the entire weekend," he said.

"You dirty dog." Her voice perked. "I'll get even with you."

"I'll make a reservation at the Pecan Tree Inn."

"It's the season. They'll be booked up. You can stay at my place if you want. I have an extra bedroom. But you'll have to make your own bed."

"Sounds perfect. That is … if it isn't too much trouble."

"No trouble. Let me know your plans. I'll pick you up at the New Bern airport."

"Perfect. I'll call you in a couple of days." He hung up and leaned back in his swivel-rocker. *Out of the blue. What was that all about? I didn't even think she remembered me.*

***

A red Porsche convertible slid to a screeching halt in front of the New Bern airport. A blonde with a UNC-W ball cap removed her huge round sunglasses. "Hey mister, want a ride?"

Steve gave Brooke a big smile. "Yeah, where do I put my bag?"

The small trunk popped opened. "It should fit in there."

Steve jammed his bag in and eased into the bucket-seat. Eyeing her, he said, "Not bad. Hot car too."

"Don't try to make amends with me." She didn't crack a smile. "Buckle up, this thing flies."

Steve pulled his old Cardinals cap down. They cruised through New Bern then she gassed it, opening it up all the way to Havelock. Zipping past Newport, his eyes bulged as the speedometer hit 120 mph.

He caught his breath at a stoplight on Arendell before bracing himself as she peeled off the line. Racing over sixty-five in the twenty-five mph zone, she flew over the Beaufort bridge and slammed on the brakes in front of a small, wood frame house.

Steve's head snapped back at the sudden stop. "Did we set a world record," he asked.

She smiled. "I broke my time by two minutes."

"What's the hurry?"

"We have reservations at the Front Street Grill in twenty minutes. I thought you might want to freshen up."

"Freshen up? I have to put on clean shorts."

She grinned. "I like that."

Steve grabbed his bag, followed her up the front porch and stepped inside. Looking around, he paused. "You're really into the arts, aren't you?"

"Performing arts. I'm studying theater."

"The artwork is very distinctive; yet, everything fits together."

"Thanks, it feels homey to me. My dad comes up a few times a year. He likes it too."

"I can see why."

She pointed to a door near the kitchen. "That's your bedroom. Fifteen minutes."

Steve shaved his five o'clock shadow then slipped on an open-collar tan shirt and a light green sports coat. Relaxing for a moment in an old overstuffed chair, his mind swirled. *I can't believe I'm here. She's the most attractive woman I've ever seen — sexy, alluring, classy.*

He heard a knock on the door. "It's time to leave."

"I'll be right there."

He glanced in the mirror one more time, adjusted his collar and opened the door. Brooke stood before him. A Greek goddess, he thought, gazing at her long blonde hair that perfectly framed her golden smile. Star-struck, he stared at Brooke's red- and purple-flowered sundress. Its graceful style caressed her slender body and shapely hips.

"You look spectacular."

"You're a sweetie." Kissing him lightly on the cheek, she took his hand and pulled him out the door.

Steve stopped on the porch and pulled her tight. "Thank you for inviting me here," he said, and kissed her softly for an extended time.

She stepped back as if not wanting to let go. "We need to leave."

***

The Front Street Grill owner glanced at Brooke then smiled at Steve. "Your table is ready."

The two followed him to a corner table overlooking the marina. The owner pulled out her chair and Steve slipped into the seat opposite.

She gazed at the harbor lights just beginning to twinkle in the dusk. "Where else in the world would you rather be."

A high-mast sailboat passed by.

Placing his hand on top of hers, Steve searched for the right words. "I can't imagine. Wherever such a paradise might be I'd want to be there with you."

Her eyes roamed over Steve's full dark hair until they connected with his warm brown eyes. "You're a very special person."

The owner filled their glasses half full and placed the bottle of Trentino in the ice bucket.

Steve raised his glass. "Here's to the most elegant woman I've ever met."

She smiled.

They clinked glasses. "And here's to the most handsome president I know."

Steve wrinkled his brow. "How did you know that?"

"I put two and two together and checked you out."

"That's not fair. You know everything about me. All I know is that I'm having dinner with Brooke Hart, the most attractive woman in the world."

She giggled. "What else would you want to know?"

The restaurant owner discreetly emptied the bottle into their glasses. "The calamari is very good. May I start you with an order?"

"Yes." Brooke nodded. "And we'll have another bottle of the pinot."

Steve searched for a point of conversation. "How did you connect me with a Civil War reenactment?"

She took a sip. "A history professor with a specialty in the Civil War," she quoted one search result.

"You did do your homework."

She looked up sheepishly. "To tell you the truth I was looking for a reason to call you."

"Really? Well, I'm glad you did. You're very straight forward, aren't you?"

"I'm not one to beat around the bush. My dad always said when you're with a friend be yourself. In business you can fool a person; being with a friend, only a fool is untruthful."

"Sounds like your father is a wise man."

"He knows everything — how to run a business, navigate a yacht, and how to deal with life. I just love him."

"Sounds like quite a guy. I hope I'll have a chance to meet him."

"Maybe you will."

"I'd like that." Steve opened the menu. "What do you recommend?"

"Everything is wonderful. The crab cakes and flounder are special but you can't go wrong with the ribeye."

"What are you having?"

"Crab cakes."

"I'm having the parmesan crusted flounder and an order of the fried green tomatoes."

She flipped her hair to the side in an absently seductive motion. "According to your website you've had a very successful year."

"Sometimes I pinch myself to make sure all of those things really happened."

"I read about that fifteen million dollar gift you received."

"Wasn't that something? The Websters are very gracious. With their contribution, next year we'll open up the new arena against Duke."

"Your basketball team is really good. They nearly beat the Tarheels."

"Everyone on campus is still talking about that."

Brooke cut into her second crab cake. "What made you become a university president?"

"It kind of happened, I worked hard and moved up as the opportunities occurred."

"I'm sure it was more than that."

"I'm lucky. I always seem to be in the right place at the right time. And I had a great mentor. Like your dad, he taught me everything."

"Bill Thornton, right?"

"Wow. You *really* did do your homework."

"Inquisitiveness is a family trait. You got divorced while you were in Arkansas. Have you met a special person since you moved here?"

"Only one."

Leaning back, Brooke frowned.

"I'm looking at her right now."

She grinned. "You're a real jokester, aren't you?"

"I got that from my mom."

"You have a dry sense of humor."

"That's from her too. She was there for me, just like your dad is to you."

Brooke grinned. "You're so sweet."

"I don't know much about Brooke Hart. Where is she from? What does she do?"

"I pretend to be from Beaufort but I live in Wilmington. I spend as much time up here as I can. I love the water. And yachting with my dad."

"A 120-footer … I could learn to like that."

"It's more than the size of the yacht. It's the freedom of solitude as you skim the ocean waves."

"Sounds exciting," Steve said, pushing his plate aside.

"I hope you left room for dessert."

Steve shook his head. "I don't think so. Would you like to take a walk?"

"That'd be perfect."

They walked hand-in-hand down the boardwalk. Brooke pointed toward the sky. "There's Orion, and over there is Polaris. Do you know where Ursa Major is?"

Steve studied the constellations. "Over there — the big dipper."

"Very good."

"It's the only one I know. Did you study astronomy?"

"A little. As a captain you need to know the map of the stars to keep your bearings."

"Right, I forgot about that."

"Ready to go home?"

Steve nodded.

Brooke took his hand and the two strolled down Queen Street. Making a turn onto her block, they walked slowly to the front porch. She kissed him on the cheek. "It's time to turn in. We'll have a busy day tomorrow."

Steve paused. "Thanks for a wonderful evening."

***

Lying wide-awake, Steve watched a moonbeam creep across his bed. *I can't believe it. Here I am in bed alone twenty feet from the most beautiful woman in the world. What could be better?*

He heard a soft rap on the door and turned. "Yes."

"I can't sleep," she said. "Would you like an after dinner drink?"

"Sure. I'll be right out."

Steve ran a comb through his hair, and slipped on his robe then opened the door and stepped out. Two candles flickered on each end of the coffee table. Brooke leaned seductively back on the sofa, her legs crossed beneath her, a short black negligée showing off her long, slender legs.

Walking slowly toward the sofa, his eyes never leaving her, Steve eased onto the other end. Posed like a fashion model, her left arm rested on top of the sofa back, her right hand held an Old Fashioned glass.

"I'm having a Grand Marnier. There's Napoleon Brandy, Kahlúa and Amaretto. Help yourself."

Steve glanced at the selections then poured Amaretto over a glass of ice. Returning to the end of the sofa, he said, "You look like a fashion model."

"Really? I did some photo shoots last month. I should hear something this week."

"I bet you'll receive an offer. I'm telling you right now, I'm buying whatever you're selling."

"You won't have to."

Taking a sip, Steve hesitated, wondering, hoping, what that meant.

"What does a president do in the summer when the faculty is gone?"

"Breathe normally." He laughed. "Seriously, it's a time to catch up."

"Do you travel much?"

"Not really. I try to squeeze in a weekend trip here and there."

"Would you pour me another Grand Marnier?"

"Certainly."

He poured a healthy measure into her glass and slid closer on the sofa. Catching a glimpse of her breast bulging from the black lacey top, an erection bulged under his robe.

"I'm thinking about going to Aruba. Have you ever been there?"

Steve shook his head. "Haven't been beyond Key West."

"I love Aruba. It's so fresh and the people are wonderful."

Brooke downed the last of her drink, got up and walked slowly toward her bedroom door. Stepping inside, she turned slightly — the moonlight silhouetted her perfectly shaped body.

He watched her unbutton her top and toss it aside. His erection shot rock-hard. He gulped the last of his drink, trying to keep things in check 'til the time was right.

"In case you're interested there are no robes or pajamas allowed in here," she said. Turning inside, she left the door open.

***

Sunlight streamed over Steve's naked body. He reached across the bed for Brooke and came up with nothing. Smelling fresh coffee, he cracked an eye, then dozed off again.

Brooke bounded in the front door with a bag of pastries in hand. She flipped her NC cap on the table and loosened her jogging suit. "Good morning," she called into the bedroom. "Did you have coffee yet?"

"No. I left my robe on the sofa last night. Would you hand it to me?"

She smiled. "Seems like you owe me."

"Owe you, what's that mean?"

"I remember … you said you'd be busy all weekend."

"I was joking."

"I didn't think it was funny."

Steve peeked around the doorway. "Come on, Brooke. I don't have any clothes in here."

"Too bad." She picked the robe up and dangled it in front of her.

Steve reached around the door frame. Brooke stepped back.

"Come on, this is not funny."

"You were naked all night. What's the difference if I see you now?"

"It's different."

All you have to do is walk out here."

"Brooke, I …"

"I'm waiting." She motioned seductively with her index finger.

"You're dressed. I don't have anything on."

She flipped off her shoes. "Step into the doorway and I'll take the rest off."

"How do I know you will?"

Slipping off her jogging suit, she stood in her running bra and panties. "The rest comes off when you come out."

Steve hesitated a moment, then stepped into the doorway — stark naked.

"Turn around."

After a long second Steve pivoted quickly around.

"Nice ass."

144

"Whataya think this is, a sex show?"

"Turn around and face me," she coaxed.

He threw his arms up. "I …"

"Turn around … hands on your hips."

"Okay, okay." Steve turned slowly and posed.

Brooke inspected him. "Hmm, I knew you were large but I didn't realize you were *that* big." She ripped off her running bra and rushed toward him.

Steve stumbled backward and they fell onto the bed. With the bed still rocking like it'd been hit by an earthquake, she leaped on top of him and kissed him wildly.

He responded with equal abandon, grabbing her slender body to help her slide over him, pushing deep inside her. They rocked in rhythm, until Steve could take no more. Moaning, he erupted with Brooke arching at nearly the same moment.

She collapsed on top of him. *Even better than last night,* he mused, as he held her to him.

CHAPTER FIFTEEN

Steve squinted at the phone trying to determine if its incessant ring was in his dream, or real. Glancing at his empty gin glass and the porno magazines scattered on the floor, his eyes finally focused on the blinking light. Picking up the phone he mumbled, "Steve Schilling."

"Steve its Charlie, I hope I didn't wake you."

"Nah, what do you want?"

"I'd like a date for the mini-retreat so I can tell Carl tomorrow."

"Hold on. I'll check my calendar." With effort, he concentrated on the little squares for the weekends in August — Lizbeth, Bev, Lizbeth, Brooke/Aruba. September was more of the same — Bev, Brooke, Bev, Lizbeth. In October — Lizbeth, Brooke, Bev, Bev. "The football team is away the last week in October. Let's plan it then, in Raleigh."

"Will do."

Steve leaned back in his lounger and skimmed the calendar again. "Damn." He pounded the armchair then walked to the bar and poured a second tall Tanqueray. He ignored the clock that told him what time of morning it was. Grabbing a bag of chips in the kitchen, he walked back and slouched in his lounger. An hour passed. He refilled his glass.

"What's wrong with you?" he shouted to the wall mirror, on his way back to sit down.

Steve painfully recalled the beating he'd endured during his dad's drunken rages, the times his dad had raped Sally, and how his father had abused his mother. *I'm just like the bastard. I've got no one. I'm alone.* Overcome with self-loathing, he flipped on a porno tape and masturbated.

It was noon on Monday when the phone woke him from his stupor. "Hello," he said, in a barely audible tone.

"Are you okay?' Joyce asked.

"I think I have a mild case of food poisoning. I'm taking today and tomorrow off. Please reschedule everything."

"Of course. Do you want me to bring you something?"

Pausing, he thought about her tight-ass skirts. "I'll be fine."

"Are you sure? I have a container of homemade soup in the fridge."

"Nah, I'm going back to bed." He hung up. Thinking about her, he pulled down his shorts, fondled himself then stroked himself back to sleep.

The next afternoon, after emptying another bottle of gin, he called Joyce. "I'm taking off the rest of the week."

"Mr. President, you've been going night and day for two years. A few days off is what you need. Are you positive there is nothing else I can do for you?"

You can come over and fuck me. "Ah, no … I'll be okay."

He fumbled with the receiver and slammed it down. *You can do something, okay. Take off that tight-ass skirt and show me what you can do.* Steve raked his hands through his hair, mumbling to himself, "Damn, she looks good."

He opened a new bottle of gin and filled his glass. *Fuckin' doctor doesn't know what he's talking about. He doesn't understand how I feel. No one cares about me. Why not? I'm a person. Who the fuck cared about my dad? He didn't give a shit about anyone ... thought he was a big shot when he whipped me.*

Steve's empty glass slipped from his hand and dropped to the floor. He dozed off.

***

Charlie hung up the phone and drove across town, thinking how bad Steve sounded. *His voice was raspy. I hope he is okay.* The car door slammed loudly as he got out and double-timed it up the sidewalk. He rang the doorbell, impatiently tapping his other hand on the side of his leg while waiting for the door to open.

No one came so he tried the door. It opened and he stepped inside.

"Steve," he called, taking a tentative half-step forward.

No response.

He called again, "Steve you okay?"

Hearing a noise from the back of the house, he hurried toward the sound. "Steve, are you in here?"

"I'm in the den," Steve grunted.

Charlie stepped into the room and gasped at the trash — bottles, beer cans and papers littered the space. "What is going on?" he asked.

"I feel like shit." Unshaven, his hair greasy, dark circles ringed Steve's eyes.

"You look terrible. When did you last shave?"

Steve rubbed his stubble. "Last week, I guess. I've got a touch of food poisoning."

Charlie took a whiff. "Food poisoning my ass. You're smashed."

"Doesn't matter. I'll fix you a drink."

"Drink hell. I'm cutting you off. Take the bottles and cans to the garage while I pick up the trash."

Steve staggered toward the kitchen with an armload of bottles and cans. Charlie followed and stopped at the kitchen table, pushed the dishes aside so Steve could set down his load, and sat in a kitchen chair. "This place smells like a pig sty. When was the last time you washed the dishes?"

"Monday … or was it Tuesday? Shit, I can't remember."

"There must be a dozen empty bottles on the counter. Find a box for them. I'll put the dirty plates in the dishwasher."

Charlie rinsed the dishes and wiped the counter. Steve carried the empty booze bottles to the garage. "At least it looks better in here. Got any room deodorizer?" Charlie asked, as he put fresh grounds into the coffeepot. "Now … what's going on?"

"Things are messed up." Steve said, staggering to the fridge. "Want a Sam Adams?"

"Stop, right there. You open that door and I'm out of here. I'm brewing coffee."

"Fuck. Isn't there anything I can do right, around here?"

"You can set your ass down and tell me what's going on."

Steve glared then plopped down at the kitchen table and pouted.

"Have you been like this all week?"

"I guess."

"Don't give me any of that 'I guess' stuff. Either you have or you haven't."

"Yeah, I have."

"Okay, let's hear it. What's going on?"

Steve rubbed a hand over his chin, feeling a scratchy, uneven beard. "How do you think things are going at the university?"

Charlie scowled. "What does that have to do with anything?"

"Shut up. I'm asking the questions."

Charlie didn't blink. "Things are going extraordinarily well. Faculty members are upbeat. Carl's doing a terrific job. We're on a big-time roll."

"How come no one ever tells me that? All I hear is piss and moan."

"People don't need to tell you. You can see it in their results." A crease crossed Charlie's forehead. "Why do you ask anyway? What's wrong with you?"

Steve stared at the floor. "I don't know."

"You have some kind of a health problem?"

"Kind of."

"Kind of?" Charlie refilled their mugs. "What's wrong?"

"It's a long story." Steve slurped his coffee. "Whataya think about Lizbeth?"

"She's wonderful. Everyone thinks the two of you are the perfect pair. And that rock she's wearing is something else."

Steve wiped his brow. "*She* bought it … she wants to have a big fuckin wedding next summer."

Charlie paused. "You okay with that?"

"Fuck, who cares."

"Are the two of you having problems?"

Steve's mouth curled down. "Lizbeth and I … problems? No way, she's the best."

"Then I ask again, what's wrong with you?"

Steve stood and paced the room. After two trips to the window and back, he plopped down across from Charlie and stared at the floor.

Charlie waited patiently, then asked, "Want to talk about it?"

Steve snarled. "Whataya want to know?"

Charlie's tone sharpened. "I want to know what's going on."

Steve tapped his fingers on the table. "I'm in love with Bev."

Charlie's mouth flew open. "You're what?"

"I love Bev. You know, the blonde I was seen with in Charleston."

"I covered your ass on that long ago."

"Charlie, you're not listening. I love Bev."

Charlie's face flushed and he stroked his shiny head. "What are you talking about?"

"I'm telling you I'm in love with Bev."

Charlie frowned. "You can't be. You just told me Lizbeth and you have wedding plans."

Steve bit his lip. "That's the problem."

Charlie looked Steve in the eye. "You can't be in love with two women."

Steve swallowed hard. "When I'm with Lizbeth she's the only one. I love her completely. And when I'm with Bev I have the same feelings for her. She's the best."

Charlie shook his head. "That's not possible. You can't be in love Lizbeth and Bev at the same time."

"You're just like Dr. Benderman, Charlie. You don't understand."

Charlie rubbed his jaw. "Okay, tell me about Bev?"

"It's Beverly Harrington."

Charlie choked on his coffee. "Beverly Harrington! You're seeing Beverly Harrington?"

Steve nodded. "Since last Christmas."

"Christmas? That's nine months ago. Have you been screwing her all that time?"

"It isn't like that."

"Sorry. Have you been sleeping with her?"

"I told you, Charlie, it isn't *like* that. I love her."

"I don't give a hoot what you call it. It's an ethical problem. She's covered for you with Hal. She ran the budget numbers. Who knows what else she may have done?"

"She hasn't done anything wrong."

"Doesn't matter. It's the perception of things. You could be in big-time trouble."

"She won't say anything."

"Jesus Christ, Steve, get your head screwed on right ... you're rationalizing."

"Charlie, you don't understand. I love Bev."

Charlie gave him a timeout sign. "Okay. You're in love with Beverly Harrington *and* you love Elizabeth Webster. Right?"

Steve nodded and gave him a sheepish grin.

Charlie wrinkled his brow. "I'm missing something here. Do I need to start over?"

"You have it right. Um, there's another one too … I"

Charlie cut him off. "*Another* one?"

"Brooke. We've been dating for three months."

"Three months. Who the hell is Brooke?"

"She's a terrific person. I can't live without her."

"What does that mean?"

"I want to be with her all the time. I love her."

"You've been out in the sun too much."

"It isn't funny, Charlie, I see one of them every weekend."

"Every weekend? What's wrong with you?"

With a loud sob Steve broke into tears. "I can't help it. I'm a sex addict."

Caught off guard, Charlie paused. "How do you know that?"

"I've seen several doctors. They all agree."

"How long have you known?"

"Four or five years, officially."

"So some of the rumors circulating in Arkansas were true?"

"Yeah, I guess. I've been under therapy since I arrived. Everything was fine at first; then the shit hit the fan."

"Like what?"

"I was working things out with my old friend, Kate, when I fell in love with Lizbeth. Then it happened again, with Bev. I thought I could handle it. Next thing I knew, I fell in love with Brooke."

Charlie looked out the window, struggling to understand Steve's confession. He turned back to Steve. "You're telling me you're in love with *three* women?"

Steve nodded. "I didn't realize the mess until you called to arrange the mini-retreat. I was booked up with them for months."

"Steve, you're going to fuck yourself to death. No, I take that back. Maybe you'll get a reprieve and one of them will shoot you."

Steve grinned. "That's the same thing a friend told me ten years ago."

"It's been going on that long …" Charlie shook his head.

"As long as I can remember."

"Who's your doctor?"

"It was Dr. Benderman in Charlotte. I stopped seeing him."

"You stopped? You have to see him again. You're out of control.

"He thought I was making progress, but I let him down. I'd be embarrassed to …"

Charlie talked over him, "Embarrassed, hell … you need help. Give me his number."

***

"Dr. McBride, it's a privilege." Dr. Benderman shook Charlie's hand. "Anyone who takes the bull by the horns like you, can't be all bad."

Charlie gave him a half smile. The doctor turned to Steve. "I've been worried about you. The demons are always out there."

"I thought I could handle it."

Dr. Benderman gave him a sympathetic grin. "You're really lucky to have a friend like Charlie."

"I know."

"Charlie says he'll be your confidant. Are you ready to start?"

"I don't have a choice. I'm about to lose my mind."

"According to Charlie you're involved with three women. Is that right?" Steve nodded. How long have you been seeing more than one?"

"Since last Christmas."

The doctor glanced at his notes. "You didn't mention a second woman when we last met."

"I couldn't, doc. I was embarrassed, it'd be like I was letting you down."

"Steve, this is not about me. We're working on your challenges. I want to fill in the blanks. Let's start with Bev."

Steve described the times he had been with her. Dr. Benderman noted each occasion. "That's it?" he asked.

Steve nodded.

"Okay, let's hear about Brooke."

Steve smiled broadly. "She's the best. I've never known anyone who makes me feel so comfortable."

The doctor took copious notes then raised his hand. "You're positive she's the best?"

"Absolutely. Why do you ask?"

"Do you realize what you've said?"

"Ah, yes … that I love Brooke."

"You said she's the best."

"What's wrong with that?"

The doctor shook his head. "You might say that to a woman but sex addicts rarely compare one woman to another."

"Sounds like an important discovery," Charlie interjected.

"Saying that about Brooke is new territory."

"Is that good?" Steve asked.

"It's something I want to pursue. Before that I want to bring Charlie up to speed on your past history, okay?"

Steve nodded. "Lay it out."

"Charlie, it's critical that you understand Steve has a permanent condition. He can control it, to a point, but it's simply a matter of time before he's back to his old behaviors."

"You mean he could have another relapse at any time?"

"Absolutely. That's why it's important for him to talk with you as often as he can. That way you can keep tabs on him and maybe together we'll be able to head off the next crisis."

"That'd be great," Steve said.

"So it requires constant attention?" Charlie asked.

"No question. The recovery rate for addicts like Steve is very low. Almost nil. Most of the time they're in a defensive mode, trying to prevent the next breakdown."

Steve sat sullenly quiet as they discussed him

"Sounds ominous," Charlie noted.

"It is. Steve doesn't realize the extent of his problem. He feels self-pity and sees himself as the victim."

"Self-pity? That's hard to imagine … a strong person like him."

Dr. Benderman smiled. "Unfortunately people don't come in neat little packages. Some of his success is a façade — he's hiding his shortcomings. He lives a double life and is in constant fear of being discovered. Down deep he doesn't trust anyone. That's why he doesn't become fully intimate with women. If he did, it'd be like letting his guard down."

Charlie scowled. "The other day he asked how things were going. I told him 'great.' He said 'all I hear is pissing and moaning.'"

"That's the point. When alone, he dwells on the negative. Then he uses sex to bolster his self-image — it makes him feel good about himself."

"As his erection goes so goes his self-esteem," Charlie quipped.

Dr. Benderman laughed. "I never thought of it that way. Sex is the symbol for love. All of his relationships with women are sexualized."

"Wow. Sounds like we have a lot of work to do," Charlie said.

"You're right. And we need to get started now. How about meeting on Saturdays for the next month?"

"Fine with me," Charlie said.

Steve looked down at the floor. "I'm booked up until November."

Dr. Benderman sighed. "Looks like another golf game down the tubes. I'll see you Thursday at two."

***

"Sorry you missed your round of golf today," Steve said as he and Charlie walked into Dr. Benderman's office. They sat down on the small leather sofa in the middle of the office.

"No problem. You made my wife happy. She handed me a long honey-do list." The doctor opened his notepad. "I want to pick up on a couple of points I made last week."

"Fire away."

"Let's discuss feeling sorry for yourself. Does that occur often?"

"Hmm, mostly when I'm down."

"What happens?"

"I feel alone, like nothing is going right."

"Then what?"

Steve squirmed and the leather squeaked. "I get depressed. Feel the need to see someone."

"That's a basic sense of emotional deprivation."

"What does that mean?"

"Simply put — you have a need that isn't being fulfilled. Your body is calling out to you; it's desperate."

"Desperate?"

"When you see a woman in a tight skirt what do you think?"

"I want to screw her."

"Do you have that feeling often?"

"All the time."

"Besides Lizbeth, Bev and Brooke, do you feel that way with others?"

"Sure, don't most guys?"

"Most men don't think about jumping in bed with every woman who walks by."

Steve's blank stare spoke volumes to the doctor.

"Those thoughts are your addiction calling out, wanting to be satisfied. When you give in, you end up in bed and feel good for the moment. After she's gone your desires start to build again. You seek refuge in another relationship. It's a vicious cycle."

"How does he avoid the temptation?" Charlie asked.

"That's where you come in. The two of you need to meet on a regular basis. You must push him, Charlie, and encourage him to talk openly about his temptations. There's a paperback — *Out of the Shadows* by Patrick Carnes. It's an easy to read primer on sex addiction. I suggest you both read it."

Steve grumbled, "I don't know, I …"

"Just give it a try. Read a chapter and tell Charlie how you feel. He can take notes and we'll go over them the next time we meet."

"That's asking a lot of Charlie," Steve said.

"Don't worry about me," Charlie assured him. "We have to take care of number one."

"That's right," the doctor interjected. "We must head off those uncontrolled behaviors. It'll require lots of work from the two of you. Are you up to it?"

Charlie looked at Steve. "I'm ready. What about you, Steve?"

"With the two of you in my corner I can't go wrong."

CHAPTER SIXTEEN

Counting the faculty senator hands as they went up, Charlie stroked his jaw — eighteen, nineteen … twenty-two. The chairman raised the gavel and hammered. "Motion to approve the operational procedures for the new tenure policy passes twenty-two to eight."

Charlie looked around the room as the meeting concluded. Senators filed out of the room without saying a word. Charlie gave the senate chairman a questioning look. *Action on tenure guidelines and no one says a word. It doesn't seem right. I don't like it.*

Carl and Charlie walked toward the president's office. "Well Carl, it looks like you pulled another one off."

"Not me. You made it happen. We're two-thirds of the way home."

"We've passed two out of three sections all right but we still have a ways to go."

"Charlie, it's a new year and we're on a roll."

"I didn't like the silence at the end of the meeting. A major vote on a tenure policy and no one says a word. It doesn't feel right. I'm going to snoop around," Charlie said, as the two walked into Steve's office.

"How'd it go?" Steve asked.

"It passed, twenty-two to eight, but Charlie's concerned."

Steve looked confused. "What is it Charlie?"

"No one said a word after the vote. They just got up and left. It doesn't smell right."

"Maybe you're overly pessimistic."

"Hmm, I don't think so."

Joyce poked her head in the doorway. "Mr. President, Chancellor Williams is on the line."

"I'll take it." Steve motioned for Charlie and Carl to leave then picked up the phone. "Eric, how are thing going in Raleigh?"

"Couldn't be better. I have terrific news."

"What is it?"

"Dr. Harrington gave me the year-end numbers. You've made a miraculous turnaround. Mountain State was headed for a fiscal watch. There was no way to avoid it. You turned the place around. Congratulations!"

"Thanks."

"Bev tells me in the years ahead, Mountain State will be one of the financially healthiest universities in the state."

"That's great news."

"Great? It's spectacular. Nobody has ever seen anything like it. We have to recognize what you've accomplished."

"That'd be super but you don't …"

The chancellor interrupted. "Steve, it's important — for both of us and for the community — have any ideas?"

"I've never had anyone ask that kind of a question."

"I'd like to start the ball rolling with something more than a typical news release. Bev thinks it'd be good for her to make a presentation to your board. What do you think?"

"That's kind of usual, isn't it?"

"That's the point. It's different. She could lay out the details at your November board meeting, if that works for you?"

"Ah … yes, that'd be fine."

"Good. I'll send an announcement to the Association of State Colleges and Universities that'll alert the national media. Hell, who knows what kind of press you might get?"

"Do you think it's that big of a deal?"

"Big deal … it's unheard of. It'll be a feather in our caps. I'll have the governor send you a letter of commendation. We might even get something from the president of the United States. She's cranking up her reelection bid. North Carolina will be big for her."

***

Charlie and Carl walked into Steve's office and sat down in the familiar overstuffed chairs in front of Steve's desk. "Why am I so honored? The two of you at the same time." Steve jested.

"We have a problem with the tenure bill," Charlie proclaimed.

Steve scowled. "I *thought* the pads were greased."

"So did I," Carl said. "Charlie's had this inkling back in the spring. I think he's right. Something is in the works."

"What is it, Charlie?"

"I had a funny feeling since the last meeting."

"Yes, I remember. You said no one said anything after the last vote."

"That and the debate, or maybe I should say the lack of debate. The most vocal critics didn't say a word."

"Maybe they've conceded to our victory."

"Those assholes — no way. They'd piss and moan about the time of day. I think they're lying in the weeds, waiting."

"Waiting for what?"

"I'm not sure. I hear rumblings about something that happened in Arkansas."

Steve scowled. "A tenure issue in Arkansas?"

"That's all I've heard."

"A tenure issue, huh?" Steve repeated the question then raked a hand through his hair. "Let me think." He paced the office then cracked a smile. "Bergmann, that's it. The fucker is back at it."

"I've heard his name but I assumed it was the issue we talked about in the search process."

"It's more than that. I blew the whistle on him when he went up for early tenure."

"Early tenure? What's that?"

"It's an old process we had in Arkansas. You could apply for tenure a year or two early. It was eliminated long ago."

"When was that?" Charlie asked.

Steve shrugged. "Twenty-five or thirty years ago."

"Geez," Carl said. "Faculty members are like elephants. They never forget."

"We used the same criteria for termination Carl is proposing."

"That's it." Charlie exclaimed. "They're going to use that to scuttle the final vote."

"After all of this work we could lose it on the last day?" Carl asked.

"Wouldn't be the first time," Charlie said.

Steve gazed out the window then turned with his fist raised over his head. "Hell no, they're not going to scuttle it!"

Charlie and Carl looked at each other in bewilderment.

He ripped open his desk drawer, pulled out three index cards and handed them to Charlie. "Here, take these."

Charlie straightened.

"Take out your pen and write one of these names on each card.

Charlie started to write. "Sharon Tice ... Melissa Carnes ... Janet Harris. Got them?"

"Yes, but ..."

Steve interrupted. "We're talking about credibility, right?"

"Of course."

"Give those names to your mole and tell him to call Bergmann about his former students."

Charlie's eyes bugged. "You mean ..."

"Right." Steve nodded. "It's time to even the score."

Two days later, Carl walked into Steve's office. "How did the senate meeting go today?" Steve asked.

"I was shocked," Carl replied. "A motion to pass the final section came out of the blue. No debate. It passed twenty-nine to two."

"What did Charlie say?"

"He cleaned his glasses, and said, 'Sometimes it's knowing who got blown rather than who you know.'"

Steve laughed. "Welcome to university life."

***

The board chairman gaveled the November meeting to order. "With the approval of my colleagues, I'd like to set the agenda aside so we can hear a special report from vice chancellor Beverly Harrington. Do I have such a motion?

"So move."

"And a second?" Three hands flew up. "All those in favor say 'aye.'" He glanced around. "Motion passes unanimously. Dr. Harrington, the floor is yours."

She rose and stepped to the podium.

"Thank you, Mr. Chairman and distinguished trustees of Mountain State University. As the chief financial officer of the State of North Carolina

Higher Education System it is my distinct pleasure to present one of the most important financial reports ever made to a board in this state."

Board members gave her their full attention. A hush fell over the audience.

She cleared her throat. "Chancellor Eric Williams had hoped to be here today but he was one of five chancellors summoned to Washington by the president of the United States. He sends his regards."

She flicked on the projector. "I have a detailed PowerPoint presentation and a handout. I'll move quickly through the slides, to focus on the more significant points." She grinned then flashed quickly through a half-dozen slides with little comment.

Beverly hesitated on the next slide. "This chart is a summary of the financial health of the university in the five years prior to Dr. Schilling's arrival. As you can see the financial decline in the two years immediately preceding his arrival was precipitous." The board members rustled. "It's obvious what was about to happen — a disaster. The next chart projects five more years, had Dr. Schilling not appeared."

She flashed it on the screen.

"Oh my God," the chairman lamented. Heads turned and the trustees mumbled.

"You're right," she said. "A major crisis was ahead. The heavy red line across the top signifies a fiscal watch. You all know what that means — financial instability — the institution is bankrupt." She looked smugly at the chairman. "That's when you receive a personal call from the governor."

Beverly gazed around the table of white-faced trustees. "Fortunately, you approved a series of actions proposed by Dr. Schilling. The turnaround by Mountain State has been spectacular."

She flashed the numbers and remained silent.

The trustees and audience oohed and ahhed.

"As you can see the financial health line dipped dangerously close to the fiscal watch line last fall then shot up on a thirty-degree angle. At this rate Mountain State will soon become one the healthiest institutions in the state."

Spontaneous applause erupted. Members in the gallery cheered. The board chairman shook Steve's hand then embraced him. Cameras flashed.

Following a long pause, Beverly flicked off the projector and smiled broadly. "In closing, it's important for all of you to know that through your collective action you've averted a campus crisis. Your action has taught every trustee in the state a lesson about strong leadership."

She waited for them to absorb her words. "On behalf of the governor, chancellor and the citizens of North Carolina, I am pleased to thank President Schilling and the board of Mountain State University. You've demonstrated extraordinary leadership. Thank you."

"Stand up, President Schilling," was heard from the gallery. "Stand up."

Steve stood and saluted his colleagues. "Thank you, thank you very much."

***

Steve shook Bev's hand after the meeting, and said, "Let's have a celebration drink before you go back to your motel."

"Maybe we shouldn't. Midville is a small town. We can have a drink in my room."

"Your picture will be all over the news tonight and in the paper tomorrow. No one will think twice about the two of us having a drink."

"Are you positive?"

"Trust me, I know a quiet place on the edge of town. It's on the way to your motel. "

Bev smiled. "Okay."

Steve helped her load her car. "You can follow me; it's only a couple of miles.

A light mist began to fall as they pulled out of the parking lot. By the time the two cars arrived at the restaurant a heavy drizzle shimmered in the late afternoon sky.

Steve parked his car, grabbed an umbrella and hurried to hers. Holding the umbrella over the door, he helped her out and they ran for the Beaver Creek Inn's canopied entrance. Seeing the two brushing rivulets of rain from their coats, the owner opened the door. "Mr. President, what brings you out this way?"

"We're celebrating. MSU just received the state's highest award. It'll be on the six o'clock news."

"Sounds like it's time for a round on the house."

"Thanks." Steve grinned. "I want you to meet Dr. Harrington."

The owner eyed her with appreciation. "A pleasure."

"She's the state vice chancellor for finance in higher education."

"A good looking doctor of finance. That's something."

Towering over him, she smiled down. He winked back. "How about a table by the window overlooking the creek?" he asked.

"Perfect," Steve said.

"Enjoy. We still have a couple of hours of daylight."

"Thank you," she said.

The owner eyed her again. "A beautiful lady, celebrating … a Ph.D. in finance you earned it."

"Wasn't he sweet?" Bev said.

"I told you. Everyone around here is like that."

"I feel like I'm back in Bemidji."

The owner delivered their drinks. "Did I hear Bemidji?"

"Yes," Bev said. "I'm from there."

"So are my wife's parents. Do you know Mrs. Earnhardt?"

"Mrs. Earnhardt? Of course, she was my fifth grade teacher."

"My God, what a small world. That my wife's mother."

"Let's order some munchies," Steve said.

"It's getting nasty out." Bev pointed to the sleet building up at the bottom of the window pane. "Maybe we should leave."

"They have great nachos. Let's have another round with some nachos. Maybe the rain will let up."

Hungry, the two scarfed downed the nachos and emptied their glasses. Steve paid the tab and waited by the front door while Bev headed for the ladies' room. The owner popped his head around the corner. "There's a freeze warning out. Do you have far to go?"

"She's staying at the Beaver Creek Motel."

"The manager from there just called, said the roads are treacherous. Tell the doctor to drive carefully. There's a bridge just after the curve at the bottom of the second hill. It's always slippery."

"Thanks, I'll let her know."

Bev returned from the restroom.

Steve helped her with her coat. "We need to go, sweetie. It's really nasty outside."

"I hate to drive when it's slippery."

"I could drive you to the motel and come back for my car in the morning."

"Hmm, someone might see your car at the motel."

"I could park mine around back and drive yours."

"I think that would be better."

"Give me your key and I'll pull yours around to the end of the canopy."

Steve pulled his coat collar around his neck and walked gingerly to his car. Parking just beyond the security light, he started back towards Bev's car and slipped twice almost falling, just grabbing the door handle of her Buick in time to keep from hitting the hard, icy asphalt.

When he stopped in front of the canopy, Bev placed her hand on the glazed aluminum support pole and reached for the door handle. Opening the door, she slipped and fell inside.

"You okay," Steve asked.

"I think so." She smiled. "The rain is freezing."

"I'll take it easy." Steve leaned over and kissed her on the cheek.

She snuggled against him, placing her arm over his shoulder. "I love you."

Steve pecked her on the cheek then pulled out of the gravel parking lot, his tires spinning. As the car hit the road, it slid across the center line. "Black ice."

"Take your time, honey. It's better to be safe than sorry."

Steve crept up the first incline and slid partway down the next hill. "Maybe we should turn around," she said.

"There's just one more hill and we'll be there."

Staring at the shiny blacktop, Steve braked gradually, easing the car down the slope. The car began to pick up speed.

"Slow down, Steve. We're going too fast."

"I'm trying to. If I brake anymore we'll go into a tailspin."

"Honey, there's a bridge and a curve at the bottom."

"I think we can make it."

Bev squeezed him tight. "We going too fast," she shouted. "Slow down."

"I can't."

The car swerved to the right then fishtailed.

"The bridge is iced we're going to crash. Oh my God," she cried.

The car hit the right side of the bridge, sparks flying, then shot across the center line and crashed headlong into the left railing. The grill tore off and flew over the top of the car as the railing stripped the left fender to shreds. Spinning around, the car rammed into the other side of the bridge — glass shattered — the back window blew out. Sliding sideways, the car left the pavement and flipped into the air. Landing on its top, more windows shattered and the car slid on its top.

Bev screamed. Steve grabbed her.

The car hit the gravel berm and catapulted over the guard rail. Flying through the air, it snapped a telephone pole then crashed to the ground, still in motion. Ripping out trees, the wreckage rolled down the wooded gully.

Debris and mud flew as the car ploughed down the steep embankment, glass and metal crunching together in screeching harmony. Their bodies banged together like two ragdolls on a runaway roller coaster.

Landing upright, it rolled to a stop in a small creek. The twisted car belched steam.

Water gushed in.

"Sssssssssssssssssssssssss."

CHAPTER SEVENTEEN

"Bev … Bev," Steve mumbled.

Silence.

He moved his left index finger then slowly twisted his wrist. *Everything hurts.* A sharp pain shot through his chest. "God, it's killing me," he gasped and tried to pull the steering wheel away from his chest.

He felt something tugging on his shoulder. Unlocking his seatbelt, Steve cracked open an eye — the driver's side door was gone and water gushed across the floorboard. "Bev, are you all right?"

He turned toward her and pulled the matted hair away from her face. "Bev," he rasped. Unable to fathom the gruesome sight — blood oozed from her mangled face — Steve rested his head on her chest and cried, "Oh Bev, I'm so sorry. I love you."

Silence.

Holding his chest, he wiped the blood from his face. "I can't stand the pain."

Gasoline. I smell gas. I'm freezing. Gotta get out of here. Slow down, slow down, breathe normally. Think. Make it look like Bev was driving. Slide her into the driver's seat.

He unlatched her safety belt and pulled her twisted body toward him. Tugging one leg at a time, he positioned her limp body on the driver's side and snapped the seat belt.

Out of breath, he panted. *Slow down, slow down … think.*

Sitting on the edge of the passenger seat, he placed one foot into the rippling creek, then the other. "Damn, it's freezing cold. I smell gas … it could blow." *I have to find my way to the motel. Room key? Find the key. Where's her purse?*

He reached into the icy water and searched the floorboard. *God, the water is cold. Here it is.* He raised her soggy purse and opened it. Rummaging through the compartments, he knew the key had to be in there. *I have it. Gotta get out of here.*

Freeing himself from the car, he stumbled and fell head-first into the creek. "Shit. It's cold." Steve scrambled to his feet and staggered upstream, one hand holding his chest and the other wiping off the mud. "Gotta get out of here before it explodes."

Stumbling and slouching from rock to rock, he slipped and fell to his knees several times. *Keep going. It's almost dark. I can barely see. Keep going.*

He spotted a light in the distance and pulled himself up the embankment toward it. *The motel. Climb ... keep going.*

Struggling for every inch, he crawled up the hillside, grabbing a scrub, then a bush, his fingers digging into the mud. Grasping a branch and tugging, he tried to rise to his knees. It broke off and he slid backward in the slush.

He laid there exhausted. Taking a deep breath, Steve forced himself to stand and made a final, painful, surge to the top — the Beaver Creek Motel sign flashed.

Resting his head on the berm, he tried to catch a breath. Stones fused to his cheek. He brushed them off and pulled himself up the side of a road sign.

A light flashed sending shockwaves down the hollow of his back, knocking him to the ground. Flames raced downstream. A fireball engulfed the car as it exploded, followed by a smaller explosion. Steve lay, dazed, on his back. Freezing ice pelted his face. "God, my chest hurts."

He wiped the blood from his forehead and turned to reach for a road sign. Losing his balance, he slid on his stomach across the ice-glazed road. Steve rolled into the ditch and came to a stop on his back, tears rolling down his cheeks. "I'm sorry, Bev."

Seeing a light in the telephone booth, he tried to collect his thoughts. *Calm down, think, plan ahead. Figure it out, call Charlie.*

Willing himself up, he grabbed the phone booth's frozen door handle, tugged at it then kicked the ice-lined door. It cracked open enough for him to ease in. Crunching the door closed, he picked up the receiver and dialed.

"McBride's," he heard Charlie say.

"Charlie," he gasped. "It's Steve."

"You okay?"

"There's been an accident."

"What happened?"

"I'll tell you later. Listen and do exactly what I say. Tell Ellen I've had an accident at home and you're going over to help me."

"Okay, I'll be right over."

"No, no, I'm not there."

"What? Where are you?"

"I'm at the Beaver Creek Motel. Do you know where it is?"

"Yes, it's east of town a mile or so, beyond the Beaver Creek Inn."

"Right. Don't talk to anyone, not even Ellen, about where you're going. Come to room number seventeen. Got it?"

"Steve, what's wrong?"

"I'll tell you later. And Charlie, be careful. Everything is iced up."

***

Steve peeked through the frosted peephole. "Charlie is that you?"

"Yes."

He opened the door and stepped back. "Come in. And don't touch anything."

"What happened to your head?"

"I was in an accident. I'll tell you about it on the way to the Beaver Creek Inn." Steve grasped his chest.

"What's wrong?"

"The pain in my chest is killing me." Steve gasped for a breath.

"That's a nasty gash on your forehead. You smell like you've been drenched in gasoline."

"I'll be okay. Don't touch anything."

"What are those towels doing on the floor?"

"I cleaned up the dirty water and mud I tracked in. I'll throw them in housekeeper's cart when we leave. Go ahead of me, I'll wipe the knob."

"Wipe the knob? What's going on?"

"Go to your car."

Charlie did as directed then drove Steve toward town. Rounding the curve, he slowed to a snail's pace. "There's been an accident up ahead. There are two or three wreckers."

"Don't stop unless you have to." Steve slid down in the seat and turned toward Charlie.

Charlie glanced at him and frowned. "What's going on?"

Steve described what had happened as they passed the sheriff's cars.

"God, that's horrible."

"We have to pick up my car at the Beaver Creek Inn."

"What's it doing there?"

"Bev and I had a drink there. I was driving her car to the motel."

"I don't like this, Steve. It's sounds like a cover-up. There's nothing wrong with driving her car."

"If someone saw me, how would I explain it? I'd be in big trouble with Lizbeth."

"Being in trouble with her is a lot better than being in a legal mess or maybe going to jail."

"I'm not going to jail."

"Leaving the scene of an accident, covering it up, I don't …"

Steve interrupted. "Charlie, I have it figured out. Follow me home. As soon as we arrive, call Ellen and tell her I have a gash on my forehead."

"Steve?"

"Tell her you're taking me to the hospital." Steve pointed to the side of the inn. "My car is around back."

Charlie pulled into the parking lot. Steve got out, scraped the ice from the windshield and headed for home. Charlie followed.

Pulling into his garage, he waited for Charlie to come in then closed the door. "Call Ellen. I have to take these clothes off and shower."

Charlie made the call and plopped on a kitchen chair.

Steve appeared a few minutes later holding a blood-soaked towel around his forehead with one hand, and a plastic bag in the other.

"What happened?" Charlie asked.

"The gash opened up in the shower. There's blood all over the bathroom. I put my smelly clothes in a doubled garbage bag. You can throw it in your trash."

"In *my* trash? Steve, that'll …"

Steve raised his hand. "Drive me to the hospital."

***

"Can you tell me what happened?" the young ER doctor asked.

"Could I have a blanket?" Steve asked. The nurse grabbed one, tucked it under his feet at the end of the gurney and pulled it up over his chest.

The doctor repeated his question.

"I was drying off after a shower. All of a sudden I had this sharp pain in my chest. I tried to catch myself … I must have blacked out. Next thing I know there's blood all over the bathroom. The pain in my chest was awful."

"On a scale of one to ten. How bad was it?"

"I had a kidney stone once. That was a ten. This had to be a twelve."

"What is your pain level now?"

"Maybe a five or six. My head is throbbing."

"Your vitals are fine. I've ordered an MRI. I'll stitch your forehead before they arrive. Looks like it'll take ten or twelve. It's along your hairline so it won't leave much of a scar."

"Good."

"Your friend is in the waiting room. Do you want him to come in?"

"Yes, thank you."

Charlie walked in and leaned over Steve. "How are you feeling?"

"Much better. There's only a dull pain in my chest. I can't feel my forehead at all."

"It's still there." Charlie laughed, pulling up a chair. "Steve, you have to tell the truth. It may help the doctors diagnose the problem."

"Charlie …"

Dr. Perry walked in. "Mr. President, I didn't expect to see you here tonight," he said, then pulled out his stethoscope. "What's going on?"

"Earnest." Steve smiled at his friend. "I took a shower after work and was drying off. All of a sudden I had a horrible pain in my chest. Next thing I know I was laying on the floor."

"Hmm." Dr Perry frowned. "That's strange."

"What do you think, doc?"

"It's hard to say. There's a large pool of fluid on top of your stomach. It's about the size of a grapefruit. I assume it's blood but I can't tell until we run more tests."

"A grapefruit? What would have caused that?"

"I'd rather not speculate right now. I'm putting you in ICU for the night. Your friend can go home. I'll check on you in the morning."

***

Charlie held *The Mountaineer* in front of Steve — STATE OFFICAL DIES IN FIERY CRASH. "Have you seen this?" he asked.

Steve shook his head. "I've been having tests all morning."

"You ought to read it. And Steve, it's important that you think about what I've said."

"I will."

"How are you feeling?"

"I'm better. They still don't know where the blood is coming from."

"A leak in the oil pan and they don't know how to find it. You ought to tell them about the accident."

"I'm sure they'll learn something from the last round of tests."

Charlie shook his head. "This is not something to mess around with. You could die."

Steve wrinkled his nose. "I'm losing a little blood. Dr. Perry isn't overly concerned."

"That's because it isn't his blood." Charlie chuckled. "When do you see him again?"

"Anytime now. He said he would stop by this morning."

Charlie gave him a forced smile, concerned about his friend's life, and his state of mind "Okay. I'll be back this afternoon."

"Don't worry, Charlie, I'll be fine."

Steve leaned back in his bed and closed his eyes, replaying the moments before the crash for the umpteenth time. *What could I have done differently? Why didn't we wait? I'm so sorry.*

***

"Sheriff. Did you see where the university president is in the hospital?" his deputy asked.

"No, what happened?"

"I'm not sure. The paper says he was admitted Friday night about seven-thirty."

"What for?"

"Don't know. They put twelve stitches in his forehead." The deputy turned the page. "Here it is; apparently he fell in the bathroom."

"That's strange," the bearded sheriff said.

"What's strange?"

"In the afternoon that woman and him were in the same meeting. Four hours later, she's dead and he's in the hospital."

"So what?"

"I have a funny feeling in my gut."

"Your wife's right." The deputy headed for the coffee pot. "You watch too much TV."

"I suppose," the sheriff said, then held his mug out for the deputy to fill. "I like him. He's been helpful in handling those student cases. Maybe I'll stop by to see him."

"That'd be nice," the deputy said.

"Yes, I'm going right now." Sheriff Jim McDonald set down his untouched coffee, snugged his tie, and walked out of the office. In the car, he flipped on the siren.

The sheriff pulled into a no parking space, left the car running, and headed inside.

At the vacant information desk, he glanced around the lobby then leafed through the computer sheets lying on the desk. Finding Steve's room number, he took the elevator to the third floor.

"How are you doing?" he asked as he walked into the room.

Steve looked up. "Sheriff, it's good to see you. Making your rounds?" he joked.

"Nah. I saw the newspaper article saying you were in the hospital and thought I'd stop in to say hi."

"Thanks, I appreciate that."

"I want you to know how much I appreciate your cooperation with my campus cases."

Steve grinned. "Hey, we're all in this together."

"That's a nasty gash on your forehead. What happened?"

"Doc Perry is still trying to figure it out. I had a pain shoot through my chest while I was in the shower Friday evening. I must have passed out and sliced my forehead. It took twelve stitches."

"What caused the chest pain?"

"They're not sure. I have a pool of blood the size of a grapefruit on the top of my stomach. I'm still losing blood."

"That doesn't sound good. It's been almost two days now."

"Sounds like a trial and error process to me."

"When did it happen?"

"Friday, between six-thirty and six-forty-five."

"That's right after that state official was killed."

"Wasn't that awful? She was a terrific person."

"Did you know her well?"

"Not really. We worked together on our school's financial problems."

"Yeah, I read about your award. That's really something."

"We had a celebration drink at the Beaver Creek Inn a little before the accident."

"Oh?"

"It was nasty outside so she cut it short. I can't believe what happened. Do you think she suffered?"

The sheriff looked around at the get-well flowers in the room. "The coroner thinks she was dead on impact. Did she have more than one drink?"

"No … a vodka and tonic, I think."

"Hmm." Sheriff McDonald turned for the door. "I hope they figure out what's going on with you."

"I'm sure Dr. Perry will."

Charlie barged in, bumping into sheriff. "Sorry."

"No problem," the sheriff said.

Charlie closed the door. "What was that all about?"

"The sheriff stopped by to see how I was doing. We've worked together several times."

"Are you positive that's all he wanted?" Charlie scowled.

"Of course. He's a good guy."

"Steve, he's the sheriff. Have you thought about what I've said?"

"Charlie, it isn't a problem."

"Steve, I think …"

"Charlie."

"Okay, okay."

Steve straightened up in bed. "One more thing."

"What's that?"

He pointed to the closet. "There's a motel key in my pants pocket."

"A motel key?" Charlie smirked as he walked to the closet and opened the door. Searching through Steve's pockets, he held up a key. "Here it is — Beaver Creek Motel, number seventeen."

"That's Bev's room key.

"Take it out to the crash site and throw it down the gully."

"Jesus Steve, no. That'd make me an accomplice."

"No one will know. All you have to do is drive by the site and toss it down the hill."

Charlie shook his head. "I'm not going to jail."

"Don't worry. I have it all worked out."

Charlie rolled his eyes. "Okay, but this is the end of it for me."

***

"Fred, come in my office," the sheriff said.

The young deputy pulled a chair out from in front of the sheriff's desk. "Whataya want?"

"Go out to the Beaver Creek Inn and ask the owner, Ed Beckwith, how many drinks Dr. Harrington had."

"What's that have to do with anything?"

"President Schilling told me he had a drink with her Friday afternoon. One's okay; but if she had three or four I need to change the report for the insurance company."

"Got it." The deputy stood and headed for the door. "While you're out that way, go to the motel and see if anyone has used her room. If not, check it out. I don't remember seeing a room key anywhere?"

"Maybe it was in her purse and melted down."

"Could be, but we need to check every angle."

"Right, anything else?"

"If the key is not at the motel, go back and walk the crash site."

"Boss, I've done that a dozen times." The sheriff gave him *the look.* "Okay, I will."

Less than an hour later, the deputy strolled into the sheriff's office. "I found the key. It was halfway down the hill, lying there in the open. It must have been under some leaves."

"Huh." The sheriff stroked his neatly trimmed beard. "What about the number of drinks?"

"She only had one. A glass of chardonnay."

"Chardonnay? You sure?"

"Do I look like Barney Fife?"

"No, but …"

***

"How are you Miss Molly?" the sheriff said to the plump silver-haired volunteer at the reception desk.

"I'm just fine, sheriff," she said in her sweet southern voice. "Can I help you?"

"I'm just passing through to see the university president."

"You better hurry, he's being dismissed. They've ordered a wheelchair."

"Thank you, Miss Molly. Like always you're on top of things." He winked.

"Thank you, sheriff," she twanged with a blush.

The sheriff walked briskly to the elevator then slowed as Dr. Perry approached. "Doc, how's it going?"

"Fine. What brings you here?"

"Thought I'd say hi to the president."

"I just released him."

"So I heard." The two men continued their conversation on the elevator. "I guess you discovered his problem."

"It was the last thing I'd ever consider. An aneurism on the duodenum artery. I've never seen one there other than when the person had been in a major crash."

"Is that right." Sheriff McDonald's forehead creased in thought.

"It's a rarity for a guy taking a shower."

The door opened. "Glad you found the problem, doc."

Dr. Perry smiled and turned down the hallway. The sheriff walked the opposite way and poked his head into Steve's room. "I hear you're checking out."

"Yes, I'm going to call my assistant and have him pick me up."

"I'll do it. A public service."

"Great."

"Dr. Perry said you had an aneurysm in the duodenum artery. Where's that?"

"It's a small artery above the stomach. Apparently, the intense pain occurred when it burst. The blood gushed until my chest cavity was full. When there was no place for the blood to go it partially sealed itself."

"You could have died."

"Any other place and I would have been a goner. This hospital's staff is top-notch. An invasive radiologist went up through a vein in my groin and closed it off."

"Just like that?"

"It took a couple of hours."

"Here's your wheelchair, sir." the transportation assistant interrupted.

"Yes … and my overnight bag. It's in the bathroom."

The three rode down in the elevator. The aid pushed Steve outside while the sheriff jogged ahead to his car. He pulled the cruiser under the canopy and opened the front door. "Watch your head, doc."

Steve laughed. "Just like TV. Does anyone ever hit their head?"

"No, but with the crazies we deal with you can't be too careful."

Steve slid in and leaned back. "It's good to be going home."

"You've had a helluva week."

"It turned out okay for me but … poor Dr. Harrington. I can't stop thinking about her."

"I hate accidents. Worse thing is following up on everything."

"Whataya mean?"

"Well … little things like you said you thought she had a vodka and tonic." Steve shifted uncomfortably in the police cruiser. "I had to check that out to see if she had more than one drink."

"Oh."

"The owner said she had a glass of chardonnay. You must have been mistaken. If she'd had three drinks everything changes — DUI implications."

"I never would have thought about that."

"Part of my training. My wife thinks I'm overly suspicious." He pulled up in front of Steve's house. "I'll walk you to the door."

"No need."

He winked. "Part of the service." The two walked up to the front door.

Stepping inside with him, the sheriff said, "Do you have an extra copy of that Harrington report? Those numbers really sounded impressive."

"There's one in my den. Hold on, I'm moving kind of slow."

"Take your time. I'll wait here in the foyer."

Steve shuffled down the hall and out of sight.

The sheriff slipped into the living room then peeked down the hallway. "Mr. President." Hearing no response, he made a beeline to the master bedroom and opened the bathroom door. Seeing blood splattered on the mirror and sink, he retreated to the foyer.

"You're in luck," Steve called as he walked through the living room and handed him the report. "If you have any questions give me a call."

"Will do … and thanks." The sheriff tucked the report under his arm. "I'll let myself out."

"Thanks for the lift."

"You deserved it."

Sheriff McDonald slid into the squad car and called his deputy. "Fred, did you find anything in the telephone usage report?"

"Yeah, it's just like the president said. There was a call at 6:58 p.m. last Friday night from his place to the phone of Charlie and Ellen McBride."

The sheriff hung up. "Damn, my gut is never wrong."

CHAPTER EIGHTEEN

"At halftime it's Mountain State thirty-nine, Elon twenty-one," the announcer exclaimed. "Stay tuned after this commercial break for an interview with MSU president, Dr. Steve Schilling."

Steve adjusted his headset and watched the announcer's hand countdown. "Well folks, we're honored tonight to have the head man at Mountain State, Dr. Steve Schilling."

"Thanks, Rich."

"Like the old saying goes, what a difference a year makes."

"It's amazing. Last year we were hoping for a win and had fewer than twelve hundred in the stands. Tonight we couldn't squeeze in one more person."

"It's an all-time record. The athletic director already announced it — 3,412."

"Terrific. We only have 3,100 seats. I'll have to find another place to sit for the second half."

"Did I see that red fedora of yours earlier, behind the basket in the south student section?"

"Sure did. I'm going to the other end for the second half."

"Good for you. So what do you see happening at the university this year?"

"We're on a roll; enrollment is up. We've increased admission standards and there are several new programs in the works. For instance, we'll soon be announcing our first doctoral program."

"That's impressive."

"Nothing more exciting than next year's home opener in the Webster Convocation Center."

"And playing Duke," the announcer interrupted. "Won't that be something?"

Steve laughed. "I suppose you'll be talking to Coach K instead of me."

"Maybe pre-game. How about we have you back at halftime?"

"Sounds good. We'll be airing our first game on the Red Hen's radio sports network."

"And opening up with Duke. How about that sports fans?"

***

Waiting in the parking lot for the traffic to clear, Steve turned on the post-game show.

"Well coach," the announcer started. "The Red Hens opened up with a twenty-seven-point win. That's quite a difference from last year."

"It was a real ball game. I thought the place was going to erupt in fan chaos at any time."

"Did you see how the players responded?"

"Yep. They were turned on all night."

"So what do you think, coach? Not a vacant seat in the house."

"Looks like the fans are with us, win or win."

"A win. We'll take that any time, right coach?"

"Hey, that's why we play the game."

"Whataya see in your crystal ball for this year?"

Bo slowed and measured his words. "Well … you know … it's a long season. We have a tough schedule and have one in the win column. Let's just leave it at that."

"Sounds good, coach. We'll be back after this commercial timeout."

"Phew, we got through that one." Steve turned off the radio and shook his head. "Bo Willard, what a guy?"

Closing his eyes, Steve's thoughts involuntarily flashed back to *that* night. He heard Bev's frightened voice. "Steve, we're going to crash!" *What if we'd left early? We should have stayed for dinner. Why did it have to happen?*

***

Steve woke up late the next morning feeling worn out and extremely tired. He trudged down the driveway and picked up *The Mountaineer.*

Returning to the kitchen, he pulled out a chair, sat down, and leafed through the paper. *Not much here.* He downed the last cup and brewed another pot. Light fluffy snowflakes turned to heavy flakes that stuck to the pane.

A reflection of Bev's mangled face looked back at him from the darkened window. He wiped away a tear that trickled down his cheek. *I can't believe she's dead.*

Turning from the window Steve gazed across the room, his eyes still playing tricks as a vision of Brooke appeared again. It happened more often. She stood naked in the glass-enclosed shower in Aruba. *God, she's beautiful.* A buzzy staccato beeping interrupted his fantasy. It took a long moment for him to realize that the telephone was not seated in the cradle. He adjusted the receiver and headed for the den.

The phone rang.

"Good morning, Steve Schilling," he said.

"Steve, its Lizbeth. Your line has been busy all morning. Is everything okay?"

"The receiver was ajar. The paper must have hit it when I tossed it aside."

"Did you hear about what happened after the game last night?"

"Ah no …" A crease formed across his brow. "I had a drink and zonked out."

"It was on the eleven o'clock news. Some guy shoved coach when he left the radio booth. It looked like Bo hit him. The two were tussling on the floor. The guy had a bloody nose."

"Shit."

"Don't worry, sweetie, the athletic director will deal with it."

"Ha, he can't deal with anything. For all I'd know he'd be rooting for Bo to slug the guy."

"Honey, let someone else deal with it. Come to the lake. We could have a bottle of wine and reminisce about last summer in France."

"Lizbeth, I can't. I don't have any confidence in the AD."

"He has to learn."

"I'm trying to help him do just that. I'm trying to teach *everyone* around here."

"The doctor said you should take it easy and phase back into things. Have Charlie handle it. You can talk to him on the phone from here. You need to rest."

"You're right, honey, but …"

"Please Steve, do it for me."

"Okay dear." Steve sighed. "I'll be there for lunch."

***

Lizbeth ran out the front door and threw her arms around Steve's neck. Planting a heavy kiss on him, she grabbed his butt. "I'm so glad you came. Charlie returned your earlier call. You can call him back. I'm putting the salmon in the broiler."

"Wonderful." Steve plopped on the sofa in the sunroom and dialed. "Charlie, how are you doing?"

"I'm snowed."

"I'm at Lake Lure with Lizbeth. What's happening with the incident?"

"The press has been trying to reach you. The shit is ready to hit the fan."

"I want you to handle it."

"Me? Geez, Steve."

"And put plenty of distance between Bo and the president's office." Steve paused. "What do you know so far?"

"I watched the scuffle on the news and have security's report. It isn't good."

"It's important to have athletics in charge."

"You mean Martin? He'll …"

Steve cut him off. "We have to give the appearance that athletics is in charge."

"That isn't easy. He comes off like one of the boys. Who knows what he'll do?"

"Tell him exactly what to say. Write the press release. Let him know that if he says *one* more word I'll fire his ass."

"Okay, I'll try."

"*One extra word* and he's gone."

"All right."

"I want you in the conference commissioner's office first thing Monday morning. And take Martin with you. We don't need him yapping with the boys downtown. Ask the commissioner what sanctions he would impose. Tell him I'll do more."

"Are you sure he'll do that?"

"Hell yes, he doesn't want to be the bad guy. He's coming up for contract renewal — he'll want to keep his nose clean."

"Okay."

"Remember my speech to the coaches?"

"Yes. You told them to stay out of the gray zone. And if there was ever a violation the university sanction would be greater than the norm."

"Right, give me a call as soon as you've talked to the commissioner. I don't want this to linger."

Steve hung up. Lizbeth threw her arms around him. "I'm so proud of you."

He frowned. "What'd I do?"

"You've always said university presidents don't act like CEOs."

"That's when we're dealing with the faculty. They're different."

"You could be my CEO anytime …"

"Work in your office? I don't think so."

She frowned; then grinned coyly. "I couldn't report to you either. The salmon is ready."

"Perfect."

The two had a leisurely lunch and topped it off with a second bottle of wine. Steve kicked off his shoes and stretched out on the sofa.

Lizbeth leaned over, showing off her full cleavage. "Want something special?"

Steve took in an eyeful. "What did you say?"

She gave him a wide Cheshire smile. "You heard me."

"I just wanted to hear it again." He laughed and jumped up. "I thought you'd never ask."

"Cool your jets. I'll be in there in a minute or two."

"Don't take too long," Steve said on his way to her bedroom.

Steve unzipped his jeans and laid them with his shirt and shorts on a side chair. Sliding under the sheet, he thought about the last two years with Lizbeth. *What could be better? She's beautiful, smart, rich, and likes everything I do. I wonder if she'll want to go to France for the wedding.*

Lizbeth walked in and stripped seductively in front of a full-length mirror. Steve watched as she moved sensually, slowly removing everything except her bra and panties. Not wanting to look like he had erected a tent, he turned on his side.

She opened the closet door, grabbed two elastic work-out bands and walked toward the headboard. "Give me your right hand," she directed.

Steve slid his arm outside the sheet and extended it toward her. "Is that all you want?"

She smiled and tied one hand then the other to headboard spindles.

Steve turned side to side, as if trying to free himself. "Poor baby," she crooned. "Do you want me to stop?"

Steve gasped as she pulled the sheet down his body, following it with her lips, "By morning."

"Dreamer."

***

Steve lay naked, the sheet pulled to his waist. Watching her wash her long silky hair, her slender fingers moved as if caressing each strand. He continued to watch as her hands slid down her sides and around her breasts. She pressed her body against the shower-stall glass; her soapy skin sliding up and down. Steve fondled himself and stroked his erection. *I love you, Brooke, you're gorgeous.*

Lizbeth called from the kitchen. "You staying in bed all day?"

"Do I have time to shower?"

"Make it quick."

Ten minutes later Steve strolled into the kitchen in a black and red tweed robe. "I can't believe it's after nine."

"I let you sleep in, honey. The doctors said it'd take a couple of months to regain your full strength. Pancakes are in the warming drawer. Do you want some juice?"

"Mmmm, V-8. I'll get it."

"Make yourself comfortable at the table; I'll be right there."

The two chit-chatted over an extended breakfast. Steve gazed at the morning sun glistening on the lake. *What could be more wonderful? Being with a beautiful woman in a setting like this.* He turned toward her. "This is paradise, Lizbeth. I love you."

"I love you, too." She caressed his hand and kissed him lightly on the cheek. They talked about France, Vegas, and other places they'd traveled.

Steve carried the plates to the counter then refilled their cups. The phone rang. He glanced at his watch. "It's almost eleven, I bet that's Charlie."

"I'll get it," Lizbeth said. In a moment she mouthed, "It's for me."

A one-sided conversation went on for several minutes, Lizbeth smiling and nodding. "That's wonderful, Brittany, I can hardly wait to tell Steve," she said, and hung up.

"What was that all about?" he asked.

"It's wonderful news I …"

The phone rang again. Lizbeth frowned and picked it up. "It's Charlie." She forced a grin and handed the phone to Steve.

"How did the meeting go?"

"It's still going on. The commissioner is right here. He dealt with a similar case five or six years ago. It got messy — the lawyers were fussing in public. He suspended the coach for three games and made him take an anger management course. And … you're right. He'd be glad to stay out of the fray."

"I figured. What do you think we ought to do?"

"The commissioner would be happy if you applied the same penalties to Bo."

"Can't do that." Steve rubbed his jaw. "How many games before we play in the holiday tournament in Chattanooga?"

"Just a minute I'll check the schedule." Charlie returned a minute later. "Five."

"Perfect. Tell the commissioner I'll give Bo a five-game suspension, a week on administrative leave without pay, and a week-long campus ban."

"That's tough; hitting him in the pocketbook. What's your thinking about the campus ban?"

"A ban — no coaching, no practice, no games — stay home."

"That'll hurt; he loves the kids. The boys downtown will go bananas. "

"Screw them, I'm running the university. Add in the anger management course and let him know if I have to deal with another incident everything doubles."

"Anything else?"

"Give Martin the script. Tell him there will be no deviations. I want the two of you to have a sit-down with Bo and then spend the rest of the mornings this week touring the downtown coffee shops. We'll have to sell this."

"Sounds like a lot of coffee."

"The downtown boosters need to understand our coaches are role models. We can't put up with any crap."

"They'll get the message."

Steve hung up and turned to Lizbeth. "I'm glad that's over. What do you think?"

"I've never seen you like that. You're a hard ass."

"Do you think I was too tough?"

She shrugged her shoulders. "You sent a clear message. I love how you handled it." She kissed him on the forehead.

"Every situation is a leadership opportunity." He hesitated. "What was your call about?"

"The national association for publishers has selected me as their person of the year. They want me to give the keynote address at our national conference in February."

"That's wonderful, dear, you're so deserving. Where is it?"

"New Orleans, the second week in February. Will you come?"

"Shoot … I'm giving a speech in Chicago then."

"It's no big deal, I'll just be accepting a plaque."

"Still, I hate to miss it."

"It'll be fine."

Steve stared out the picture window then turned. "I'm thinking about putting Charlie in charge of athletics. What do you think?"

"You should. It'll take some of the pressure off you."

"I know but …"

Lizbeth cut him off. "You've always said the athletics department is a ticking bomb waiting to explode. Now would be a perfect time to make a change. Charlie will be a good buffer." She refilled their cups then asked, "What's your schedule like for the remainder of the year?"

"I have a budget retreat coming up with the VPs. As soon as the semester is over I'm taking some time off. I'm not answering the phone over the holidays."

"Good for you."

"When are your grandkids coming for Christmas?" Steve was genuinely interested.

"Christmas eve. They're staying four nights."

"That'll be a fun time for you."

She squeezed his hand. "I've never felt this way before. Everything you do makes me feel warm inside. I just want to grab you and kiss you all over. I want to take the next step."

His eyes connected with hers. "Lizbeth, I've wanted to say that for so long. To hell with everything. We ought to get married."

"But Steve … our lives are so different. Do you really think we could work it out?"

"People have all types of relationships. Last year you had a tumor on your brain. I just had an aneurysm. Who knows what's next?

"I think about that all the time. It's kind of scary."

"You can't go on like this forever. You need a break too."

"I don't need to be a CEO. Look at my dad. He just keeps on trucking — it's this event then that one. At night he's back home and there's nothing. I don't want to end up like that. I want to spend the rest of my life with you."

"My life is nothing without you." Steve stood and caressed her for the longest time, his hands gently roaming over her. "I want to be with you forever."

"Let's set a date for next summer. We can honeymoon in France."

"Perfect," Steve said, gently tugging her toward the bedroom.

***

Two days before Christmas Steve waited at Douglass International for the delayed flight from New Bern. *This is the last flight into Charlotte. If she's not on it I'll have to stay here all night.* He watched as the tired-looking passengers departed. Waiting patiently, his heart skipped a beat when he saw her pass through security.

"Brooke, over here." He waved.

She rushed toward him. "Did the Jacksonville flight leave yet?"

"I don't think so. Everything is running late."

"Do I have time to go to the bathroom?"

"Probably; there's one by the gate, I'll stall the plane if I have to." Steve and Brooke ran through the airport. First Steve tugged her then she pulled him.

Rushing up to the gate, they saw the flashing light — FLIGHT DELAYED.

"At least we didn't miss it." She sighed. "I'm going to the bathroom."

Steve checked in with the agent at the counter.

Brooke returned and threw her arms around his neck. "How long do we have?"

"An hour.

"I'm starved."

"We passed a Chili's not long ago. Want a burger?"

"That'd be great."

The two hurried back to the restaurant. Steve pulled out a chair then sat across the table from her. The waitress quickly took their orders.

"I'm so excited," Brooke said. "Four nights in St. Augustine, the holiday lights, and world-class restaurants. And most of all being with you."

Steve pulled a small package from his jacket pocket. "Here's a little something for the most beautiful woman in the world."

"Steve, we agreed not to get each other presents."

"It's not Christmas. It's just a travel gift."

"Sure …" She unwrapped the box and opened the bottle of perfume — Beautiful — it's smells wonderful."

"I can't imagine anything better than being with you."

CHAPTER NINETEEN

Brittany walked into Lizbeth's office. "Did you enjoy the holidays?" Lizbeth asked.

Brittany wrinkled her nose. "It was okay. How about you?"

"It was wonderful. I had four days with the grandkids."

"Sounds like fun. Did you see Steve?"

"No. We agreed not to see each other so he could have some time off."

"Good for him. I don't see how the two of you maintain the pace."

"That's something I want to talk about."

Recognizing Lizbeth's serious tone, Brittany waited for her to continue.

"I'm making some changes," Lizbeth declared.

Brittany looked puzzled. "What kind?"

"Steve and I have decided to modify our schedules so we can spend more time together."

"That's wonderful." Brittany wondered what that meant for her.

"Life is too short. We need to find more time for the two of us."

"Terrific." Brittany glanced through Lizbeth's personal calendar. "Your schedule is jammed for the next three months. And we're hosting that huge fundraiser for President Stetson. In February you'll be in New Orleans to receive the award."

"Clean out the clutter. I've talked to daddy. We're promoting you and giving you an assistant."

"Geez, thank you but …"

"Start freeing up every other Friday. Steve and I are taking some long weekends."

***

Waiting for Steve to arrive at his favorite water hole, Charlie nursed a Sam Adams.

"Want another one," the barmaid asked.

Charlie took the last slug and slid the mug down the bar. "How long have you worked here?" he asked the attractive brunette.

"Seventeen years."

"I bet you've seen it all."

"That and more. How do you like your boss?"

"He's great. I'm waiting for him to stop by."

"He's really something, isn't he?"

"I never noticed."

"I hope not." She laughed. "I've noticed his wandering eyes."

Steve walked in.

Charlie grinned. "Talk about the devil."

The barmaid eyed him.

Charlie pointed to the other side of the room. "Let's take that table in the corner. Want a beer?"

Pulling a chair out from the table, Steve nodded. "I'll have what you're having."

"Another Sam Adams," Charlie called.

Steve loosened his tie. "You know what those assholes want now?"

Charlie shook his head. "I can't imagine."

"A seven percent raise. Can you believe it? We just eliminated two hundred positions and avoided a fiscal watch. Do they think it grows on trees?"

"They think you can do anything. Sounds like a vote of confidence."

"Vote of confidence, hell. They're a bunch of greedy bastards."

"Maybe so, but what's the reason for our meeting today?" Charlie asked.

"For me to complain about the fuckers." Steve chuckled. "No, seriously, Lizbeth and I've been talking …"

Charlie cut him off. "Are you going to announce a wedding date?"

"Hmm, not yet."

"Well then, I hope you're at least going to slow down."

Steve looked surprised. "You nailed it. We're going to modify our calendars so we can be together more often."

"I was just kidding. The two of you slowing down. Ha! I don't see that happening."

"That's why we're here. Lizbeth had a similar conversation with her assistant. You're both getting promotions."

Charlie pulled his wire-rim glasses off and set them on the table. "Sounds like more work to me."

"I'm giving you athletics."

"Athletics? Deal with Martin and the rest of those jerks on a regular basis?"

"You did a great job with the Bo incident."

"That was a one-time issue. I don't need that kind of shit every day."

"Lizbeth and I are taking more time off and this is a good way to free up some time."

"I don't see how the two of you are going to do it."

"For her part, she's moving her son up in the family business. Life is too short. We need to make this happen."

***

Fantasying about their upcoming getaway, Steve stood outside the airport security checkpoint waiting for Brooke's smiling face. *I love her so much. I can't wait till we're together again.* Seeing her large sunglasses turn the corner, he waved and blew her a kiss.

Her smile broadened and she rushed to throw her arms around him. "It's been so long."

"I can't believe how long two weeks can seem."

"I can't wait until we're alone."

"It won't be long before we're at the ski lodge in Blowing Rock."

Steve picked up her bag. She grabbed his arm. "I've missed you so much."

"I want the next four days to be special."

"You always make things special."

Steve tossed her bag in the trunk and started the engine. Brooke slid in beside him and snuggled, kissing him on the neck and ear.

Pulling onto the freeway ramp, he gassed it. "I can't get there fast enough."

"Maybe I can help you," she said, slipping her hand inside his shirt, softly stroking his chest.

"I'll give you a half hour to quit," he quipped.

She smiled and unbuttoned his shirt. "Really?"

Steve scowled. "That was a joke."

"It didn't sound like a joke to me." She loosened his belt and unzipped his pants.

"Brooke, we're still in town."

She pulled her hands back and pouted.

"I didn't mean it that way."

"No problem," she said. "I understand." She leaned back on the seat.

Steve drove west on I-85 then turned north on US Route 321. The traffic thinned. Darkness set in.

Brooke placed her hand on Steve's right thigh. He didn't give her a glance, and kept both hands on the wheel. Slowly she moved her hand up, caressing his leg, then fondling his bulging boxers.

Steve gasped and tried to catch a breath. "Brooke, I-I …"

She leaned down and gently kissed his shorts.

"Jesus Brooke, I'm going to explode."

She looked up with a megawatt smile, "Have you ever had a blow job while you're driving?"

"Ah, once."

Sounding surprised, she asked, "When was that?"

"On spring break during college while I drove across a bridge over the Mississippi River."

"Perfect timing. How long did you last?"

"Geez, I don't know." Steve scrunched his shoulders. "Three or four minutes."

"Not much of a record."

"I wasn't trying to set a record. I was trying not to crash."

Brooke teased him then rested her head on his lap. "I'm shooting for a half hour."

"A half hour? Do you think I'm made of steel?"

She grinned. "Don't worry. I'll save the best until we're in the lodge."

***

The first couple of days Brooke skied rings around Steve. A natural, he thought. Not to be outdone, he gave it his all and by the fourth day he matched her pace. Finishing up that day, she stopped at the bottom of the sloop and hugged him. "I can't believe how much you have improved."

He grinned. "I didn't have a choice. It was either that or sit in the café all day and drink hot chocolate."

"You weren't that bad. Just a little rusty."

"Rusty? That reminds me … I can't believe how many Rusty Nails you downed last night."

"I only had two."

"Two? You must have failed math or had a memory lapse."

She blushed. "Okay, three. I was just keeping pace with the number of your Tanquerays."

"Talk about keeping pace, wait till you see where we're eating tonight."

Strolling back to their room, they talked and window shopped, taking time to enjoy the ambiance of the small community. Stepping inside their room, Brooke said, "I'll take a quick shower and be ready to go in no time."

"I'll slip in with you. That way you'll have plenty of time."

"You sure that's the only reason?" She giggled.

"Of course. Reservations are for eight."

At quarter of eight Brooke opened the bathroom door and stepped out. "Oh my God," Steve said. "You look gorgeous."

She flashed her perfect smile. "Thanks."

Steve took her hand and they sauntered down Main Street. Arriving at the Storie Street Grille, he stopped and with exaggerated flair, opened the door for her.

"Oh Steve, what a lovely restaurant. I didn't expect anything like this. What a great choice for our last evening."

He kissed her on the cheek. "I knew you would like it."

The waitress directed them to the small booth Steve had selected earlier in the day.

"This place is so comfortable … and romantic."

"The menu looks good too."

"Would you like a drink before dinner?" the waitress asked.

"A bottle of Trentinio Pinot Grigio. And we'd like to take our time."

Brooke nodded. "Thanks, for saying that, Steve. I don't want tonight to end."

"Can you imagine four more perfect days of skiing, dining, and drinks around the fireplace?"

"I thought the nights were wonderful."

"Wonderful? You were fabulous."

He laughed. "You weren't half bad yourself."

"Monday's dinner at the Gamekeeper Restaurant was tremendous," she said. "My ostrich was outstanding."

"How about that plate of charcuterie appetizers — ostrich terrine, duck rillettes, and liver mush. I've never tasted anything like it."

With a warm smile, Brooke mused, "Do you realize it's almost been a year since the first time we met?"

"Funny. I didn't even think you noticed me."

"Oh, I noticed you all right." She grinned shyly. "I didn't know how to react. I'd never had that feeling."

"I bet you've said that to lots of guys."

She shook her head. "There's never been anyone like you."

"It's the same for me. I love your smile — everything — how you act, your walk, what you say, your personality."

"You're so sweet. I want to be with you all of the time. Two weeks is too long to wait."

"Geez, honey, I …"

Brooke cut him off. "I could come to your place once in a while."

"I'd like to say yes but …"

"Just once in a while, please. I'll do anything you want."

Steve hesitated. "Okay."

Brooke leaned over the table and pecked him on the cheek.

"Wait, that doesn't mean right away."

"Whatever you say will be terrific."

"I'm jammed until spring break. Maybe we could meet part way, like in Greensboro."

"Wherever you say, I'll be there."

"My schedule will lighten up after commencement."

"I knew you'd find a way."

***

"How's it going, Steve?" Dr. Benderman asked.

"I'm making progress."

"I like to hear that."

"I feel better about myself, sorting things out, and drinking less."

"That's good. Most addicts have multiple compulsive behaviors — gambling, drinking or smoking. Dealing with one often helps with the other."

"Are you still troubled by Bev's passing?"

"Hmm, I think about her once in a while, but she's gone. I can't change that."

"What kind of thoughts do you have about her?"

"Mostly how good she was in bed."

"What else do you miss?"

Steve shrugged his shoulders. "The things we did, I guess."

The doctor flipped a page in his notepad. "Do you still have strong feelings for Brooke?"

"They're stronger than ever. She has the same feelings for me. I want to marry her."

"Marry her? What about Lizbeth?"

Steve rubbed his jaw. "I don't know how to explain it, doc. I love being with Brooke. She's wonderful. We have great times."

"Are you still seeing Lizbeth on a regular basis?"

"We're engaged; getting married this summer."

"Steve, you can't say you want to marry Brooke when you're planning to marry Lizbeth. Have you thought about that?"

"Not really."

"How can you not think about it?"

Steve stared blankly at the doctor.

"You can't be in bed with one then jump on top of another and not think about it. You can't treat them like objects. They're not pieces of art for you to enjoy."

"I'm not treating them that way. They're beautiful women. I love each one for different reasons.

"You've said you love Brooke in many ways. Do you feel the same about Lizbeth?"

Steve shrugged. "I never thought about it."

"Steve you can't go on like this; someone is going to get hurt … again."

***

Standing at an auxiliary bar in the back of Charlotte's Omni ballroom, Steve struck up a conversation with the tall, clean-cut guy next to him. He kept his eyes glued on the receiving line forming in the front of the room. Steve glanced around and noticed a dozen or so more — dark suits and tie, short haircuts. *Secret service I bet.*

A roar rumbled through the room as the ten-foot double doors opened. The agent's eyes sharpened. People pressed in. Spontaneous applause broke out. Cheers filled the room.

The crowd shouted, "Stetson. Stetson … reelect Stetson!"

The United States Marine Band struck "Hail to the Chief."

Walking arm-in-arm, Lizbeth paraded with Janet Stetson, the President of the United States, making a full circle around the room, to finish at the end of the receiving line.

Steve smiled, watching her staff doing the Texas two-step — dressed in tight khaki shorts and half-buttoned silky, dark green blouses, with a Stetson hat and Western boots. Each one looked like she was on the way to work at Hooters.

Lizbeth motioned for Steve to join her in the receiving line.

"Later," he mouthed, then made his way to the round table reserved in front of the podium. He extended his hand to Mr. Webster. "Good evening, sir. Is this seat taken?"

"Please join me. They'll have to adjust their seating chart." He laughed.

Steve looked around, and asked, "Where's the head table?"

"The president doesn't like them. It reminds her of the good ol' boys," Mr. Webster said.

"Good for her."

"She's a Stetson and makes no bones about it. And don't let that pretty little smile fool you. She's as tough as nails."

"She looks good to me."

"Don't let Lizbeth hear you say that." The old man laughed, knowing his daughter's possessive feelings about Steve. "How's my arena coming?"

"It's right on schedule. The seats will go in next week."

"I can hardly wait to see it."

"I'll give Lizbeth some pictures so you can have a sneak preview."

"I'd appreciate that. Looks like that Bo fella is off to another good start."

"They lost three close ones early, to some big schools, but that'll help them in the long run."

"He's no dummy, a no horse-shit kind of guy. I'd like to meet him sometime."

"I'll do more than that. You'll be sitting next to him at the Duke game."

"Really. Does Lizbeth know about this?"

"No. It's our secret."

The old man smiled. "My lips are sealed."

"A blue-suiter leaned between them. Turning slightly to Lizbeth's father, "Are you Mr. James Webster?" he asked.

"Yes."

The agent looked to Steve on his other side. "And are you Steve Schilling?"

"Yes." He explained their presence at the front of the room. "Mr. Webster gave a million dollars to the president's last campaign and is paying for tonight."

The suit made some markings in his small black notepad. "Have a nice evening."

Mr. Webster winked at Steve. "That's quite a rock Lizbeth is wearing. When I was your age I couldn't have afforded something like that."

"Things haven't changed much."

Picking up on the inference, he gave Steve a sly look out of the corner of his eye. "You're smarter than you look, having her buy the ring. I like that."

Lizbeth guided the president toward the two men. "Here they come," Mr. Webster whispered. "We'd better shape up." The two men stood.

"Madam President, I'd …"

She interrupted. "It's Janet."

Lizbeth smiled. "Janet, I'd like for you to meet the two most important men in my life."

The president stepped toward Mr. Webster. "Sir, it's a privilege." She extended her hand and thanked him for his generosity, then turned to Steve. "Mr. President, Lizbeth told me all about you. You're a lucky person."

"I'm the luckiest man in the world," Steve agreed.

"Smooth, too." She pushed by Lizbeth, "Mind if I sit between the two of you?" she asked the men.

Mr. Webster rolled his eyes towards the suit. "You'd better check with Mr. Flattop."

"He's okay." The president smiled and motioned for Steve to sit beside her. "Lizbeth tells me you're the best president in the state and that you know more about education than anyone."

"She's a little biased."

"From what I've heard, I don't think so." The president gazed into his dark brown eyes then glanced away. "Education will be my major platform in next year's campaign. Would you mind if my assistant gives you a call? I want her to pick your brain."

"It won't take long." He laughed.

She eyed him. "A sense of humor, too. I like that."

CHAPTER TWENTY

Taking in the beauty of the beaded cut-glass chandeliers and hand-painted ceiling insets, Karen Holmes walked slowing through the lobby of New Orleans' Monteleone Hotel. For most visitors the French motif would be overwhelming, but for her the memories of that night several years ago were still etched in her mind.

The short blonde bangs of that cute young reporter had grown into to a sophisticated sweep of hair to the side. Wearing a dark blue suit, she looked every bit the young executive she became — assistant editor of *The Times-Picayune*. Karen paused for a moment by one of the massive columns and reflected on that confusing night. She had covered the most important story of her career and interviewed him over a late lunch. Several times during the encounter, she pinched herself to make sure she was talking to the man of her dreams. When he asked her out for dinner, something told her she shouldn't accept, but she couldn't say no.

Dressed in her sexiest black knit dress, she was mesmerized through a seductive dinner at a famous restaurant. Before she realized it they were upstairs in his room — she parading around in her bra and panties. *Why did I let that happen? How disgusting, falling for him hook, line and sinker. I was a damn fool.*

"Ms. Holmes?"

Karen blinked and extended her hand. "Elizabeth Webster, I presume."

"A pleasure."

"The pleasure is mine. Did you have a good trip?"

"Yes. Brittany and I … sorry, my administrative assistant and I had plenty of time to catch up. I've had a hectic schedule this year."

"How has your recovery been?"

"Thanks for asking. It's gone amazingly well. I have more energy than ever."

"That's terrific. I'd like to hear more about that. I've reserved a small conference room on the second floor. Would you follow me, please?"

Elizabeth nodded, and the two walked briskly up the stairs.

"Are you from New Orleans?" Elizabeth asked.

"Born and raised, right here. I received my degree in journalism from the University of Missouri, worked for a PR firm in St. Louis for a while and then as a reporter. I've been back home for three years. I love the city."

"New Orleans is a wonderful place."

"Most people only see the French Quarter. There's so much more. I wouldn't live anywhere else." Karen opened the conference room door. "Would you like a bottle of water?"

"Yes, thank you."

Karen took a bottle from the tray and handed it to her. "Ms. Webster, I'd like to …"

She was interrupted. "Please, it's Lizbeth. Ms. Webster and Elizabeth are for the story."

"Of course. How does it feel being named person of the year by your national association?"

"It's surreal. An honor. I never thought anything like this would happen," she began; then answered Karen's long list of questions. The two chatted for nearly an hour and by the end they were more like old friends than two professionals engaged in a high-powered interview.

"One last question," Karen said. "Who was the single most important influence on your career?"

"That's easy." Lizbeth grinned. "My dad. As the only child he figured I was his only hope to carry on the family tradition. I learned it all from peddling newspapers, working in the pressroom (when we had those), to running the boardroom. He was awesome."

"Sounds like it."

Lizbeth shifted the focus as their meeting wound down. "Tell me about your career."

"I owe a lot to my parents too. My dad gave me preciseness, order and drive. Mom, bless her heart was always there standing tall for what was proper and right."

"Who could ask for more?"

"You're right." Karen hesitated. "There is something else."

Lizbeth gave her a quizzical look. "What's that?"

"I'm on the program this week."

"Terrific. Is it your first national presentation?"

"Yes. Thursday morning at nine o'clock. I'm so excited."

"You should be." Lizbeth glimpsed at her personal calendar. "Darn, I have an executive committee meeting then. I'll send Brittany."

"That's very thoughtful but it isn't necessary."

"I want to. People like you are important to the future of our profession."

***

Brittany waved. "Over here, Lizbeth."

Lizbeth gave her the "hi" sign and squeezed through the crowded Monteleone coffee shop. "Have you been waiting long?"

"Maybe ten minutes. I figured they'd be busy so I came down early."

"Good thinking."

"Your speech last night was terrific. I can't tell you how many positive comments I've heard. Have you seen the lead story in *The Times-Picayune?*"

"No."

"Look." She slid the paper across the table. "Your picture on the front page."

Lizbeth glanced at it. "My gosh, I didn't know that much was showing."

"It's the angle — sells papers you know." Brittany smiled. "You should hire Karen Holmes as your press agent. I've never read a better review."

"Coffee, first."

"I have a carafe ready." Brittany filled her cup. Lizbeth read the two-page story then laid the paper down. "You're right, I couldn't have done better." She sliced into a cherry Danish. "Ms. Holmes is on the program tomorrow at nine o'clock. I have a conflict so I'd like for you to go."

"What's the title of her presentation?"

"Just a minute I'll look." Lizbeth pulled the program from her purse and flipped a couple of pages. "Here it is, 'Investigative Research: A Novice's Approach.'"

"Sounds interesting."

Karen sat at a small table next to the podium waiting for the clock's hand to reach nine. Not many people here she thought as the program representative stood and introduced her.

She stepped to the lectern and nervously said, "Good morning, ladies and gentleman, I'm Karen Holmes." Pausing, she looked at the fifteen or so sleepy-eyed individuals. "My father once told me 'necessity is the mother of all creation.' Today I want to share with you how that phrase guided a young reporter to uncover the wrong doings of a prominent leader. I've modified the events for anonymity, but the strategies are real."

Brittany listened intensely, taking precise notes and printing several key phrases in caps. By the time Karen had finished, she'd filled three pages in her pad. Brittany stood and applauded then looked around at the few remaining souls.

"Great job," she called as she walked toward the podium.

"Thanks. I guess it wasn't too exciting. Not enough to get people here for the early session."

"You were wonderful. It isn't your fault everyone was still hung over from last night. I'm Brittany Hayward, Lizbeth's assistant. Do you have time for a coffee?"

"Yes, I'd love one."

The two chatted on the way to the elevator. Brittany continued to discuss Karen's presentation on the way to the coffee shop. Karen seemed overwhelmed by the attention. Pulling out a chair, Brittany asked, "How did you learn to do all of that stuff?"

"I just did what came naturally. Every step of the investigation presented a new challenge. At night I worked my way through the next situation. It was exciting."

"I can imagine." Brittany refilled her cup. "I'm intrigued by this guy."

"A lot of women were."

"No, not in that way. Would you mind if I asked you a couple of questions about him?"

"That'll be fine as long as it isn't something that might reveal his identity."

"No problem. Other than the hussy who blackmailed him, the other four were classy women, right?" Karen nodded. "Why do you think they fell for him?"

"That's beyond me." Karen shrugged. "You'll have to ask a psychologist."

"I'm sure you've thought about it. What's your take?"

"Sure, I've given it serious thought. A lot of women romantize about prominent men — movie stars, TV personalities, athletes — and lose track of reality."

"You're telling me. Listening to my girlfriends, you'd think half of them had been in bed with Tom Cruise or Richard Gere. But … this guy seems to have something more."

Karen nodded her head. "He was charismatic, easy going and so sincere. He had a certain extra appeal though, that was difficult to define."

"Sex appeal?"

"Not exactly. It was his eyes. They were like magnets, disarming, drawing you closer. He followed every word you said and respond sincerely. Before you know it you're waiting in anticipation for his next sentence."

"He sounds mesmerizing."

"Hmm, it was more than that."

Brittany cocked her head. "Did you go to bed with him?"

"No, of course not."

"The way you just described him … are you sure?"

"Well …"

"Come on, you can tell me. I don't know any of your friends."

"Hmm, I …"

"It's just the two of us."

Karen hesitated. "Okay, between the two of us … I had a big-time crush on him. I was young and infatuated." She glanced away as if drifting into the past.

"You were alone with him, weren't you?" Karen blushed. "It was here … in this hotel, wasn't it?"

Karen bit her lip. "Room 812," she whispered.

"Did you go to bed with him?"

"No. We had a wonderful dinner at Commander's Palace and came back here. God, I can't believe it."

"Believe what?"

"I can't believe I said that. I've never told anyone."

"You were with this stud and you never told anyone?"

"He wasn't a stud …"

"Sorry, I guess you did have it in for him."

"It's hard to explain."

"What was he like when you were alone?"

"Funny, that's the same question I asked each one of the women. They all said the same thing, 'you'll never understand him unless you've been with him.'"

"Is that true?"

"I don't …"

"Come on, fess-up."

Karen pursed her lips then unloaded. "I tingled when he walked into the room. My nipples got hard. I wanted to jump him."

"Did you have that feeling from the beginning?"

"No. It was kind of subtle. He talked openly and seemed so sincere. In one of my interviews I was asking my third question when I realized that I hadn't taken a single note."

"Wow."

"After that I could hardly wait for my next interview. I must have fussed an hour or more trying to decide what to wear. That's when the tingles started," Karen said, her voice trailing off.

"Don't stop now it's just getting interesting."

Karen looked around, as if concerned someone might be listening. "I started fantasizing about him — at night with a glass of wine, in bed, and in the shower."

"You must have had it bad."

"Bad? For the next interview I wore my tightest sweater."

"Did he notice?"

"He had to. I pulled my shoulders back and gave him a couple of profile shots."

"Did he say anything?"

"No, but I can't believe how I flaunted myself. I'd never done anything like that."

"No wonder he wanted to get you into bed."

"It was more than that."

"What happened that night?"

Karen swallowed. "I was looking at the dessert menu and realized that his hand was moving up my thigh. It was almost right *there*."

"You mean?" Karen nodded. "What did you do?"

"I-I … didn't move."

"You just let him do it?"

"Part of me wanted to slide my chair away. The other half wanted to scoot closer. Then I felt his finger inching along the edge of my panties and circling …"

"You had an orgasm at the table?" Brittany interrupted.

"It was unreal. I bit my lip trying to hold off then glanced over at him. He pressed his lips together like he was giving me a kiss."

"And."

"I lost it."

"You came in the restaurant and you didn't go to bed with him … come on."

"I wanted to. God did I."

"Then what?"

"I slipped on a robe when we got to his room. We had champagne. And I played out my sexiest fantasy dance. Letting the robe fall to my feet, I stood there in my Victoria's Secret black panties and bra."

"And then … and then," Brittany urged her on.

"Memories of my mother's lectures rushed through my brain. I panicked and took off."

"You took off … just like that?"

"I didn't know what to do. I was messed up for the next two or three months. One night I'd fantasize about him and the next day I thought my mother was right."

"Sounds like he really got to you."

"Ha. *Then* I got the assignment to investigate him."

"That must have been a shocker."

"A shocker? I was so upset I couldn't think straight. I was pissed at him. Pissed at myself — the world. All I could think about was nailing him."

Brittany shook her head. "Why do you think those women stayed with him? They must have had their own suspicions."

"You wouldn't believe the stories the women told me. Each felt he was so sincere and loving. They kept saying, 'I've never met a man like him. He treats me like I'm the only one he cares about.'"

"He must have really snowed them."

"In his mind, I think he loved them, at least loved having sex with them. They repeated, 'He's caring and considerate, treats me special.' One told me she had a sore neck and he gave her an hour-long, fully-body massage. She was lying in her panties, lathered with moisturizer, trying to hold off, not wanting him to stop. She was ready to make it when he slowed. She begged him not to stop. He moved easy for a second then a third time before she exploded."

"Wow. He sounds like a miracle man."

"You'd think so. He builds a fire in them. And when he calls, writes or drops by, it's like rekindling the flame. They can't wait to get him in bed."

"Was he good?"

"I didn't have to ask. That's all they wanted to talk about."

"Did he have a big one?"

"I guess so … but it was more than his size. He fulfilled them time and time again. One orgasm was never good enough."

"Shit. I haven't had one in six months."

Karen grinned. "Welcome to the club."

Brittany drained the last few ounces of coffee from the carafe. "What about his actions? He proposed to each of them. How could he do that? Didn't he have any scruples?"

"That's the hardest thing for me to understand. Somehow he's able to stay focused on the one he's with. Like she's a separate part of his life."

"Separate … how so?"

"It's crazy … maybe he has a switch he can flip when he's with each woman, to shut off the others."

Brittany laughed. "You'd think he'd short-out sooner or later."

"It's like he could read their minds."

"I wish I could meet a guy like that."

"Making them happy is his only goal."

"I'll take one of those too." Brittany shook her head. "But marriage …"

Karen cut her off. "I don't think he ever had an intention get married — that'd be a commitment. It's all about sex for him. Turn them on … watch them squirm …make them happy. Everything is golden — I'm happy!"

"Sick, if you ask me."

CHAPTER TWENTY-ONE

"Welcome to March Madness, folks, this is Brent Musburger," the TV blasted. "Sixty-four of the nation's top basketball teams are ready to rumble. The countdown continues tonight with the number three seeded Louisville Cardinals and their 25–5 record against the number fourteen seed, Mountain State Red Hens with a 20–10 record. Dick, what can we expect tonight?"

"On paper the Red Hens don't have a chance but I remember last year. The Red Hens lost to top seeded North Carolina by only one. The Red Hens have upgraded their schedule so who knows?"

"Last year I said we might be going home early. Tonight, I'm a believer," Musburger chimed in. "These mountain boys might have a chance. What do you think Dick?"

"After listening to the Cardinals' coach Rick Pitino I think the boys from Mountain State are in for a forty-minute lesson."

"Dick, you know Rick is a big city guy."

"You're telling me. He said the only mountain he saw growing up in New York was a pile of garbage."

"That ought to get the attention of the boys from the Smokies. Whataya think Coach Bo will have to say about that?"

"Good question. Here he comes right now, I'll ask him." Vitale turned to the coach. "Two years in a row in the big dance, coach. How does it feel?"

"Same as last year," Coach Willard said in his usual drawl. "We're proud to be here."

"Your team got off to a slow start this year. How do you explain that?"

"Does it matter? We're in the tournament and haven't lost a game."

"Coach Pitino said the only mountain he saw growing up in New York City was garbage. Whataya think about that?"

"Don't know, never seen garbage piled that high."

"Coach. This is Brent Musburger in the booth. Last year at halftime against the Tarheels you said you were going to pound it inside. You almost pulled it off. What's your strategy tonight against a bigger Louisville team?"

"We're playing strong defense and going inside."

"They're averaging ninety-four points a game."

"We're slowing it down and pounding it inside."

"Good luck on that." Musburger rolled his eyes. Dick Vitale shrugged.

***

"With the Red Hens down 32–29 at halftime, it'll be interesting to hear what Coach Willard has to say now," Musburger said. "Here come the Red Hens."

"Coach, neither team shot very well in the first half," Dick Vitale said. "What are you going to do differently in the second half?"

"We're down by three, to one of the best teams in the county. We're gonna pound it inside."

"Coach, your big man has three fouls. How are you going to protect him?"

"I'm sitting him on the bench the first ten minutes. After that we'll see what happens."

"You'll have a 6-3 center going up against their 6-11 man. How's he going to handle that?"

"Hmm, maybe our team will do jumping jacks."

***

"This place is going crazy, Dick. We have two seconds to go. Louisville is up 48–47. And here's a time out by the Red Hens. We're staying right here, Dick, what do you think?"

"The Red Hens need a long inbound pass and a prayer. The Cardinals will probably put their big man on the inbound passer, so he can't pass over him."

"Dick, what's happening on the Red Hen bench?"

"It looks like Coach Willard is thanking everyone."

"The crowd is chanting something. It sounds like … 'ring, ring.'"

"His players are waving to the crowd. What a great gesture. Everyone in the arena is standing, even Louisville folks are applauding. The outmanned Red Hens deserve it."

"Well, here we go. Two seconds. The official motions to the Red Hen player that he can run the baseline. He hands the ball to the Red Hen guard. He fakes to the right, takes three steps to the left and sprints back to the right. There's a whistle — a foul. The Louisville big man ran over the other Red Hen guard. It's a one-and-one. Dick, what happened?"

"They ran the sting. I haven't seen it in years."

"What are you talking about?"

"I think it's an old Bobby Knight play. When the inbounder ran left, the off guard slides from the free-throw line to the baseline. The Louisville big man couldn't stop, and ran over the Red Hen guard."

"The guys in the media truck figured it out. The fans were chanting 'sting … sting,' Dick."

"Makes sense. And the players were trying to shush them."

Mountain State has a chance to pull off the first major upset of the tournament. They'll be at the free-throw line for a one-and-one."

"I'll tell you, Dick … Bo Willard has coached a great game."

"And they have a chance to win."

"Here's the first free-throw. The ball is up, bounces around and drops in. We're tied at forty-eight."

"This could be one of the biggest free-throws in college history," Musburger prognosticated.

"Here's the next one. It's up and *good*. The Red Hens win! Red Hens win! This place is going wild. The fans are mobbing the team."

***

Steve sat in his office, reflecting on the NCAA tournament. They lost to Georgetown by twelve two nights later, but everyone remembered the sting. *People will talk about this forever. I can't wait until we open up next fall against Duke.*

Charlie walked in. "You wanted to talk about next week's budget meeting?"

"We have to work out a strategy with the VPs."

"Before the committee meeting with faculty and staff?"

"Yes. I want the administration to come off like a team."

"You're going to orchestrate the meeting?"

"Why not?" Steve asked.

"It could be trouble if word gets out. What if someone leaks it?"

"We'll have to hire a new VP."

"Steve, it isn't cricket."

"Who cares if it's cricket or not? It's an old strategy my mentor used. We hammered out the tough stuff behind closed doors so when we were in open session everything ran smoothly."

"It may look good but it still isn't cricket."

"I want everyone to be on the same page. And, give our employees a raise."

"A raise … why? People are happy. They're not expecting it."

"That's why I want to."

"So why did you asked me about a strategy?"

"I wanted to hear your thoughts."

"What are your other priorities?"

"I want to double the operations budget of the library and increase support for women's athletics by fifty percent. And put some money in a pot so there'll be funds at the end of the planning cycle. Otherwise, people will say 'what's the use — there's no reward at the end of the pipeline.'"

"Those are laudable goals, Steve, but where are you going to find the money?"

"The financial vice president will find it."

"Ed 'Penny' Pincher? I don't think so."

"Like every financial VP he has money tucked away in fringe benefits and maintenance accounts. We'll give him the credit for making it happen. That'll puff him up."

"Fine, but you need to carry the ball on the library and women's athletics. They're big winners. The academics will applaud a library increase. And all of the women on campus will be on board with the increase for women's athletics."

"I knew you'd agree."

Charlie grinned. "How are things going with Lizbeth?"

"We're doing very well, thanks for asking. We're spending spring break together."

"Good for you."

***

Steve pulled into Lizbeth's driveway and popped the trunk. Gazing at Lake Lure, he thought about the changes they had made in their schedules. *Best of all, it was working out.* They'd had several long weekends together. Charlie had picked up the slack for him. And Lizbeth had adjusted her workload too. *Last time we were together we didn't even talk shop. It was just the two of us. What could be better?*

He slid out of the car, walked up the steps, and unlocked the door. "Darling, I'm here," he called.

"Come in, sweetheart. I'll be right there."

"The car is loaded with rations. I'll bring the bags in."

"Can that wait?" she asked, stepping out of the bedroom in a sheer black negligee.

"Lizbeth …"

She slinked his way, twisting to the right then the left. "How was your week, dear?" she cooed.

"Nothing like this."

"I hope not." She extended her hand. "Champagne is on ice in the bedroom. Care to join me?"

"I'm on the way."

She pulled him inside and closed the bedroom door. Smelling the incense, Steve paused, adjusting to the dim light flickering from the candles on the bedside tables.

"Where is the champagne?"

She pointed to the far corner. Steve squinted then headed that way. "We need a little warmer upper," Lizbeth said, and pushed him gently against the armoire. She kissed him softly around the neck and ear. "I love to watch you turn on."

"I'm for that."

She unbuttoned his shirt, tossed it aside and ran her fingers across his hairy chest. Her mouth followed closely behind, kissing every inch, nibbling on one nipple, then the other, causing a tingle down Steve's spine.

"This could get interesting," he quipped, kicking off his shoes.

She loosened his belt and fondled his tented boxers. "Would you like champagne?"

"Champagne? I thought we were …"

She pulled back. "I would like some."

"Now?"

"There's something I want to talk about."

Steve sighed and rolled his eyes. "Okay, I'll open it." He popped the bubbly then handed her a full glass. "For the lady."

She clinked his glass. "Here's to the man I want to be with forever."

"I'll drink to that. And here's to the love of my life."

"Tell me more about being the first lady."

"Now?"

"I've been thinking about it all week. I want to know more."

"You'll be a wonderful one."

"It makes me a little nervous."

"You, nervous, the CEO of a Fortune 500 corporation?"

"It's different. I've been in the business all of my life. I've never been a first lady."

"Geez, can't we talk about it later?"

She held her empty glass out. "Is there a book or something I can read?"

"Hmmmm, yes." He refilled her glass. "The president's wife at Cincinnati wrote one some time ago. I'll get you a copy. Anything else?"

"I'd like to talk to someone who's been one."

Steve scratched his head. "There's an AGB meeting coming up. They always have several sessions for spouses. It's in Chicago. Do you want to go?"

"Would I have time to shop?"

"Shop? It's at the Marriott on the Magnificent Mile. There's a Neiman-Marcus, Saks Fifth Avenue, Bloomingdales and a slew of boutiques."

"Sounds wonderful."

"That settles it. I'll have Joyce make the reservations." He emptied his glass. "*Now* can we go to bed?"

She looked at him. "Did you buy any ice cream?"

"Oh my God, I forgot. It's in the car."

***

Steve filled two glasses with ice, poured Crown Royal in one and fixed himself the usual. He placed her drink on a stone coaster next to the hors d'oeuvres on the coffee table then walked to the glass sliders and looked down at the intersection of Michigan Avenue — the shoulder-to-shoulder crowd had not yet thinned for the evening. Further down the side street, he spotted a dozen sailboats scooting along on Lake Michigan.

The room door clicked and he turned to face it. "How was your day, Lizbeth?"

"Wonderful," she said as she stepped inside. "I have to make a pit stop. I'll tell you more in a minute."

"Fine." Steve turned back to the sailboats.

Snuggling up behind him, Lizbeth stood on her tiptoes to give him a peck on the cheek. "Phew, the elevator must have stopped on every floor. The closer I got the more I had to go."

"I don't understand why that happens." He chuckled. "So tell me about your day."

"It was the best ever. I went to three programs. The last one was terrific."

"Really? Your drink is by the sofa. Let's have some appetizers while you update me."

Lizbeth settled onto the couch and took a sip. "That tastes good." She licked her lips and sighed. "The last speaker was Lin Cochran."

"From Youngstown State?" he interrupted.

"How did you know?"

"I've heard her husband speak. He's initiated several exciting changes up there."

"He wears a red fedora to football games just like you."

"Oh no!" He laughed in mock dismay. "My secret is out."

"Your secret?"

"I saw him wearing one years ago on an ESPN clip. What a great idea, I thought. So I bought one. It's been my signature ever since."

She giggled at his monkey-see-monkey-do story. "You're smarter than you look."

"I know a good thing when I see it." He leaned over and kissed her on the cheek.

She shook her head. "I can't believe it, sweetie. You always say the right thing."

"Tell me about the session."

"She was fabulous. And very attractive. She wears a different red hat to every game."

"Maybe you ought to do that too."

"I'm going to follow her lead on everything. She presented the steps she took in transforming how presidential events were run on campus."

"Transformed?"

"Yes, she says she has upgraded everything. When they arrived the president served hot dogs and popcorn in the box at football games. Staff members sat around and talked to each other, rather than working the crowd."

"What do they do now?"

"You won't believe it. Within a few games the VPs and deans were schmoozing potential financial contributors. Every staff member had an assignment. They invited seventy-five to eighty community leaders to the president's loge. She had food services prepare different gourmet selections for every game. It was a *happening*. In no time, it was the place to be."

"Sounds terrific. Maybe you could start something like that when we open the Webster center."

"Oh Steve, could I? I'd love to do that."

CHAPTER TWENTY-TWO

Two fortyish men, wearing tattered MSU football jerseys, walked into the small bar off the lobby of the Beaver Creek Inn. Plopping down on stools by the doorway, the short stocky one ordered, "We'll have a couple of Buds."

"Yeah, and some pretzels too," the other one, resembling Jabba the Hutt, added.

Watching *Monday Night Football*, they hooted and hollered, and downed three more rounds before half time. The big guy glanced down the bar at a couple talking quietly at the other end. "Hey buddy, you and that broad want a beer?"

Bo continued to talk to her, ignoring his loud intrusion. The bruiser got up in a huff and, passing four vacant stools with some difficulty, staggered toward him. He tapped Bo on the shoulder. "Who the fuck do you think you are?"

Bo looked his way then turned back to the weathered barfly.

"Hey, I'm talking to you."

Bo glanced over his shoulder. "Well, I'm not talking to you."

The grubby guy grabbed Bo's arm. "Look at me when I'm talking to you." Bo pushed his hand away. "What the fuck is wrong with you?"

"I'm fine," Bo said. "You're the one with the problem."

"Whaddaya mean by that?"

"Forget it … have another beer."

"Don't tell me what to do. I'll do what I please."

Bo turned to the stringy-haired woman. "You know this guy?"

She frowned. "We've gone out a few times. He used to play football at the university. Ignore him, coach."

"Coach? What the hell do you coach?" the guy slurred.

Bo continued to snub him and spoke quietly with the once-attractive brassy blonde.

"Hey, boy," the drunk said, grabbing Bo's shoulder.

Bo firmly removed the man's hand, hoping that would be the end of it. But once again the bruiser raised his hand and clamped it onto Bow's neck, spinning him around on the stool.

"Lay off," Bo said.

"Fuck you." He pulled Bo from the stool and wrestled him to the floor then landed a right on Bo's jaw, splitting his lip.

The broad screamed. "Ed, Ed, come out here." She jumped on the bruiser. "Stop, stop, he's not bothering you."

Jabba shoved her away, ripping her blouse.

"That's no way to treat a lady," Bo exclaimed.

"Lady? What the fuck do you know? She's no more of a lady than your mother."

Bo pushed him in the face. The guy wailed on him, bloodying Bo's nose and slicing his left eyebrow.

Two guys slid out of a booth, grabbed the man's arms and pulled him off Bo. Ed, the inn manager, shoved the guy toward a corner chair. "Sit down," he said, "What's wrong with you?"

"That coach guy took a swing at me."

"Shut up."

Ed helped Bo up and checked the cut. "That looks nasty. You'll need stitches."

"I don't want any. It'll be fine."

"I'll have my wife clean it up."

An hour later Ed motioned Steve to a small office off the front lobby and closed the door. "I'm glad you could come right over."

"No problem. What happened?"

"There was a scuffle in the bar. Coach didn't do anything. He was talking to a regular — a woman — when this loud-mouth drunk interrupted. I think the he'd picked her up a time or two, so thought he had the right to butt in."

"Is he still here?"

"No. A friend took him home. I told him to keep his mouth shut or I'd ban him for life. He won't be a problem."

"How's coach?"

"He has a deep cut over his left eye. My wife put three butterflies on it. He's in a booth in the bar. Want to talk to him?"

"In a minute. First, I want to hear the whole story."

"Starting when?

Steve frowned. "At the beginning. Before today."

"Coach started coming in a couple times a week, after the tournament ended and has been stopping by regularly ever since."

"Has he been drinking a lot?"

"Yeah, I think he's an alcoholic. When he gets started he can't stop."

"Anything else?"

"That's it until tonight."

"Thanks, I'll talk to him now," Steve said, and headed for the bar.

Seeing Bo in the far booth, he walked toward him and slid in across from him. "How are you doing, coach?"

"I'm okay I guess."

"You look terrible."

"If you'd had a tackle pounding on you, you wouldn't look good either."

"What happened?"

"I was talking to this woman. Next thing I know some big fat guy was all over me. I didn't do no wrong, doc."

"That's what Ed said." Steve looked Bo in the eye. "How long you been coming out here?"

Coach lowered his head. "Two, maybe three weeks."

"Ever since the season ended, right?"

"I hate it when the season ends. It's like falling off a cliff."

"It was a high for everyone on campus. Falling off a cliff … I don't get it."

"Falling off the cliff, falling off the wagon it doesn't matter. I'm an alcoholic."

"I've never seen you out drinking."

"I've learned how to manage it during the season. I've been smashed ever since the Georgetown loss."

"How long has this been going on?"

Bo hung his head then looked up, sheepishly. "All my life."

"All your life?"

"My dad was a drunk. By the time I was eighteen I was hooked. You know much about addiction?"

"A little."

"It doesn't matter if it's drinking, gambling, whatever. It's always there. You might stop for a while but sooner or later it's back."

"Isn't there anything you can do about it?"

"I stop for a while then I go on a binge. Next thing I know, I hurt someone."

"You hurt someone?"

"That's what addicts do. They're so wrapped up in their own situation they can't see how they're affecting others. Sooner or later it happens — they hurt the one closest to them. Maybe not physically, but emotional pain is just as devastating."

"Sounds like you know a lot about addicts."

"I do but I can't do anything about it. I've destroyed everything around me. My wife divorced me after seventeen years of this shit. I never see my kids. And they won't let me be around my grandkids."

"I'm sorry to hear that. You've hidden it pretty well throughout the school term. What about past jobs?"

"I've been reprimanded countless times, got fired from my last three. I figured this was my last chance." A tear escaped down Bo's cheek. "You gonna fire me, doc?"

"No. I'm finding you some help."

***

Dr. Benderman walked into his smaller office and pulled up a chair across from Steve. "How's it going?"

"I'm doing fine; but need a favor for my friend."

"What kind of a problem does he have?"

"He's an alcoholic?"

"Did he tell you that?"

"Yes."

"That's a first step. What else do you know?"

"He's destroyed everything around him — his career, wife, kids — everything."

"You ever think about the lives of people *you* may have messed up?"

Steve frowned. "Not really, why?"

218

"I'll come back to that in a minute. Let's see what I can do for your friend." The doctor walked over to his desk and twirled his Rolodex. "Yes, here's the doctor I'm thinking about," he said, jotting a phone number on an index card then handing it to Steve. "Now, let's make a list of the women you've loved and what happened to them."

"Right now?"

"Yes. I want you to think about them … and how your actions affected their lives. Were their more than Suzanne and Kate? "

"There were lots. But I never laid a hand on any of them."

"And nothing happened to any of them, right?"

Steve hesitated. "Well …" He shifted uncomfortably. "There was Mary Lou in high school. She got pregnant. Her parents put her in a convent."

Steve paused and bit his lip. "But there was nothing I could do about it," he said flatly.

"There were others, weren't there?" Steve nodded. "Go ahead."

"There was Rhonda in college. She had a kid and all kinds of problems; she eventually committed suicide. Our daughter, Stephanie, jumped off a bridge. But I didn't even know about her, at first." Steve sniffled then pulled a handkerchief from his pocket and blew his nose.

"Go on."

Steve slid forward on the chair. "Sandra jumped off a cliff, and you know about Bev's car accident. It's wasn't my fault," he said; then paused. "I guess I've hurt several women."

"And I bet the list is even longer. Your addiction is not just about you, it's about everyone around you."

Steve stared out the window without seeing the bluebird perched on a tree limb.

"I've been telling you all along, you can't keep saying you're in love with two women — or more. Something is going to happen."

"I won't let anything bad happen."

"Steve, you're not listening. You destroyed the lives of Rhonda, your daughter Stephanie, and the others — it will happen again."

"No, I don't want it to."

The doctor paused before trying to reason with Steve again. "How's it going with Lizbeth?"

"We're spending more time together. We're getting married in late summer or early fall. She's going to step down and become a full-time first lady."

"That's a big step for her. Do you realize the kind of commitment she's making?"

"Yes, we're in love; we're changing our lives."

"You're changing?" Dr. Benderman frowned. "What about Brooke?"

"What about her?"

"You know what I mean."

Steve's eyes wandered around the room. "I guess …"

"You guess what?"

"If I marry Lizbeth I can't continue to see Brooke."

"Well?"

Steve shook his head. "I can't stop. Brooke is vivacious, creative and loves the ocean. We have so much in common. I know she's the right person for me."

The doctor pursed his lips. "Steve, look at me. Do you know what you have just said?"

"Of course, I love Brooke."

"You've described your feelings for her — more than physical traits — you just talked about her personal qualities. That's something I want to pursue."

***

Steve picked up the office intercom. "Yes, Joyce, what is it?"

"Coach Willard is here. He'd like to see you for a minute."

"Of course, send him in."

Steve met Bo halfway to the door. "Is that a new suit, coach?"

"A new shirt and tie too. What do you think?"

"The players won't recognize you." Steve laughed. "How's it going?"

"That's what I wanted to tell you. Do you have a minute?"

"Sure, by all means." Steve motioned for Bo to take a chair then joined him. "Have at it."

"It's been six weeks since that night at the inn. I've had eight sessions with the doctor you suggested. She's fabulous. Got me thinking again and doing things I haven't done in years."

"Good for you."

"I've taken an important step forward and I want to say thanks. You could have fired me. I would have been washed up. Who knows what would have happened to me."

"Bo, I gave you her name. You're the one who acted on it and made a difference."

"You helped me see the importance of basketball; and if I lost that I'd have nothing."

"So what are you doing differently?"

Bo shook his head. "Everything. In the morning I count my blessings then lay out my plan for the day. When I get home at night I have my Snickers treat; then attend the Alcoholics Anonymous meeting. I haven't had a drink since my first meeting with her."

"That's terrific."

Bo stood and extended his hand. "Thanks, Mr. President. Thanks for being a friend."

"My pleasure, coach. And good luck."

Bo left.

Steve eased into his swivel-rocker, feeling good about himself. He reflected on what Dr. Benderman had said about his feelings for Brooke. *I know she's the one.* He chuckled to himself. *Sometimes what you tell others may be the best advice you can give yourself.* He picked up the phone and called Brooke.

"Hello," she answered in her usual chipper manner.

"What are you doing this weekend?"

"Nothing, it's a normal, boring weekend when you're not here."

"How about I fly over?"

"Oh my gosh, would you?" her voice chimed. "That'd be wonderful."

"Friday night at the New Bern airport, six o'clock. Be there," he said.

"My motor is running."

"I hoped it would be." He laughed and hung up.

"Joyce," he called.

"I'll be right there." She appeared at the doorway, her pad in hand. "Yes, Mr. President."

"Call Brittany and have her tell Lizbeth that I won't be there this weekend. Something very important has come up. I have to be out of town."

"Oh-Okay."

***

Brooke waved to Steve as he exited security then planted a wet kiss on his lips. "I'm so happy you could change your schedule. Seeing you three weeks in a row is special."

"It's better than special. It's the way it should be."

Brooke wrapped an arm around his waist and snuggled against him all the way to the car.

"I hope you're not going for another world's record," he said.

"Not on the way home." She giggled. "I have something special planned for you when we get there."

"For dinner?"

"No. We're picking up a pizza on the way home."

"Sounds good." Steve squeezed his bag into the trunk.

Brooke put the car in gear and pulled slowly out of the parking lot.

"At this speed we'll never arrive."

Brooke gave him *the look* then slammed her Porsche into low gear and peeled down the street. "Is that better?" she asked. Steve held on tight until they came to a screeching halt at the pizza shop.

She jumped out and was back in a flash. Gassing it, she slid around the corner to her house in no time then slammed on the brakes before Steve could say a word.

She ran in. "You can hang your clothes in my closet. Want something to drink?"

"A beer sounds good."

She tossed the pizza on the table, pulled a couple of Yuenglings from the fridge and crunched into a cheesy slice. "Hurry up, sweetie."

Steve walked into the kitchen and pulled up a chair. "What's the rush?"

"I told you I have plans."

"What kind?"

"A style show."

"You're putting me on."

"I know how much you like them. I picked up several outfits this week."

"Wonderful. What do you want me to do?"

"Just sit on a chair in the middle of the living room."

"That's it?"

"Between each outfit you have to take something off."

"Me?" Steve frowned.

"You know … your shoes, socks, shirt."

"Are you going to strip too?"

"Let's just say you'll see more of me each time I come out."

"Sounds good."

"You can clean up the kitchen while you're waiting."

"Gladly." Steve did his chores then eased into the chair. "I'm ready," he called.

Brooke poked her head around the bedroom doorway. "Take off your shoes and socks."

"You got it."

Brooke turned the music on then slinked out in a long, navy blue gown. The halter bodice accentuated her slender, graceful neck. "Wow, you look fabulous."

She didn't say a word as she paraded around the room, sliding her hands sensually up and down her sides then lightly across her breasts. Slow dancing around him, she ran her fingers through his hair and kissed the back of his neck.

Steve swallowed hard.

She disappeared into the bedroom and the music stopped.

He heard a muffled tone. "What?" he asked.

"Did you take your pants off yet?"

Steve pulled them off and tossed them on the sofa. He sat back down in his boxers. "Okay."

The music started. Brooke appeared before him in a short, dark green cocktail dress that hugged her shapely hips. A provocative line of buttons paraded down the front.

"It's beautiful ... you look terrific."

She moved as if each step had been choreographed perfectly; then loosened the last button, letting her dress fall to the floor. Stepping aside, she danced in her skimpy, flesh colored panties and bra.

He reached for her.

"Not so quick," she said. "You still have a shirt on."

She slipped into the bedroom. The music stopped.

Steve unbuttoned his shirt and flipped it on a chair.

A slow melody began to play. Brooke stepped before him wearing a sheer white cover-up over a dark halter top and shorts. Dancing in her sexiest manner yet, she slowly removed the overlay, showing off her bulging halter top.

Steve's arousal peaked.

She ran her hands over his body and stroked his boxers.

The music stopped. Brooke disappeared into the bedroom.

Steve sat waiting; his urges firing.

As the music started again Brooke strutted boldly out like a model on the runway, her bikini barely noticeable.

Moving in front of him, she pressed her body against his, then slid down into his lap, straddling his legs. Lap-dancing, she removed her top and, smothering him with her breasts, slid up and down on his erection.

"Brooke, I'm going to explode."

She stood and slinked around him.

"Let's go to bed," he whispered.

She pulled the string on her bikini bottom and let the last handkerchief-sized cloth fall. Standing naked, she said, "I thought you'd never ask."

CHAPTER TWENTY-THREE

"How much longer will it be?" Brooke asked.

"Not long. The Waynesville exit is three miles ahead."

"Last week seemed like an eternity. I can't wait."

Steve blew her a kiss. "How did you hear about the Old Stone Inn?"

"From my dad. He used to go there when it was a hunting lodge."

Steve pulled onto the exit. "Do you know the way?"

"I think so. Stay on this road until you come to Dellwood then take a right." Brooke pointed. "There's Dellwood." Steve slowed and turned. "Take a right and follow Dolan up the mountain. It narrows into one lane and becomes very steep and winding."

"Here's Dolan." Steve turned. "I feel like we're in the wilderness, seeing nothing but trees."

"There's a clearing ahead."

"I see it." Steve pulled into the small gravel lot and pointed to the right. "The office is over there. Wanta go in with me?"

"Sure. I'll pick up whatever literature they have about the area."

Steve checked in and turned to Brooke. "Our room is on the second floor of the main lodge, over the dining room. "Let's check it out."

She grabbed the key and ran ahead. "I can't wait to see it." Steve jogged to catch up.

Brooke opened the lodge door and stepped in. "It's just like daddy described — a timber ceiling and a carved handrail going upstairs."

"Look at the stonework on the fireplace. It must have cost a fortune."

"It's so quaint, Steve. I just love it."

He pointed to the left side of the room. "I'm reserving that table in the corner for dinner tonight."

"Fine. I'm going upstairs to our room.

"I'll be up as soon as I make dinner reservations."

Steve talked to the chef then walked up the hewed-log stairs and opened the door.

He saw Brooke laying on the bed in her bra and panties.

"I can't wait much longer," she said, motioning for him to hurry up.

He locked the door, stripped to his shorts and slid in next to her.

"What took you so long?"

"The chef wanted to know if you had any allergies. He's putting a special seasoning on the rack of lamb. It's the house specialty."

"Daddy said it used to be great."

She ran her fingers across his pecks then climbed on top and kissed him wildly.

"Brooke, slow down."

"I'm just warming up."

"At this rate I won't last five minutes."

She grinned and pushed his arms over his head. "Hold on to the headboard."

"Brooke … I-I."

"Grab the spindles with your hands."

"Don't say I didn't warn you."

"Poor baby." She kissed his nose, lightly around his mouth, then gently probed for a French kiss.

She eased up and looked into his eyes. "Now we're getting somewhere." She ran her lips across his chest and worked her way down. She pulled off his boxers, tossing them to the floor, and teased his rock-hard organ.

Steve gasped. "Brooke, take it easy."

"I am." She slipped off her panties, pulled herself up and straddling him, eased down.

Steve glanced at the bear skin hanging on the wall, not wanting to come too soon. He tried to catch his breath.

She grabbed his shoulders and pulled him tight into her pelvis. He joined her slow, easy rhythm. Brooke increased the pace, slamming against him again and again.

"Oh my God, Brooke … I can't hold off any longer."

"Go for it sweetie."

Panting, he lost it. "I love you Brooke."

She slowed for a moment then franticly pounded his body with every ounce of strength she had left. Her hair flew about her face; she arched her back and jammed against him. "Oh Steve, I love you too." Her arms weakened and she wilted on top of him.

Snuggling her head on his chest, she ran her fingers through his hair. "I want to be with you night and day, all the time."

"I wish that were possible."

"Being together every other week is not enough. I want more."

"I want more too, but honey …"

She placed her hand over his mouth. "I'll give up everything. I'll buy a place in the mountains. There has to be a way."

Steve closed his eyes knowing anything he said would sound like a commitment. She gave him a peck on the cheek and dozed off.

***

The two lovers walked single-file down the narrow handcrafted stairs. At the bottom Steve took Brooke's hand and led her toward the table. He slid his chair next to hers so both of them had a view of the fireplace.

"This is the best night ever," she said.

Steve grinned. "You make every day my best one ever."

"I could watch the fire all night. It's so mesmerizing."

"I could watch you all night." Steve placed his hand on top of hers and caressed her fingers. "I love you, Brooke, more than I've ever loved anyone."

She snuggled closer and whispered in his ear. "I'm yours, anytime, all the time."

He kissed her lightly on the lips. "Whatever you want, dear. I'll work it out."

"Oh, Steve, you're so sweet."

"Would you like a drink before dinner?" the waiter interrupted.

Steve turned to Brooke.

She paused. "I'll have a Tanqueray on the rocks with three olives, please."

Steve stared at her. "Are you sure?"

"I've been practicing, just for you."

Steve raised an eyebrow. "Make it two."

"How's the rack of lamb tonight?" she asked.

"It's special. The chef is using his father's secret seasoning. You'll love it."

"Sounds perfect."

Steve gave her his full attention. "Tell me about your dad. Did he come here often?"

"As long as I can remember. This was his favorite place. He came with his buddies two or three times every year."

"Wow, it must have been special."

"Sometimes I think he came here to get away from mom. She could be a tyrant."

"I'm sure she wasn't that bad."

"Most of the time she wasn't but when she didn't get her way she could be a Jekyll and Hyde."

"I'm having the lamb too. Want a bottle of red wine?"

"Hmm." Brooke hesitated. "Yes, why not?"

The waiter appeared. "Wine with your dinner?"

"Yes, we'll have a bottle of the Old Vine Zin from Sonoma Valley."

"Excellent." The waiter looked at Brooke. "Rack of Lamb?"

"Yes, we're both having it."

"Perfect."

Brooke looked into Steve's eyes. "You'll never know how much I love you."

"Why do you say that?"

"You're so understanding. Other than my dad I've never known anyone like that."

"What about your mother?"

Brooke pursed her lips. "My mother … she never listened to me. Everything was all about her and what she wanted."

"How so?"

"When I was young she entered me in beauty contests. The more I won the more she wanted. She decided everything — what I'd wear, how I'd fix my hair, how I walked and talked. She even put on my makeup."

"That's hard to imagine."

"It got worse when I grew up. No boy was good enough. She ran them off. I couldn't breathe. I don't know what I would have done had it not been for my dad.

"It's hard to believe she was so controlling."

"It didn't stop there. She wanted me to go to Agnes Scott College in Atlanta."

"Agnes Scott? That's a very uppity school."

"It's where my grandma and she went. She thought it was an important tradition. It didn't matter what I thought."

"What did you do?"

"I played along. Loaded my stuff in the car and took off. When I got to the freeway I turned the other way and got an apartment in Wilmington."

"How did you manage?"

"Daddy set up a bank account. I talked to him every week. That's when we started boating on our own. He's the best."

"Sounds like it."

"I got a part-time job in a movie studio there and went to school at UNC-Wilmington. And here I am."

"I'm glad. What about your mom?"

"His helping me was the final straw. They got divorced and I never saw her again. We haven't talked in eleven or twelve years."

"Don't you miss her?"

"Sometimes I think I should make amends. Then I think about the times she was such a bitch." Brooke reached across the table and squeezed his hand. "I don't want to talk about her." She gazed into his eyes. "You're what's important to me."

He caressed her hand. "I'll find time so we can be together more often."

"Oh Steve, I could kiss you all over."

"Really?"

She tugged on his hand. "Want to go upstairs?"

"What about the bread pudding?"

"Well." She giggled. "I guess I can wait fifteen minutes."

***

Charlie plopped down in the stuffed wingback in Steve's office. "Summer will soon be over."

Steve signed a letter and looked up. "I can't believe it's the first of August already."

"That wedding date must be getting close. How are things with Lizbeth?"

Steve gave him a scowl. "We're okay. Why do you ask?"

Charlie shrugged. "Joyce mentioned she had changed several dates and was having difficulty working out times for you."

"Why did she tell you that?"

"I guess she thought you might want to talk."

Steve walked over to the window and stared across campus for the longest time then turned. "It's Brooke … I love her."

"I thought you were working that out with Dr. Benderman."

"He doesn't know anything."

"How can you say that? Last time we talked you were singing his praises."

"I'm back to the same point. I'm always back to the same point — I can't be in love with both of them, he says."

"Steve, you know he's right. He's helped you a lot. You're making progress."

"Progress, huh? I'm like I've always been."

"Steve, you're not. You're better. You're just having a bad day."

"It isn't just a bad day. It's like this every day. I'm in love with both of them."

"We've been through this before. You have to keep working on your problem. You can't give up."

"Shit Charlie." He threw his arms in the air. "I want to marry Brooke."

"Steve? You …"

Steve cut him off. "Charlie, she's different. We talk and have fun. I love her in so many ways."

"Dr. Benderman said you're confusing sex with love. You're only seeing physical attributes."

"That's what I'm trying to tell you. It isn't like that with Brooke. We talk about personal things, her childhood, how she feels about life. She's caring and has a charming, upbeat personality. We share mutual feelings. I love everything about her."

"And Lizbeth? What about her?"

"I love her too."

"Here we go again."

"Charlie, you don't understand."

"Are you going to marry Lizbeth in the fall?"

"We haven't talked about it in the last month or two."

"You haven't talked about it?"

Steve stared blankly at the wall behind Charlie.

"When was the last time you were together?"

"I stopped by her place at the lake two weeks ago, Sunday."

"You stopped by? I thought you were seeing her for extended weekends."

"I was with Brooke on Friday and Saturday."

"You banged Brooke on Friday and Saturday then screwed Lizbeth?"

"It isn't that."

Charlie shook his head. "I know … you're in love. What do you think Dr. Benderman will say about that?"

"He'll be upset and say the same thing — 'You can't have them both.'"

"You don't need them. You *want* them. There's a difference. It's like he's said, you're only feeding your addiction. You need to talk with him again about your feelings."

"I can't."

Charlie scowled. "Why not?"

"I stopped seeing him last month."

"You what? I'm calling him right now. You need to get back on track."

"Charlie …"

He ignored Steve's plea and double-timed it out of his office.

***

Steve and Charlie waited outside Dr. Benderman's office, watching him balance the tray of three large coffees and a bag of donuts.

"Can I help?" Charlie called.

"You can hold the coffee when I get to the door."

Charlie grabbed the tray. The doctor unlocked the door and led the way, flipping the light switches as he hustled down the hallway. "I have a ten-forty-five tee-off time so we need to be finished by ten."

"No problem," Charlie said. "We really appreciate you squeezing us in on a Saturday morning."

The doctor ripped the bag open and set it on the small round table. "Help yourself."

Steve grabbed a double chocolate.

Dr. Benderman pulled up a chair. "Tell me what you said to Charlie about Brooke."

Steve's vacant stare shifted across the room.

"Come on Steve, let's hear it."

Steve hesitated then repeated everything he'd told Charlie. "She's special, doc."

Dr. Benderman's brows furrowed. He clasped his hands together in front of his mouth in thought, then leafed through his notes. He read a page and looked up. "Some time ago you told me Rhonda was very special."

"Yes, she was." Steve beamed.

"Was there ever anyone else special like her?"

"No."

"Why didn't you marry her?" Steve fidgeted in his chair and downed a donut. "Steve?"

He shrugged his shoulders. "Cause I married Suzanne."

"I know you married Suzanne but why didn't you marry Rhonda? She was 'the best' wasn't she?"

Steve bit his lip and nodded.

The doctor continued as Steve stared at his loafers, "So why didn't you marry *her*? Why did you marry Suzanne?"

"I-I ..." Steve raised his eyebrows and pursed his lips in confusion. "I guess I ..."

"Steve, no guessing. Why didn't you marry Rhonda?" Steve sat motionless, frozen in place. Dr. Benderman waited.

"Because I knew," he whispered.

"You knew what?"

He wiped a tear from his cheek. "I knew she expected a full commitment."

"A full commitment? What does that mean?"

Steve rolled his eyes. "A total commitment — no screwing around."

"And what would have happened if she caught you screwing around?"

"She would have killed me."

"So you married Suzanne so you wouldn't have to marry Rhonda, right?"

"Yes," Steve sobbed.

"And all along you knew you could get away with anything with Suzanne."

Steve nodded then burst into tears.

Charlie sat teary-eyed. Waiting patiently, Dr. Benderman sipped the last of his coffee.

Steve composed himself. "So what about Brooke?"

The doctor gave him a half smile. "You really want to hear my prediction?"

"Yes."

"You won't marry her."

"Why not? I love her."

"Down deep you know you can't. Your addiction won't allow you to commit to a woman like her — it needs sex. Brooke is just like Rhonda and you know it. She won't take any crap. Making a full-fledged commitment to her means being intimate, and closing the door to everyone else. Right?"

Steve nodded.

"It'd be like cutting off your sex supply."

"But doc, I love her. I want to marry Brooke."

The doctor shook his head. "You'll find a way to weasel out of it just like always."

"No, I won't. I don't want to go through all of that pain again."

"Steve, I've told you before 'nothing will change until you change.'"

"I've tried."

"You have to do more. It won't happen overnight; it's a long, step-by-step process that takes years, as it has already."

Charlie interrupted. "Steve, you don't have a choice. We have to keep working, talking, reading, trying — there's no other option."

Steve stood and shook Charlie's hand. "I know ... you're right. Thank you."

CHAPTER TWENTY-FOUR

Long-standing chief legal counsel, Thaddeus Abbott, walked slowly out of his one-on-one session with Elizabeth wondering about a gnawing feeling in his gut. Back inside his office he pulled a volume from his personal law library, skimmed the table of contents then read several articles. Still feeling uncomfortable, he called an old colleague and took copious notes.

At seventy-seven Thaddeus had overseen corporate and family matters since Elizabeth was in grade school. In addition to legal counsel, he'd been her father's only confidant; yet, questioned whether he should call Mr. Webster on this one. He reflected on his friend's advice then buzzed his administrative assistant.

"Yes, Mr. Abbott," she answered.

"Would you ask Brittany Haywood to come in for a few minutes?" His office was one floor down from hers and Elizabeth's.

"Yes, sir."

Moments later his assistant poked her head in the door. "She'll be right down."

"Thank you, Lenore."

Thaddeus paced his office then extended his hand to Brittany. "Thanks, for dropping whatever you were doing. Please, have a chair."

He gestured to the two brown leather chairs with gleaming brass studs, in the corner. "Would you like a bottle of water?"

Having never been summoned to his office, she eased in to the furthest chair. "Ah, no thank you," she managed in an insecure tone.

"You can relax, Brittany, this is not about you." He smiled. "I've heard many positive comments about your work. Congratulations on your outstanding career with us."

She leaned back and took a breath. "Thank you."

"I'm concerned about Elizabeth."

Brittany raised her eyebrows slightly. "Elizabeth?"

"She seems to be under a lot of pressure."

"She's always balancing a hundred and one projects."

Thaddeus took the chair next to Brittany and stroked his full, white beard. "Have you noticed any changes in her during the last few months?"

Brittany shrugged. "Not really."

"Maybe it's me. It seems like there's something on her mind."

"Hmm, now that you mention it she hasn't been her normal, outgoing self."

"What's different?"

"She seems more serious, matter-of-fact about everything."

"I've had that sense too. Has she said anything to you?"

"Quite the opposite. We haven't talked at all. She's gives me an assignment and ends it curtly."

"Has she ever done that before?"

"No. We used to talk like close friends, almost like sisters."

"Do you have any idea what may be troubling her?"

Brittany pursed her lips then shook her head.

"Do you think she's had an argument with Steve?"

"I can't imagine that. They're always holding hands and talking about their plans to be married. She changed her work schedule so they can be together more often."

"Is it working out?"

"They're together almost every other weekend."

"Almost?"

"Recently Steve cancelled a couple of times and cut another weekend short."

"When was that?"

Brittany had carried her daily portfolio to Mr. Abbott's office, just in case. She pulled out her calendar and flipped through the past couple of pages. "All of them have been in the last two months."

"Did she give any reason for his action?"

"Not that I recall."

"Never anything specific?"

"No."

"Hmm." He finger-combed his beard. "What about earlier in the year? Anything different or unusual happen?"

Brittany stared blankly, in thought. "Not that I can recall."

"Start with January and walk me through each week of the year."

Brittany flipped Lizbeth's calendar to the beginning of the year and shared the entries. "The big thing in February was her receiving the national award in New Orleans."

"What happened there?"

Brittany counted the official meetings Elizabeth had attended. "She attended four executive committee meetings, two technology meetings and the media awards meeting."

"Did she say anything about them?"

"No. I have the minutes for each one if you want to read them."

"Just walk me through the week for now."

"Monday morning she was interviewed about her award by a reporter from *The Times-Picayune*. She wrote a wonderful article. Do you want a copy?"

"Not now."

"Lizbeth was so impressed, she asked me to attend her presentation."

"And?"

"It was outstanding. The reporter outlined an investigative project she undertook when she was a cub reporter in Arkansas."

"Do you remember the name of the town?"

"No but I checked her out after the meeting. She was a reporter in Ruston."

"Ruston … that's interesting." He paused, as if reflecting. "What was her presentation about?"

"She uncovered the wrong-doings of a community leader."

"Wrong-doings?"

"The guy had five affairs."

"Five? How did he find time for work?" Thaddeus laughed. "Anything else?"

Brittany shook her head. "No, I don't believe so."

***

"I'd like authorization for expenses to go to Ruston, Arkansas," Thaddeus said.

Mr. Webster stared at him. "Ruston? Why?"

"I'm pursuing a hunch."

"A hunch? I need to know more than that. What's going on?"

"I'd rather not say. I'm hoping you'll trust me, for now."

Mr. Webster stared at his long-time confidant. "How many times have you asked me that?"

Thaddeus was firm in his answer. "Never."

"A hunch." The old man stroked his chin then nodded. "You got it."

Thaddeus walked back to his office and asked his secretary to make travel arrangements to Memphis.

Two weeks later he sipped a glass of wine at Molina's in downtown Ruston. Reflecting on his interviews thus far, he wondered if he'd overreacted. *Maybe Elizabeth's mood change was a result of her surgery, or she's menopausal. Maybe I'm getting old and paranoid.*

He thought about his meeting earlier in the morning with Howard Clark and his daughter, Christina. Both were highly supportive of Steve — the football stadium was named after Howard and the athletic training facility after her. For a half hour Howard had touted Steve's virtues. Christina said little and, for the most part, remained aloof from the conversation. Well-endowed and attractive, she reminded him of Elizabeth. *Who wouldn't want to have an affair with her? You're grasping for straws.*

"Oh well," he mumbled, then paid the bill and headed for his car. "Maybe all of this was a wild goose chase." He drove to the parking lot of the First National Bank, took the elevator to the top floor and headed for the suite marked Don Cagney, President. After introducing himself to the receptionist he took a chair.

Moments later Mr. Cagney appeared. "Mr. Abbott, to what do I owe this privilege?"

"I'm doing background research on Steve Schilling. He's being considered for an appointment on our board."

"Impressive to send the head legal counsel to Ruston on such an assignment."

"Mr. Webster, our board chairman, is quite thorough."

"He must be," Don said. "How may I help you?"

"I'm interested in your views of Dr. Schilling — his style, values and ethics."

"What can I say? He was a top notch leader. He's engaging and personable. He made quantum academic improvements at EAU."

"What is your opinion of why he left?"

"He'd been highly successful and got divorced. Maybe he thought it was time to move on."

"Was his divorce messy?"

"No. They simply agreed to go separate ways."

"And no one else was involved?" Don gave him a questioning look. "You didn't sense something else may be going on?"

"Going on?"

Thaddeus decided not to beat around the bush. "Like he was fooling around."

"Steve Schilling? Nah."

"Anything you haven't mentioned that you think I ought to know about him?"

"He'll be an outstanding board member."

***

Dr. Molly Green walked out of her office and shook Thaddeus's hand. "Good morning, Mr. Abbott," the president of Eastern Arkansas University said.

Struck by her stateliness and beauty, he smiled. "Good morning to you, Madam President."

"Enough of that. It's Molly. Would you like a soda?"

"No. I'm fine."

"Please have a seat." She pointed to the settee on her left. He took a straight-back chair. She joined him in the loveseat across the coffee table. "I understand you're considering Steve Schilling for an appointment to your board. How may I help you?"

"Yes. We're a Fortune 500 corporation. I'm doing a comprehensive background check on him."

She grinned. "Coming to Ruston, Arkansas … I guess so."

"What can you tell me about him?"

"Steve and I were in college together. I was a cheerleader and the first black on campus, he played football. We were good friends and talked a lot."

"Did you ever go out with him?"

"No, I had my own agenda and was very focused; thought I had to be perfect in every way."

"What can you tell me about him?"

She shrugged. "Steve Schilling is Steve Schilling. From what I know he hasn't changed one iota. He's friendly and outgoing, won't hurt a flea or make a negative comment about anyone. He's bright and articulate. He'd make a great board member."

"There's nothing negative in his background?"

"Shoot no, I'd love to have him on my board."

"Hmm." Thaddeus stood. "Well, thank you for taking time out of your busy schedule."

"No problem. It's always a pleasure to talk about Steve."

Thaddeus closed his notebook and headed downtown for his last interview.

"I guess this is the end of the line," he said to himself.

Pulling into the *Daily Gazette* parking lot, he walked down the sidewalk to the front of the building and stepped inside. Noting the editor's office off to the right, he walked over to the receptionist, and said, "I'm Thaddeus Abbott to see Mr. Coleman."

"Yes, he's waiting for you. Please have a chair."

Within seconds Jerry Coleman appeared in the doorway, wearing his customary bow tie, and extended his hand. "Mr. Abbott, please come in."

Thaddeus shook his hand and gave Jerry his card. Mr. Coleman motioned him to the chair in front of his desk. "How may I help you?"

"I'm doing background research on Steve Schilling. We're considering him for an appointment to our board."

Staring at the business card, Jerry hesitated. "A board appointment, huh?" Thaddeus nodded. "The head legal counsel for a Fortune 500 corporation is in Ruston, Arkansas, performing a background check." He frowned. "Forgive me, but I don't think so."

"Our chairman is precise."

"Have you done a search on him?"

"Yes, and I've read all of the articles you've printed."

"Then why are you here?"

"I thought you might share some personal insights about him?"

Jerry bristled. "Personal?"

"You know what I mean."

"Not really. You will need to be more specific."

"I'm interested in his ethics. Is there any reason to question his values?"

"You know the code of ethics I follow. If I have an opinion I write an editorial."

"What about his divorce? Was there anything …"

Jerry cut him off. "The notice of his divorce was printed in the paper like anyone else's."

"No, I mean …"

"Mr. Abbott, I'm not sure what you're trying to accomplish but you need to pursue your agenda elsewhere." Jerry stood. "Anything else?"

"I-I guess not."

***

Thaddeus ordered a Manhattan, straight up, and opened the menu. I might as well enjoy a steak dinner on my last night here, he thought, then turned to the waitress. "I'll have a New York strip, rare."

"Baked potato?" the plump, fiftyish waitress asked. "House salad with blue cheese?"

"That'll be fine."

She brought the salad. Thaddeus looked up. "Have you lived in Ruston long?"

"All of my life."

"Do you remember EAU's President Schilling?"

"Of course. He wore a red fedora to all of the football games."

"Do you recall anything else?"

"He was very popular. I never understood why he got a divorce."

"Did you ever hear any rumors about him?"

"Rumors?"

"You know, about him fooling around?"

"There was some but I didn't pay no attention. There's all kinds of talk on campus."

"If you wanted to find out if someone was having an affair, where would you go?"

She pressed her lips. "The County Line Tavern. It's the hottest place in town. A lot of people out there are fooling around."

"Where is it?"

"Five or six miles north of town on Mill Creek Road."
"Thanks, I think I'll head out there after dinner."
"You can't go dressed like you are."
Thaddeus frowned.
"You need to wear jeans and an old shirt."

***

Thaddeus pulled up a barstool and ordered a draft.
"You from out of town?" the Tavern owner asked.
"Out east. I'm visiting a friend here, checking out the local scene."
"You're a little old for the stuff in here … unless you're willing to pay for it."
"Some friends at the university said there might be some people from the campus out here."
"We don't get many university-types. Marie Cabrera in that booth is the only one." He pointed to a dark-haired busty woman wearing a tight red sweater.
"She's really stacked."
"And she knows it too." The bartender laughed.
"Do you think she'd talk to me?"
"She'll talk to anyone. But I'll warn you she can be brash as hell. She'll tell you to fuck off without blinking an eye."
"Thanks, for the tip."
Thaddeus picked up his beer and walked across the bar. "Mind if I join you?" he asked.
Marie glanced up. "I'm not running a geriatric ward."
He grinned. "I hear you know everything about the university."
"I work there."
"I have a couple of questions. Do you mind if I join you?"
She scowled. "What's on your mind?"
"I'm doing a little research on Steve Schilling. Do you know anything about him?"
"Who wants to know?"
Thaddeus handed her his card. "We're considering him for an appointment to our board."
"A corporate lawyer, huh?"
He prodded her again. "Can you tell me anything about him?"

"Shit, I could write a book about him."

"A book … about what?"

"The biggest asshole I ever met."

Thaddeus raised his eyebrows. "Asshole. I've not heard him called that."

"Guess you've been talking to the wrong fuckin' people."

"The wrong people?"

"Yeah, the ones downtown. They live in a cocoon. I bet they told you how wonderful he was — a great leader, an outstanding fundraiser, and all of that bullshit."

Thaddeus nodded. "You're close."

"Close? Fuck, I'm right on target."

He smiled.

"What do you want to know?"

"Everything. To start with why did you call him an asshole?"

She smirked. "I fucked a lot of guys but he snowed me; said he wanted to marry me. And I believed the son-of-a-bitch."

"Want to talk about it?"

She licked her lips. "How much are you willing to pay?"

"Pay … for what?"

"For the fuckin information. Whataya think?"

"What kind of information do you have?"

"Shit, I just told you. He proposed to me after fucking him for three years."

Thaddeus straightened. "He what?"

"You heard me. I fucked him just like he fucked the others."

"Others?"

"Four sluts. That's why he had to get his ass out of town."

Thaddeus pulled five folded hundred dollar bills from his shirt pocket and slid them across the table. "What can you tell me about him?"

She scowled. "Five more Ben Franklins and I'll tell you more than you ever dreamed possible."

CHAPTER TWENTY-FIVE

Mr. Webster motioned Thaddeus in. "How was your trip?"

He shook his head. "You won't believe it."

"Well, let's have it."

"I talked to several community leaders and came up with nothing."

"What are you talking about?"

"Steve Schilling."

"Steve, what does he have to do with Ruston, Arkansas?"

"He was the president of the university there."

"So … I don't know where you're going with this."

"Hold on, it will take a while to explain."

Mr. Webster leaned back in his chair. "I have all day."

"It started several months ago when I picked up some changes in Elizabeth's behavior …"

"Elizabeth?" Mr. Webster interrupted.

"Let me finish."

Mr. Webster bit his lip. "Okay."

Thaddeus described the changes he'd perceived — her pensiveness and unusual brooding — his follow-up meeting with Brittany, and how he'd made the Ruston connection. "Because of your relationship with Steve I was reluctant to tell you what I suspected."

"Just as well."

"On the last night of my stay I struck up a conversation with a waitress at a local restaurant. She'd heard some rumors about Steve and suggested I go to a tavern outside of town."

"And?"

"Turns out a hussy there was proud to tell me how many times she'd fucked him."

"She what?"

"And that's not all. He had several other affairs."

"No … you're putting me on."

"I gave her a thousand bucks and she spilled the beans. She worked in the mailroom at the university and intercepted his love letters. He was banging four others."

"Five women? You sure she didn't make it up?"

"Absolutely. She had too much detail and talked nonstop."

"And the community leaders had no knowledge of this."

Thaddeus shook his head. "Not so far as I could determine. I talked to several prominent community leaders and came up with nothing," he said, then described the specifics of each meeting. "There wasn't a hint of impropriety."

"My God," the old man said. "What do you think we ought to do?"

"I was hoping you'd have some sage advice."

"Think we should talk to Arnold and ask him to do some local research through the newspaper?"

"Hmm, he may be her ex, but he still loves her. I think he'd lose it."

"You're probably right. What about Elizabeth?"

"Hell no, she'd go off like a Chinese New Year firecracker," her father said. "Then she'd be pissed at you for interfering in her life and would want me to fire you."

"I checked that out with the best legal minds. 'Pursuing the best for the corporation' gives me plenty of leeway."

"Leeway, hell. If she has a hissy-fit you're on the highway."

"I suppose you're right."

"What about telling Brittany? Maybe she could help us."

"She has a level head but that's a lot to ask of someone in her position."

"She could keep a close eye on Lizbeth," her father said.

"Hmm, maybe, I could play it soft and chat with her once in a while."

"I like that. Do you have any other thoughts?"

Thaddeus stoked his beard. "I've thought about hiring a private investigator to see if he's doing the same thing here but I …"

The old man cut him off. "That's dangerous. If Lizbeth finds out it'd be the end of the world."

"No doubt about that. Why don't we wait a week or two. There's no need to rush into it."

"Sounds good."

***

Lizbeth buzzed Brittany.

"Yes," she said then hustled in.

"Call Steve and tell him that I can't make it tonight. It's going to take another four or five hours to finish this report. Tell him I'll meet him at the Omni tomorrow afternoon."

"It's kind of late. He may have already left."

Lizbeth glared. "I doubt it. He's late a lot recently."

"I'll stop by the Omni on the way home and put the hors d'oeuvres back in the containers."

"Do you think that's necessary?"

"I'd feel better. Room service usually delivers them around five. I'll make sure everything is sealed so they'll be fresh for the two of you on Saturday."

"Fine."

Brittany cleaned her desktop and headed for the Omni. Unlocking the door, she made a beeline for the fridge then placed the olives, pickles, and other delicacies that had been left ready to eat, in plastic containers, and slammed the door.

"Who's there?" A voice sounded from the bedroom.

She turned that way. Steve appeared, a shirt and hanger in hand. "What are you doing here?" he asked.

"I was wondering the same thing."

"I'm waiting for Lizbeth." He finished hanging the shirt in the closet and walked in the living room.

"Oh, I'm sorry. She's not coming."

"Why, what happened?"

"She's working late. I left a message for you saying she'd be here tomorrow afternoon. You must have missed it. I stopped by to put the hors d'oeuvres away. I can get them out again if you'd like."

"Yes, I'd like that. I'm having a drink. May I fix you one?"

"No thanks I'm on my way to the spa."

Steve smiled to himself then poured a gin and fixed a vodka and tonic for Brittany.

She rearranged the appetizers and added green garnish.

"Should I put them on the coffee table?"

"That'll be fine," he said, walking behind her.

She placed the platter on the table and turned.

Steve handed her the glass. "Vodka and tonic as I recall."

"I don't …"

Steve pushed the glass into her hand. "You might as well have some hors d'oeuvres to tide you over till dinner."

"I really must go."

"Come on, one drink isn't going to hurt."

Glancing at her watch, she took a sip. "Well, just one." She eased onto the end of the sofa.

Pointing to the appetizers, Steve slid to the center of the sofa. "Fix yourself a plate."

She placed two crackers with cheese on her plate, while Steve loaded his and stuffed a large piece of salmon in his mouth. Still chewing, he asked, "How long have you worked for Lizbeth?"

"Almost five years," she said, pensively.

"You must know her very well."

Brittany nodded.

"What do you like most about her?"

"What's there not to like? I admire her drive and commitment. When she sets her mind on something you know it's going to happen."

"How's it to work for her?"

"Great. She has high expectations and demands a lot but I like that. She applies the same standards to everything she does. That pushes me to do more."

"Good for you. What do you do in your spare time?"

"Not much, I guess I'm a stay-at-home."

"An attractive young woman like you, I bet you have men standing in line."

"I'm afraid not. They're either too short, too nerdy or …"

"Or what?"

She pursed her lips. "Or, all they can think about is jumping in bed."

Steve laughed. "Maybe you're looking in the wrong places."

"I don't think so." She leaned over and filled her plate. "What made you decide to become a university president?"

He hesitated. "I really didn't decide. It kind of just happened."

"Happened … I don't understand."

"That's a long story. Let it suffice to say I had a great mentor who guided me on every step."

She stood. "Would you excuse me, please?"

"Of course." He grinned and pointed. "The powder room is the first door on the left."

Steve refilled his gin and poured her another. She sat down and looked at her full glass. "I really must go; I have a massage appointment."

"Let me see if I can help." Steve moved next to her and pressed his fingers into her shoulders.

"No, that's okay …"

"Just relax." He caressed her left shoulder then massaged the base of her neck. "You have a lot of tension in your shoulders and neck."

"It's been building up all week."

"With your workload, I can imagine."

She pulled her shoulder back and crunched several vertebras. "That feels better already."

"I've barely started," he said. "Turn to the side so I can massage the other shoulder."

She slid sideways.

"Perfect." Steve placed his hands on her shoulders and moved easy — going through a routine he'd done hundreds of times. After working his fingers around each vertebra, he asked, "How does that feel?"

"You're a real pro. Great hands. I've never felt better."

"Could you handle being alone for a minute while I refresh our drinks?"

She grinned. "I think so."

Steve went to the bar and fixed her a double. Walking back, he paused and gazed into her eyes. "Here's to a very attractive woman."

She clinked his. "Thank you, Mr. President."

"It's Steve."

She took a sip and rolled her head side to side. "My shoulders feel much better, Steve."

"Your back had a thousand knots," he said, sliding closer to her. Circling her shoulder blades with one hand then the other, he inched his fingers below her bra-line.

She moaned involuntarily, and leaned her head back against his chest. "That feels wonderful."

Steve kissed her lightly on the neck then grazed his lips around her right ear. Pulling her tight, he slid his hands around her sides and loosened the buttons on her blouse. She undid her front-hooking bra and closed her eyes. Steve cupped his hands over her modest breasts, teased her right nipple then the other.

Arching her back, she pressed her breasts into his hands. Steve kissed her firmly on the neck and shoulders, then with one hand, unbuckled her belt.

She swallowed hard.

His fingertips slid along the top of her panties and took a downward turn. She placed her hand on his and pressed his index finger inward.

He felt her body tense.

"Oh my God," she called out in a low sigh. "I can't believe it."

***

Brittany waited outside of Thaddeus's office. *Surely he doesn't know anything.* He stepped into the anteroom and extended his hand. "How have you been?" he asked.

"Ah … fine." *I guess so, after four orgasms in one night.*

"Have a chair," he said, graciously. She followed him toward a leather straight-back chair.

He paced the room. "I've been thinking about Lizbeth. My concerns for her have increased. Do you think her recent behavior is related to her surgery?"

"Hmm, all of her MRI's have been clear. Dr. Beamer gave her a clean bill of health — she's as good as ever, maybe better."

"And you haven't noticed anything since we last talked?"

"Not really … she cancelled her Friday night meeting with Steve. Said she was working on a big project."

"That's right. The entire team was here until eleven."

"Anything else?"

"Not that I can think of."

"Maybe I'm looking for something that isn't there. Let me know if anything unusual pops up, please."

"Of course. I'll give you a call."

***

"Brittany, would you mind if I talked to you about something personal?" Lizbeth asked.

"Of course." Brittany followed her into her office, sat in the chair in front of Lizbeth's desk and gave her a pleasant smile. "How may I help?"

"You're such a dear. I don't know what I'd do without you."

Brittany grinned sheepishly, though Lizbeth wouldn't know why. "Thank you."

"I'm having second thoughts about my wedding plans. Since there's no one in my family to talk to, I hope you don't mind."

"Of course not, say whatever you want."

"It's about Steve."

Brittany tensed. "Okay."

"He's wonderful and I love him but I'm afraid it isn't working out." Brittany stared without saying a word. "We can't seem to make the kind of changes that we need to make things work."

"You've modified your schedules. You're spending lots more time together."

"I know," Lizbeth said. "But it doesn't feel right. He's trying hard; but lately he's cancelled out or been late. Two weeks ago I was too busy … I'm feeling awkward."

"You can't change overnight. Maybe you're expecting too much. Give yourselves more time. There's no requirement that you be married this fall."

"You're right." Lizbeth nodded. "Thanks for listening."

***

Steve stood in front of the picture window watching a pontoon boat float by. Lizbeth put the last dinner plate in the dishwasher.

"Do you want to walk by the lake?" she asked.

"I'd love to," Steve said. "I have to make a pit stop. I'll meet you out back."

Seeing Lizbeth staring at the sunset, he stepped up behind her and kissed her on the neck. "I love you, darling."

"I love you too, sweetheart. I never want to leave you."

He frowned. "Am I going somewhere?"

She took his hand and the two strolled down to the lake. "No. It's just that I've been thinking."

"Thinking … is something wrong?"

"No. Things are so right — that's the problem."

"I'm … I'm missing something."

"It isn't easy to say what I'm feeling."

He stopped and turned toward her. "Take your time, darling. I'm all ears."

She took a deep breath. "I feel like I'm rushing you."

"Rushing me about what?"

She hesitated. "And maybe, I'm rushing myself."

Steve squeezed her hand. "Lizbeth, what is it?"

She sighed. "I guess … maybe … I don't know."

"Slow down, Lizbeth." He stopped her by the water's edge.

"Maybe we should postpone our wedding plans."

"Is that all?"

Lizbeth wondered how he meant that.

"Lizbeth, I love you. But I've had the same feelings. The harder I try the more difficult it becomes to create more time for each other. I hate to call and say I can't make it. I *do* want to see you."

"Oh Steve, you're so understanding. I just love you."

She hugged him tighter than she had in a month.

"Let's play it by ear. In the meantime, we're here, and I want to make love to you all night."

"Now we're getting somewhere." He tugged her toward the house.

CHAPTER TWENTY-SIX

Brooke parked her Porsche outside her father's office and ran in. Rushing past the secretary, she bolted into his office and closed the door. "Hi Daddy."

He looked up from his third-generation oak desk. "What's going on?"

"I have to talk."

"Right now? I'm in the middle of a big project."

"It's important."

He rolled his eyes and leaned back in his old swivel-rocker. "Draw up a chair. So, what's on your mind?"

"I'm getting married."

His eyes bugged. "You're what?"

"That's what I want to talk about."

Struggling for words, he said, "You've always said you'll never get married. What's going on?"

"Things have changed."

He took a deep breath. "Well, let's hear it."

"I've been dating this man for over a year. I've never felt this way about anyone."

Arnold raised his hand. "Does he have a name?"

She paused. "No name. Not just yet."

"Okay then, tell me about Mr. No Name."

"He's so much like you."

"I hope he's not as old as me."

"Not quite."

"Not quite." Her dad scowled. "What does that mean?"

"I'll tell you later."

Mr. Hart threw up his arms in dismay. "All right … say what you want, you're going to anyway."

"He's the best ever. He's smart, an outstanding leader and is involved in all kinds of exciting things.

"Does he love you?"

"Oh, yes. I've never met anyone like him."

"You're positive he loves you?"

"Absolutely. I can tell by the way he treats me. I feel like a queen in a fairytale."

"You're sure he's the right one."

"Yes, yes, we like the same things, we joke and laugh all the time."

"Is he good in bed?"

"Daddy!"

"Well is he?"

"He's wonderful. He makes me happy."

Her dad smiled. "So what do you want from me?"

"I want Marco to take us to Bermuda on the yacht."

"To Bermuda, why?"

"I remember the diamond store you took me to there."

"Diamonds International."

"Yes, I want everything to be special."

"That qualifies."

"Can Marco take us? Can he, Daddy, please?"

"When do you want to go?"

"In three or four weeks."

"Three or four weeks, which is it?"

"I'm not sure. I haven't asked him yet."

Her father frowned.

Brooke decided, "Four weeks."

"You're getting married but … he hasn't asked you … and you haven't asked him to go. But something is going to happen in Bermuda in four weeks."

"Yep, that's it."

He shook his head. "You haven't changed a bit."

"You always said I was a lot like you."

"Well, yes …"

"Does that mean you'll do it?"

254

"I suppose … I'll call Marco in the morning."

Brooke jumped up and planted a smacker on his cheek. "You're the best."

***

Thaddeus ran a finger down his schedule for the day and stopped at noon — lunch with Arnold at Sullivan's. He picked up the phone and called Mr. Webster.

"Jim, it's Thaddeus, do you have a minute?"

"Sure, go ahead."

"When we talked about Elizabeth we agreed not to mention anything to Arnold."

"Yes, I recall."

"I'm having my monthly meeting with him at noon. Do you think I should say something?"

"Funny you ask; I've had second thoughts too. I think we loop him in."

"Agree. It's better for him to hear it from one of us than through the grapevine."

"If he heard it second hand he'd really be upset with me."

"I'll give you a call after we meet."

"Thanks."

Thaddeus hung up and gazed out the window. *This is not going to be easy. Arnold still loves her. When he hears about Steve he's liable to go berserk.* Thaddeus shoved the brief he was working on to the side of his desk and left early.

Sipping on a Manhattan, Thaddeus motioned to Arnold when he walked in. Arnold waved and headed toward him. "How have you been?" he asked.

"Quite well," Thaddeus said. "Thanks for asking. How about you?"

"I'm doing fine, I think."

"You think?"

"I had a real shocker last Friday when Brooke came by."

"How's she doing anyway?" Thaddeus interrupted.

"By her definition, fabulous."

"Her definition? What's going on?"

"She met Mr. Right and is going to be married."

"Brooke … married? I thought that was the furthest thing from her mind."

"So did I; figured she'd save me a lot of money."

"Who is he? What does he do? How long has she known him?"

"Don't know. Don't know. One year. All I know is he's older and she's in love with him."

"When is it happening?"

"Don't know."

"Sounds like Brooke."

"I guess she's a lot like me. They're going to Bermuda on the yacht so he can buy her a ring."

"That sounds more like her mother. Planning the fairytale moment."

"Don't mention that to Brooke or you'll be in a dog fight."

Thaddeus laughed. "You're telling me."

"What's happening on your end?"

Thaddeus looked around the room.

"Something on your mind?" Arnold asked.

"We have a big problem."

"What kind?"

"Steve Schilling. I think he's …"

"What about him?" Arnold interrupted in an elevated tone.

"Bear with me." Arnold pressed his lips. "Last month Jim and I talked about Elizabeth."

"About what?"

"Her demeanor. Recently she's seemed aloof … disengaged. Brittany felt much the same."

"Brittany? Why did you ask her?"

"I had this nagging feeling and wanted to check out every possibility."

"What did you do?"

"I did some digging."

"You investigated Lizbeth?"

"Not really …"

"You better be right or you'll be in real trouble."

"Wait till you hear what I learned."

"I'm waiting," Arnold said, impatiently.

"It started when I traced Lizbeth's calendar back to a research program Brittany had attended for her in New Orleans."

"Research on what?"

"A reporter made a presentation on some investigative research she'd completed when she worked in Arkansas."

"What kind of investigation?"

"A community leader who was fooling around. After the presentation Brittany checked out the reporter. Turns out that she had worked in Ruston."

"Ruston? That's where Steve Schilling is from."

"Wait, you're getting ahead of me." Arnold zipped his mouth. "Jim authorized me to go to there and check things out."

"Why didn't one of you tell me?"

"We talked about that but didn't want to raise your hackles unless we were positive."

"Positive about what?" Arnold said, in a sharp tone.

"I found a source who admitted to having an affair with Steve. And, hear this … she was aware of four others."

"Steve Schilling … that seems a little far-fetched. Are you positive?"

"Yes. She described everything in great detail. There's no question Steve was the guy referenced by the reporter."

"Shit, I knew he was too good to be true." Arnold threw his hand in the air and signaled the waiter. "We'll have another round, please." He scooted closer to Thaddeus. "I want to hear everything."

Thaddeus nodded and for the next hour he described his findings. Arnold probed every point and asked: "Are you sure about the banker? Do you think the editor really knew something? Why was the floozy so willing to talk? You're positive about all of this?"

Thaddeus responded to every point, assured him of his finding's authenticity, then concluded, "I'm telling you, Arnold. There's no question … it's true."

"Crap." Arnold shook his head. "So what are you going to do?"

Thaddeus leaned closer. "Jim and I agree we should hire a private investigator."

"What about Lizbeth?"

"We can't tell her … at least for now. She won't believe us unless we have documented proof … and plenty of it."

"I can't imagine what she'd do if all of this is true."

"Do you think we should pay for the detective out of corporate funds?"

"No way. Lizbeth checks on every detail. Besides, if we found something damaging we'd have to take it to the board. All hell would break loose. It's better to keep it at my level. I'll run it through my personal account at the newspaper."

"Are you sure?" Thaddeus asked.

"I don't see any other option. Hire the PI and send me the bill."

***

Carl La Russa looked around the tired bar then headed toward Charlie's wave.

"What kind of a beer do you want?" Charlie asked.

Carl glanced at his empty Sam Adams. "I'll have one of those."

Charlie signaled the barmaid for two. "So what's on your mind?"

"The general education program is the pits."

"Big deal. Let it ride for the year."

"It's something out of the dark ages. Who cares about Shakespeare nowadays? Students should be learning about computers, critical thinking and problem solving."

Charlie took a long sip. "You just wrapped up tenure. Write an article, let the faculty have a breather."

"The best thing we could do is toss out the entire program and start over."

"Carl, I'm telling you, back off. Everyone is happy."

"The bastards have been teaching from the same yellow notes for twenty years, Charlie."

"We'd have to create a new academic structure with new goals, objectives, and a helluva lot more. It'd take three or four years to restructure the core program."

"We can't ignore it just because it will take a lot of work. We're supposed to be preparing students for a fast-moving technological society."

"Hurray, everyone agrees." Charlie snickered. "You know as well I, making changes like these generally don't have one iota to do with students. It's about jobs and protecting turf."

Carl glanced at Charlie's half-rusted 1957 license plate. "What was the general education program like when you came here?"

Charlie rolled his eyes. "The same as it is today."

"No changes?"

"No changes."

"Charlie, the world has changed. We've got to update gen ed."

"You don't have to convince me. You're the chief academic officer; you know better than I. I'm just pointing out reality."

"Why shouldn't I recommend to Steve that we press forward?"

Charlie scratched his head. "You're really serious, aren't you?"

"Damn right. If I don't take it on it'll be another decade before the question surfaces again. That's another ten years of us failing to provide our students the best possible education."

"I'll tell you what." Charlie downed the last of his beer.

Carl straightened in his chair. "I'm all ears."

"Give me a couple of weeks. I'll chat with some key faculty members and get their assessment."

Carl thrust his hand across the table. "Deal."

***

Midville recorded the hottest August ever — twenty consecutive days over ninety degrees — and no rain. The brown mountain slopes prompted officials to post fire alerts. Charlie walked into his old stomping grounds and bellied up to the bar.

Wiping his brow, he said, "Another week of this and I'll die."

"You can say that again," the barmaid grinned. "It's on the house. What'll you have?"

Charlie's glance caught a reflection of Carl returning from the men's room. He slid onto a barstool next to Charlie as the barmaid asked, "Sam Adams or Heineken?"

Carl loosened his tie. "Heineken."

"Make it two," said Charlie.

"I thought summers were supposed to be cooler up here," Carl complained.

"This is the worst I've ever seen."

The two Ph.D.'s settled into their usual round of academic philosophizing. After a second beer, Charlie raised the question. "Do you still believe you have to change the world?"

"Maybe not the world but we need to reform general education."

Charlie shook his head. "What is it about you academics? You're never satisfied. You always think you can create a perfect place."

"Charlie. I'm the provost; if I don't propose the change no one will."

"You're right about that."

"Will you support me if I take it to the president?"

Charlie rubbed his glistening bald head. "I'd say 'no' if I didn't like you so much." He wiped his high forehead with a handkerchief. "You're smart enough to pull it off. And there's a core of faculty who think it's time. Yes, I'll support you."

"Terrific." Carl clinked Charlie's mug. "Bartender, another round."

CHAPTER TWENTY-SEVEN

Sitting on a harbor-side park bench, Brooke stared at her daddy's 120-footer thinking about her fantasy trip to Bermuda. She'd had the same thoughts countless times; recently her dreams had turned more erotic — tying him to the bedpost, screwing him in the shower, seducing him at the dinner table, and watching him squirm, naked, on the sundeck. Her nipples hardened.

Steve returned with two Rocky Road ice cream cones. "What are you thinking about?"

She patted him on the butt. "Your ass."

"Let's hear more about this." He handed her a cone. "Well?"

"It's a woman's thing."

"Even better."

"It isn't the right time."

Steve glanced at his watch. "It's 9:47 …when will it be the right time?"

She giggled. "You're so cute."

Steve placed a hand on her jaw and tilted her face toward him. "Brooke, I love you more than anyone in the world. I want to be with you the rest of my life."

"You're not just saying that, are you?"

"Brooke, I want to be with you forever. I love you."

"Oh, Steve." She kissed him firmly on the lips. "I want to be with you, too."

"Since that's settled can we get back to my ass?"

"It wasn't really your ass." She giggled. "It's a fantasy I've had for years."

"Is my ass in it?"

"Sort of."

"Come on, tell me."

Brooke sighed. "It's about yachting to Bermuda, picking out a ring at a fabulous diamond store there, and that kind of stuff."

Steve kissed her lightly on the cheek. "I want to hear more."

"Are you sure?"

"Of course. I've never been on a 120-foot yacht. What's it like."

"It's like living in a mini-palace. There's paneling and marble throughout; columns in the dining room, etched-glass doors and huge windows. It's pure elegance."

"Sounds spectacular."

"And best of all we don't have to do anything. Captain Marco will be in charge and his wife will prepare the meals."

"Sounds like you've given it a lot of thought. Why wait?"

"Would you go?" she said, hesitantly.

"Sure. My schedule is flexible the rest of the month."

"Can you get away September third?"

"Perfect. That's Labor Day weekend."

Brooke hugged him with all her might. "I can hardly wait."

"One last question."

She gave him a questioning look.

"How is my ass involved in all of this?"

Brooke smiled. "You'll have to wait and see."

***

Brooke guided the yacht out of Beaufort harbor. Captain Marco stowed the lines and joined her at the helm. "I'll take it from here, Miss Brooke."

She turned to Steve. "Do you want to steer?"

"Maybe later."

"Okay, I'll show you around." Brooke gave him a walking tour of the yacht, ending up in the master suite. "What do you think about this?"

"It's more luxurious than any bedroom I've ever seen — mahogany paneling, a king-size bed and a sitting area. The dressing table must be five feet long."

She unbuttoned her blouse. "I could stay here forever."

"Brooke, we're barely out of port."

"So, we're on our way." She grabbed him and kissed him passionately. Steve stepped back, gasping for a breath. "Take off your shirt and pants."

"Just like that? What kind of a man do you think I am?" he asked with a smile of false modesty.

She pointed to the bed.

"Okay." He quickly stripped and crawled in. "Now what?"

"Handcuffs or rope?"

"Are you serious?"

"I told you, I've had this fantasy for a long time."

"Your fantasy … your choice." Steve stretched out spread-eagle.

She cuffed his hands to the bedposts. He watched her shed her clothes, down to her bra and panties, and slide in bed. Snuggling next to him, she caressed his chest then headed south.

Steve gazed at the shifting shadows in the room as the ship turned and headed out to sea. She watched him twist and turn in hesitating ecstasy. Reaching her goal, she toyed with him; her quick but firm strokes teasing his senses.

Trying not to come too soon, Steve stared at the large photo of the yacht on the wall across from the foot of the bed. Brooke eased on top and pushed him in and took her time riding him, moisture flowing from every pore on her body as she quickened the pace.

Trying to stop, Steve counted to ten then gasped. "Oh … my … *God*."

"Go for it, babe."

Spent, he lay on the bed like her helpless prey. She continued to pump then gave a final heave and gasped, "I love you, Steve."

When she slid off him, he smiled. "Don't forget the handcuffs."

She acted like she already had. "Oh yes." She loosed one then the other.

"I'm ready for a nap."

"No time. We need to hit the sundeck."

"The deck? It's only ten in the morning."

"And you're lily white. You can't take the afternoon sun. I'll have to load you up with lotion as it is. The robes are in the bathroom. Take the large one. I'll be up in a minute."

"Where are the swimsuits?"

Brooke stared at him. "Swimsuits? We're going to the sundeck."

He stripped then slipped on a robe and headed for the spiral stairs.

After making his way up the narrow steps, he positioned the lounger toward the sun and stretched out.

Brooke poked her head over the deck. "What are you doing? Take that robe off."

Turning away, he stood and flipped his robe on a small table.

"Turn around. I've already seen everything."

Standing naked, he turned back to her and placed his hands on his hips. "Does that make you happy?"

She eyed him. "Very much. You can lay on your back now." She pulled the other lounger next to his and began to fondle.

"Geez Brooke, we just did it an hour ago."

"So what? The morning is almost over."

"Do you think I can get up again just like that?"

"I bet you can," she said, rubbing her breast across his face.

"Come on, Brooke."

She looked down and teased his traitorous erection. "Looks like you're doing fine."

"You think I'm made out of steel?"

She pressed his abs with her hand. "Hmm, maybe something more exciting. Turn over and I'll put lotion on your back."

He nudged on his side then laid on his stomach. "How's that?"

"Nice ass." She filled one hand with lotion, rubbed her hands together, loaded his shoulders up with the white cream, then slowly worked her way down - perspiration streamed down his sides, mixing with the lotion.

"How are you doing?" she asked.

"I'm totally relaxed."

"Wait till I get started." She giggled. "Turn over on your back and slide each leg over the side so your feet are touching the deck."

He glimpsed up. "What are you going to do?"

"I'm going riding, cowboy style."

"What?"

"You'll see."

His eyes rolled back. "You practicing for a western movie?"

"You may think so by the time I'm done."

She threw a leg over the lounger and stood above him, his erection aimed for the promised land. Slowly she eased down, pulling him in.

Steve gasped. "Holy shit."

She smiled, pushed him further in then eased back.

"Come on, Brooke, don't tease."

"I'm not, sweetie. I'm warming up the horse."

"Warming up … I don't get it."

"A cowboy can't ride at full speed without easing in to it," she said, shoving her pelvis firmly against him and picking up the pace. She slammed against him.

"Oh my God," he gasped, trying not to come.

She was relentless, pressing his flesh, not giving him a chance to relax. Gasping, Steve lost control.

She smiled watching him unload. And she joined him. "Hi-ho, Silver," she shouted, waving one arm in the air, like a bronco-rider.

***

Captain Marco sounded the all clear horn. "All hands on deck," he boomed on the PA.

Startled from dozing in the warm sun, Steve jumped up off the lounger. "What's happening?"

Brooke set her margarita on the end table. "We're in the Gulf Stream. The water is warmer here. We're going deep sea fishing." Brooke fluffed her hair and tied her blouse around her bare midriff.

"You look great. What time is it?"

"One o'clock."

"One?" He rubbed his eyes.

"Take a quick shower and put on your fishing gear. It's on the bed. I'll be aft."

"Aft?"

"In the back."

Steve watched her disappear down the spiral staircase. At the bottom she grabbed a pair of binoculars and scanned the horizon.

He headed for a shower then joined her in a muscle shirt and shorts. "What are you doing?"

"I'm watching a whale pod. They're headed our way. Want to see them?" she asked. "Here, take the binoculars they're about three o'clock."

Steve focused the binoculars. "They're huge. It looks like three of them."

"They're sperm whales. They get up to sixty feet long."

"Sperm?"

"Not that kind." She pointed to the swivel chair bolted to the floor. "You know anything about deep-sea fishing?"

He laughed. "I used a cane pole the last time I went fishing."

She scowled prettily. "Come over here and I'll help you get your line out."

Steve sat in a chair and braced his feet against the hull. "I'm ready."

"Sure, you are." The captain slowed the engines and she cast his line out. "When a tuna or mackerel hits, give the pole a tug to set the hook. After that happens keep the line taut and reel it in." She cast out her line.

"Sounds like a piece of cake." He downed a beer then opened another one. "How much longer?"

"You have to wait until the fish is ready, silly." Her pole bent in half and she jerked. "I have one," she shouted. "Reel your line in so we don't get tangled up."

Steve did as told then laid his pole down. "Is it a big one?"

"Ah, maybe thirty or forty inches."

"Forty inches? Sounds big to me."

She reeled in the fish then pointed. "There it is … a mahi-mahi. Looks like dinner tonight."

***

Steve stood in a blue and white horizontal-striped shirt and white slacks gazing out the dining-room window. What a spectacular sunset he thought. *Spectacular ... nothing matches her. And the setting — pure opulence — a glass dining room table for eight. Indirect lighting in the ceiling and etched-glass doors. They've thought of everything.*

Brooke strolled in wearing a short, dark blue cocktail dress, the V-top showing off her cleavage. It complemented her long blonde hair and warm tan. Steve stared, unable to speak.

Turning full circle, she asked. "Well, what do you think?"

"You're beyond words … fabulous. I can't describe how beautiful you are."

She stepped closer and kissed him on the cheek.

"What do I smell?" he asked, then took a deep whiff. "Beautiful."

"I love it." She pecked him on the cheek. "Ready for some champagne?"

"I'm ready for whatever."

She licked her lips. "You didn't sound like that this morning."

"Geez, I can't keep it up all day."

She gave him a sly look. "Not bad for an old guy."

"I made a comeback." He poured the champagne and handed her a glass. "Here's to the most beautiful woman in the world … and the sexiest too."

She clinked his glass. "And here's to the man of my dreams." She stepped next to him and kissed him lightly on the lips.

When they finished their drinks, she asked, "Ready for dinner?"

"Absolutely." Steve pulled a chair out for her in front of one of the two place settings and joined her.

Brooke rang the crystal dinner bell. The plump captain's wife appeared with two large shrimp and lettuce salads. She sat them on the table and poured the white wine.

"Are we having Trentinio tonight?"

Brooke grinned. "It's something a little nicer … a 1989 Jean Laurent, Brut White Chardonnay."

"Sounds fancy."

"You might say that. It's very good."

The two talked over dinner and a second bottle of wine. Steve offered up a list of the things he liked most — walking on the beach, traveling, shopping …

"All of those sound like fun," she said, then started on hers. "Of course, yachting is number one and … I love to play cards."

"What do you like to play best?"

"Blackjack and poker."

"I could play blackjack all night."

"I've done that many times."

"What kind of poker do you like?"

"Hmm, the wild card games, 'deuces are wild.'"

"How about strip poker?"

"I'm awful." She giggled. "I lose every game."

Steve grinned. "Maybe we should play tonight?"

"I have other plans."

Steve raised an eyebrow. "What do you have in mind?"

"You'll see." She leaned over the table and gave him a peck on the cheek. "Would you like an after dinner drink?"

"That'd be perfect."

Brooke rang the bell. Captain Marco's wife appeared, drying her hands on a kitchen towel. "Would you bring the liqueur tray?"

"Yes, Miss Brooke."

A few minutes later she sat the tray before them and disappeared.

"Amaretto or something different tonight?" Brooke asked.

Steve surveyed the array. "Hmm, maybe Grand Marnier."

"That's what I'm having too."

Steve shook his head. "It's unreal how many things we both enjoy."

Brooke poured the drinks and continued to chatter. Looking at her cleavage, his mind wandered. *Perfectly shaped. What could be better? She's the best.* Feeling an erection coming on, he realized her hand was fondling him. *Holy shit. I could blast off right here.*

He swallowed, their eyes connected.

"Are you ready for bed?" he asked.

"If you're up to it."

He gave her his signature Cheshire-smile. "I'll do my best."

***

"Are you going to sleep all day?" Brooke asked.

Steve looked up at her and surveyed her outfit. "Don't tell me there's a tennis court on board."

"No, silly. It was something handy in the closest, I slipped on this morning. Lunch will be ready in an hour. Let's take a shower."

Steve rubbed his eyes. She stripped and was in the shower before he crawled out of bed. "Come on, the water is great."

He slid open a glass panel etched with dolphins, and stepped in. "This is big enough to be a carwash."

"Almost." She glanced at the master bathroom. "Don't you just love all of the marble? It's like living in a palace."

"And I have my own princess."

"Brooke snuggled her head on his chest. "I don't ever want to leave."

"Being in a place like this, who does?"

"No, I mean I never want to leave you."

"I love you, Brooke," he said, then kissed her on the neck and caressed her shoulders.

"Not so fast," she said, easing down on her knees.

"I've thought about this for a long time."

Steve braced his hands against the wall.

She moved easy, taking her time.

***

The two stood at a taxi stand outside the entrance to St. George's Harbour in Bermuda. A soft breeze blew through her long golden hair. "You look like a model in an advertisement."

"Thanks, I just did a pose like this in a photo shoot." She pushed her hair away from her eyes and gave him a sexy profile shot.

"Be careful or you'll end up back in the master suite."

She smiled. "Captain Marco said you ordered a car for today. Where are we going?"

"Not to a motel," he jested then pointed down the street. "Here comes the limo."

Pulling to a stop, the driver jumped out, ran around the car and opened the door. She stepped in and Steve joined her in the backseat.

"Now can you tell me where we're going?"

"It's a secret."

The driver drove slowly through the city streets for a while, then stopped. Steve opened the door. A red carpet unfurled from the building doorway to the car. People lined the way. Drums rolled, "Dada, da … da."

Brooke stared at smiling faces then saw the store marquee. "Diamonds International." She jumped out of the limo and threw her arms around his neck. "How did you know? I didn't say a word."

"Not a word? You've been making innuendos and dropping hints ever since we left."

She blushed.

"You seduced me every hour in every location possible. What did you expect?"

"Poor baby. And here I thought you were enjoying it."

"How could I think about anything other than being with you for the rest of my life?"

Extending his arm to her, the store manager said, "Right this way. We have a special showroom set up for you. Would you like a glass of champagne?"

She glimpsed at Steve. "Might as well," he said as they sat down on a plush settee. "It looks like we'll be here for a while."

"There must be a hundred different ring styles." She snuggled against him, and marveled at the sparkling display. "I love you, sweetie."

***

Brooke loaded a mini trailer and headed for the mountains. Gassing up in Monroe, she grabbed a soda in Gastonia and pulled into a driveway five miles north of Midville.

Steve leaped from the porch of the new log cabin.

She waved and ran toward him.

"How was your trip, sweetie?" he called.

"A little long."

He pointed to the trailer. "Where did you get that? It looks like a little kid's wagon."

"Isn't it cute. It's specially designed for sports cars. It holds more than you'd think. I have my extra dishes, pots and pans and everything I need to wear for a long weekend or a special time when I might be here."

"Sounds perfect." Steve grabbed her hand. "Let me show you around."

"I can hardly wait. Daddy said he bought the place for a song."

Steve lifted his eyebrows. "A high-fluting melody if you ask me."

"Funny. When you called me about a log cabin, I wasn't too excited." She brushed the hair from her face. "Daddy checked it out, said a millionaire owned it and wanted to unload it. I figured it couldn't be too bad."

"Too bad? Wait till you see the inside," he said, opening the door and motioning her in.

Brooke took two steps inside and covered her mouth. "The stone fireplace is huge! And look at the kitchen. It must have every appliance known to man."

"Wait until you see the deck out back." Steve opened the French doors.

She rushed outside and looked over the hand railing at the rippling stream below. She turned and threw her arms around him. "Thanks, for everything."

"I only told you about it. Your dad did the rest."

"Steve, it's perfect."

"Want to unload the trailer tonight?"

She gave him a sly, sexy look. "In the morning."

CHAPTER TWENTY-EIGHT

Thinking about the look Lizbeth gave her earlier in the morning, Brittany sat at her desk fiddling with a pen. *She has never looked at me with such obvious irritation. Does she know something?*

Lizbeth appeared in the doorway to Brittany's office. "Would you come in," she said in a harsh tone.

Brittany followed her, without looking up, and took a chair in front of Lizbeth's desk. Lizbeth tossed a file aside and looking up at Brittany, forced a smile. "I want to talk about Steve."

"Okay." Brittany froze in place — *Fire me now. I don't know what got into me.*

"We've decided to delay our wedding plans."

Taking a breath, Brittany sighed. "I'm sorry to hear that."

"No reason to be sorry. It's for the best."

"You're okay with it?"

"It was my idea. Steve agreed."

"Are you going to say anything to your friends?"

"No, people will talk anyway."

"Is there anything I can do?"

"Ah, keep your ears open. I'm interested in what you hear in the rumor mill."

"Yes, of course. Anything else?"

"No, that's it."

Brittany stood and returned to her desk. She thought about Steve the rest of the afternoon; then left early for her spa appointment.

Nursing a cheap bottle of chardonnay that night, she continued to ruminate about him. *Why did Lizbeth and he decide not to marry? Have they actually split? Did I have anything to do with it? How does he feel about me?*

Her phone rang. "Brittany Hayward."

"Brittany, its Steve."

Her heart fluttered. She covered her mouth, trying to catch her breath.

"Brittany?"

"Yes, I'm sorry, I was moving some furniture," she fibbed.

"Would you rather I call back?"

"No, I've finished now."

"How are you doing?"

"I'm fine."

"I think so too."

She hesitated. "Steve, I shouldn't have stayed. I don't think we should be talking."

"Why not?"

"Lizbeth and you are getting married. I shouldn't have …"

"That's why I'm calling you," he interrupted. "Things with Lizbeth and I have been cooling for some time," he lied. "She's been hanging on. I've told her it wasn't going to work."

"I thought …"

Steve talked over her. "We've agreed to go our separate ways. We're not saying anything to anyone right now. After a while it'll become obvious. I wanted to tell you at the Omni but it didn't seem right," he said, adding another silky strand to his web.

"I'm confused, Steve, I don't know what to think."

"For good reason. There's no way you would have known."

"Lizbeth mentioned I should schedule her calendar as usual."

"She's putting a good face on. You know how she is."

"You are right about that."

"I'd like to see you again," he said. "Would you meet me Friday night at the Omni?"

The phone was silent.

Steve waited patiently, letting the thought sink in.

"Brittany, I'd love to meet with you. Will you be there?" He paused and waited for another long moment. "I won't take no for an answer." He heard her sigh.

"Yes," she said meekly.

"Terrific. I'll call you after I check in."

***

Steve cracked the door and motioned Brittany in. Her mid-back length blonde hair flowed softly over a red satin cocktail dress.

"You look ravishing." He gave her a peck on the cheek. "Want a drink?" She nodded and walked timidly toward his makeshift bar. "A vodka and tonic?"

"Make it a double."

Steve raised his brow. "Did you have a rough day?"

"Kind of." She pushed her hair to the side. "I had second thoughts all day."

"Second thoughts. Why?"

"Lizbeth …"

"Brittany, I told you she is history."

"I know but …"

"Brittany, I don't need someone else running my life. I called you because I want to be with you. You're a very striking woman and I'm attracted to you."

"You're very appealing too, Steve, but you're much older. I …"

"Brittany," he interrupted. "Age makes a difference when you're young — ten to twenty years are like night and day — you're a beautiful woman. And as adults, age doesn't matter one iota."

"That's how I feel too, but you're a university president. You have a Ph.D. You're a leader in the state. I'm just a …"

He placed his fingertip over her lips and framed her face with his hands. "Brittany, we are two people. Titles and ages don't mean a hill of beans, it's how we feel about each other."

"Oh, Steve, you're so sweet." She kissed him on the lips.

"I bet you know a lot about me, don't you?"

She pressed her lips and nodded, agreeing.

"If you have any questions … anything at all, I hope you will ask."

He lowered his eyelids suggestively.

Picking up on the signal, she took a long sip then placed her glass on an end table. Stepping closer toward him, she loosened his tie, pulled him tight and locked her lips on his.

He responded, kissing her again and again.

Brittany ran her tongue across his teeth to part them for a long, sexy French kiss.

"Wow." Steve stepped back to put his emotions in check. "Would you like some hors d'oeuvres?"

"Sounds great."

"I ordered one of their special packages with bacon-wrapped chestnuts."

"They're one of my favorites."

Steve looked her in the eye. "I want you to know that I meant everything I said." He squeezed her hand then followed her to the sofa. "Tell me more about you — where did you grow up? What do you like to do?"

"There's not much to tell. I was a skinny kid with waist-long pigtails."

"Have you always had long hair?"

"Not in high school. I was on the swim team so I wore it short."

"Did you swim in college?"

"No. I went to the Fashion Institute of Technology and majored in merchandise management."

"They're one of the best."

"I thought I was going to be an executive in the fashion industry."

"No wonder you know so much about management."

"I'm glad for the training. It takes a lot to stay up with Lizbeth." She held her glass high. "Would you freshen my drink, please?"

He took her glass and placed it on the coffee table. "There's something else I'd rather do."

With a coquettish half-smile, she looked into his eyes. "What's stopping you?"

***

Charlie waited in Steve's anteroom watching the minutes tick by — 11:20.

"I don't have you on his schedule," Joyce said. "What time was your meeting supposed to be?"

"Eleven. We set it up on his way out of town Friday."

"He shouldn't be much longer he has a luncheon meeting."

"Fine, I'll wait."

Charlie picked up the recent issue of *The Chronicle of Higher Education.* Reading the lead story on the challenges of reforming general

274

education, he wondered if he should reconsider. "Nope," he said to himself. "I like Carl's plan. I think he can pull it off." *I'm more concerned about Steve. My gut says things are not right. He's irritable, out of touch. He's not his normal self.*

Steve burst in the door, his hair curled on his neck, dark circles hanging under his eyes. Looking at Charlie, he asked, "What are you doing here?"

"I had a meeting with you at eleven."

"I forgot. Have Joyce reschedule it for this afternoon."

Charlie looked at Joyce and shrugged his shoulders.

"Three o'clock," she said.

"Okay."

Steve picked up his notebook and barged back out the door.

Charlie frowned. "Has he been acting that way for long?"

"Maybe a month or so. He's gotten worse in the last week or two."

"Hmm, I have to run now. I'll be back as soon as I can, so we can talk.

"I'm worried about him."

"Me too."

Charlie cut his meeting short and returned at quarter to three. "What kind of changes have you noticed in him?" he asked Joyce as he sat in a chair next to her desk.

"He's stressed all the time. Small issues are major crises."

"That's not like him. He has enormous tolerance for petty annoyances."

"Maybe you can say something to him. I'm afraid he won't listen to me."

"I'll try."

Steve burst into the room and motioned Charlie into his office. "What do you want?"

"I want your undivided attention."

"What's that mean? You have a fuckin' secret?"

Charlie ignored his harsh tone. "I want to talk about a couple of items."

Steve slammed down a report. "What the fuck is it?"

"I have two questions."

"Shit. Don't just sit there, what are they?"

"Your state of the university address is three weeks away. Anything you want me to do?"

"Fuck no. I'll write it when I have time."

"I'd be glad to draft something."

Steve raised his voice. "I said I'd get to it. Second question?"

Charlie gazed quietly at Steve for a moment, trying not to react. "Carl and I have had several conversations about the general education program. It's a shambles. We agree it's time for an overhaul."

"Revise general education? You're fuckin' nuts. The faculty will be all over my ass."

"Carl has a good plan."

"Fuck, no plan is that good."

"You've said we have to take on a biggie every year."

"Not this year. I don't need a bunch of assholes clamoring about the curriculum. The answer is no ... hell no."

"The movers and shakers are lined up."

"Lined up? If you have already decided, why the fuck are you asking me?"

"I haven't decided. I've checked the pulse of the campus like you've always asked."

"I can't handle any more shit. I'm already stressed out."

"Stressed? The campus is quiet. Carl put tenure to bed and everyone is excited about the upcoming game with Duke. Now's the time to strike with a new goal."

"Fuck then, why did you ask me?"

"I want your approval."

"Fine, you got it."

Charlie stared at him. "Can I ask another question?"

"You asked your two." Steve looked disgusted. "What the fuck is it?"

"You've said 'fuck' a half dozen times in five minutes. What's wrong with you?"

"I'm dealing with a lot of issues."

"I can see that. You've gained weight and need a haircut. You're wearing the same shirt you wore on Friday. What's going on?"

"Things are fucked up."

"That's seven times." Steve smirked at the count as Charlie asked, "Are things okay with you and Lizbeth?"

"We've decided to slow down the process."

"Maybe that's good. You still seeing Brooke?"

"Whenever I can. She just bought a place north of town up in the mountains."

"Here?"

"That's what I said. You have a fuckin' hearing problem?"

"That's eight."

"Who gives a shit?"

"I'm concerned about you. You're acting like when we first met with Dr. Benderman."

"Benderman — poof," Steve waved his hands in the air like a magician. "He repeats the same fuckin' stuff every time I see him — you can't be in love with multiple women at the same time."

"Multiple?" Charlie scowled. "I thought it was two."

Steve wiped his brow. Lizbeth, Brooke and … Brittany."

"Brittany? Who the … who is she?"

"She Lizbeth's assistant."

"Her assistant? Are you crazy?"

"Lizbeth will never know."

"How long have you been seeing her?"

"Two months."

"You need to visit Dr. Benderman."

"I'm not going through all of that shit again."

Charlie shook his head. "Did you read the chapter he told us to read?"

"I haven't had time."

"You haven't had time. I've read it twice."

"Probably a bunch of that touchy-feely stuff."

"It's very practical. He said we ought to discuss a section and he'd use that as a basis for your next session. Six weeks ago, remember? We were supposed to talk about it and I'd make notes for the next session."

"Fuck yes, I remember."

"I've marked a few sentences," Charlie said, more forcefully. "Would you at least listen?"

Steve looked distastefully at Charlie then sighed. "Okay, I'll listen."

Charlie opened the book and read a passage. "Sexual behaviors of an addict are usually connected with other addictive behaviors he or she may have."

"Big deal."

"Listen to the characteristics of a sex addict. 'He works until he's exhausted. He justifies sexual activity with multiple partners. He reads sex magazines and watches porno videos.'"

"How do you know that about me?"

"I've seen the magazines at your house, and from what I've read I assume you're watching videos."

"I thought you were my friend."

"That's why I'm telling you all of this. And drinking and cruising are mutually intoxicating, like binge eating. Does that sound familiar?"

Steve stared down at the book.

"There's more." Charlie continued. "'Addicts argue, use excuses and justify circular reasoning to rationalize their behavior.' That mean anything to you?"

Steve's faced flushed.

"And what about this?" Charlie continued. 'Multiple relationships often evolve as the addict attempts to fulfill his appetite for sex.' Steve, you need to get back on a regular schedule with Dr. Benderman."

Steve's eyes glazed. "I can't help it, Charlie," he groaned, then burst into tears.

Charlie sat motionless, waiting for Steve to regain his composure. After a long hesitation, Steve wiped his face with a handkerchief. "I guess you're right. I need to see him."

"Good." Charlie nodded. "I'll set up a meeting for the two of us to meet with him as soon as he can make time."

***

Charlie turned the doorknob and led the way into Dr. Benderman's half-lit office. "Anyone home?" he called.

"I'm in the back. Follow the green arrows."

Charlie led the way. Steve lagged behind.

Charlie poked his head in a large, bright office. Dr. Benderman extended his hand. "Charlie, it's good to see you. How have you been?"

"Thanks for coming in on Saturday. The guy behind me is in sad shape."

The doctor extended his hand to Steve. "I heard it's time for us to get down to brass tacks."

278

Steve gave him a partial smile. "I guess."

"I've been worried about you."

"You and Charlie are the only ones."

Dr. Benderman made a note. "Charlie told me about the sentences he quoted from the book and that you're willing to take another stab at it."

"I don't have a choice."

"We all have choices. That's what I want to talk about." Steve didn't move. "Charlie tells me you've met another woman." He paused, waiting for Steve's response.

Steve hesitated. "Brittany."

"Want to tell me about her?"

"She's Lizbeth's assistant."

"And?"

"She's tall, maybe 5-10, slender, with long, blonde waist-length hair. And great legs."

"Anything else?"

Steve shrugged. "She's a wonderful person."

Dr. Benderman smiled. "How does she stack up with Lizbeth?"

"You can't compare them. They're different. I love both of them."

"And Brooke?"

"You can't compare her with the others."

"I thought the quotes in the book about multiple relationships were right on target." Steve's eyebrows drew close together as the doctor asked, "How did it start with Brittany?"

"It just happened."

"*Happened*? Tell me what *happened*?"

"Lizbeth cancelled our meeting at the hotel. I didn't get the message and went to the hotel as scheduled. Brittany arrived at the room to put the hors d'oeuvres away."

"And then?"

"We had a drink and she complained about her back. I gave her a massage … it *happened*."

"Steve, things don't just happen. When you saw Brittany that night you starting thinking about having sex with her. Didn't you?"

Steve looked away.

"Steve?"

"Yes, I thought about fucking her. I've thought about fucking her for a long time."

"Even while you're in love with Lizbeth and Brooke."

"Sure ... so what?"

"You're not in love with her. You just want sex."

Steve sat motionless, staring at the tips of his shoes.

"This is about your addiction."

"Shit, I didn't know she was going to appear."

"This time, maybe not. But you need to use restraint and avoid things like this from occurring."

"How am I going to do that?"

"Be careful what you say and do; don't invite the situation. Think about things before you say them."

The doctor let Steve think about that while he skimmed his calendar. "You've cancelled several appointments or were a no-show. What's that all about?"

Steve shrugged his shoulders. "I don't know."

"That's not good enough. Why were you a no-show?"

"Embarrassment," he said sheepishly. "I didn't want to let you down."

"That may be what you told Charlie, but it isn't the real reason." Steve hesitated. Dr. Benderman urged him, "Come on, Steve."

"I couldn't face reality."

"That's called delusional thinking. You're trying to convince yourself that you don't have a problem. You want to feel like you're in control. Does that make sense?"

Steve bit his lip. "It's always there."

"And what do you have to do?"

"Be on guard ... fight it continuously."

"Right. Every addict must understand his compulsive behavior pattern. Do you understand?" Steve shrugged.

The doctor pushed for an answer. "What is yours?"

Steve frowned as if the question was in a foreign language. "Can you repeat that?"

Dr. Benderman grinned and asked again, "What's the basis for your compulsive behavior?"

Steve shook his head. "I don't have a clue."

"Read the next chapter. That's where we start our next session."

"Fine."

On the way home Charlie stressed the importance of saying no.

"I got it," Steve insisted. "Don't worry."

Steve dropped Charlie off at his place and headed home. Walking into the den, he saw the phone's blinking light. He pushed the button. The computer droned, "You have one new message. 'Steve, its Brittany. I've a great idea. Give me a call.'"

He glanced at his watch — 9:54 — then dialed her number.

"Brittany Hayward," she said in her bubbly tone.

"Brittany, its Steve."

"Thanks for calling back. Something exciting happened today."

"What was that?"

"A corporation cancelled their reservations at the Omni. They missed the cancellation deadline — everything is paid for. Can you come for the weekend?"

"Geez, I'm not sure. There are so many …"

Brittany interrupted, "Steve, we'll have the pool, everything."

"Ah …"

"Please." He paused. "Honey, it's all arranged. It'll be perfect."

Silence.

"Okay. I'll see you Friday around seven."

CHAPTER TWENTY-NINE

Sitting under the 1957 license plate, Charlie waved to Carl. "Can you believe what we just witnessed?"

Carl shook his head. "I've never seen anyone have the audience eating out of the palm of his hand like that, not even Bill Clinton."

Charlie smirked. *He's more like Bill Clinton than anyone might realize.*

"He was amazing. Not an 'ah' or 'um.' He weaved the institutional goals, academic planning, and general education reform together like they were parts of a puzzle. It sounded like he had a plan in mind all along."

"Two weeks ago I asked him about his state of the university address. He didn't know what planet he was on. And today he sounded like a savior."

"You would have thought he was the biggest advocate for general education reform ever."

Charlie downed a Sam Adams and ordered another round. "It's a good lesson for us."

"You can say that again."

"He can throw fits all week; but put him at the podium and he'll never let us down."

Charlie toasted Carl with his cold mug. "Where did he come up with all of that jargon on general education reform?"

Carl recalled their many due diligence reports. "He must have read all of the stuff we gave him. I'll have to watch his video again to make sure I don't say the wrong thing."

Charlie laughed. "And to think you're the resident expert."

"Me? He sounded like the world-renowned leader; I'm just the behind-the-scenes guy."

"You'll have to shorten your timeframe and strike while the iron is hot."

"I'm with you on that."

***

Steve couldn't get his mind off Brittany as he sped toward the Omni. *I can't wait to see her. She's really hot. Fucks all night.* He exited I-85, passed the valet area and parked in the garage.

Following Brittany's instructions, he picked up the key for the room adjacent to the Webster suite then took the elevator to the penthouse level.

Glancing at his watch, he figured it'd be at least an hour before Brittany would arrive. *Time to take a shower, slip on a robe and unwind.* The warm, pulsing shower relaxed his muscles. He stretched out on the bed and dozed off.

What was that noise?

He raised his head and shook the cobwebs. He heard it again.

A knock on the door?

Steve looked toward the front door then heard the door between the adjoining suites unlock.

He scrambled up. "Yes, I'm on my way."

The doorknob turned. He grabbed it and flung open the door. "Brittany! You look great."

Wearing an emerald green dress that clutched tightly around her hips, she sashayed through the doorway and flung her arms over his shoulders. She thrust her slender body against him, kissing all over his head and neck; then grabbed his ass, pulling his pelvis against her. She ran her fingers through his hair as they moved towards the bedroom together and fell onto the bed.

"Oh Steve," she said. "The last three weeks have seemed like an eternity."

"I've missed you too, Brittany."

She flipped her hair aside. "Wait until you see what I have for you tonight — shrimp cocktail, salmon and cold cuts."

"Sounds terrific."

"The rooftop pool is available — no swimsuits allowed."

Steve pulled her tight. "And then?"

She giggled. "The party begins."

"I can't wait."

She gazed into his eyes. "Well then, I'll give you a preview."

Leaning over him, she untied his robe and threw it open. Looking at him lying there in his boxers, she rose off the bed, slowly unzipping her dress, and laid it on a chair. Brittany paraded around the bed, slipped off her panties and climbed on top of him.

"That was quite a preview. I can't wait for the real stuff."

She smiled down at him. "The preview hasn't started."

Steve raised his eyebrows. "You mean …"

Her finger brushed across his lips. "You'll see." She bent over and smothered him with a long, wet kiss then snuggled against his chest. "What do you like best about having sex?"

Steve squinted curiously at her then shrugged his shoulders. "I don't know."

"Come on. When you're on top of a woman, what gets you excited?"

He pursed his lips. "Turning her on and … watching her squirm."

"And then?"

"Ah … slowing down and doing it again."

She ran her hand across his shorts and lightly teased his balls. She was rewarded with an erection.

Pulling his shorts off, she focused her attention on his growing organ. First fondling softly, followed by gentle kisses that escalated to steady sucking.

"I'll give you a half hour to stop," he jested between gasps.

She giggled. "I bet you don't last ten minutes." She nibbled and teased some more.

Steve closed his eyes; his body involuntarily twitched then began to move with her pace. His breaths shortened and he panted. "Brittany … Brittany, I can't … wait …"

She paused then pulled herself up and placed her hands on his shoulders. "Did you say something?" she purred.

He gasped, "You know what I said."

"Say it again."

"I can't wait. I want you."

"You want me … let's see what I can do about that." She pushed her pelvis against his and slowly eased him in. Steve's eyes rolled back. She increased the pace then banged forcefully against him.

"Oh my God."

"Is that better?"

"Oh God, don't stop." She slowed and raised up. "Oh Brittany, don't stop …please."

"Please." She gave him a Cheshire smile. "I like that."

"Please Brittany, I-I can't take any more."

"Remember … this is only a preview." She giggled.

He grabbed her cheeks and pulled her butt tightly against him. "I can't wait," he shouted, then jerked out of control.

***

Sitting in his robe at the kitchen table, Steve sorted through his weekend mail and sucked down a second cup of coffee. *God, I've never met anyone like her. She's more than I ever anticipated — her arms and legs were all over me. She fucked all night.* He pressed his fingertips into his temples. *There's so much going on … I can't handle it. I have to talk to someone.*

He thought about calling Charlie. *It's Sunday morning; that's his time with Ellen. There's no one I can talk to. I hate being alone.*

He tossed in three olives, chucked a water glass full of ice and filled it with gin. Taking a sip, visions of Brittany, Lizbeth, and Brooke raced through his mind. Shuffling down the hallway, he opened the door to the den and flopped down in his recliner. He opened *The Hustler* and stared at the boobs of a woman then the ass of another woman. He read a story in the latest issue of *Perfect 10* and absently fondled himself. An erection formed. Steve turned on a porno video, and stroked until he masturbated. Lying there, he shouted to the walls, "What the fuck is happening to me?"

Half dazed and still gasping from self-sex, he stared at the ringing phone for a long second before picking it up. "Steve Schilling," he mumbled.

"Steve, its Lizbeth. Are you okay?"

"I must have dozed off," he said, a little groggy. "And I'm kind of down …."

"I'm feeling the same, have been wondering if you could squeeze in a short getaway."

He perked up. "What do you have in mind?"

"My six-month MRI is coming up. I thought we might spend an extended weekend in Baltimore."

"Baltimore … that'd be perfect," he said, enthusiastically. "We'll have some time to get back in our old routine."

"Exactly."

* * *

Steve and Lizbeth followed the bellman to the fourteenth floor of the Baltimore Hyatt Regency. After listening to his spiel, Steve handed him a twenty and locked the door. He motioned for Lizbeth to join him in front of the sliders. "Isn't the view spectacular?"

"I love the inner harbor."

"Maybe we should take a harbor cruise tomorrow after your MRI."

"I'd like that." Lizbeth pulled Steve tight and caressed his butt. "I'm so happy when I'm with you."

"We have to find more time to be together like this."

"Absolutely. Life is too short."

"I'll fix us a drink. How about I order some hors d'oeuvres?"

"Sounds perfect. I'll slip into something more comfortable."

Steve fixed his usual and poured her a Crown Royal on the rocks. He kicked off his shoes and sunk into a large plush sofa. *Here I am with the most beautiful woman in the world overlooking the inner harbor. God, I love her.* A vision of Brooke naked, her breasts pressing against the glass shower wall flashed quickly through his mind. He fantasized about her; then his daydreaming turned into Brittany swimming naked in the pool.

He heard a knock at the door.

"I'll get it, dear," he called, as he unhooked the door latch, turned the knob, and stepped back. A waiter carrying a silver tray over his head entered and walked into the center of the room. "You can put it on the coffee table."

"Yes, sir," the dark-skinned man said, and accepted Steve's tip.

After closing the door, Steve returned to the coffee table and peaked under the sterling cover. "Darling, the seafood platter is here."

"I'll be right out."

He plopped down on the settee facing the water and waited.

Lizbeth paraded toward him in a hot pink, thigh-length silk negligee.

"You look like a 'hot' Greek goddess."

"It's a robe-de-chambre," she said in fluid French. "I picked it up on my last trip to Paris."

"What else did you find in Paris?"

"There's a little something underneath … for later."

"Maybe we should pass on the appetizers."

"Gourmet seafood hors d'oeuvres. I don't think so."

Steve uncovered the platter. "Looks good to me."

She joined him on the settee and gave him a soft kiss on the cheek. "It looks wonderful. Would you fix me a plate?"

"Of course, my love."

The two talked the rest of the afternoon as if their recent issues had not occurred. Steve updated her on the final touches for the Webster center. She rambled about going back to France.

***

Dr. Beamer walked into the examining room with a grin. "Your MRI is clear. There's no sign of reoccurrence."

"Thank God."

"Your brain is slowly moving back to its original location." He hesitated. "But it may never refill the space once occupied by the tumor."

"Is that a problem?" Lizbeth asked.

"Not at all. Your brain was under immense pressure for so long it may never fully return to its original shape," the doctor said. "You may end up with a small, inconsequential vacancy in your skull."

She turned to Steve with a lopsided smile and shook her finger. "And don't you start calling me an airhead."

"That was the furthest thing from my mind." He grinned. "Whatever would give you that thought?"

"I know you."

"You're good to go for another six months," the doctor said.

"Thanks so much," she said, and gave him a parting goodbye.

The two took the elevator to the lobby, grabbed a taxi and headed for the inner harbor. "Let's postpone the cruise. I'm starved."

"How about an early dinner at the Rusty Scupper? They have wonderful food and a great view."

"Can't do better," the cabbie added. "Sunset is in an hour. The harbor lights will be beautiful." The friendly taxi driver pulled into the parking lot.

"Thanks," Steve said, giving him a larger tip than normal.

Lizbeth led the way up the steps, pausing as they stepped inside the restaurant. She gazed at the white-tablecloth dining room. "Isn't this delightful?"

Steve nodded and slipped the maître d' a twenty. "We'd like a table by the window."

"Yes, right this way." The smartly dressed man guided them to a corner table overlooking the harbor.

"Oh Steve, this is perfect," Lizbeth exclaimed.

"You're the perfect one … maybe a little spacey, but …"

"Don't start that." She wheeled her index finger. "That's our little secret."

"Yes, dear." He ordered a bottle of Sauvignon Blanc from Domaine Thomas et Fils Sancerre, Loire Valley.

They chatted, gazing at the twinkling harbor lights. Steve dug into the crab dip. She reached across the table and caressed his hand. "There's something I've been thinking about."

"Oh?" he said, without looking up then placed another scoop of dip on his plate.

She paused, waiting for his full attention. Steve took a cracker and looked up. "What is it, dear?"

"I think we should get married."

"Married? I thought …"

She interrupted. "I see my dad with no one to share things. He goes home at night and waits for the next big event. In a few weeks he'll be at the Duke game. Then what … nothing."

"I never thought of it that way."

"Before I got the results of the MRI all I could see were roadblocks. I rationalized why it wouldn't work. When the doctor talked about my 'vacancy' I said to myself, how crazy."

"It put a different perspective on things for me, too."

Steve ordered another bottle of wine. He turned toward her and their eyes connected.

"I don't want to live the rest of my life like my dad."

He clasped his hands on top of hers. "You don't have to convince me."

"You're so sweet. I love you."

He held her eyes a moment longer and said softly, "We don't have to tell anyone just yet."

“That’d be fine with me.”

“Let’s just take off over Christmas and get married. We could go to Paris … anywhere you want.”

“Paris sounds great. I just want to be with you the rest of my life.”

“I love you, Steve. Let’s go back to the hotel.”

CHAPTER THIRTY

Sitting with his feet propped up on the desk in his den, Steve grinned to himself. He had nailed another state of the university address. The arena will open on schedule. And Lizbeth. *I've never met a woman like her. She's perfect. Everyone loves her. She'll be a wonderful first lady. I can't wait until we're married.*

He refreshed his gin and leaned back in his swivel-rocker. The phone rang. He placed his glass on an old cork coaster and picked it up. "Good evening, this is Steve Schilling."

"Steve, its Brooke."

"Brooke? How are you?"

"I've barely had time to think."

"You need a break."

"That's for sure."

"I've been thinking about taking the yacht out one last time this year. We're having a late Indian Summer and have a couple of weeks of good sailing left."

"Sounds terrific."

The following week, Steve threw the lines to the deckhand at Palmetto Dunes Marina. "Hilton Head," he shouted to Brooke.

"I'll be down as soon as Captain Marco and I finish," she called.

Wearing white shorts and a white blouse, jauntily knotted to reveal her midriff, Brooke ran down the dock with a large white hat and sunglasses in her hand. She gave him a quick kiss on the cheek and slipped her glasses and hat on. Looking like a picture out of *Vogue,* she grabbed Steve's arm and they strolled leisurely toward the marina restaurant.

Steve ordered a Heineken; she had a glass of white wine. He munched on a pound of peel 'n' eat shrimp while she enjoyed a basket of tortilla chips with tasty guacamole.

Sitting on the outdoor patio lined with bright red umbrellas, Brooke seemed unusually quiet. Steve nudged her leg. "What are you thinking about?" he asked.

"Ah, nothing."

"Come on, no secrets."

"Are you sure?"

"Yes. I want to know."

She took off her sunglasses and looked him in the eye. "What do you think about going to France on our honeymoon?"

Steve was startled. "Ah, France … that'd be wonderful."

"It didn't sound like it. Are you positive?"

"Of course. You just caught me off guard."

"I love Lyon and the wine country north of there."

"What's it like?" he asked.

"There are several quaint little towns with lots of boutique shops."

"Sounds perfect. Nothing better than a fine bottle of Beaujolais."

She frowned. "Have you been there?"

"Only to Lyon," he lied. "I signed a university exchange program there."

"Oh, that's right."

She changed the subject. "What would you like for dinner tonight?"

"Dinner? I couldn't eat one more bite."

She ginned. "In an hour you'll be starved."

"Do you have a favorite place here?"

"It depends on the atmosphere you'd prefer. There's upscale, casual or low country."

"Dinner tonight, lunch and dinner tomorrow. Let's do all three."

"I like that. We'll start with low country tonight — Chef Davis's Roastfish & Cornbread."

"Is that really the name of the place?"

"Yes. And they have wonderful seafood, sweet potato cornbread and collard greens."

"Great. What about tomorrow?"

"We'll do the Old Fort Pub for lunch. It's very comfortable. And the Skull Creek Boathouse for dinner. They have the most beautiful sunsets around."

"I'm ready for a shower and maybe a little nap."

"A nap? You can take a nap anytime."

***

"Ready to cast off," Steve shouted.

"Go ahead," Captain Marco said. "Come on up, you can steer us out of port."

Steve tossed the last line on the dock and raced up the narrow metal stairs. "Aye, aye, captain."

Captain Marco motioned for him to take the helm.

"All alone?"

"You have to learn some time. Keep your eye on that piling on the starboard."

"Starboard?"

"To the right silly," Brooke jested. She had followed him up to watch.

Steve held the wheel tight like a teenager's first try, and gingerly guided the ship into open waters where Captain Marco took over the helm. Steve turned to Brooke and leaned down on one knee.

"Steve, what are you doing?"

"I thought it'd be a good time to make it official. We have a witness."

"Are you serious?"

"You've been talking about it all weekend, why not?"

"No reason … it is one of my favorite places in the world."

Steve reached in his pocket and pulled out a small velvet box.

"Wait," Brooke shouted. "Marco, have your wife bring us some champagne. I'm going to get my camera."

Marco smiled. "She's right behind you with champagne and camera."

"Oh Steve, you think of everything," Brooke said, her face a glow.

***

"Welcome to the season opener," TV announcer Brent Musburger said. "Tonight we are in Midville, North Carolina, for the kickoff of the NCAA basketball season.

"Midville?" Dick Vitale shouted. "We might as well be in Nowheresville. It's an hour's drive from anywhere."

"Can you imagine?" Musburger spouted.

"We're not in Madison Square Garden. Rupp Arena. Or, the Forum in LA. We're in Midville." Vitale laughed. "As they say around here 'who would have thunk it?'"

Musburger chimed in. "Three years ago the Red Hens from Mountain State were in their first NCAA tournament and they almost knocked off the University of North Carolina. Last year they upset Louisville, and tonight they're opening up a new twelve thousand-seat arena against Duke. It's been a fairy-book story since Coach Bo Willard arrived."

The camera panned courtside then zeroed in on Dick Vitale. "Tonight the twenty-ninth ranked Red Hens are taking on the third ranked Duke Blue Devils, and their coach is standing beside me. Coach K, what do you think about the atmosphere here tonight?"

"It's wild but to tell you the truth I'd rather be at home in Cameron."

"I guess so. You've won thirty-two in a row there. What do you think about Coach Willard's Red Hens?"

"They're talented. And he'll have them ready to play. I expect he'll throw in a new wrinkle or two to try and slow us down. You can count on that."

"Thanks coach and good luck. Right after this TV timeout we'll have Coach Willard with us for his take on the night's event."

The camera switched to New York sports central and after several commercials, panned the capacity crowd at Webster Convocation Center. Dick Vitale's smiling face filled the screen. "Well coach, it's a big night, huh?"

"Every game is a big night," Coach Willard said in his trademark drawl.

"You have to be excited about playing Duke."

"We are proud of our new arena. I want to say a special thanks to our fans and president Schilling. He did a great job getting us here."

"You're ranked twenty-ninth in the nation. Whataya think about that?"

"Doesn't mean a thing. We haven't played a game this season."

Vitale nodded. "Do you have a secret plan for the game tonight?"

"Wouldn't say if I did; if I did it wouldn't be a secret."

Watching from the president's loge, Steve smiled and squeezed Lizbeth's hand. She placed her arm around Steve. "This is wonderful, darling."

Turning to her father, she said, "Don't you love it, daddy?"

Mr. Webster flashed a big smile. "It's better than I'd ever imagined."

Steve slid into the seat next to Mr. Webster. "Well sir, it's your night. Any final thoughts before the usher takes you courtside?"

"It's fabulous, Steve. The arena, playing Duke, sitting by Bo and capping it off with what Lizbeth told me … couldn't be better."

Steve leaned back. "I'm sorry, sir. I didn't get that last point."

The old man grinned then whispered, "Lizbeth told me. I'm looking forward to calling you son."

"Thanks, dad. You can call me whatever, whenever. I'll be there and I'll never let Lizbeth down."

"I appreciate that Steve. Welcome aboard, son."

Lizbeth pulled her dad close and snuggled to Steve. "You're the only men in my life. I love both of you."

Ed Barkley joined the threesome. "I hope I'm not interrupting anything."

"Not at all," Steve said. "We were having a personal celebration."

"Hey, you all deserve it. This place is first class. Whataya think of my reception center?"

Mr. Webster grabbed Ed by the arm and pulled him into the next seat. "I want to thank you for going above and beyond in the reception center. There is nothing like it in the state. You must be proud of it."

"Proud." He laughed. "I should be, it cost me a million dollars."

"It looks like five million."

"We've got one guy to thank for that." Ed looked around. "Steve, get your ass over here. You can talk to Lizbeth later."

Mr. Webster nearly fell off his chair, laughing. "You're alright, Ed."

The arena lights flashed then a single beam circled the American flag. A hush fell over the arena, and the PA announcer urged solemnly, "Ladies and Gentlemen, please stand and remove your caps for Barbara Mandrell's rendition of the 'The Star-Spangled Banner.'"

Steve walked down the driveway, pulled the Sunday paper from its plastic sleeve and opened to the front page — RED HENS OUT-DUKED BY LATE SURGE

He grinned. *We were up by ten with two minutes to go. We could have beat their ass.* Steve fixed a pot of coffee then peeked in on Lizbeth. *A raven-haired beauty, lying there in her black bra and panties.* He closed the door.

Starting a second pot, he heard the bedroom door open. He tossed the paper aside and looked up. "Lizbeth, you're up early."

"I couldn't sleep. I kept thinking about last night."

"Want some coffee?"

"Do you have any orange juice?"

"I'll provide whatever you want."

She gave him a questioning look. "Orange juice will be fine."

The two sat in silence reading the paper. Steve skimmed the sports page again then reread the lead story. Lizbeth leafed through the ads and travel section.

"I'm fixing French toast. Want anything else?"

She admired his big brown eyes. "Sausage, please. I'm taking a shower. Give me a call when it's ready."

Steve took his time, knowing it would be at least an hour. He downed a Bloody Mary then made a round for both of them. "Darling, breakfast is almost ready," he called into the bedroom.

"I'll be right there."

Fifteen minutes later, he knocked lightly on the door, "It's ready."

She pranced out in a form-fitting black knit ensemble.

"Are you going to a style show?"

"Hmm, maybe later."

"Sounds good to me." He pulled out a chair.

"Breakfast looks wonderful."

"So do you, dear."

She smiled. "You always say and do the right things."

"It's easy when I'm with you."

She took a sip of juice then sliced into the French toast. "I didn't know you were a chef too."

"You'll be surprised what I can do."

She shook her head knowingly. "I don't think so."

"Last night you had a taste of what it'll be like to be the first lady. What do you think?"

"I considered that all through the game. People treated me like a queen."

"Well, you are."

"It was the entire atmosphere."

"The people love you."

"The people were sincere. I felt so proud — I just wanted to kiss you all over."

"Now we are getting somewhere."

"Be serious, Steve. I want you to know how I feel."

Steve leaned back and gave her space. She replayed every conversation she'd had with boosters and board members then rambled on, telling him stories she'd heard from a banker, ski-lift owner and lumber barren. "These are real people, not pompous asses. They tell it the way it is."

"That's the quality I like most about the people of western North Carolina. They're down to earth. And if they shake your hand you can count on them."

"What a contrast to what happens in my life. I talk to the same old people about the same old issues. What a bore. When I talked with someone last night, I learned something. And they wanted to know about you and the university. How refreshing."

"What did you think about the game?"

"For the first time in my life the game was secondary. Most of the time I was talking with people. I only watched the last five minutes."

"You're sounding like a first lady already."

Lizbeth reached across the table and squeezed his hand. "You're the best."

"It isn't me. It's you." He blew her a kiss. "But you know, being the first lady is not all fun and games. There is a lot of behind-the-scenes work — planning events, selecting menus, tasting food. It's like a full-time job except you don't get paid."

"Who cares … it'll be a blast."

"That's the same attitude I have. It's what drives me."

"I'm sure there are ups and downs but the people are so appreciative. You can see it in their eyes."

"You connected with the people. You'll make a perfect first lady."

"I can hardly wait. I'm going to start noting other university events to attend, on my calendar."

"Starting January first there'll be an event nearly every night. You'll need to pick and choose what you want to attend."

"The first? Maybe we should come back early."

"Lizbeth, it's our honeymoon. When we're back we'll be consumed. We're coming back on the ninth. You can start planning activities for the tenth."

"You're so sweet." Lizbeth snuggled close for a moment, then tugged him toward the bedroom.

CHAPTER THIRTY-ONE

Arnold slapped the private investigator's report on his desk then clasped his hands over his face. *That SOB is involved with some rich bitch on the coast. And maybe another one in Charlotte. He must be crazy.* Trying to put the pieces together, he wondered how all of this could be true. He thumbed the report again and reread the summary. *Why would Steve do this? How could he betray Lizbeth? She'd do anything for him.*

He slid the report back into the brown envelope, re-taped it and then used his black-marker to letter across the front — Thaddeus Abbott.

"Sharon," he called.

"Yes," his secretary replied from the reception area. "I'm on my way."

Arnold handed her the envelope. "Please take this to Thaddeus and ask him to stop by around nine in the morning."

"Will do."

Arnold tried to piece the details together. *Five affairs in Arkansas. How could he do it? Doesn't he have any scruples?* "Why?" he asked himself again and again, periodically throughout the day.

Sitting alone at home that night was more of the same.

Right on time Thaddeus knocked and walked into his office. Arnold closed the door and motioned him to the overstuffed leather chair by the coffee table. A carafe of coffee and two mugs waited.

Arnold filled the mugs, slid one slowly across the table, and eased into a matching chair. "I guess a tiger never changes his stripes."

"He sure knows how to pick them — attractive and rich. How does he do it?"

"How? My question is why? There's no one better than Lizbeth."

"Sounds like he found a thirty-year old version."

"I guess." Arnold took a sip of steaming coffee. "What do you think we ought to do?"

"The case on Miss Hotsy-Totsy is cut and dried. He's been screwing her all over the state. I want to talk to the private investigator about the other one. She doesn't fit his modus operandi — staying in a room at the Omni all weekend, never going out for dinner. I don't get it."

"You're right."

"I've scheduled a meeting with the PI this afternoon. Maybe he can shed some light on it."

"I hope so. I'll spring for coffee in the morning at nine again," Thaddeus said, then left.

Over the next hour, Thaddeus explored every plausible situation and reconsidered every option he could think of.

Walking into the Omni with a blank note pad, he spotted the private eye nursing a drink. He pulled out a high-back stool and slid up to the contemporary black granite bar.

"What are you having?" he asked.

"Jack Daniels."

The bartender stepped in front of him. "Whataya have?"

"A Manhattan on the rocks. And give my friend another," he said, nodding to the detective.

"Thanks," the Colombo look-alike snarled. "It's your nickel."

Thaddeus nodded. "Walk me though the times our guy was at the Omni."

"There's not much to say; it's always the same. He checks in, goes up to the executive-suite level and doesn't come out for the weekend."

"You're positive?"

"Absolutely. I sit right here with my eye on the elevator and stairwell. He leaves every Sunday morning between ten and eleven."

"Does he check out?"

"Nope. He tosses the key on the counter and takes off."

"Does he use the valet?"

"Nope."

Thaddeus frowned. "Anything else you can tell me?"

"Nope. It's all in the report."

"Can you show me the room he stays in?"

"Sure, we'll have to go across the street."

"That's fine." Thaddeus motioned to the bartender. "Give us another round."

They finished their drinks with minimal talking, and walked across the street. The detective pointed to the single window in the center of the top floor. "That's it."

"You're sure?"

"Of course; I'm positive. After he comes in I stand out here and watch. A couple of minutes later the light goes on. And at eleven o'clock the light goes out, just like clockwork."

"I don't remember reading that."

"Reading what?"

"That the light goes out at eleven."

"Guess I forgot to mention it."

"Anything else you forgot?" The detective let out a disgusting sigh. Thaddeus asked, "Why do you think he turns the light out at eleven every night?"

"Damned if I know. Maybe he watches a movie and gets laid on schedule. How in the hell would I know?"

"I thought you might have a theory."

"Never thought about it."

Thaddeus turned toward the PI with his hand outstretched. "I guess that'll be it."

The detective shook his hand, then looked at his watch. "Forty-five minutes."

"Round it off to an hour."

"You sure you don't want the pictures of the broad on the beach for five thousand more?"

"Nah, it doesn't matter what she looks like."

"I have some terrific shots of her — great body."

"I'll send you a check for the hour."

"Thanks for the drinks."

***

Arnold placed a steaming mug in front of Thaddeus and sat down. "Find out anything?"

"I'm not sure."

Arnold frowned. "What's that mean?"

"The detective said that when at the Omni, Steve turns off the light every night at eleven o'clock."

"So?"

"That's kind of strange. He stays in the room all weekend and turns off the light at the same time every night. That doesn't add up."

"None of this makes sense. He eats at the finest restaurants and orders top-notch wines with the other one. And here he's a monk."

"I have to give this some thought," Thaddeus said. "I told the detective to prepare two reports. They don't belong together. If separated, perhaps more details will be revealed."

Arnold shrugged. "Fine with me."

Thaddeus walked back to his office pondering what he'd learned. *He's on a schedule ... eleven o'clock every night. What am I missing?* He leaned back in his black leather executive swivel-rocker and rubbed his forehead. *No food. No sight of a woman. What's going on?*

He paced his office and ended up in front of his secretary's desk. "Bring me the file on the Mecklenburg suite."

"It'll take a couple of minutes. I think it is in Ms. Webster's office."

"That's fine. Bring it in when you find it."

A few minutes later the secretary handed him the file. "Thanks," he said.

Shuffling through the file, he pulled out the usage schedule and compared it to the dates in the PI's report — every date matched. He leaned back with a scowl. *How can that be?*

He checked Lizbeth's calendar. She was out of town on each of the weekends mentioned in the report. *What the shit? Who's using it?*

***

That afternoon Brittany sat outside Mr. Abbott's large walnut door waiting for him to appear. *I wonder if he has learned any more about what is bugging Lizbeth?*

The knob turned and Thaddeus walked out. Looking stern, he motioned her to the chair in front of his desk and closed the door.

A feeling of uneasiness swept over her; her skin crawled with prickly anticipation. He stared at her with his gray eyes of steel. Brittany bit her lip, sensed a storm brewing.

He paced to the window and back. "We have a problem," he said, coldly.

Brittany's face turned lily-white. She swallowed hard. "What kind?" she squeaked out.

"I've reviewed the usage of the Mecklenburg suite."

Brittany gasped.

"You've authorized its use a number of times when Elizabeth was out of town. Would you explain that?"

Brittany froze in the chair. She pursed her lips. "I … I-I can't." Trying to hold back her emotions, she burst into tears.

Thaddeus eased back in his swivel-rocker and gave her plenty of space. She tried to compose herself then broke down again.

"Brittany, I want the truth."

"I'm sorry." She stared at the floor. "I'll resign. I'll pay for everything."

"I want to know the truth, not your resignation."

"I can't believe I did it. I'm so ashamed."

"Brittany, let's talk … just the two of us."

She looked up through blurry eyes.

"Tell me the truth and it'll stay with me. No one else will know."

"Mr. Abbott, it's horrible. I can't …"

He cut her off. "Brittany, I won't tell anyone. And you won't lose your job."

She took a deep breath. "You promise?"

He smiled and handed her a tissue. "I promise."

Brittany sighed. "It started several months ago. I had the suite set up for Lizbeth and him. At the last minute on Friday she cancelled and asked me to call him. I left a message at his office and at home." Sobbing, she paused. "The hors d'oeuvres were already on the platter so I stopped by the Omni to put them back in their containers." She bit her lip. "He was there."

"Steve Schilling?"

She nodded. A tear ran down her cheek. Thaddeus slid a box of Kleenex in front of her. Brittany sat distraught then slowly regained her composure. She described how she'd become involved with Steve.

Thaddeus listened and responded like a caring father soothing his young daughter.

"I knew it was wrong but I couldn't stop. He was so kind and gentle. He made me feel special, like I've never felt before," she sobbed. "I don't know what else to say."

"You don't have to say anything." Thaddeus stood. "I do have one final question."

She looked up, mascara streaking her cheeks.

"Why did the lights go off in the adjoining room every night at eleven o'clock?"

She smiled timidly. "That was his idea. He said, 'We need to be careful. I want to make sure no one ever connects the two of us.'"

Brittany's eyebrows drew closer together as she thought about it. "Why did you ask about that?"

"Our private investigator indicated that Steve never went out to eat and turned the lights off every night at the same time. I thought that was strange."

"They're on a timer."

"Funny. But that's what triggered my investigation."

"What's going to happen to me?"

Thaddeus smiled benevolently. "I suspect you'll have some long nights trying to unravel your thoughts and feelings. You'll work your way through it and someday you'll find the right person. All of this will become a faint memory."

"That may take a long time." She sniffled. "What about my job and the expenses?"

With compassion he said, "That's between the two of us. I promised. The charges have been paid. And you've learned your lesson. You have enough to do in putting your life back together without him." He glanced at his watch then nodded to her. "It's almost noon, maybe you should take a long lunch."

"Really … that's it?"

He smiled. "Unless you want to work through lunch."

***

Sitting in Dr. Benderman's office, Steve stared at the floral impressionist painting. Not knowing if it was a Degas or Monet, he loved the vivid reds, oranges, and yellows. They reminded him of the bright-colored dresses Brooke wore. *God, I love her.*

The receptionist called his name and he followed her to the usual small office — painted a light mint-green — with two leather chairs and a couple of end tables. He took the larger chair on the right and settled in.

The doctor appeared minutes later. "Steve, you're looking better. How have you been?"

"Busy, as usual."

"How's your personal life going?"

"Lizbeth and I are going to be married after Christmas. We're honeymooning in France."

"She's a wonderful person, but Steve … you know you'll have to make serious changes."

"She's stepping down at Webster International to become a full-time first lady."

"Good for her. She deserves her own time. People at the university will love her." Dr. Benderman paused. "I guess that means you've ended your relationship with Brooke."

"Ah …"

"Steve, you *have* stopped seeing her, haven't you?"

"I haven't worked that out yet."

"You mean you haven't tried. Things are going on like always, aren't they?"

Steve shifted uncomfortably in the warm leather chair. "I proposed to her."

"You what?" The doctor leaped up and began to pace. "Steve, you can't. We've talked about you being with more than one woman. That's your addiction talking."

"It isn't. I love her. She bought a place near the university so we can be together more often."

The doctor placed his hands over his face. Steve sat motionless. After several moments of silence, Dr. Benderman raised his head and spoke. "Did you ever think about the feelings of these women?"

"They love me."

"Not that. What about their feeling when one finds out about the other? Since you've asked them both to marry you, it's going to happen soon. Doesn't that bother you?"

Steve didn't respond.

"You're going to hurt Lizbeth, or Brooke, or likely both."

Steve frowned. "Why did you say both?"

"If you marry one ..." Dr. Benderman stopped. "Why did you ask that question?"

"I don't know." Steve shrugged. "I wondered why you said both." Steve looked down at his tasseled loafers and fidgeted with his fingers.

"You're still seeing Brittany, aren't you?" Frozen, Steve couldn't reply. "Look me in the eye."

Steve's eyes wandered aimlessly around the room; then fell back on the doctor. "Yes. She's wild ... has orgasms all night."

"And ... what else?"

Steve shrugged. "She has beautiful, long blonde hair down to her waist. I love being with her."

"Doesn't that sound familiar?"

"I don't know."

"You do know." Steve gazed across the room. The doctor waited a moment and prompted him again, "Steve."

"I know," he sighed. "It's my addiction. I'm confusing sex with love. It's all about sex. How many times have I heard that?" Steve took a deep breath. "I'm back to where I started, right?"

"At least you recognize the problem. Now, one more time. Who's going to get hurt?"

"No one. I don't want to hurt anyone. I love each one."

"Steve, that isn't realistic. What happens when you marry Lizbeth? What will Brooke do? Do you think she'll feel hurt? And what about Brittany when she makes Lizbeth's travel arrangements for the honeymoon? How do you think she'll feel?"

Steve bit his lip; a tear ran down his cheek. "I don't want to hurt anyone," he cried.

"Steve, you're not being truthful with yourself. You're going to hurt someone."

"No, I'm not."

"You're in denial, Steve." The doctor picked up Steve's file and leafed through his history. "You didn't want to hurt Sandra. And Martha and Christina; did you hurt them? And how do you think Kate felt when she learned that you had betrayed her?"

"I don't know."

"You've hurt others and you're going to do it again."

Steve didn't move.

"You've hurt others, haven't you, Steve?"

Steve pursed his lips. "Stephanie, my daughter."

The doctor shuffled through Steve's file. "Oh yes, Rhonda and you had a child."

"Rhonda Williams, I loved her more than anyone. We dated for two years in college. She got pregnant."

"What happened?" Though he'd heard these stories before, Steve needed to re-tell them in order to make progress toward accepting and modifying his addiction. The doctor nodded his head toward Steve to continue.

Steve hesitated, glanced down at the floor. "Ah …"

"Why didn't you marry her?"

"I-I couldn't"

"You couldn't. Why not?"

"I couldn't do it."

"What did you do?"

"I told her I was marrying Suzanne."

"Suzanne? You said you loved Rhonda. Why did you tell her that?"

He shrugged. "Had you talked before about marrying Suzanne?"

"No."

"Did you propose to Suzanne?"

"Yes. And a few months later we were married."

"You're in love with Rhonda. She got pregnant so you married Suzanne. What was going through you mind?"

"Being married and raising a kid seemed like such a commitment. I couldn't do it. I couldn't."

"You couldn't what?"

"I just couldn't."

"You couldn't give up the others, right?"

"I guess."

"That was your addiction again. You rationalized your marriage to Suzanne as a way to continue to have sex with other women. Isn't that so, Steve?"

Steve shook his head then nodded. "I guess so. I don't know. Yes."

"Let's go back to your daughter, Stephanie. You said you hurt her. How?"

"I never sent her any money, never called. Didn't participate in her life. Then her mother overdosed."

"So you contributed to that to?"

"Yes. And then Stephanie committed suicide."

"How do you feel about it?"

"Awful. I wish I had married Rhonda."

"How do you think all of this connects with today?"

"I never thought about it."

"Might Lizbeth and Brooke be like Suzanne and Rhonda? And might Brittany be a substitute for one of the others?"

"Geez, I don't know … I guess." Steve covered his face with his hands for several seconds, then looked the doctor in the eye. "I'm going to hurt one of them, aren't I?"

"Steve, you need to face reality. If not for yourself, for others, for those closest to you."

Steve sighed. "What do I do?"

"You must start thinking rationally — face reality — and not let your desire for sex make decisions for you."

"What does that mean?"

"Be truthful with yourself. You can't continue to live in the fantasy world you've constructed. You need to be truthful with each one of them."

"I can't. They'll leave me."

"That's the same thing you've been saying for thirty years — it isn't logical. If you aren't truthful you'll end up hurting them, one by one. Your addiction will keep calling for more sex and you'll go on to the next woman and then another. It'll never end."

Steve fell back against the chair and wiped the moisture from his cheeks. "I never realized how my actions affected others."

"Remember when you met with Dr. Jones? He said, 'It is going to take a long time to sort this out.' You are at that point."

"Now what?"

"It is time to do what you should have done thirty years ago. You must decide which woman is right to spend the rest of your life with. And you can't base your decision on whose best in bed. Consider her personality, your common interests, and all the other factors that go into a loving relationship."

"Will I be well then?"

"I wish I could say yes." Dr. Benderman grinned. "Steve, you will never be well. The addiction will always be there. You'll have to be on guard the rest of your life. Just like I've said before … it doesn't matter if you're a smoker or a gambler, the urge will always there. You'll have to continually ask yourself, what am I doing to my life? … to *her* life? What about my wife or woman friend? Whoever the other person might be you have to think about them."

"That's a lot to consider."

"Look how far you've come in the past four years. You understand your challenge."

"Where do I start?"

"Again, you have to be truthful with yourself; describe what you want out of your life and then take one step at a time to achieve it."

"Someone has to go — Brittany … Lizbeth … or Brooke?"

"Steve, I can't tell you who, how many, or how. All I can do is help you through the process. You have to decide what you want to do."

"You may be right, but I can't."

A crease crossed the doctor's forehead. "What do you mean you can't?"

"I just can't." Steve stood and walked out.

"Wait, we have to talk this through."

Steve barged out the door. "I can't."

CHAPTER THIRTY-TWO

Arnold met Thaddeus outside his office and the two men walked in. Arnold closed the door and asked, "Well Thaddeus, how'd your meeting with the private investigator go?"

"Quite well. The case on the rich blonde is a slam-dunk."

"I figured."

"He walked me through every step with the other one. I checked hotel records, couldn't find anything that would hold water so I told him to drop that reference. No sense complicating the case with circumstantial evidence."

"Makes sense. So what's next?"

Stroking his beard, Thaddeus hesitated. "We need to confront Lizbeth."

"Shit." Arnold paused. "I suppose that 'we' means me."

"No, if it comes from you she'll have a hissy-fit."

"What's new?" Arnold lamented. "She holds everything against me anyway."

"I'll do it and keep your name out of it. If she asks I'll tell her I did it on my own and that no one else knows."

"She'll lambast you."

"Probably so. She'll be over it in a week or two."

***

Brittany's face flushed when Thaddeus stepped in front of her desk. "Is Elizabeth in?" he asked.

"Ah …"

"It isn't about you," he whispered then smiled. "You have my word."

Brittany started breathing again. "Her conference call should be finished anytime."

"I'll wait." He took a straight-back chair next to Brittany's desk. "How are you doing?" he asked softly.

"Okay. An old friend asked me out."

"And?"

"I had a good time. We're going out for dinner this weekend."

"Good for you."

Lizbeth's door opened and she charged out with a file and a handful of papers. "Thaddeus, how nice. I ..."

He interrupted. "Finish what you're doing. I'll wait."

"I'll be but a minute."

Lizbeth handed Brittany a stack of papers, gave her instructions then turned with a fake grin to her visitor. "C'mon in."

Thaddeus followed her and closed the door.

She turned with a sneer. "Don't tell me there's more crap."

"I'm afraid so. Can we sit in your meeting area?"

"Do I need a pad?"

"No." He raised the report in his hand. "I have everything right here."

She leaned back in the leather chair across from him. "You look rather stern. Is it that bad?"

"It's worse than bad."

Elizabeth gave him her full attention. "Okay, let's hear it."

"I've had growing concerns about your behavior over the past several months ..."

"My behavior," she cut him off. "What are you talking about?"

"Elizabeth, I want you to listen, please."

She pouted. "Fine. Five minutes."

"I've had misgivings about ..."

"About what?"

"Elizabeth. It's my five minutes."

She sighed.

"Quite frankly, you haven't been your normal self."

She began to interrupt. He raised his hand. "Now hear me out."

She bit her tongue.

"You've seemed distant, sometimes short, like your mind was elsewhere on unpleasant thoughts."

"I can't be perfect all of the time."

"I considered that but you've been totally out of character."

Elizabeth mocked him with a lady-like sneer.

"I did my own investigation and hired a private detective."

"You what?" she shouted. "You're not authorized ... I could fire you."

"I used my authority," he quoted, "'to take whatever action was necessary to protect the corporation.'"

"You hired someone to follow me, to protect the corporation? Are you crazy?"

"It wasn't you."

"Who then?"

He hesitated then looked her in the eye. "Steve Schilling."

"Steve! Why in the world would you do that?"

"Some information came to light that concerned me about him."

"Christ, we're getting married. You could have had the common decency to say something."

"I didn't have another option; and in the scope of the corporation I thought it in your best interest."

"You're beyond the scope of the corporation. You're into my personal life."

"Maybe so."

"You can't do that." She jumped up and waved her index finger at him. "I'll have none of that."

Thaddeus raised his voice to her for the first time, ever. "Elizabeth Webster, stop right there. And sit down."

She glared at him then eased back down onto the edge of her chair. "You're out of line," she exclaimed loudly. "This better be good."

He held up a document. "This report is all about him."

She frowned. "What does it say?"

He hesitated. "Steve is having an affair with another woman."

"I don't believe that." She shook her head emphatically. "It isn't possible."

Thaddeus held the report high. "It's all here ... times, dates and places."

"Give me that." She grabbed it from his hand and read the first page. The more she read the more her mouth curled down. Paging through the report, she paused on the last page. "That will be all Thaddeus."

"Elizabeth, I can explain."

Her eyes brimmed with fury, her mouth quivered. She said evenly, "Thaddeus that will be all."

***

Elizabeth stood in the doorframe to Thaddeus' office.

He looked up. "Come in, dear."

She closed the door and walked slowly to his window. Gazing out, she ran her fingertips over her lips and then turned. "What lead you to hire a private investigator?"

He stroked his beard.

"Did Arnold have anything to do with this?"

"No, I did it on my own."

"Why? What triggered it?"

"I told you about my concerns about your behavior …"

She interrupted. "There had to be more. Why did you hire a detective?"

"It started three or four months ago." He hesitated and began to clean his glasses.

"Well, get on with it."

"I checked your calendar and asked Brittany about your mood."

"Brittany? You had no right. She's my assistant."

"She's an employee."

"She's my personal assistant …"

Thaddeus cut her off. "Elizabeth, I had no choice." He paused. "And I might say, she's quite loyal to you. You're very fortunate to have someone like her."

"What did you find out?"

"She told me about a program she attended for you in New Orleans."

"Yes, I recall; I had an executive meeting and asked her to go in my place."

"Well, based on what she told me, I followed a hunch and did some digging. The young woman giving a presentation about researching a high-level businessman had been a cub reporter in Ruston, Arkansas."

"Ruston, that's where Steve was …"

"You got it. I went there."

"You went there, why?"

"To see if he was the person the reporter investigated. I had to confirm it."

"I don't believe it." She covered her mouth and stifled a sob. "It isn't true."

"Elizabeth, I had a conversation with one of the women. She confessed to having an affair with him and provided compelling testimony about four others."

"Five affairs ..." her voice trailed away in disbelief.

"I'm sorry, Elizabeth, it is true."

"Five affairs."

She stared at him then wiped a tear from her cheek and headed for the door.

"Elizabeth, if there's anything I can do ...."

***

Elizabeth entered an old building on a side street in downtown Charlotte and walked up three flights. Seeing Edward Flasker, Private Detective, painted in black on the frosted pane, she opened the door.

A gray-haired secretary looked up from her stacks of paper. "May I help you?"

"Yes, I called this morning. I have a two o'clock appointment."

"Have a chair. Mr. Flasker will be with you in a minute."

Elizabeth turned and sat in one of the straight-back wooden chairs lined against the wall. She wrinkled her nose. *Thaddeus could have picked a PI with a more pleasant office. The artificial plants haven't been dusted in years. And the floor ... what a pig sty.*

His door opened and a short Italian man, his collar open and tie hanging loose, walked toward her. "Good afternoon, I'm Eddy Flasker, c'mon in."

Elizabeth followed him in and closed the door behind her.

"Have a chair," he said. "What can I do for you?"

"I'd like to talk about the report you prepared for Mr. Abbott."

"Yes, he called, said you might be stopping in."

"The pictures for the exhibits were not included. I'd like to see them."

"That's not possible."

She scowled. "Not possible? I am Elizabeth Webster. This report was done for my company and I want to see the pictures."

315

"I know who you are. I told Mr. Abbott that would be an added cost. He said they weren't necessary so I disposed of them."

"You disposed of them?"

"Yes. I almost got shot one night by a distraught wife trying to catch her husband in the act. She came to my office with a gun and demanded the file photos. From then on I pledged to myself — no pictures are maintained on file unless they are in the contract."

"Describe her," Elizabeth demanded, angrily.

The sixtyish, black-haired detective gave her the once-over and smiled, looking at her décolletage. "She's blonde about your height, nice boobs like yours, thirtyish with a great smile. And hot as hell."

"Hot? What do you mean ... why that?"

He shrugged. "She's a knockout. A real turn-on for most guys."

Elizabeth stared at him without emotion. "I want her out of his life."

He grinned. "I'm sure you do."

"No, I'm serious. I want her out of his life. Do you understand?"

"M-Ms. Webster ..." Eddy stammered. "I don't get involved in that kind of stuff. One slip-up and I'm in jail for life. It isn't worth it."

She pulled a letter-size envelope from her purse and threw it on his desk. "There's twenty-five thousand dollars in there Mr. Flasker, I want her out of his life."

Eddy's fingers tapped the desk. "Ms. Webster, I can't."

"You know people who will."

He hesitated. "Yes."

"Well then, take care of this."

"Ms. Webster that's very risky stuff. I can't."

"How much more does it take?"

"I don't want to ..."

She pounded his desk. "I'll make it fifty. Twenty-five thousand now and twenty-five later."

Mr. Flasker stared at her then picked up the envelope. "I'll be in touch."

CHAPTER THIRTY-THREE

I'm glad this week is over Arnold thought as he headed east on US Route 74. "I'll grab a bite to eat in Wilmington and will be to Beaufort before dark," he said aloud, and shook his head. *I can't believe he two-timed Lizbeth. Christ, she would do anything for him. And all for some hot floozy.*

He gassed up in Whiteville, grabbed a burger in Wilmington and headed north on US Route 17. Arriving in Beaufort for another perfect sunset, he dropped his bags at the house and walked to the marina. Marco had his bourbon on ice beside a plate of crackers and his favorite Dubliner sharp cheese.

Arnold took a long sip. "What could be better than chatting with an old friend and watching the sunset?"

"Sitting with a beautiful woman."

"Ha, that's all you would be doing."

Marco laughed. "At least I can look. Tomorrow we'll be preparing the yacht for winter storage. How many years in a row have we done this?"

"Must be close to twenty. Brooke was just a little tyke."

Arnold smiled. "She grew up to be quite a woman."

"I'm really happy for her."

"Happy?"

"Yeah, Steve and she are making plans to be married."

"Steve, is that his name?"

"Yes."

"What's his last name?"

"Hmm, I can't recall. I don't think she said."

"She mentioned he was older."

"Fiftyish."

"Fiftyish? That old … what's he like?"

"Fit and trim. Athletic type. He was a good hand on board. I liked him."

"On board?"

"You told me to take her to Bermuda and any place else she wanted to go. I figured you knew all about him."

"You know when Brooke says something I …"

"Daddy's girl, I know. They've been up and down the east coast this summer — Hilton Head, Myrtle Beach, Savannah — they've done it all."

"Anything in particular you remember about him?"

"Nice looking, a real lady's man."

"A lady's man?" her dad frowned.

"You know, he does all of the little things — opens the door for her, pulls out her chair, kisses her on the cheek for no reason, treats her like a queen. He's some kind of a bigwig in the western part of the state."

"How do you know that?"

"He always flies into New Bern from Charlotte. He lives west of there. I have a picture of him proposing to her in my cabin. Want to see it?"

"Yes. But please pour me another bourbon, first."

"Will do."

Marco filled their glasses with ice and booze then headed for his cabin. When he returned Arnold had dozed off. Marco went to the galley, grabbed a couple of steaks and fired up the grill.

Twenty minutes later, he called. "Your Caesar and New York strip will be ready in two minutes. Want to freshen up?"

Arnold jumped, startled from his nap. "I'll be right there."

The two old friends sat down on the back deck. Marco lifted his glass and toasted Arnold. "Here's to the luckiest guy in the world. You have it all and now your prize possession is about to be married. Salute."

Arnold clinked his glass. "And here's to my best friend."

"With Brooke getting married, I suppose she won't be taking many trips with this old guy. I'll miss that."

"Maybe Steve and she will continue the tradition."

"It won't be the same. Did you find that picture?"

"Yes. I have it right here." Marco pulled it from his shirt pocket and handed it to Arnold. "What do you think?"

Arnold stared at the photo of Steve on his knee proposing to Brooke. "Where did you get this?!" he shouted.

Marco backed up. "I took it when we were leaving Hilton Head. Brooke said it was her favorite place."

"Do you know who this is?"

Marco frowned. "Steve."

"Do you know anything about him?"

Marco shrugged. "Just what I told you."

"He's Steve Schilling, president of Mountain State University."

"I told you he was a bigwig from western Carolina."

"I can't believe this." Arnold dug his fingertips into his temple.

"What's wrong?

"*He's* engaged to Elizabeth. They're supposed to be married after Christmas."

"Steve? You must be mistaken, Arnold."

"Mistaken? The guy has been screwing Lizbeth for two years. Don't you think I'd recognize him?"

"You mean he's been …"

Arnold nodded. "He's been screwing my daughter and fuckin' my ex."

"Jesus Christ, what kind of a guy is he?"

"Who knows?"

"I'm so sorry, Arnold."

"Did Brooke say anything about what she was going to do?"

"Not that I recall. She couldn't stop cooing over him."

"Come on, Marco, think. She must have said something."

Marco scratched his head. "Oh yeah, the two of them talked about telling her mother."

"Lizbeth … Jesus Christ, no."

"Brooke told him that she hadn't talked to her in years. He convinced her that she should make up. Brooke said she was going to drive up to Lake Lure Saturday."

"Tomorrow?"

"Yes."

"Holy shit. I have to get there before she arrives."

"You'll need to leave early."

"I'll catch some shuteye and leave first thing in the morning."

***

Arnold was up well before his alarm sounded and passed Wilmington before daybreak. *How am I going to tell Lizbeth? What am I going to say? God, she'll go berserk. What will I say to Brooke? All of these years waiting for the right guy ... how could this happen?*

Arnold floored the pedal.

Flying past Laurinburg and Polkton, he gassed up in Charlotte and headed on for Lake Lure.

It was almost nine when he pulled onto a county road, a mile away from Lizbeth's mountain home. *Gotta be there before Brooke arrives. What if she's already there? What if they've already talked?* He slowed at the entrance to the driveway and turned in.

Two state police cars, lights flashing, were parked in front. Arnold's heart leaped. *What are they doing here? Did Lizbeth have a problem? Is she okay?*

He took the steps two at time but was stopped by an officer at the front door.

"Is Lizbeth okay?" he asked.

"Are you referring to Elizabeth Webster?"

"Yes, she's my former wife."

"There's been a problem, sir. You'll have to speak to the officer over there." The deputy pointed inside. "By the fireplace."

Arnold walked slowly toward the fireplace. Approaching the officer, he gave Arnold a "Sh" sign.

"What's the problem officer?" he asked.

The officer frowned.

"Is Lizbeth okay? I'm her ex, what's happening?"

"Her daughter was killed in an auto accident early this morning."

"Brooke? God, no." He grabbed his chest. "She's my daughter, too."

"I'm sorry to hear that, sir."

Arnold doubled over and collapsed on the nearest chair. "I need my ... my geo ... geo-glycerin. Water ... water." His head flipped side to side. "The pills are in my pants pocket ... left side."

The young deputy franticly searched his pocket. "Here they are, sir." He shook one out of the bottle and handed it to Arnold. "Drink the water."

Arnold leaned his head heavily back on the chair — the room spun in a crazy, misshapen circle. "What ... what happened?" He stared at the ceiling.

"Sir, are you okay?" Arnold's head wobbled a bit and he blinked. "What happened … the accident?"

"We're not sure. It looks like she lost control or her brakes failed on a curve about ten miles northwest of Rutherfordton."

"Oh my God, I saw two wreckers there when I went by."

Arnold covered his face with his hands. "Can I get you something else, sir?" the young officer from the door asked.

"More water will be fine."

Arnold stared across the room in disbelief. *How could this happen? She had so much to live for. Why? Poor Lizbeth. What can I say?*

An older officer interrupted his thoughts. "Are you Mr. Webster?"

"We're divorced. I'm Arnold Hart. Brooke was my daughter, too," he repeated for him.

"My condolences, sir. I wish there was more I could say."

Arnold forced a partial smile. "Is Lizbeth okay?"

"The doctor gave her a sedative. She'll sleep for a few hours. Do you want me to leave an officer here?"

"No, we'll be fine. Thank you very much."

The officer tipped his hat and directed the others to leave.

CHAPTER THIRTY-FOUR

Arnold filled his coffee mug and eased onto the sofa in the sunroom. Staring at Lake Lure, he recalled the times Lizbeth and he had sat in this very spot, watching Brooke grow up — swimming in the lake, throwing the football, sunbathing. *What happened to those years? Why did our perfect world crumble and fall? How had we let issues of no consequence grow into irresolvable conflicts? Why did I allow Lizbeth to pound a wedge between herself and Brooke? There had been so many opportunities for me to forge a positive relationship. Why didn't I pursue them?*

He heard a rustling behind him and turned. Lizbeth staggered toward him. He stood and extended his arms. She fell into his embrace and squeezed him tight.

"I can't believe what happened," she sobbed.

"I know, dear, it's a nightmare come true."

"I'm so pleased you're here. I don't know what I would do without you."

He gave her a feeble, false grin. "It's something we have to work our way through."

"Oh Arnold." Tears gushed down her cheeks. "All of these years I just wanted her to come home so I could tell her how I felt."

"I wanted that too."

"I'm so sorry," she said, pulling him tight. Arnold comforted her.

"Want a cup of coffee?"

She nodded. He filled her mug and guided her to the sofa. The late morning sun streaked across the room.

"How? How did I mess up so badly?" she asked. "Things at the office went so well; but nothing I did was right for her."

"There's plenty of fault to go around. Sometimes things just happen …"

"It's my fault," she talked over him. "I forced her to grow up without a mother."

"That's not true, Lizbeth. You're being too hard on yourself."

Lizbeth shrugged. "I didn't do anything with her. You were the best part of her life. She loved you, wanted to be with you all the time. As a mother, I did everything wrong."

"Lizbeth, that's not fair. Think about the good times."

"Maybe when she was a baby; but after that I was just a busy ogre."

"That's not true. She watched you from the sidelines, talked about your accomplishments and the awards you won."

"Those didn't have anything to do with being a mother. She needed *me* not a CEO."

Arnold gave her a peck on the cheek.

"Why don't you shower and we'll take a walk on the beach like we used to?"

"I'd like that."

***

Pacing outside, Arnold tried to figure out how he'd tell Lizbeth about Steve and Brooke. *She's gone through so much. Maybe I should wait. If not now, when? What if Steve convinces her that none of this is true? There's no way she wouldn't fall for that. He's so smooth. And what if she ended up marrying the bastard? I can't let that happen.*

Lizbeth stepped onto the deck wearing a dark navy jogging suit, large oval sunglasses, and a floppy straw hat. "I'm ready," she said, extending her hand.

"You look nice," he said, patting her hand comfortingly.

"It's the only thing I could find."

They walked hand-in-hand and Lizbeth squeezed his affectionately for the first time in years. "Remember when we used to stroll down the beach and stop by that picnic table?"

"By the picnic table? I remember one night *on* the table."

"You were a crazy man." She gave him a half smile. "How did all of that slip away?"

"We forgot about the important things in life."

"Sad, isn't it? Somehow our lives became all about going places, doing things. We weren't a family; we did things that looked good. Why didn't I let Brooke grow up like a normal little girl … with two parents?"

"You wanted the best for her."

"And look what I got. Nothing. I never saw her happy."

"She was happy." Arnold paused, thinking about that day in the office when Brooke had told him about her plans. "She especially loved the ocean. We laughed and joked when we were yachting."

"That was Brooke and you. I was never a part of her life."

"You were a bigger part of her life than you realize. There are lots of things we can talk about." Arnold hugged her tight. "Let's head back to the house."

Lizbeth took his hand. "I don't know what I'd do without you."

"I'll always be here."

She sighed. "I have to do something. I can't just wallow in sadness. What can I fix you for breakfast?"

"I'm not very hungry."

"How about we split an omelet."

"Perfect. I'll make the toast and pour some juice. Orange okay?"

"Fine."

The two had breakfast and lingered at the table, reminiscing about Brooke and the good times they'd shared.

"We have to make plans for a funeral," Arnold noted.

"God, no. I can't go through that."

"We can't ignore our responsibility."

Lizbeth grit her teeth. "Make it small, private, maybe in Beaufort. We can have her cremated, and Marco could spread her ashes in the ocean."

"I'll take care of it," Arnold said, looking for the right time to tell her the rest of the story. Lizbeth stood up and kissed him on the cheek. "I need a nap."

"I'll make a pot of my special chili for later."

"Sounds wonderful … light on the hot peppers."

***

After two bowls of chili that afternoon, Arnold took Lizbeth by the hand and led her to the sofa.

"That was the best chili you've ever made. I can't believe you had two bowls."

"I only had part of an omelet for breakfast," he jested, trying to lighten the atmosphere. He sat down beside her and clasped her hands.

Lizbeth gave him a quizzical look. "I know that look Arnold, what is it?"

"There's something I have to tell you."

"What is it, dear?"

"It's about the report Thaddeus shared with you."

"He told me you didn't know anything about it."

"That's what we had agreed to say … before."

"Before what?" Lizbeth interjected.

"Before … things are different now."

"Don't beat around the bush." With a sudden thought, Lizbeth covered her mouth. "Oh my gosh, I forgot to tell Steve about the accident. I have to call him."

Lizbeth started to rise. Arnold grabbed her arm and softly pulled her back onto the sofa. "Honey, you don't need to call Steve."

She scowled. "The report is not right. Maybe he saw someone a few times. I know it was nothing … he loves me … I know it, Arnold."

Arnold bit his lip. "He doesn't."

"How can you say that? We've done everything together, gone places, shared experiences, made plans …"

He interrupted. "I have proof."

"Proof?"

Lizbeth straightened. "What kind of proof?"

"A picture of him and …"

"The detective said he got rid of them."

"He didn't take this one."

"Let me see it?"

"There's something I have to say first." Arnold hesitated then reached for the picture in his shirt pocket.

Before he could explain Lizbeth snatched it out of his hand. "Where did you get that? What is Brooke doing with Steve?"

"Marco took it in Hilton Head."

"Hilton Head?" She scowled. "What were they doing there?"

Arnold looked Lizbeth in the eye. "Brooke was the other woman."

Lizbeth stared hard at him, unable to grasp his meaning. Her mouth turned down. Her hands shook, and she mumbled, "No. That isn't possible. He loves *me*."

"That isn't true."

She pushed Arnold in the chest. "Why would you ever say something like that? I can't believe you'd ..."

Arnold clasped his hand gently over her mouth. "This time you're going to listen to me."

She shook her head, trying to free herself. He spoke firmly, directly. "He does not love you."

Lizbeth struggled free. "I don't believe you. Why would you make up a story like that about Brooke?"

"I didn't make it up. She was coming here to tell you that Steve and she were getting married."

"No. No!" she screamed. "No, no, it can't be." Lizbeth flailed her arms. Arnold grabbed her around the waist and held her tight. "Let me go. Let me go! It isn't true."

"It happened just like the detective described it."

"It can't be." Lizbeth shouted. "I didn't mean to ..."

Arnold cut her off. "Lizbeth, it's nothing you did. You can't change what happened."

"You don't understand."

"Lizbeth, it was an accident."

"It wasn't. I killed her!" She flung her arms wildly in the air, her distress overwhelming.

Arnold tried to console her. "Lizbeth. Lizbeth."

She slammed her hands against his shoulders then pounded on his chest. "Why, why ... I didn't mean for that to happen."

"Take it easy, honey. It'll be alright."

"It won't! You don't understand."

"Lizbeth, slow down ... what're you trying to say?"

She took a deep breath to compose herself then burst into tears. "I killed Brooke," she sobbed.

"Honey, it was an accident, you ..."

She shouted. "It wasn't an accident I paid someone ..."

Arnold cut her off. "You what?"

Lizbeth gasped trying to catch her breath. "I wanted the other woman out of his life."

"Lizbeth, you're not making sense."

She covered her face.

Arnold backed up and waited for her explanation.

Slowly, she composed herself. "I read Thaddeus' report again and again. It didn't make sense. I had to find out for myself. So I went to Mr. Flasker's office and confronted him. He had documentation for everything in the report. I panicked."

"You panicked?"

"I wanted 'that woman' out of his life. I gave him twenty-five thousand dollars.

Arnold's eyes opened wide. "You paid him to have her killed?"

Lizbeth nodded. "Twenty-five thousand then and another twenty-five afterward."

"Oh my God, Lizbeth, how could you do that?"

"I don't know … I just did."

"Maybe Brooke really had an accident."

"No way. She drove fast but she was an excellent driver. She's gone around that curve a hundred times. It wasn't an accident, I'm sure of it."

"Oh my God, Lizbeth … she was my reason for living."

"I know dear. She thought the world of you."

Lizbeth placed her head on Arnold's chest and sobbed. "What are we going to do?"

"I need to think. You need to take your medication and rest."

"I can't. I could go to prison."

"Lizbeth, you're not going to prison. Just relax. We need to think our way through this."

"Pour me a Crown Royal, please."

"Lizbeth?

"A large glass."

"Okay, we'll both have a regular size glass."

Arnold filled two glasses with ice and Crown Royal then joined her in the sunroom.

"What's going to happen to me?"

"Nothing is going to happen to you." Arnold raised his hand. "Stop thinking that way. Brooke had an accident." He tried to conceal his devastation.

"Arnold, I can't. I killed my daughter."

"Lizbeth, listen to me. We have to put our personal feelings aside."

"Arnold, I can't. I killed her!"

He shook his head. "Jesus Christ, Lizbeth, you can't say that."

"It's true."

"True or not, it doesn't matter … *Brooke died in an accident* — plain and simple."

"No, no, that isn't true."

Arnold grabbed her face and held her so she had no choice but to look in his eyes. "Lizbeth, listen to me … Brooke died in an automobile accident. Repeat that to me."

"Brooke …" she sobbed, "died in an accident."

"Again."

"Brooke died in an automobile accident."

"Good."

Arnold paused and walked away to give her space. "You're okay now."

Lizbeth bit her lip then said, "What about the detective?"

"I'll take care of that first thing Monday."

"Arnold, … a cover up?"

"We don't have a choice. Our daughter is dead. We need to fulfill our family obligations. Think how devastating this would be to your dad. We must keep this between the two of us."

"Oh no, poor Brooke."

"Brooke didn't know. Marco said he'd never seen her so happy. The last two weeks were the happiest time of her life."

"I wish I could have had the same happy feelings for her."

"We have to end everything right here and now. If any of this ever gets out the media will crucify us. It'd be the downfall of everything we've worked for."

"I suppose." Lizbeth sighed then shook her head. "How could Steve do this to me? To Brooke?"

"I can't imagine a person doing what he has done. Has he no feelings for others."

"Arnold, he was so loving, so sincere …"

"It was all a façade — he's a fake."

"You must be right." Lizbeth straightened. "I hate the bastard. I don't want to ever see him again."

"I understand that dear, but again, we have obligations — to the university, a broadcasting contract — we just can't end things overnight."

"I don't care what you do. I don't want to see him … ever again … I don't want anything to do with him."

"Lizbeth put your CEO hat on. You have corporate responsibilities you can't ignore."

"Who cares? Arnold, he was with my daughter *and* me, maybe on the same day. How can I not care about all of that? He's sick. I can't stand the thought of him."

"But we cannot turn our backs on your dad and what your family has accomplished."

"Get rid of him." She sniffled. "You're good at fixing things — make it happen."

"Lizbeth, I can't snap my fingers and make a university president disappear."

"I don't care how you do it." Lizbeth paused. "Call the president in Washington. Tell her you need a favor."

"President Stetson?"

"Yes," Lizbeth said, "Remind her of my daddy's million dollar contribution."

"What am I supposed to say?"

"Tell her you have the right man to head up her commitment to reform public school education. He's turned around two universities and received national accolades. Tell her it'd be a real coup if she could tap him."

"Hmm, not bad. What's going to make her agree?"

"Arnold, I'm sure she's expecting another million, maybe two; tell her it's payback time."

***

Carl stared at the '57 license plate and turned in time to watch Charlie saunter in the bar's door.

Carl ordered two Sam Adams then slapped the special edition of *The Mountaineer* on the table. Charlie smirked. "What do you think about that?"

"It's a good life if you don't weaken."

Charlie laughed. "You learned your lessons well."

"I remember the first time Steve said that to me."

Charlie grinned. "Don't we all?"

"I thought about it all night then concluded, how prolific."

"Absolutely. If you stand tall on principle you'll always come out on top."

"And if you weaken," Carl said, "you'll end up with the shitheads."

Charlie ginned. "How many times did we hear that?"

"I lost track." Carl shrugged. "With Bergmann, on tenure, general education, God, who knows?"

Charlie unfolded *The Mountaineer* so the front page spread across the table. "Can you believe that — his picture and headlines cover the whole page — SCHILLING NOMINATED FOR HIGH-RANKING FEDERAL POST!"

"Practically the entire issue is devoted to him and his presidential exploits."

"And look at this," Charlie interrupted, "quotes from our nation's president. She calls him 'one of the foremost educators in the country — an innovator, a change agent — a man who can lead the reform effort of our failing public schools.'"

"Wait until she sees him at the podium — he'll have the audience eating out of his hand.

Charlie chuckled. "Can you imagine President Stetson taking a back seat to *him*?

"I wouldn't mind taking her in the back seat."

"Carl, I can't believe you said that."

"I'm only human."

"Human? You're the provost — that's an oxymoron."

COMING IN 2015

Book three of a trilogy

PRESIDENTIAL AFFAIR

CHAPTER ONE

Standing in front of a full-length mirror, the President of the United States unzipped her dark green evening gown and, letting it curl to her feet, admired her shapely body. She removed her cultured freshwater pearl torsade necklace and matching earrings, and placed them on an end table. Unhooking her bra, Janet ran her hands around her breasts — *a full-size larger than in college and as firm as ever.* Sensuously, her hands slid over rounded hips — her smile turned down, a crease crossed her forehead. *I can't believe I've added weight there. That's always been the least of my worries.*

She turned toward him. "What do you think, darling?"

"You look fabulous," Steve said. "Every red-blooded man in the country voted for you. Who could ask for more?"

"That was two years ago." Turning back to the mirror, she murmured, "I have to lose a couple of inches off my hips."

"They look fine to me," he said, motioning for her to step closer.

She slinked his way, locking a sultry stare on his soft brown eyes. As she grew closer, her gaze took in his graying temples and five o'clock shadow. *He's so sexy and distinguished looking; I could mount him right now.*

Janet stopped a few feet in front of him.

He loosened the gold braided belt on his blue velvet robe, slid his legs off the chaise lounge, and planted his feet on the soft carpet. Beckoning her near, he spread his legs and pulled her between his knees.

"What are you doing?"

"I'm researching."

She scowled prettily as he ran his hands around her hips then slipped his fingers under the elastic of her bikini panties. Wrapping his hands around her cheeks, he pulled her stomach against his lips and nibbled her waist.

"That's more like searching. I know where you're heading."

"Seriously, I'm checking the size of your hips."

She pursed her lips in a half-fake pout. "Sure, you are."

"No, really, I can tell — you need to lose an inch-and-a-half."

"Get out of here." Bristling, she pushed his head away. "I know what you're after."

He gave her a sly smile, thought it best to change the subject. "How about a drink?"

"That'd be perfect. I'll slip on my robe."

Janet Stetson walked slowly to the bathroom, her wobbly gait revealing extreme fatigue.

Steve scurried around the bedroom — dimming the lights, turning on Smooth Jazz 105.9 and prepping the bed. Filling two Old Fashioned glasses with ice, he added three olives and Tanqueray to his, took a short sip, and filled her glass with Jack Daniels.

He reached for the Duncan Phyfe coffee table, admiring its smooth curved legs and gilt-brass feet, and placed her glass on a crystal coaster. Taking a long sip of his drink, Steve quickly added a splash of gin and kicked back on the lounger.

He thought about the year they'd just had — it'd been a whirlwind pace — traveling around the country. He recalled laying her on the seaside balcony in Miami — the pounding surf muffling her moans and groans — it was ecstasy, almost like doing it on the beach.

He remembered that night in Dallas, too, when she'd had three orgasms for the first time. *I thought she was going to lose her mind. And how could I ever forget that night in San Diego's Coronado Hotel when she'd tied my hands to the bedpost and stripped me naked? She'd teased and fondled 'til I blew my mind. God, I still can't believe it!*

Hearing the bathroom door crack open, he stared that way. She stepped into the doorway, looking like a goddess, wearing a loosely tied purple silk robe. The plunging neckline of her negligee beneath revealed more than a hint of her deep cleavage. *Brains and beauty, no wonder she's been elected twice. They ought to change the law so she can run again.*

Janet took a couple of steps toward him then gazed across the shadowed room. Flickering candles lead her eyes to his square shoulders and two-hundred-and-ten-pound frame. Quite a specimen for a guy in his mid-fifties, she thought. *George Clooney couldn't compare to him.*

Picking up on the beat of the smooth jazz, she moved her hips in sync with the sounds then looking around, she asked, "What have you done? This looks like a love nest."

"Only the best for the president," he said, his eyes twinkling.

She grinned and still a few feet away, leaned over, showing off everything but her nipples.

His desires perked. "I do have a request," he whispered lustily.

Seemingly surprised, she asked, "What's that, dear?"

"Next time could you have secret service provide scented candles and champagne?"

"Sure." She laughed then picked up her glass and eased onto the winged-back chair across from him. "Did you do anything special while I was out?"

"Not really, I read mostly … watched part of the Academy Awards."

"Gosh, I forgot all about them." She took an extra-long sip. "Did *Titanic* win?"

"Best picture and a slew of other Oscars. Jack Nicholson won best actor."

"I figured he would. I loved his performance in *As Good as It Gets.*

"Helen Hunt won the best actress award too."

"The two of them seemed to feed off each other."

Steve changed the subject back to her. "How did the reception with the European prime ministers and presidents go?"

"Quite well. They're about ready to agree on the Euro as their single currency. That'll be a big step forward." She winced as she stood to refill her glass.

"You okay?"

"My feet are killing me." She smoothed her brow again, gave him that sexy look and winked. "Would you be a dear?"

I thought she'd never ask. "It'd be my privilege." He jumped up and headed for the bathroom. "I'll get the lotion and a hand towel."

"Do you want me on my stomach or back?"

"Your stomach will be fine."

When he returned she was face down on the bed — her rounded ass inviting him like never before. His psychic senses went into high gear. Having done his routine countless times on numerous women, he smiled, knowing exactly where he was headed.

He eased his rear onto the end of the bed. *Move easy. Take her to the top then ease her down. Take your time, make her squirm — have an orgasm — then make her squirm again.* He filled one hand with lotion then rubbed his hands together to warm it.

Stroking her right ankle gently, then worked his way down her foot, caressing every bone, he watched her unwind as if he'd released the air from a balloon.

She moaned. "Oh Steve, that feels wonderful."

"I've saved the best for last," he announced.

"I can hardly wait."

He grinned to himself, knowing what was next. *Besides she doesn't have a choice. Before I'm done, she'll be like putty in my hands.* He moved to her toes, gently massaging each one several times, slowly, sensually. She moaned with every touch.

Adding a dab of lotion to his hand, he tenderly massaged her left foot and watched the tension release from her body. Steve slid onto the bed and inched his fingers up her calves to the backs of her knees. He moved his hands slowly, rhythmically, gliding soothingly up and around the back of her legs. Her body melted into the bed.

"Perfect," he said under his breath. *Time to get down to business.* He slipped his fingers under the elastic band of her short negligee bottoms. Slipping them off, he doubled a pillow under her pelvis. He ran his fingers around, then between, her perfectly-shaped cheeks, and smugly watched their tightening reflex.

Her soft moans and increasing body thrusts let him know she was getting close. He slowed and took it easy. Her cheeks moved in concert with his fingers, sliding up and down, between her cheeks then teasing her private parts. Her body rose then slammed against the bed. She called out, "Please Steve, I can't hold off any longer."

Grinning, he honored her request fondling her G-spot gently, watching her ass bounce out of control. "Oh my God," Janet screamed into her pillow. Gasping, she melted like butter.

Knowing he was almost home, he waited for her to unwind and cool. His urges fired, and unable to delay any longer, he pulled himself on top of her. He caressed and fondled, fingered every part he could reach. Again, her cheeks moved in tandem with his touch.

Steve grazed his erection between her cheeks then eased it, ever so slowly, inside. The two locked and fell into a slow, easy rhythm.

Losing control; he quickened his pace.

Her body tensed. "Please, Steve." She panted. "Fuck me … fuck me."

***

A year and a half earlier, Senator Kennedy (D) had convened the Health, Education, Labor and Pension Committee. After his introductory remarks, he looked across the room at Steve. "It is my privilege to welcome one of the nation's foremost educators — and President Stetson's designate for Deputy Secretary of Education — Steve Schilling. His turnaround efforts of universities in Arkansas and North Carolina are well documented as is his KidsStyle program — a public school model for dealing with bullying and character development."

The senator speechified his long-standing commitment to education then commended the president for making the reform of education her highest priority. He paused, gathered his thoughts, and said, "I yield to my colleague on the other side of the aisle."

Senator Enzi (R) from Wyoming nodded and delivered equally laudatory comments citing Steve's leadership and fundraising successes. Following his oratory, Chairman Kennedy welcomed Senator Dale Bumpers (D) from Arkansas who introduced Dr. Steven Schilling. He touted Steve's many accomplishments at Eastern Arkansas University then turned to him. "It's a privilege to present my good friend Steve Schilling, the next Deputy Secretary of Education."

Steve shook his colleague's hand, closed his folder of notes with a flourish, then made an impeccable presentation. Making eye contact with each member, he connected his comments with the accomplishments of each senator — making the proceedings sound more like an ol' boys' club than a confirmation hearing — the senators sat in awe as he praised their endeavors.

An hour later, Senator Kennedy acknowledged Steve's sterling performance. "You've obviously done your homework, Dr. Schilling. That kind of attention to detail will serve you well as the next deputy secretary."

"Thank you, Mr. Chairman."

Senator Kennedy raised the gavel. "The committee will recess until the Q and A session tomorrow at ten o'clock."

Senator Bumpers stood and shook his hand. "Congratulations, Steve, you're home free."

Senator Kennedy motioned for Steve to approach the dais then leaned over, and said, "I've heard lots of speeches over the years ... none better." He pressed his hand on Steve's shoulder and whispered. "Whenever you want something, remember I'm only a phone call away."

Steve raised an eyebrow. "Thank you, Senator ..."

He winked. "It's Ted ... call anytime."

"I appreciate that," Steve said, then turned and walked toward the smiling faces waiting for him behind the table.

Department staff members spilled into the empty area. "I can't believe it," one said. "You didn't use a single note."

Steve gave the team a megawatt smile. "You briefed me ... what'd you expect?"

A cute young intern with dark bangs pushed herself firmly against his side. "You connected with each of the fifteen senators here today. How did you keep them straight?"

He gave her a Cheshire grin. *I know what she wants.* "A trade secret."

The group laughed.

Sherry Holmgren, the Secretary of Education's personal assistant, who'd been assigned to guide him through the confirmation process, tugged on his hand. "It's time to go. We have to prepare for tomorrow."

Steve nodded and followed her to the door. Feeling a burst of adrenaline, he walked briskly from the Dirksen Senate Building to Constitution Avenue. Turning, he found Sherry struggling twenty-five feet behind on her high heels, trying to balance a briefcase and an armful of files.

"I'm sorry," he said, rushing back to grab the files. "I was fired up."

"For good reason. You did an outstanding job."

He grinned and stepped onto the street, waving for a taxi.

Traffic buzzed by.

A traffic light a block away turned and another pack of cars approached. They too, streamed past Steve, still waving to no avail.

"Hold this," Sherry said, handing the briefcase to him. She bolted to the center lane and waved, placed two fingers in her mouth, and let out a shrilling whistle.

A cab heading in the other direction slammed on its brakes, made a U-turn and wheeled between the two of them. She jumped in the backseat on the driver's side. Steve slid in on the passenger's side.

"Where to?" the cabbie asked. Steve fumbled to close the door. "Hey buddy, I don't have all day."

"I'm starved," Steve said, turning to Sherry. "How about a quick lunch?"

"Where *to* buddy?" the driver asked again, impatiently.

"The Wall Street Deli is right next to our office building," Sherry said.

Steve wrinkled his nose. "I walked past there the other day. I was thinking of something a little nicer."

She shrugged. "The Capital Grill and 701 are upscale restaurants on our way back."

Steve glimpsed in the rear-view mirror. "Whataya think, buddy?"

The taxi driver turned and eyed Sherry, looking terrific as usual in her business attire. "The Capital Grill for business. An attractive lady — 701."

She blushed.

"701 it is."

***

Checking in with the hostess, Steve lagged behind, watching Sherry's gait — *what an ass*. He followed her through the maze of tables. Gazing up at the hanging shaded lamps that filled the ceiling, he said, "Great choice. It has the warmth and ambiance of a private club."

Dressed in black long sleeves and a muted-burgundy vest, the hostess stopped at a white-clothed table for two. Steve pulled out Sherry's chair and slid onto the chair across from her.

"The black and gold accents add a touch of class. It looks pricey," she said. "Let's go Dutch."

"No way," Steve said. "You worked your tail off, it's my treat."

She frowned.

"I insist," he emphasized.

"Just this once. It's Dutch next time."

"I need a drink," he exclaimed. "How about you?"

"I usually don't drink at …"

Steve cut her off. "Come on, this is a big day."

"Cocktails today?" a slender waitress asked.

"Yes." He pointed to Sherry. "You first."

She hesitated. "I'll have a Manhattan, straight up, light on the vermouth."

The waitress turned to Steve. "And you, sir?"

"Tanqueray on the rocks, three olives."

Sherry grinned. "I know … you drink gin for the olives."

Steve gave her a questioning look. "What made you say that?"

"My dad always said, he 'loves olives and orders gin just so he can eat them.' I just thought it was funny."

"It's true for me too … that's why I drink Tanqueray."

"Sure." She looked him in the eye then changed the subject. "You were fabulous today."

"Me? Your team made it happen."

"I can't believe how smooth you were. It's like you knew what questions were coming up."

"Thanks again to you. I felt like I did."

She smiled broadly, showing her perfectly-shaped white teeth. "I've been at this a while."

"Tell me about your career," he said. "Where are you from? Where did you go to college?"

"I grew up in Steubenville, Ohio."

"Where's that?"

"On the state line between Ohio and West Virginia — it's the finger area that divides Ohio and Pennsylvania."

"That's a big industrial area, isn't it?

"It used to be — coal and steel. Now, it's part of the rust belt."

"I bet you were popular with the guys."

"Not really. I was a cheerleader and honor student."

Steve laughed. "None of the cheerleaders I dated were honor students."

"Ha, that was the problem. I was on a mission to change the world. Went to Youngstown State and graduated with a 4.0."

"Wow, a four-point. The only one I ever had is when I added my first two semesters."

She giggled. "I'm positive you did better than that."

"Not much." He stared into her bright blue eyes. "Did you go to grad school?"

"Yes, Ohio State. I received a law degree there and headed for Washington."

"What's happened since you've been here?"

She finished her drink. Steve ordered another round over her mild protest.

"I had several offers, ended up taking a position in the Office of Inspector General for the Department of Education — twenty-two years ago — been here ever since."

"Inspector General? What does that office do?"

"They conduct internal investigations for fraud and inappropriate action.

"I bet you've seen it all."

"Sure have," she agreed.

"Anything I should be thinking about for the Q and A session tomorrow?"

"We covered almost everything yesterday. Senator Enzi is a stickler for details. He submitted ten questions. Staff has prepared a twenty-five page response."

"Twenty-five pages?" Steve wrinkled his nose. "Too long … I want two pages."

"We can't do that. The introduction is three pages."

"Forget about the introduction — two pages. "Tell them to start with the phrase 'since we agree on 80% of the issues, I'll focus my comments on the other 20%.'"

"Steve ..."

He cut her off. "Just do it. I've heard him use that phrase; it'll shock the hell out of him."

She rolled her eyes. "Okay."

"Anything else?"

"Senator Hatch will ask several budget-related questions. It'd be a good time to mention your leadership in the financial turnaround at Mountain State and how frugal your mother was."

"My mother?"

"They like to hear about your mother — what you learned from her, the values she instilled in you. They'll eat it up."

"You sure?"

"Positive."

He took a sip of his gin. "Do you mind if I ask you a business question?"

Sherry glimpsed at her watch — 2:10. "You're on government time."

He pursed his lips. "The Secretary has asked my opinion about naming you as my Senior Advisor."

She smiled.

"Why are you interested in the position?"

Sherry wet her lips.

"You don't have to respond if you don't want to."

"No, I'll tell you." She took a moment to compose herself. "I'll never lie, cover up or tell you something just because I think it's what you want to hear. I'll do my best and tell you what I think. After that, it'll be your decision."

"I appreciate that."

"To your point." Sherry brushed her blonde-streaked hair to the side. "Whether it's me or someone else, the naming of the Senior Advisor for Educational Reform is the most important internal decision you'll make."

Steve cocked his head. "Why do you say that?"

"Two reasons." She sipped her Manhattan. "Senior Advisors are part of The Secretariat."

"The Secretariat?"

"That's the Secretary's immediate staff — they have his ear twenty-four hours a day. It's composed of his Chief of Staff, the Senior Advisors and the Liaison to the White House."

"How many Senior Advisors are there?"

"Four; with the addition of educational reform there'll be five."

"And the second reason is?"

"Senior Advisors have department-wide responsibilities. They speak on behalf of the Secretary at department meetings. The Senior Advisor will be your lead person in communicating with all forty-five hundred staffers."

"Wow, there's that many employees in the department?"

"Probably more … that's the official count."

Steve raised his brow. "Sounds like that person would have considerable power."

"It isn't about power. Think about it as your right arm. You'll have plenty to do representing the president, attending meetings, and making speeches across the country."

"So you'd be running internal operations?"

"Not really. I'd rather say I'd be your agent."

Steve paused. She fidgeted, not knowing what else to do or say.

"Well then," he said, "if you're going to be my Senior Advisor we'd better get started."

"Really?" Her face glowed. She reached across the table and touched his hand. "You're really naming me?"

"Yes." He clasped her hands. "Congratulations."

She paused then gave him a questioning look. "You knew all the time, didn't you?"

He looked up with a sly smile. "The Secretary and I talked."

"You ratfink, I'll get even with you."

Steve finger-combed his dark hair. "Ready to order?"

"Yes, but I'm also ready to explode. You'll have to excuse me." She straightened her ruffled blouse and tugged on the back of her tweed jacket.

"Of course."

She stood and walked toward the restrooms.

Steve eyed her red high-heels then zeroed in on her tight-ass skirt. *Holy shit, I can't remember when I last saw a piece of ass like that!*